STEPHEN KING

REVIVAL

A NOVEL

SCRIBNER

New York London Toronto Sydney New Delhi

SCRIBNER
A Division of Simon & Schuster, Inc.
1230 Avenue of the Americas
New York, NY 10020

This book is a work of fiction. Any references to historical events, real people, or real places are used fictitiously. Other names, characters, places, and events are products of the author's imagination, and any resemblance to actual events or places or persons, living or dead, is entirely coincidental.

First Scribner hardcover edition November 2014

Interior design by Erich Hobbing
Jacket design by Tal Goretsky
Jacket photographs: Lightning © D. GLEITER/Robertstock/Aurora Photos; mountains © Brett Maurer/Moment Open/Getty Images

Manufactured in the United States of America

1 3 5 7 9 10 8 6 4 2

Library of Congress Control Number: 2014005950

ISBN 978-1-4767-7038-3
ISBN 978-1-4767-7040-6 (ebook)

This book is for some of the people who built my house:

Mary Shelley

Bram Stoker

H. P. Lovecraft

Clark Ashton Smith

Donald Wandrei

Fritz Leiber

August Derleth

Shirley Jackson

Robert Bloch

Peter Straub

And ARTHUR MACHEN, whose short novel *The Great God Pan* has haunted me all my life.

That is not dead which can eternal lie,
And with strange aeons, even death may die.

—H. P. Lovecraft

REVIVAL

I

Fifth Business. Skull Mountain. Peaceable Lake.

In one way, at least, our lives really are like movies. The main cast consists of your family and friends. The supporting cast is made up of neighbors, co-workers, teachers, and daily acquaintances. There are also bit players: the supermarket checkout girl with the pretty smile, the friendly bartender at the local watering hole, the guys you work out with at the gym three days a week. And there are thousands of extras—those people who flow through every life like water through a sieve, seen once and never again. The teenager browsing graphic novels at Barnes & Noble, the one you had to slip past (murmuring "Excuse me") in order to get to the magazines. The woman in the next lane at a stoplight, taking a moment to freshen her lipstick. The mother wiping ice cream off her toddler's face in a roadside restaurant where you stopped for a quick bite. The vendor who sold you a bag of peanuts at a baseball game.

But sometimes a person who fits none of these categories comes into your life. This is the joker who pops out of the deck at odd intervals over the years, often during a moment of crisis. In the movies this sort of character is known as the fifth business, or the change agent. When he turns up in a film, you know he's there because the screenwriter put him there. But who is screenwriting our lives? Fate or coincidence? I want to believe it's the latter. I want that with all my heart and soul. When I think of Charles Jacobs—my fifth business, my change agent, my nemesis—I can't bear to believe his presence in my life had anything to do with fate. It would mean that all these terrible things—these *horrors*—were meant to happen. If that is so, then there is no such thing as light, and our belief in it is a foolish illusion. If that is so, we live in darkness like animals in a burrow, or ants deep in their hill.

And not alone.

Claire gave me an army for my sixth birthday, and on a Saturday in October of 1962 I was gearing up for a major battle.

I came from a big family—four boys, one girl—and as the youngest I always got lots of presents. Claire always gave the best ones. I don't know if it was because she was the eldest, because she was the only girl, or both. But of all the awesome presents she gave me over the years, that army was by far the best. There were two hundred green plastic soldiers, some with rifles, some with machine guns, a dozen welded to tubelike gadgets she said were mortars. There were also eight trucks and twelve jeeps. Perhaps the coolest thing about the army was the box it came in, a cardboard footlocker in camouflage shades of green and brown, with PROPERTY OF U.S. ARMY stenciled on the front. Below this, Claire had added her own stenciling: JAMIE MORTON, COMMANDER.

That was me.

"I saw an ad for them in the back of one of Terry's comic books," she said when I was done screaming with delight. "He didn't want me to cut it out because he's a booger—"

"That's right," Terry said. He was eight. "I'm a big brother booger." He made a fork with his first two fingers and plugged his nostrils with them.

"Stop it," our mother said. "No sibling rivalry on birthdays, please and thank you. Terry, take your fingers out of your nose."

"Anyway," Claire said, "I copied the coupon and sent it in. I was afraid it might not come in time, but it did. I'm glad you like it." And she kissed me on the temple. She always kissed me there. All these years later, I can still feel those soft kisses.

"I love it!" I said, holding the footlocker against my chest. "I'll love it forever!"

This was after breakfast, which had been blueberry pancakes and bacon, my favorite. We all got our favorite meals on our birthdays, and the presents always came after breakfast, there in the kitchen with its woodstove and long table and our hulk of a washing machine, which was always breaking down.

"Forever for Jamie is, like, five days," Con said. He was ten, slender (although he bulked up later), and of a scientific bent, even then.

"Nice one, Conrad," our father said. He was dressed for work in a clean coverall with his name—RICHARD—stitched in gold thread on the left breast pocket. On the right breast it said MORTON FUEL OIL. "I'm impressed."

"Thanks, Daddy-O."

"Your silver tongue wins you the opportunity to help your mother clean up breakfast."

"It's Andy's turn!"

"It *was* Andy's turn," Dad said, pouring syrup on the last pancake. "Grab a dishtowel, Silver Tongue. And try not to break anything."

"You spoil him rotten," Con said, but he grabbed a dishtowel.

Connie wasn't entirely wrong about my concept of forever. Five days later, the Operation game Andy gave me was gathering dust bunnies under my bed (some of the body parts were missing, anyway; Andy got it at the Eureka Grange rummage sale for a quarter). So were the jigsaw puzzles Terry gave me. Con himself gave me a ViewMaster, and that lasted a little longer, but it eventually wound up in my closet, never to be seen again.

From Mom and Dad I got clothes, because my birthday falls near the end of August, and that year I was going into first grade. I found new pants and shirts about as exciting as a TV test pattern, but tried to say thanks with enthusiasm. I imagine they saw through that with no trouble; false enthusiasm does not come easily to six-year-olds . . . although, sad to say, it's a skill most of us learn fairly rapidly. In any case, the clothes were washed in the hulk, hung on the clothesline in the side yard, and finally folded away in my bureau drawers. Where, it's probably needless to add, they were out of sight and mind until September came and it was time to put them on. I remember there was a sweater that was actually pretty cool—it was brown with yellow stripes. When I wore it I pretended I was a superhero called the Human Wasp: evildoers, beware my sting!

But Con was wrong about the footlocker with the army inside. I played with those guys day in and day out, usually at the edge of the front yard, where there was a dirt strip between our lawn and Methodist Road, which was itself dirt in those days. With the exception of Route 9 and the two-lane leading to Goat Mountain, where there was a resort for rich people, all the roads in Harlow were dirt back then. I can remember my mother on several occasions weeping about all the dust that got into the house on dry summer days.

Billy Paquette and Al Knowles—my two best friends—played army with me on many afternoons, but on the day Charles Jacobs appeared in my life for the first time, I was on my own. I don't remember why Billy and Al weren't with me, but I do remember I was happy to be by myself for a change. For one thing, there was no need to split the army into three divisions. For another—this was more important—I didn't have to argue with them about whose turn it was to win. In truth, it seemed unfair to me that I should ever have to lose, because they were *my* soldiers and it was *my* footlocker.

When I advanced this idea to my mother one hot late-summer day shortly after my birthday, she took me by the shoulders and looked into my eyes, a sure sign that I was about to receive another Lesson in Life. "That *it's-mine* business is half the trouble with the world, Jamie. When you play with your friends, the soldiers belong to all of you."

"Even if we play-fight different sides?"

"Even if. When Billy and Al go home for their dinner and you pack the soldiers back into the box—"

"It's a *footlocker*!"

"Right, the footlocker. When you pack them away, they're yours again. People have many ways to be lousy to one another, as you'll find out when you're older, but I think that all bad behavior stems from plain old selfishness. Promise me you'll never be selfish, kiddo."

I promised, but I still didn't like it when Billy and Al won.

On that day in October of 1962, with the fate of the world dangling by a thread over a small tropical spit of land called Cuba, I was fighting both sides of the battle, which meant I was bound to come out on top. The town grader had been by earlier on Methodist

Road ("Moving the rocks around," my dad always grumbled), and there was plenty of loose dirt. I scraped enough together to make first a hill, then a big hill, and then a *very* big hill, one that came up almost to my knees. At first I thought of calling it Goat Mountain, but that seemed both unoriginal (the real Goat Mountain was only twelve miles away, after all) and boring. After consideration, I decided to call it Skull Mountain. I even tried to poke a couple of eye-like caves in it with my fingers, but the dirt was dry and the holes kept caving in.

"Oh, well," I told the plastic soldiers tumbled in their footlocker. "The world is hard and you can't have everything." This was one of my father's favorite sayings, and with five kids to support, I'm sure he had reason to believe it. "They'll be pretend caves."

I put half of my army on top of Skull Mountain, where they made a formidable crew. I especially liked the way the mortar guys looked up there. These were the Krauts. The American army I arranged at the edge of the lawn. They got all the jeeps and trucks, because they would look so groovy charging up the steep slope of the mountain. Some would turn over, I was sure, but at least a few of them would make it to the top. And run over the mortar guys, who would scream for mercy. They wouldn't get it.

"To the death," I said, setting up the last few of the heroic Americans. "Hitsmer, you are next!"

I was starting them forward, rank by rank—and making comic-book-style machine-gun noises—when a shadow fell over the battlefield. I looked up and saw a guy standing there. He was blocking the afternoon sun, a silhouette surrounded by golden light—a human eclipse.

There was stuff going on; at our house on Saturday afternoons, there always was. Andy and Con were in our long backyard, playing three-flies-six-grounders with a bunch of their friends, shouting and laughing. Claire was up in her room with a couple of *her* friends, playing records on her Imperial Party-Time turntable: "The Loco-Motion," "Soldier Boy," "Palisades Park." There was hammering from the garage, too, as Terry and our dad worked on the old '51 Ford Dad called the Road Rocket. Or the Project. Once I heard him call it a piece of shit, a phrase I treasured then and still use now. When you want to feel better, call something a piece of shit. It usually works.

Plenty going on, but at that moment everything seemed to fall still. I know it's only the sort of illusion caused by a faulty memory (not to mention a suitcase loaded with dark associations), but the recollection is very strong. All of a sudden there were no kids yelling in the backyard, no records playing upstairs, no banging from the garage. Not a single bird singing.

Then the man bent down and the westering sun glared over his shoulder, momentarily blinding me. I raised a hand to shield my eyes.

"Sorry, sorry," he said, and moved enough so I could look at him without also having to look into the sun. On top he was wearing a black for-church jacket and a black shirt with a notched collar; on the bottom blue jeans and scuffed loafers. It was like he wanted to be two different people at the same time. At the age of six, I put adults into three categories: young grownups, grownups, and old people. This guy was a young grownup. He had his hands on his knees so he could look at the opposing armies.

"Who are you?" I asked.

"Charles Jacobs." The name was vaguely familiar. He stuck out his hand. I shook it right away, because even at six, I had my manners. All of us did. Mom and Dad saw to that.

"Why are you wearing that collar with the hole in it?"

"Because I'm a minister. When you go to church on Sundays

from now on, I'll be there. And if you go to Thursday-night MYF, I'll be there, too."

"Mr. Latoure used to be our minister," I said, "but he died."

"I know. I'm sorry."

"It's okay, though, because Mom said he didn't suffer, only went straight to heaven. He didn't wear a collar like that, though."

"Because Bill Latoure was a lay preacher. That means he was sort of a volunteer. He kept the church open when there was no one else to do it. That was very good of him."

"I think my dad knows about you," I said. "He's one of the deacons in the church. He gets to take up the collection. He has to take turns with the other deacons, though."

"Sharing is good," Jacobs said, and got down on his knees beside me.

"Are you going to pray?" The idea was sort of alarming. Praying was for church and Methodist Youth Fellowship, which my brothers and sister called Thursday Night School. When Mr. Jacobs started it up again, this would be my first year, just like it was my first year at regular school. "If you want to talk with my dad, he's in the garage with Terry. They're putting a new clutch in the Road Rocket. Well, my dad is. Terry mostly hands him the tools and watches. He's eight. I'm six. I think my mom might be on the back porch, watching some guys play three-flies-six-grounders."

"Which we used to call rollie-bat when I was a kid," he said, and smiled. It was a nice smile. I liked him right away.

"Yeah?"

"Uh-huh, because you had to hit the bat with the ball after you caught it. What's your name, son?"

"Jamie Morton. I'm six."

"So you said."

"I don't think anyone ever prayed in our front yard."

"I'm not going to, either. What I want is a closer look at your armies. Which are the Russians and which are the Americans?"

"Well, these ones on the ground are Americans, sure, but the ones on Skull Mountain are Krauts. The Americans have to take the mountain."

"Because it's in the way," Jacobs said. "Beyond Skull Mountain lies the road to Germany."

"That's right! And the head Kraut! Hitsmer!"

"The author of so many evils," he said.

"Huh?"

"Nothing. Do you mind if I just call the bad guys Germans? 'Krauts' seems kind of mean."

"No, that's great, Krauts are Germans, and Germans are Krauts. My dad was in the war. Just the last year, though. He fixed trucks in Texas. Were you in the war, Mr. Jacobs?"

"No, I was too young. For Korea, too. How are the Americans going to take that hill, General Morton?"

"Charge it!" I shouted. "Shoot their machine guns! Pow! Budda-budda-budda!" Then, going down way low in my throat: "Takka-takka-takka!"

"A direct attack on the high ground sounds risky, General. If I were you I'd split your troops . . . like so . . ." He moved half of the Americans to the left and half to the right. "That creates a pincers movement, see?" He brought his thumb and forefinger together. "Drive on the objective from both sides."

"Maybe," I said. I liked the idea of a head-on attack—lots of bloody action—but Mr. Jacobs's idea appealed to me, just the same. It was sneaky. Sneaky could be satisfying. "I tried to make some caves, but the dirt's too dry."

"So I see." He poked a finger into Skull Mountain and watched the dirt crumble and bury the hole. He stood up and brushed the knees of his jeans. "I've got a little boy who'd probably get a kick out of your soldiers in another year or two."

"He can play right now, if he wants to." I was trying not to be selfish. "Where is he?"

"Still in Boston, with his mother. There's lots of stuff to pack up. They'll be here Wednesday, I think. Thursday at the latest. But Morrie's still a little young for soldiers. He'd only pick them up and throw them around."

"How old is he?"

"Just two."

"I bet he still pees his pants!" I yelled, and started laughing. It probably wasn't polite, but I couldn't help it. Kids peeing their pants was just so funny.

"He does, at that," Jacobs said, smiling, "but I'm sure he'll grow out of it. Your father's in the garage, you say?"

"Yeah." Now I remembered where I had heard the man's name before—Mom and Dad at the supper table, talking about the new minister that was coming from Boston. *Isn't he awfully young?* my mother had asked. *Yes, and his salary will reflect that*, my dad replied, and grinned. They talked about him some more, I think, but I didn't pay any attention. Andy was hogging the mashed potatoes. He always did.

"You try that enfilading maneuver," he said, starting away.

"Huh?"

"Pincers," he said, tweezing his thumb and finger together again.

"Oh. Yeah. Great."

I tried it. It worked pretty good. The Krauts all died. The battle wasn't what I'd call spectacular, though, so I tried the frontal assault, with trucks and jeeps tumbling off the steep slope of Skull Mountain, plus Krauts tumbling off the back with deathcries of despair: "*Yaaaahhh!*"

Mom, Dad, and Mr. Jacobs sat on the front porch while the battle raged, drinking iced tea and talking about churchy things—in addition to my dad being a deacon, my mom was in the Ladies Auxiliary. Not the boss of it, but the next-to-boss. You should have seen all the fancy hats she had in those days. There must have been a dozen. We were happy then.

Mom called my brothers and sister, along with their friends, to meet the new minister. I started to come, too, but Mr. Jacobs waved me back, telling Mom we'd already met. "Battle on, General!" he called.

I battled on. Con, Andy, and their friends went out back again and played on. Claire and her friends went back upstairs and danced on (although my mother told her to turn the music down, please and thank you). Mr. and Mrs. Morton and the Reverend Jacobs talked on, and for quite awhile. I remember often being surprised at how much adults could yak. It was tiring.

I lost track of them because I was fighting the Battle of Skull Mountain over again in several different ways. In the most satisfying scenario—adapted from Mr. Jacobs's pincers movement—one part of the American army kept the Germans pinned down from the front while the rest looped around and ambushed the Germans from behind. "*Vat is zis?*" one of them cried, just before getting shot in the head.

I was starting to get tired of it and was thinking of going in for a slice of cake (if Con and Andy's friends had left any), when that shadow fell over me and my battlefield again. I looked up and saw Mr. Jacobs, holding a glass of water.

"I borrowed this from your mother. Can I show you something?"

"Sure."

He knelt down again and poured the water all over the top of Skull Mountain.

"It's a thunderstorm!" I shouted, and made thunder noises.

"Uh-huh, if you like. With lightning. Now look." He poked out two of his fingers like devil horns and pushed them into the wet dirt. This time the holes stayed. "Presto," he said. "Caves." He took two of the German soldiers and put them inside. "They'll be tough to root out, General, but I'm sure the Americans will be up to the job."

"Hey! Thanks!"

"Add more water if it gets crumbly again."

"I will."

"And remember to take the glass back to the kitchen when you finish the battle. I don't want to get in trouble with your mother on my first day in Harlow."

I promised, and stuck out my hand. "Put er there, Mr. Jacobs."

He laughed and did so, then walked off down Methodist Road, toward the parsonage where he and his family would live for the next three years, until he got fired. I watched him go, then turned back to Skull Mountain.

Before I could really get going, another shadow fell over the battlefield. This time it was my dad. He took a knee, being careful not to squash any American soldiers. "Well, Jamie, what did you think of our new minister?"

"I like him."

"So do I. Your mother does, too. He's very young for the job, and if he's good, we'll only be his starter congregation, but I think he'll do fine. Especially with MYF. Youth calls to youth."

"Look, Daddy, he showed me how to make caves. You only have to get the dirt wet so it makes kinda almost mud."

"I see." He ruffled my hair. "You want to wash up good before supper." He picked up the glass. "Want me to take this in for you?"

"Yes, please and thank you."

He took the glass and headed back to the house. I returned to Skull Mountain, only to see that the dirt had dried out again and the caves had collapsed. The soldiers inside had been buried alive. That was okay with me; they were the bad guys, after all.

These days we've become gruesomely sensitized to sex, and no parent in his or her right mind would send a six-year-old off in the company of a new male acquaintance who was living by himself (if only for a few days), but that is exactly what my mother did the following Monday afternoon, and without a qualm.

Reverend Jacobs—Mom told me I was supposed to call him that, not Mister—came walking up Methodist Hill around quarter to three and knocked on the screen door. I was in the living room, coloring on the floor, while Mom watched *Dialing for Prizes.* She had sent her name in to WCSH, and was hoping to win that month's grand prize, an Electrolux vacuum cleaner. She knew the chances weren't good, but, she said, hope springs infernal. That was a joke.

"Can you loan me your youngest for half an hour?" Reverend Jacobs asked. "I've got something in my garage that he might like to see."

"What is it?" I asked, already getting up.

"A surprise. You can tell your mother all about it later."

"Mom?"

"Of course," she said, "but change out of your school clothes first, Jamie. While he does that, would you like a glass of iced tea, Reverend Jacobs?"

"I would," he said. "And I wonder if you could manage to call me Charlie."

She considered this, then said, "No, but I could probably manage Charles."

I changed into jeans and a tee-shirt, and because they were talking about adult things when I came back downstairs, I went outside to wait for the schoolbus. Con, Terry, and I attended the one-room school on Route 9—an easy quarter-mile walk from our house—but Andy went to Consolidated Middle and Claire all the way across the river to Gates Falls High, where she was a freshman. ("Just don't be a fresh *girl*," Mom told her—that was also a joke.) The bus dropped them off at the intersection of Route 9 and Methodist Road, at the foot of Methodist Hill.

I saw them get off, and as they came trudging up the hill—squabbling as always, I could hear them as I stood waiting by the mailbox—Reverend Jacobs came out.

"Ready?" he asked, and took my hand. It seemed perfectly natural.

"Sure," I said.

We met Andy and Claire halfway down the hill. Andy asked where I was going.

"To Reverend Jacobs' house," I said. "He's going to show me a surprise."

"Well, don't be too long," Claire said. "It's your turn to set the table." She glanced at Jacobs, then quickly away again, as if she found him hard to look at. My big sister had a wicked crush on him before the year was out, and so did all her friends.

"I'll have him back shortly," Jacobs promised.

We walked down the hill hand in hand to Route 9, which led to Portland if you turned left, to Gates Falls, Castle Rock, and Lewiston if you turned right. We stopped and looked for traffic, which was ridiculous since there were hardly any cars on Route 9 except in the summer, and then walked on past hayfields and cornfields, the stalks of the latter now dry and clattering in a mild autumn breeze. Ten minutes brought us to the parsonage, a tidy white house with black shutters. Beyond it was the First Methodist Church of Harlow, which was also ridiculous since there was no other Methodist church in Harlow.

The only other house of worship in Harlow was Shiloh Church. My father considered the Shilohites moderate to serious weirdos. They didn't ride around in horse-drawn buggies, or anything, but the men and boys all wore black hats when they were outside. The women and girls wore dresses that came down to their ankles, and white caps. Dad said the Shilohites claimed to know when the world was going to end; it was written down in a special book. My mother said in America everyone was entitled to believe what they liked as long as they didn't hurt anybody . . . but she didn't say Dad was wrong, either. Our church was larger than Shiloh, but very plain. Also, it had no steeple. It did once, but a hurricane came along back in the olden days, 1920 or so, and knocked it down.

Reverend Jacobs and I walked up the parsonage's dirt driveway. I was interested to see that he had a blue Plymouth Belvedere, a very cool car. "Standard shift or push-button drive?" I asked.

He looked surprised, then grinned. "Push-button," he said. "It was a wedding present from my in-laws."

"Are in-laws like outlaws?"

"Mine are," he said, and laughed. "Do you like cars?"

"We all like cars," I said, meaning everyone in my family . . . although that was less true of Mom and Claire, I guessed. Females didn't seem to totally understand the basic coolness of cars. "When the Road Rocket's fixed up, my dad's going to race it at the Castle Rock Speedway."

"Really?"

"Well, not him, exactly. Mom said he couldn't because it's too dangerous, but some guy. Maybe Duane Robichaud. He runs

Brownie's Store along with his mom and dad. He drove the nine-car at the Speedway last year, but the engine caught on fire. Dad says he's looking for another ride."

"Do the Robichauds come to church?"

"Um . . ."

"I'll take that as a no. Come in the garage, Jamie."

It was shadowy and musty-smelling. I was a little afraid of the shadows and the smell, but Jacobs didn't seem to mind. He led me deeper into the gloom, then stopped and pointed. I gasped at what I saw.

Jacobs gave a little chuckle, the way people do when they're proud of something. "Welcome to Peaceable Lake, Jamie."

"Wow!"

"I got it set up while I'm waiting for Patsy and Morrie to get here. I should be doing stuff in the house, and I *have* done a fair amount—fixed the well-pump, for one thing—but there's not a whole lot more I *can* do until Pats gets here with the furniture. Your mom and the rest of the Ladies Auxiliary did a terrific job of cleaning the place up, kiddo. Mr. Latoure commuted from Orr's Island, and no one's actually lived here since before World War II. I thanked her, but I wouldn't mind if you thanked her again."

"Sure, you bet," I said, but I don't believe I ever passed that second thanks on, because I barely heard what he was saying. All my attention was fixed on a table that took up almost half the garage space. On it was a rolling green landscape that put Skull Mountain to shame. I have seen many such landscapes since—mostly in the windows of toyshops—but they all had complicated electric trains running through them. There was no train on the table Reverend Jacobs had set up, which wasn't a real table at all, but sheets of plywood on a rank of sawhorses. Atop the plywood was a countryside in miniature, about twelve feet long and five feet wide. Power pylons eighteen inches high marched across it on a diagonal, and it was dominated by a lake of real water that shone bright blue even in the gloom.

"I'll have to take it down soon," he said, "or else I won't be able to get the car in the garage. Patsy wouldn't care for that."

He bent, planted his hands above his knees, and gazed at the rolling hills, the threadlike power lines, the big lake. There were plastic sheep and cows grazing near the water (they were considerably out of scale, but I didn't notice and wouldn't have cared if I had). There were also lots of streetlamps, which was a little peculiar, since there was no town and no roads for them to shine on.

"I bet you could have quite a battle with your soldiers here, couldn't you?"

"Yeah," I said. I thought I could fight an entire war there.

He nodded. "That can't happen, though, because in Peaceable Lake, everyone gets along and no fighting is allowed. In that way it's like heaven. Once I get MYF going, I plan to move it to the church basement. Maybe you and your brothers would help me. The kids would like it, I think."

"They sure would!" I said, then added something my father said. "You betchum bobcats!"

He laughed and clapped me on the shoulder. "Now do you want to see a miracle?"

"I guess," I said. I wasn't actually sure I did. It sounded like it might be scary. All at once I realized the two of us were alone in an old garage with no car in it, a dusty hollow that smelled as if it had been closed up for years. The door to the outside world was still open, but it seemed a mile off. I liked Reverend Jacobs okay, but I found myself wishing I had stayed home, coloring on the floor and waiting to see if Mom could win the Electrolux and finally get the upper hand in her never-ending battle with the summer dust.

Then Reverend Jacobs passed his hand slowly above Peaceable

Lake, and I forgot about being nervous. There was a low humming sound from under the makeshift table, like the sound our Philco TV made when it was warming up, and all the little streetlights came on. They were bright white, almost too bright to look at, and cast a magical moony glow over the green hills and blue water. Even the plastic cows and sheep looked more realistic, possibly because they now cast shadows.

"Gosh, how did you do that?"

He grinned. "Pretty good trick, huh? 'God said, Let there be light, and there was light, and the light was good.' Only I'm not God, so I have to depend on electricity. Which is wonderful stuff, Jamie. Such a gift from God that it makes us feel godlike every time we flip a switch, wouldn't you say?"

"I guess so," I said. "My grandpa Amos remembers before there were electric lights."

"Lots of people do," he said, "but it won't be long before all those people are gone . . . and when that happens, nobody will think much about what a miracle electricity is. And what a mystery. We have an idea about how it works, but knowing how something works and knowing what it *is* are two very different things."

"How did you turn on the lights?" I asked.

He pointed to a shelf beyond the table. "See that little red bulb?"

"Uh-huh."

"It's a photoelectric cell. You can buy them, but I built that one myself. It projects an invisible beam. When I break it, the streetlights around Peaceable Lake go on. If I do it again . . . like so . . ." He passed his hand above the landscape and the streetlights dimmed, faded to faint cores of light, then went out. "You see?"

"Cool," I breathed.

"You try it."

I reached my hand up. At first nothing happened, but when I

stood on tiptoe my fingers broke the beam. The humming from beneath the table started up again and the lights came back on.

"I did it!"

"Betchum bobcats," he said, and ruffled my hair.

"What's that humming? It sounds like our TV."

"Look under the table. Here, I'll turn on the overhead lights so you can see better." He flipped a switch on the wall and a couple of dusty hanging lightbulbs came on. They did nothing about the musty odor (and I could smell something else as well, now—something hot and oily), but they banished some of the gloom.

I bent—at my age I didn't have to bend far—and looked beneath the table. I saw two or three boxy things strapped to the underside. They were the source of the humming sound, and the oily smell, too.

"Batteries," he said. "Which I also made myself. Electricity is my hobby. And gadgets." He grinned like a kid. "I love gadgets. Drives my wife crazy."

"My hobby's fighting the Krauts," I said. Then, remembering what he said about that being kind of mean: "Germans, I mean."

"Everyone needs a hobby," he said. "And everyone needs a miracle or two, just to prove life is more than just one long trudge from the cradle to the grave. Would you like to see another one, Jamie?"

"Sure!"

There was a second table in the corner, covered with tools, snips of wire, three or four dismembered transistor radios like the ones Claire and Andy had, and regular store-bought C and D batteries. There was also a small wooden box. Jacobs took the box, dropped to one knee so we'd be on the same level, opened it, and took out a white-robed figure. "Do you know who this is?"

I did, because the guy looked almost the same as my fluorescent nightlight. "Jesus. Jesus with a pack on his back."

"Not just any pack; a battery pack. Look." He flipped up the top of the pack on a hinge not bigger than a sewing needle. Inside I saw what looked like a couple of shiny dimes with tiny dots of solder on them. "I made these, too, because you can't buy anything this small or powerful in the stores. I believe I could patent them, and maybe someday I will, but . . ." He shook his head. "Never mind."

He closed the top of the pack again, and carried Jesus to the Peaceable Lake landscape. "I hope you noticed how blue the water is," he said.

"Yeah! Bluest lake I ever saw!"

He nodded. "Kind of a miracle in itself, you might say . . . until you take a close look."

"Huh?"

"It's really just paint. I muse on that, sometimes, Jamie. When I can't sleep. How a little paint can make shallow water seem deep."

That seemed like a silly thing to think about, but I didn't say anything. Then he kind of snapped to, and put Jesus down beside the lake.

"I plan to use this in MYF—it's what we call a teaching tool—but I'll give you a little preview, okay?"

"Okay."

"Here's what it says in the fourteenth chapter of Matthew's Gospel. Will you take instruction from God's Holy Word, Jamie?"

"Sure, I guess so," I said, starting to feel uneasy again.

"I know you will," he said, "because what we learn as children is what sticks the longest. Okay, here we go, so listen up. 'And straightaway Jesus constrained his disciples'—that means he commanded them—'to get into a ship, and to go before him to the other side of the water, while he sent the multitudes away. And when he had sent the multitudes away, he went up into a mountain to pray—' Do *you* pray, Jamie?"

"Yeah, every night."

"Good boy. Okay, back to the story. 'When evening was come, he was there alone. But the ship was now in the midst of the sea, tossed with waves, for the wind was contrary. And in the fourth watch Jesus went unto them, walking on the sea. And when the disciples saw him walking on the sea, they were troubled, saying, It is a spirit; and they cried out for fear. But straightaway Jesus spake unto them, saying, Be of good cheer; it is I; be not afraid.' That's the story, and may God bless his Holy Word. Good one, huh?"

"I guess. Does *spake* mean he talked to them? It does, right?"

"Right. Would you like to see Jesus walk on Peaceable Lake?"

"Yeah! Sure!"

He reached under Jesus's white robe, and the little figure began to move. When it reached Peaceable Lake it didn't sink but continued serenely on, gliding along the top of the water. It reached the other side in twenty seconds or so. There was a hill there, and it tried to go up, but I could see it was going to topple over. Reverend Jacobs grabbed it before it could. He reached under Jesus's robe again and turned him off.

"He did it!" I said. "He walked on the water!"

"Well . . ." He was smiling, but it wasn't a funny smile, somehow. It turned down at one corner. "Yes and no."

"What do you mean?"

"See where he went into the water?"

"Yeah . . ."

"Reach in there. See what you find. Be careful not to touch the power lines, because there's real electricity running through them. Not much, but if you brushed them, you'd get a jolt. Especially if your hand was wet."

I reached in, but cautiously. I didn't think he'd play a practical joke on me—as Terry and Con sometimes did—but I was in a strange place with a strange man and I wasn't completely sure. The water looked deep, but that was an illusion created by the blue paint of the reservoir and the lights reflecting on the surface. My finger only went in up to the first knuckle.

"You're not quite in the right place," Reverend Jacobs said. "Go a little bit to your right. Do you know your right from your left?"

I did. Mom had taught me: *Right is the hand you write with*. Of course that wouldn't have worked with Claire and Con, who were what my dad called southpaws.

I moved my hand and felt something in the water. It was metal, with a groove in it. "I think I found it," I told Reverend Jacobs.

"I think so, too. You're touching the track Jesus walks on."

"It's a magic trick!" I said. I had seen magicians on *The Ed Sullivan Show*, and Con had a box of magic tricks he got for his birthday, although everything but the Floating Balls and the Disappearing Egg had been lost.

"That's right."

"Like Jesus walking on the water to that ship!"

"Sometimes," he said, "that's what I'm afraid of."

He looked so sad and distant that I felt a little scared again, but I also felt sorry for him. Not that I had any idea what he had to feel sad about when he had such a neat pretend world as Peaceable Lake in his garage.

"It's a really *good* trick," I said, and patted his hand.

He came back from wherever he'd gone and grinned at me. "You're right," he said. "I'm just missing my wife and little boy, I guess. I think that's why I borrowed you, Jamie. But I ought to return you to your mom now."

When we got to Route 9, he took my hand again even though there were no cars coming either way, and we walked like that all the way up Methodist Road. I didn't mind. I liked holding his hand. I knew he was looking out for me.

Mrs. Jacobs and Morris arrived a few days later. He was just a little squirt in didies, but she was pretty. On Saturday, the day before Reverend Jacobs first stood in the pulpit of our church, Terry, Con, and I helped him move Peaceable Lake to the church basement, where Methodist Youth Fellowship would meet every Thursday night. With the water drained, the shallowness of the lake and the grooved track running across it were very clear.

Reverend Jacobs swore Terry and Con to secrecy—because, he said, he didn't want the illusion spoiled for the little ones (which made me feel like a big one, a sensation I enjoyed). They agreed, and I don't think either of them peached, but the lights in the church basement were much brighter than those in the parsonage garage, and if you stood close to the landscape and peered at it, you could see that Peaceable Lake was really just a wide puddle. You could see the grooved track, too. By Christmas, everyone knew.

"It's a big old fakearoonie," Billy Paquette said to me one Thursday afternoon. He and his brother Ronnie hated Thursday Night School, but their mother made them go. "If he shows it off one more time and tells that walking-on-water story, I'm gonna puke."

I thought of fighting him over that, but he was bigger. Also my friend. Besides, he was right.

II

Three Years. Conrad's Voice. A Miracle.

Reverend Jacobs got fired because of the sermon he gave from his pulpit on November 21, 1965. That was easy to look up on the Internet, because I had a landmark to go by: it was the Sunday before Thanksgiving. He was gone from our lives a week later, and he went alone. Patsy and Morris—dubbed Tag-Along-Morrie by the kids in MYF—were already gone by then. So was the Plymouth Belvedere with the push-button drive.

My memory of the three years between the day when I first saw Peaceable Lake and the day of the Terrible Sermon are surprisingly clear, although before beginning this account, I would have told you I remembered little. After all, I would have said, how many of us remember the years between six and nine in any detail? But writing is a wonderful and terrible thing. It opens deep wells of memory that were previously capped.

I feel I could push aside the account I set out to write and instead fill a book—and not a small one—about those years and that world, which is so different from the one I live in now. I remember my mother, standing at the ironing board in her slip, impossibly beautiful in the morning sunshine. I remember my saggy-seated bathing suit, an unattractive loden green, and swimming in Harry's

Pond with my brothers. We used to tell each other the slimy bottom was cowshit, but it was just mud (*probably* just mud). I remember drowsy afternoons in the one-room West Harlow school, sitting on winter coats in Spelling Corner and trying to get poor stupid Dicky Osgood to get *giraffe* right. I even remember him saying, "W-W-Why sh-should I have to suh-suh-*spell* one when I'll never suh-suh-*see* one?"

I remember the webwork of dirt roads that crisscrossed our town, and playing marbles in the schoolyard during frigid April recesses, and the sound the wind made in the pines as I lay in my bed, prayers said and waiting for sleep. I remember my father coming out of the garage with a wrench in his hand and his MORTON FUEL OIL cap pulled low on his forehead, blood oozing through the grease on his knuckles. I remember watching Ken MacKenzie introducing Popeye cartoons on *The Mighty 90 Show*, and how I was forced to give up the TV on the afternoons when Claire and her friends arrived, because they wanted to watch *American Bandstand* and see what the girls were wearing. I remember sunsets as red as the blood on my father's knuckles, and how that makes me shiver now.

I remember a thousand other things, mostly good ones, but I didn't sit down at my computer to put on rose-colored glasses and wax nostalgic. Selective memory is one of the chief sins of the old, and I don't have time for it. They were not all good things. We lived in the country, and back then, country life was hard. I suppose it still is.

My friend Al Knowles got his left hand caught in his father's potato grader and lost three fingers before Mr. Knowles could get the balky, dangerous thing turned off. I was there that day, and remember how the belts turned red. I remember how Al screamed.

My father (along with Terry, his faithful if clueless acolyte) got the Road Rocket running—God, what a gorgeous, blasting clatter it made when he revved the engine!—and turned it over to Duane Robichaud, newly painted and with the number *19* emblazoned on its side, to race at the Speedway in Castle Rock. In the first lap of the first heat, the idiot rolled it and totaled it. Duane walked away without a scratch. "Accelerator pedal must have stuck," he said, grinning his foolish grin, only he said it *ass*-celerator, and my father said the only ass was the one behind the wheel.

"That will teach you to ever trust anything valuable to a Robichaud," my mother said, and my father stuffed his hands so deep into his pockets that the top of his underwear showed, perhaps to ensure they would not escape and go someplace they weren't supposed to.

Lenny Macintosh, the postman's son, lost an eye when he bent down to see why the cherry bomb he'd put in an empty pineapple tin didn't go off.

My brother Conrad lost his voice.

So, no—they weren't all good things.

On the first Sunday that Reverend Jacobs took the pulpit, there were more people present than had been there in all the years fat, white-haired, good-natured Mr. Latoure had kept the church open, preaching his well-meant but obscure sermons and reliably welling up at the eyes on Mother's Day, which he called Mother's Sunday (these details came courtesy of my own mother, years later—I barely remembered Mr. Latoure at all). Instead of twenty congregants there were easily four times that number, and I remember how their voices soared during the Doxology: *Praise God from Whom all blessings flow, Praise Him ye creatures here below*. It gave me goosebumps. Mrs. Jacobs was no slouch on the pedal organ, either, and her blond hair—held back with a plain black ribbon—glowed many colors in the light falling through our only stained glass window.

Walking home from church *en famille*, our good Sunday shoes kicking up little puffs of dust, I found myself just behind my parents, so heard Mom expressing her approval. Also her relief. "I thought, him being so young and all, we'd get a lecture on civil rights, or banning the draft, or something like that," she said. "Instead we got a very nice Bible-based lesson. I think people will come back, don't you?"

"For awhile," my father said.

She said, "Oh, the big oil baron. The big cynic." And punched his arm playfully.

As it turned out, they were both sort of right. Attendance at our church never slumped back to Mr. Latoure levels—which meant as few as a dozen in winter, huddled together for warmth in the drafty, woodstove-heated church—but it dropped slowly to sixty, then fifty, and finally to forty or so, where it hovered like the barometer on a changeable summer day. No one ascribed the attrition to Mr. Jacobs's preaching, which was always clear, pleasant, and Bible-based (never anything troubling about A-bombs or Freedom Marches); folks just kind of drifted away.

"God isn't as important to people now," my mother said one day after a particularly disappointing turnout. "A day will come when they'll be sorry for that."

During those three years, our Methodist Youth Fellowship also underwent a modest renaissance. In the Latoure Era, there were rarely more than a dozen of us on Thursday nights, and four were named Morton: Claire, Andy, Con, and Terry. In the Latoure Era I was considered too young to attend, and for this Andy sometimes used to give me head-noogies and call me a lucky duck. When I asked Terry once what it was like back then, he gave a bored shrug.

"We sang songs and did Bible drills and promised we'd never drink intoxicating liquor or smoke cigarettes. Then he told us to love our mothers, and the Catlicks are going to hell because they worship idols, and Jewish people love money. He also said to imagine Jesus is listening if any of our friends tell dirty jokes."

Under the new regime, however, attendance swelled to three dozen kids between six and seventeen, which necessitated buying more folding chairs for the church basement. It wasn't Reverend Jacobs's mechanical Jesus toddling across Peaceable Lake; the thrill of that wore off rapidly, even for me. I doubt if the pictures of the Holy Land he put up on the walls had much to do with it, either.

A lot of it was his youth and enthusiasm. There were games and activities as well as sermons, because, as he pointed out regularly, most of Jesus's preaching happened outside, and that meant there was more to Christianity than church. The Bible drills remained, but we did them while playing musical chairs, and quite often someone fell on the floor while searching for Deuteronomy 14, verse 9, or Timothy 2:12. It was pretty comical. Then there was the ball diamond, which Con and Andy helped him create out back. On some Thursdays the boys played baseball and the girls cheered us on; on alternate Thursdays it was the girls playing softball and the boys (hoping some of the girls would forget it was their turn and come in skirts) cheering *them* on.

Reverend Jacobs's interest in electricity often played a part in his Thursday-night "youth talks." I remember one afternoon when he called our house and asked Andy to wear a sweater on Thursday night. When we were all assembled, he called my brother to the front of the room and said he wanted to demonstrate the burden of sin. "Although I'm sure *you're* not much of a sinner, Andrew," he added.

My brother smiled nervously and said nothing.

"This isn't to frighten you kids," he said. "There are ministers who believe in that kind of thing, but I'm not one of them. It's just so you'll know." (This, I've learned, is the kind of thing people say just before they try to scare the living crap out of you.)

He blew up a number of balloons and told us to imagine that each one weighed twenty pounds. He held the first up and said, "This one is telling lies." He rubbed it briskly on his shirt a few times, and then held it against Andy's sweater, where it stuck as if it were glued there.

"This one is theft." He stuck another balloon to Andy's sweater.

"Here's anger."

I can't remember for sure, but I think it likely he stuck seven balloons in all to Andy's homemade reindeer sweater, one for each of the deadly sins.

"That adds up to over a hundred pounds of sin," he said. "A lot to carry! But who takes away the sins of the world?"

"Jesus!" we dutifully chorused.

"Right. When you ask Him for forgiveness, here's what happens." He produced a pin and popped the balloons one after another, including one that had drifted free and needed to be stuck back on. I think we all felt that the balloon-popping part of the lesson was quite a bit more exciting than the sanctified static electricity part.

His most impressive demonstration of electricity in action involved one of his own inventions, which he called Jacob's Ladder. It was a metal box about the size of the footlocker my toy army lived in. Two wires that looked like TV rabbit ears jutted up from it. When he plugged it in (this invention ran on wall current rather than batteries) and flipped the switch on the side, long sparks almost too bright to look at climbed the wires. At the top, they peaked and disappeared. When he sprinkled some powder above this device, the climbing sparks turned different colors. It made the girls ooh with delight.

This also had some sort of religious point—at least in the mind of Charles Jacobs, it did—but I'll be damned if I remember what it was. Something about the Divine Trinity, maybe? Once the Jacob's Ladder wasn't right there in front of us, the colored sparks rising and the current fizzing like an angry tomcat, such exotic ideas had a tendency to fade away like a transient fever.

Yet I remember one of his mini-lectures very clearly. He was sitting on a chair that was turned around so he could face us over the back. His wife sat on the piano bench behind him, hands folded demurely in her lap, head slightly bowed. Maybe she was praying. Maybe she was just bored. I know that a lot of his audience was; by then most of the Harlow Methodist Youth had begun to tire of electricity and its attendant glories.

"Kids, science teaches us that electricity is the movement of charged atomic particles called electrons. When electrons flow, they create current, and the faster the electrons flow, the higher the voltage. That's science, and science is fine, but it's also *finite.* There always comes a point where knowledge runs out. What *are* electrons, exactly? Charged atoms, the scientists say. Okay, that's fine as far as it goes, but what are atoms?"

He leaned forward over the back of his chair, his blue eyes (they themselves looked electric) fixed on us.

"*No one really knows!* And that's where religion comes in. Electricity is one of God's doorways to the infinite."

"I wish he'd bring in a lectric chair and fry up some white mice," Billy Paquette sniffed one evening after the benediction. "*That* would be in'dresting."

In spite of the frequent (and increasingly boring) lectures on holy voltage, most of us looked forward to Thursday Night School. When he wasn't on his hobbyhorse, Reverend Jacobs could give lively, sometimes funny talks with lessons drawn from Scripture.

He talked about real-life problems we all faced, from bullying to the temptation to cheat answers from someone else's paper during tests we hadn't studied for. We enjoyed the games, we enjoyed most of the lessons, and we enjoyed the singing, too, because Mrs. Jacobs was a fine pianist who never dragged the hymns.

She knew more than hymns, too. On one never-to-be-forgotten night she played a trio of Beatles songs, and we sang along with "From Me to You," "She Loves You," and "I Want to Hold Your Hand." My mother claimed that Patsy Jacobs was seventy times better on the piano than Mr. Latoure, and when the minister's young wife asked to spend some of the church collection money on a piano tuner from Portland, the deacons approved the request unanimously.

"But perhaps no more Beatles songs," Mr. Kelton said. He was the deacon who had served Harlow Methodist the longest. "The children can get that stuff on the radio. We'd prefer you to stick to more . . . uh . . . *Christian* melodies."

Mrs. Jacobs murmured her agreement, eyes demurely cast down.

There was something else, as well: Charles and Patsy Jacobs had sex appeal. I have mentioned that Claire and her friends were gaga for him; it wasn't long before most of the boys had crushes on her, as well, because Patsy Jacobs was beautiful. Her hair was blond, her complexion creamy, her lips full. Her slightly uptilted eyes were green, and Connie claimed she had witchly powers, because every time she happened to shift those green eyes his way, his knees turned to water. With those kind of looks, there would have been talk if she had worn more makeup than a decorous blush of lipstick, but at twenty-three, that was all she needed. Youth was her makeup.

She wore perfectly proper knee- or shin-length dresses on Sundays, even though those were the years when ladies' hemlines started their climb. On MYF Thursday nights, she wore perfectly proper slacks and blouses (Ship 'n Shore, according to my mother). But the moms and grandmoms in the congregation watched her closely just the same, because the figure those perfectly proper clothes set off was the kind that made my brothers' friends sometimes roll their eyes or shake a hand the way you do after touching a stove burner someone forgot to turn off. She played softball on Girls' Nights, and I once overheard my brother Andy—who would have been going on fourteen at the time, I think—say that watching her run the bases was a religious experience in itself.

She was able to play the piano on Thursday nights and participate in most of the other MYF activities because she could bring their little boy along. He was a biddable, easy child. Everyone liked Morrie. To the best of my recollection even Billy Paquette, that young atheist in the making, liked Morrie, who hardly ever cried. Even when he fell down and skinned his knees, the worst he was liable to do was sniffle, and even that would stop if one of the bigger girls picked him up and cuddled him. When we went outside to play games, he followed the boys everywhere he could, and when he was unable to keep up with them, he followed the girls, who also minded him during Bible Study or swung him around to the beat during Sing Time—hence the nickname Tag-Along-Morrie.

Claire was particularly fond of him, and I have a clear memory—which I know must be made up of many overlaid memories—of them in the corner where the toys were, Morrie in his little chair, Claire on her knees beside him, helping him to color or to construct a domino snake. "I want four just like him when I get married," Claire told my mother once. She would have been going on seventeen by then, I suppose, and ready to graduate from MYF.

"Good luck on that," my mother replied. "In any case, I hope yours will be better looking than Morrie, Claire-Bear."

That was a tad unkind, but not untrue. Although Charles Jacobs was a good-looking man and Patsy Jacobs was a downright beautiful young woman, Tag-Along-Morrie was as plain as mashed potatoes. He had a perfectly round face that reminded me of Charlie Brown's. His hair was a nondescript shade of brunet. Although his father's eyes were blue and his mother's that entrancing green, Morrie's were plain old brown. Yet the girls all loved him, as if he were a starter-child for the ones they would have in the following decade, and the boys treated him like a kid brother. He was our mascot. He was Tag-Along-Morrie.

One February Thursday night, my four siblings and I came back from the parsonage with our cheeks red from sledding behind the church (Reverend Jacobs had set up electric lights along our run), singing "I'm Henry the Eighth" at the top of our lungs. I remember that Andy and Con were in a particularly hilarious mood, because they'd brought our toboggan and put Morrie on a cushion at the front, where he rode fearlessly and looked like the figurehead on the prow of a ship.

"You guys like those meetings, don't you?" my father asked. I think there was mild wonder in his voice.

"Yeah!" I said. "We did about a thousand Bible drills tonight, then went out back on our sleds! Mrs. Jacobs, she sledded, too, only she kept falling off!"

I laughed and he laughed with me. "That's great, but are you *learning* anything, Jamie?"

"Man's will should be an extension of God's will," I said, parroting that night's lesson. "Also, if you connect the positive and negative terminals of a battery with a wire, it makes a short circuit."

"True," he said, "which is why you always have to be careful when you're jump-starting a car. But I don't see any Christian lesson in that."

"It was about how doing something wrong because you thought it might make something else better doesn't work."

"Oh." He picked up the latest issue of *Car and Driver*, which had a cool Jaguar XK-E on the cover. "Well, you know what they say, Jamie: The road to hell is paved with good intentions." He thought for a moment, then added: "And lit with electric lights."

That made him laugh, and I laughed with him, even though I didn't get the joke. If it was a joke.

Andy and Con were friends with the Ferguson brothers, Norm and Hal. They were what we called flatlanders, or folks from away. The Fergusons lived in Boston, so the friendship was ordinarily restricted to summer vacations. The family had a cottage on Lookout Lake, only a mile or so from our house, and the two sets of brothers met at another church-related event, in this case Vacation Bible School.

The Fergusons had a family membership at Goat Mountain Resort, and sometimes Con and Andy would go with them in the Fergusons' station wagon to swim and have lunch in "the club." The pool, they said, was about a thousand times better than Harry's Pond. Neither Terry nor I cared much about this—the local swimming hole was fine by us, and we had our own friends—but it drove Claire wild with envy. She wanted to see "how the other half lived."

"They live just like us, dear," Mom said. "Whoever said the rich are different was wrong."

Claire, who was running clothes through our old washing machine's wringer, scrunched her face into a pout. "I doubt *that*," she said.

"Andy says the girls who swim in the pool wear bikinis," I said.

My mother snorted. "They might as well go swimming in their bras and underpants."

"I'd like to have a bikini," Claire remarked. It was, I suppose, the sort of provocation girls of seventeen specialize in.

My mother pointed a finger at her, soap dripping from one short-clipped nail. "That's how girls get pregnant, missy."

Claire returned *that* serve smartly. "Then you ought to keep Con and Andy from going. They might *get* a girl pregnant."

"Zip your lip," my mother said, cutting her eyes in my direction. "Little pitchers have big ears."

Like I didn't know what getting a girl pregnant meant: sex. Boys lay down on top of girls and wiggled around until they *got the feeling*. When that happened, a mysterious something called jizz came from the boy's dink. It sank into the girl's belly, and nine months later it was time for diapers and a baby carriage.

My parents didn't stop Con and Andy from going to the resort once or twice a week during the summer in spite of my sister's dog-in-the-manger barking, and when the Fergusons came up for February vacation in 1965 and invited my brothers to go skiing with them, my parents sent them off to Goat Mountain without a qualm, my brothers' scarred old skis strapped to the station wagon's roof right along with the Fergusons' gleaming new ones.

When they came back, there was a bright red weal across Con's throat. "Did you drift off-course and run into a tree branch?" Dad asked when he came home for supper and saw the mark.

Con, a fine skier, was indignant. "Gosh no, Dad. Me n Norm were racing. We were side by side, going like hell's kitchen—"

Mom pointed her fork at him.

"Sorry, Mom, like heck's kitchen. Norm hit a mogul and just about lost his balance. He stuck out his arm like this"—Con demonstrated, almost knocking over his glass of milk—"and his ski pole hit me in the neck. It hurt like . . . you know, bad, but it's better now."

Only it wasn't. The next day the red mark had faded to a necklace-like bruise, but his voice had gotten hoarse. By that night he could hardly speak above a whisper. Two days later, he was completely mute.

A hyperextension of the neck resulting in a stretched laryngeal nerve. That was Dr. Renault's diagnosis. He said he'd seen them before, and in a week or two, Conrad's voice would begin to come back. By the end of March Connie would be as right as a trivet. Nothing to worry about, he said, and there wasn't. Not for him, at least; *his* voice was fine. This was not true of my brother. When April rolled around, Con was still writing notes and making gestures when he wanted something. He insisted on going to school, even though the other boys had started making fun of him, especially since he had solved the problem of class participation (to a degree, anyway) by writing YES on one palm and NO on the other. He had a pile of file cards with more communications written on them in block letters. The one his classmates found particularly hilarious was MAY I USE THE RESTROOM.

Con seemed to take all this in good spirits, knowing that to do otherwise would only make the teasing worse, but one night I went into the room he shared with Terry and found him lying on his bed and weeping soundlessly. I went to him, asking what was wrong. A stupid question, since I knew, but you have to say *something* in that situation, and I *could* say it, because I wasn't the one who'd been struck across the throat with the Ski Pole of Destiny.

Get out! he mouthed. His cheeks and forehead, studded with newly arrived pimples, were flaming. His eyes were swollen. *Get out, get out!* Then, shocking me: *Get the fuck out, cocksucker!*

The first gray began to appear in my mother's hair that spring.

One afternoon when my father came in, looking more tired than usual, Mom told him that they had to take Con to a specialist in Portland. "We've waited long enough," she said. "That old fool George Renault can say whatever he likes, but I know what happened, and so do you. That careless rich boy ruptured my son's vocal cords."

My father sat down heavily at the table. Neither of them noticed me in the mudroom, taking an inordinate amount of time to lace up my Keds. "We can't afford it, Laura," he said.

"But you could afford to buy Hiram Oil in Gates Falls!" she said, using an ugly, almost sneering tone of voice I had never heard before.

He sat looking at the table instead of at her, although there was nothing on it except the red-and-white-checked oilcloth. "That's *why* we can't afford it. We're skating on mighty thin ice. You know what kind of winter it was."

We all knew: a warm one. When your family's income depends on heating oil, you keep a close eye on the thermometer between Thanksgiving and Easter, hoping the red line will stay low.

My mother was at the sink, hands buried in a cloud of soapsuds. Somewhere beneath the cloud, dishes were rattling as if she wanted to break them instead of clean them. "You had to have it, didn't you?" Still in that same tone of voice. I hated that voice. It was as if she was egging him on. "The big oil baron!"

"That deal was made before Con's accident," he said, still not looking up. His hands were once more stuffed deep into his pockets. "That deal was made in August. We sat together looking at *The Old Farmer's Almanac*—a cold and snowy winter, it said, coldest since the end of World War II—and we decided it was the right thing to do. You ran the numbers on your adding machine."

The dishes rattled harder under the soapsuds. "Take out a loan!"

"I could, but Laura . . . listen to me." He raised his eyes at last. "I may have to do that just to make it through the summer."

"He's your son!"

"*I know he is, goddammit!*" Dad roared. It scared me, and must have scared my mother, because this time the dishes under the cloud of suds did more than rattle. They crashed. And when she raised her hands, one of them was bleeding.

She held it up to him—like my silent brother showing YES or NO in class—and said, "Look what you made me d—" She caught sight of me, sitting on the woodpile and staring into the kitchen. "Buzz off! Go out and play!"

"Laura, don't take it out on Ja—"

"*Get out!*" she shouted. It was the way Con would have shouted at me, if he'd had a voice to shout with. "*God hates a snoop!*"

She began to cry. I ran out the door, crying myself. I ran down Methodist Hill, and across Route 9 without looking in either direction. I had no idea of going to the parsonage; I was too upset to even think of seeking pastoral advice. If Patsy Jacobs hadn't been in the front yard, checking to see if any of the flowers she'd planted the previous fall were coming up, I might have run until I collapsed. But she *was* out, and she called my name. Part of me wanted to just keep on running, but—as I think I've said—I had my manners, even when I was upset. So I stopped.

She came to where I was standing, my head down, gasping for breath. "What happened, Jamie?"

I didn't say anything. She put her fingers under my chin and raised my head. I saw Morrie sitting on the grass beside the parsonage's front stoop, surrounded by toy trucks. He was goggling at me.

"Jamie? Tell me what's wrong."

Just as we had been taught to be polite, we had been taught to keep our mouths shut about what went on in the family. It was the Yankee way. But her kindness undid me and it all came pouring out: Con's misery (the depth of which I'm convinced neither of our parents comprehended, in spite of their very real concern), my mother's fear that his vocal cords had been ruptured and he might never speak again, her insistence on a specialist and Dad's on how they couldn't afford it. Most of all, the shouting. I didn't tell Patsy about the stranger's voice I had heard coming from my mother's mouth, but only because I could not think how to say it.

When I finally ran down, she said: "Come around to the back shed. You need to talk to Charlie."

Now that the Belvedere had taken its proper place in the parsonage garage, the back shed had become Jacobs's workshop. When Patsy led me in, he was tinkering with a television set that had no screen.

"When I put this puppy back together," he said, slinging an arm around my shoulders and producing a handkerchief from his back pocket, "I'll be able to get TV stations in Miami, Chicago, and Los Angeles. Wipe your eyes, Jamie. And your nose could use a little attention while you're at it."

I looked at the eyeless TV with fascination as I cleaned up. "Will you really be able to get stations in Chicago and Los Angeles?"

"Nah, I was kidding. I'm just trying to build in a signal amplifier that will let us get something besides Channel 8."

"We get 6 and 13, too," I said. "Although 6 is a little snowstormy."

"You guys have a roof antenna. The Jacobs family is stuck with rabbit ears."

"Why don't you buy one? They sell them at Western Auto in Castle Rock."

He grinned. "Good idea! I'll stand up in front of the deacons at the quarterly meeting and tell them I want to spend some of the collection money on a TV antenna, so Morrie can watch *Mighty 90* and the missus and I can watch *Petticoat Junction* on Tuesday nights. Never mind that, Jamie. Tell me what's got you in such a tizzy."

I looked around for Mrs. Jacobs, hoping she'd spare me the job of having to tell everything twice, but she had quietly decamped. He took me by the shoulders and led me to a sawhorse. I was just tall enough to be able to sit on it.

"Is it Con?"

Of course he'd guess that; a petition for the return of Con's voice was part of the closing prayer at every Thursday-night meeting that spring, as were prayers for other MYFers who were going through hard times (broken bones were the most common, but Bobby Underwood had suffered burns and Carrie Doughty had had to endure having her head shaved and rinsed with vinegar after her horrified mother discovered the little girl's scalp was crawling with lice). But, like his wife, Reverend Jacobs hadn't had any idea of how miserable Con really was, or how that misery had spread through the entire family like an especially nasty germ.

"Dad bought Hiram Oil last summer," I said, starting to blubber again. I hated it, blubbering was such a little kid's trick, but I couldn't seem to help it. "He said the price was too good to turn down, only then we had a warm winter and heating oil went down to fifteen cents a gallon and now they can't afford a specialist and if you could have heard her, she didn't sound like Mom at all, and sometimes he puts his hands in his pockets, because . . ." But Yankee reticence finally kicked in and I finished, "Because I don't know why."

He produced the handkerchief again, and while I used it, he took a metal box from his workshop table. Wires sprouted from it every whichway, like badly cut hair.

"Behold the amplifier," he said. "Invented by yours truly. Once I get it hooked up, I'll run a wire out the window and up to the eave. Then I will attach . . . *that*." He pointed to the corner, where a rake was propped on its pole with its rusty metal tines sticking up. "The Jacobs Custom Antenna."

"Will it work?" I asked.

"I don't know. I think it will. But even if it does, I believe the days of television antennas are numbered. In another ten years, TV signals will be carried along the telephone lines, and there will be a lot more than three channels. By 1990 or so, the signals will be beamed down from satellites. I know it sounds like science fiction, but the technology already exists."

He had his dreamy look, and I thought, *He's forgotten all about Con*. Now I know that wasn't true. He was just giving me time to regain my composure, and—maybe—himself time to think.

"People will be amazed at first, then they'll take it for granted. They'll say 'Oh yes, we have telephone TV' or 'We have earth satellite TV,' but they'll be wrong. It's all a gift of electricity, which is now so basic and so pervasive we have a way of ignoring it. People like to say 'Thus-and-such is the elephant in the living room,' meaning a thing that's too big to be ignored, but you'd even ignore an elephant, if it was in the living room long enough."

"Except when you had to clean up the poop," I said.

That made him roar with laughter, and I laughed along with him, even though my eyes were still swollen from crying.

He went to the window and looked out. He clasped his hands at the small of his back and didn't speak for a long time. Then he turned to me and said, "I want you to bring Con to the parsonage tonight. Will you do that?"

"Sure," I said, without any great enthusiasm. More praying was what I thought he had in store, and I knew it couldn't hurt, but there had been a lot of praying on Con's behalf already, and it hadn't helped, either.

My parents had no objections to our going to the parsonage (I had to ask them separately, because that night they were barely talking to each other). It was Connie who took convincing, probably because I wasn't very convinced myself. But because I had promised the Reverend, I didn't give up. I enlisted Claire for help, instead. Her belief in the power of prayer was far greater than my own, and she had her own powers. I think they came from being the only girl. Of the four Morton brothers, only Andy—who was closest to her in age—could resist her when she got all pretty-eyed and asked for something.

As the three of us crossed Route 9, our shadows long in the light of a rising full moon, Con—just thirteen that year, dark-haired, slender, dressed in a faded plaid jacket handed down from Andy—held up his notepad, which he carried everywhere. He had printed while he walked, so the letters were jagged. THIS IS STUPID.

"Maybe," Claire said, "but we'll get cookies. Mrs. Jacobs always has cookies."

We also got Morrie, now five and dressed for bed in his pj's. He ran directly to Con and jumped into his arms. "Still can't talk?" Morrie asked.

Con shook his head.

"My dad will fix you," he said. "He's been working all afternoon." Then he held his arms out to my sister. "Carry me, Claire, carry me, Claire-Bear, and I'll give you a kiss!" She took him from Con, laughing.

Reverend Jacobs was in the shed, dressed in faded jeans and a sweater. There was an electric heater in the corner, the elements glowing cherry-red, but his workshop was still cold. I supposed he had been too busy tinkering away on his various projects to winterize it. The temporarily eyeless TV had been covered with a mover's quilt.

Jacobs gave Claire a hug and a peck on the cheek, then shook hands with Con, who then held up his pad. MORE PRAYER I SUPPOSE was printed on the fresh page.

I thought that was a little rude, and by her frown I could see Claire felt the same, but Jacobs only smiled. "We might get to that, but I want to try something else first." He turned to me. "Whom does the Lord help, Jamie?"

"Them that help themselves," I said.

"Ungrammatical but true."

He went to the worktable and brought back what looked like either a fat cloth belt or the world's skinniest electric blanket. A cord dangled from it, going to a little white plastic box with a slide-switch on top. Jacobs stood with the belt in his hands, looking at Con gravely. "This is a project I've been tinkering with on and off for the last year. I call it the Electrical Nerve Stimulator."

"One of your inventions," I said.

"Not exactly. The idea of using electricity to limit pain and stimulate muscles is very, very old. Sixty years before the birth of Christ, a Roman doctor named Scribonius Largus discovered that foot and leg pain could be alleviated if the sufferer stepped firmly on an electric eel."

"You made that up!" Claire accused, laughing. Con wasn't laughing; he was staring at the cloth belt with fascination.

"Not at all," Jacobs said, "but mine uses small batteries—which *are* of my invention—for power. Electric eels are hard to come by in central Maine, and even harder to put around a boy's neck. Which is what I intend to do with this homemade ENS gadget of mine.

Because Dr. Renault might have been right about your vocal cords not being ruptured, Con. Maybe they only need a jump-start. I'm willing to make the experiment, but it's up to you. What do you say?"

Con nodded. In his eyes I saw an expression that hadn't been there in quite awhile: hope.

"How come you never showed us this in MYF?" Claire asked. She sounded almost accusing.

Jacobs looked surprised and a tiny bit uneasy. "I suppose I couldn't think how it connected to a Christian lesson. Until Jamie came to see me today, I was thinking of trying it out on Al Knowles. His unfortunate accident?"

We all nodded. The fingers lost in the potato grader.

"He still feels the fingers that aren't there, and says they hurt. Also, he's lost a good deal of his ability to move that hand because of nerve damage. As I said, I've known for years that electricity can help in matters like those. Now it looks like you'll be my guinea pig, Con."

"So having that handy was just a lucky break?" Claire asked. I couldn't see why it mattered, but it seemed to. To her, at least.

Jacobs looked at her reproachfully and said, "*Coincidence* and *lucky break* are words people with little faith use to describe the will of God, Claire."

She flushed at that, and looked down at her sneakers. Con, meanwhile, was scribbling on his pad. He held it up. WILL IT HURT?

"I don't think so," Jacobs said. "The current is very low. Minuscule, really. I've tried it on my arm—like a blood-pressure cuff—and felt no more than the tingle you get when your arm or leg has been asleep and is just beginning to wake up. If there *is* pain, raise your hands and I'll kill the current right away. I'm going to put this thing on now. It will be snug, but not tight. You'll be able to breathe just fine. The buckles are nylon. Can't use metal on a thing like this."

He put the belt around Con's neck. It looked like a bulky winter scarf. Con's eyes were wide and scared, but when Jacobs asked if he was ready, he nodded. I felt Claire's fingers close over mine. They were cold. I thought Jacobs might get to the prayer then, asking for success. In a way, I suppose he did. He bent down so he could look Con directly in the eyes and said, "Expect a miracle."

Con nodded. I saw the cloth around his throat rise and fall as he swallowed hard.

"All right. Here we go."

When Reverend Jacobs slid the switch on top of the control box, I heard a faint humming sound. Con's head jerked. His mouth twitched first at one corner, then at the other. His fingers began to flutter rapidly and his arms jerked.

"Does it hurt?" Jacobs asked. His index finger was hovering over the switch, ready to turn it off. "If it hurts, hold out your hands."

Con shook his head. Then, in a voice that sounded as if it were coming through a mouthful of gravel, he said: "Doesn't . . . hurt. *Warm.*"

Claire and I exchanged a wild glance, a thought as strong as telepathy flowing between us: *Did I hear that?* She was now squeezing my hand hard enough to hurt, but I didn't care. When we looked back at Jacobs, he was smiling.

"Don't try to talk. Not yet. I'm going to run the belt for two minutes by my watch. Unless it starts to hurt. If that happens, hold out your hands and I'll turn it off at once."

Con didn't hold out his hands, although his fingers continued to move up and down, as if he were playing an invisible piano. His upper lip lifted a few times in an involuntary snarl, and his eyes went through spasms of fluttering. Once, still in that grating, gravelly voice, he said, "I . . . can . . . *talk* again!"

"Hush!" Jacobs said sternly. His index finger hovered over the switch, ready to kill the current, his eyes on the moving second hand of his watch. After what seemed like an eternity, he pushed the switch and that faint hum died. He unloosed the buckles and pulled the belt over my brother's head. Con's hands went immediately to his neck. The skin there was a little flushed, but I don't think that was from the electric current. It was from the pressure of the belt.

"Now, Con—I want you to say, 'My dog has fleas, they bite his knees.' But if your throat starts to hurt, stop at once."

"My dog has *fleas*," Con said in his strange grating voice. "They bite his *knees*." Then: "I have to spit."

"Does your throat hurt?"

"No, just have to spit."

Claire opened the shed door. Con leaned out, cleared his throat (which produced an unpleasantly metallic sound like rusty hinges), and hocked a loogie that to me looked almost as big as a doorknob. He turned back to us, massaging his throat with one hand.

"My dog has *fleas*." He still didn't sound like the Con I remembered, but the words were clearer now, and more human. Tears rose in his eyes and began to spill down his cheeks. "They bite his *knees*."

"That's enough for now," Jacobs said. "We'll go in the house, and you'll drink a glass of water. A big one. You must drink a lot of water. Tonight and tomorrow. Until your voice sounds normal again. Will you do that?"

"Yes."

"When you get home, you may tell your mother and father hello. Then I want you to go into your room and get down on your knees and thank God for bringing your voice back. Will you do that?"

Con nodded vehemently. He was crying harder than ever, and he wasn't alone. Claire and I were crying, too. Only Reverend Jacobs was dry-eyed. I think he was too amazed to cry.

Patsy was the only one not surprised. When we went into the house, she squeezed Con's arm and said in a matter-of-fact voice, "That's a good boy."

Morrie hugged my brother and my brother hugged him back hard enough to make the little boy's eyes bug out. Patsy drew a glass of water from the kitchen tap and Con drank all of it. When he thanked her, it was almost in his own voice.

"You're very welcome, Con. Now it's well past Morrie's bedtime, and time for you kids to go home." Leading Morrie to the stairs by the hand, but not turning around, she added: "I think your parents are going to be very happy."

That was the understatement of the century.

They were in the living room, watching *The Virginian*, and still not talking. Even in my joy and excitement, I could feel the freeze between them. Andy and Terry were thumping around upstairs, grousing at each other about something—business as usual, in other words. Mom had an afghan square in her lap, and was bending over to unsnarl the yarn in her basket when Con said, "Hello, Mom. Hello, Dad."

Dad stared at him, mouth open. Mom froze, one hand in the basket and the other holding her needles. She looked up, very slowly. She said, "What—?"

"Hello," Con said again.

She screamed and flew out of her chair, kicking the knitting basket over, and grabbed him the way she sometimes had when we were little, and meant to give one of us a shaking for something we had done wrong. There was no shaking that night. She swept Con into her arms, weeping. I could hear Terry and Andy stampeding down from the second floor to see what was going on.

"Say something else!" she cried. "Say something else so I don't think I just dreamed it!"

"He's not supposed to—" Claire began, but Con interrupted her. Because now he could.

"I love you, Mom," he said. "I love you, Dad."

Dad took Con by the shoulders and looked closely at his throat, but there was now nothing to see; the red mark had faded. "Thank God," he said. "Thank God, Son."

Claire and I looked at each other, and once more the thought didn't need to be spoken: Reverend Jacobs deserved some thanks, too.

We explained about how Con was supposed to use his voice sparingly to start with, and when we told about the water, Andy went out to the kitchen and came back with Dad's oversize joke coffee cup (printed on the side was the Canadian flag and ONE IMPERIAL GALLON OF CAFFEINE), filled with water. While he drank it, Claire and I took turns recounting what had happened, with Con chipping in once or twice, telling about the tingling sensation he'd felt when the belt was turned on. Each time he interrupted, Claire scolded him for talking.

"I don't believe it." Mom said this several times. She couldn't seem to take her eyes off Con. Several times she grabbed him and hugged him, as if she was afraid he might sprout wings, turn into an angel, and fly away.

"If the church didn't pay for his heating oil," Dad said when the tale was finished, "Reverend Jacobs would never have to pay for another gallon."

"We'll think of something," Mom said distractedly. "Right now we're going to celebrate. Terry, fetch the ice cream we were saving for Claire's birthday from the freezer. It will be good for Con's throat. You and Andy put it out on the table. We'll have all of it, so use the big bowls. You don't mind, do you, Claire?"

She shook her head. "This is better than a birthday party."

"I have to go to the bathroom," Connie said. "All that water. Then I'm supposed to pray. Reverend said so. The rest of you stay out while I do it."

He went upstairs. Andy and Terry went into the kitchen to serve out the Neapolitan (which we called van-choc-straw . . . funny how it all comes back). My mother and father subsided into their chairs, staring at the TV without seeing it. I saw Mom grope out with one hand, and saw Dad take it without looking, as if he knew it was there. That made me happy and relieved.

I felt a tug on my own hand. It was Claire. She led me through the kitchen, where Andy and Terry were squabbling over the relative size of the portions, and into the mudroom. Her eyes when she looked at me were wide and bright.

"Did you see him?" she asked. No—demanded.

"Who?"

"Reverend Jacobs, stupid! Did you see him when I asked why he never showed us that electric belt in MYF?"

"Well . . . yeah . . ."

"He said he'd been working on it for a year, but if that was true, he would have showed it off. He shows off *everything* he makes!"

I remembered how surprised he had looked, as if Claire had caught him out (I had on more than one occasion felt the same expression on my own face when *I* had been caught out), but . . .

"Are you saying he was lying?"

She nodded vigorously. "*Yes!* He was! And his wife? *She knew it!* Do you know what I think? I think he started right after you were there. Maybe he already had the idea—I think he has thousands of ideas for electrical inventions; they must pop around in his head like corn—but he hadn't done anything at all on this one until today."

"Gee, Claire, I don't think—"

She was still holding my hand, and now she gave it a hard and impatient yank, as if I were stuck in the mud and needed help to get free. "Did you see their kitchen table? There was one place still set, with nothing on the plate and nothing in the glass! He skipped his supper so he could keep working. Working like a demon, I'd guess from the look of his hands. They were all red, and there were blisters on two of his fingers."

"He did all that for Con?"

"I don't think so," she said. Her eyes never left mine.

"Claire! Jamie!" Mom called. "Come for ice cream!"

Claire didn't even look toward the kitchen. "Of all the kids in MYF, you're the one he met first, and you're the one he likes the best. He did it for you, Jamie. He did it for you."

Then she went into the kitchen, leaving me to stand by the woodpile, feeling stunned. If Claire had stayed a little longer and I'd had a chance to get over my surprise, I might have told her my own intuition: Reverend Jacobs had been as surprised as we were.

He hadn't expected it to work.

III

The Accident. My Mother's Story. The Terrible Sermon. Goodbye.

On a warm and cloudless midweek day in October of 1965, Patricia Jacobs popped Tag-Along-Morrie into the front seat of the Plymouth Belvedere that had been a wedding present from her parents and set out for the Red & White Market in Gates Falls—"She gone groceryin," the Yankees at that time would have said.

Three miles away, a farmer named George Barton—a lifelong bachelor known in town as Lonesome George—pulled out of his driveway with a potato digger attached to the back of his Ford F-100 pickup. His plan was to drive it a mile or so down Route 9 to his south field. The best speed he could manage with the digger attached was ten miles an hour, so he kept to the soft shoulder, thereby allowing any southbound traffic to pass safely. Lonesome George was considerate of others. He was a fine farmer. He was a good neighbor, a member of the school board, and a deacon of our church. He was also, as he would tell people almost proudly, "a pepileptic." Although, he was quick to add, Dr. Renault had prescribed some pills that controlled the seizures "just about perfect." Maybe so, but he had one behind the wheel of his truck that day.

"Probably shouldn't have been driving at all, except maybe in the fields," Dr. Renault said later, "but how can you ask a man in George's line of work to give up his license? It's not as if he has a wife or any grown kids he can put behind the wheel. Take away his driving ticket, you might as well ask him to put his farm up for sale to the highest bidder."

Not long after Patsy and Morrie set out for the Red & White, Mrs. Adele Parker came down Sirois Hill, a tight and treacherous curve where there had been many wrecks over the years. She was creeping along, and so had time to stop—barely—before striking the woman staggering and weaving up the middle of the highway. The woman had a dripping bundle clasped to her breast with one arm. One arm was all Patsy Jacobs could use, because the other had been torn off at the elbow. Blood was pouring down her face. A piece of her scalp hung beside her shoulder, bloody locks of hair blowing in the mild autumn breeze. Her right eye was on her cheek. All her beauty had been torn away in an instant. It's fragile, beauty.

"Help my baby!" Patsy cried when Mrs. Parker stopped her old Studebaker and got out. Beyond the bloody woman with the dripping bundle, Mrs. Parker could see the Belvedere, on its roof and burning. The stove-in front end of Lonesome George's truck was pushed against it. George himself was slumped over the wheel. Behind his truck, the overturned potato digger was blocking Route 9.

"Help my baby!" Patsy held the bundle out, and when Adele Parker saw what it was—not a baby but a little boy with his face torn off—she covered her eyes and began to scream. When she looked again, Patsy had gone to her knees, as if to pray.

Another pickup truck came around Sirois Hill and almost slammed into the back of Mrs. Parker's Studebaker. It was Fernald DeWitt, who had promised to help George with the digging that day. He jumped from the cab, ran to Mrs. Parker, and looked at the woman kneeling in the road. Then he ran on toward the site of the collision.

"Where are you going?" Mrs. Parker screamed. "Help her! *Help this woman!*"

Fernald, who had fought with the Marines in the Pacific and seen terrible sights there, did not pause, but he *did* call back over his shoulder, "She and the kid are gone. George might not be."

Nor was he wrong. Patsy was dead long before the ambulance arrived from Castle Rock, but Lonesome George Barton lived into his eighties. And never got behind the wheel of a motor vehicle again.

You say, "How could you know all that, Jamie Morton? You were only nine years old."

But I do know it.

In 1976, when my mother was still a relatively young woman, she was diagnosed with ovarian cancer. I was attending the University of Maine at the time, but took the second semester of my sophomore year off, so I could be with her at the end. Although the Morton children were children no more (Con was all the way over the horizon in Hawaii, doing pulsar research at the Mauna Kea Observatories), we all came home to be with Mom, and to support Dad, who was too heartbroken to be useful; he simply wandered around the house or took long walks in the woods.

Mom wanted to spend her final days at home, she was very clear about that, and we took turns feeding her, giving her her medicine, or just sitting with her. She was little more than a skeleton by then, and on morphine for the pain. Morphine's funny stuff. It has a way of eroding barriers—that famous Yankee reticence—which would otherwise be impregnable. It was my turn to sit with her on a February afternoon a week or so before she died. It was a day of snow flurries and bitter cold, with a north wind that shook the house and screamed beneath the eaves, but the house was warm. Hot, really. My father was in the heating oil business, remember, and after that one scary year in the mid-sixties when he looked bankruptcy in the face, he became not just successful but moderately wealthy.

"Push down my blankets, Terence," my mother said. "Why are there so many? I'm burning up."

"It's Jamie, Mom. Terry's out in the garage with Dad." I turned down the single blanket, exposing a hideously gay pink nightgown that seemed to have nothing inside it. Her hair (all white by the time the cancer struck) had thinned to almost nothing; her lips had fallen away from her teeth, making them look too big, and somehow equine; only her eyes were the same. They were still young, and full of hurt curiosity: *What's happening to me?*

"Jamie, Jamie, that's what I said. Can I have a pill? The pain is awful today. I've never been in such a hole as this one."

"In fifteen minutes, Mom." It was supposed to be two hours, but I couldn't see what difference it made at that point. Claire had suggested giving her all of them, which shocked Andy; he was the only one of us who had remained true to our fairly strict religious upbringing.

"Do you want to send her to hell?" he had asked.

"She wouldn't go to hell if *we* gave them to her," Claire said—quite reasonably, I thought. "It isn't as if she'd know." And then, nearly breaking my heart because it was one of our mother's favorite sayings: "She doesn't know if she's afoot or on horseback. Not anymore."

"You'll do no such thing," Andy said.

"No," Claire sighed. She was closing in on thirty by then, and was more beautiful than ever. Because she was finally in love? If so, what a bitter irony. "I don't have that kind of courage. I only have the courage to let her suffer."

"When she's in heaven, her suffering will only be a shadow," Andy said, as if this ended the matter. For him I suppose it did.

The wind howled, the old panes of glass in the bedroom's single window rattled, and my mother said, "I'm so thin, so thin now. I was a pretty bride, everyone said so, but now Laura Mackenzie is so thin." Her mouth drew down in a clown-moue of sorrow and pain.

I had three more hours in the room with her before Terry was due to spell me. She might sleep some of that time, but she wasn't sleeping now, and I was desperate to distract her from the way her body was cannibalizing itself. I might have seized on anything. It just happened to be Charles Jacobs. I asked if she had any idea where he'd gone after he left Harlow.

"Oh, that was a terrible time," she said. "A terrible thing that happened to his wife and little boy."

"Yes," I said. "I know."

My dying mother looked at me with stoned contempt. "*You* don't know. You don't understand. It was terrible because it was no one's fault. Certainly not George Barton's. He simply had a seizure."

She then told me what I have already told you. She heard it from the mouth of Adele Parker, who said she would never get the image of the dying woman out of her head. "What I'll never get out of mine," Mom said, "was the way he screamed at Peabody's. I didn't know a man could make a sound like that."

• • •

Doreen DeWitt, Fernald's wife, called my mother and gave her the news. She had a good reason for calling Laura Morton first. "You'll have to tell him," she said.

My mother was horrified at the prospect. "Oh, no! I couldn't!"

"You have to," Doreen said patiently. "This isn't news you give over the phone, and except for that old gore-crow Myra Harrington, you're his closest neighbor."

My mother, all her reticence washed away by the morphine, told me, "I gathered up my courage to do it, but I was caught short as I was going out the door. I had to turn around and run to the toidy and shit."

She walked down our hill, across Route 9, and to the parsonage. She didn't say, but I imagine it was the longest walk of her life. She knocked on the door, but at first he didn't come, although she could hear the radio inside.

"Why would he have heard me?" she inquired of the ceiling as I sat there beside her. "The first time, my knuckles barely grazed the wood."

She knocked harder the second time. He opened the door and looked at her through the screen. He was holding a large book in one hand, and all those years later she remembered the title: *Protons and Neutrons: The Secret World of Electricity*.

"Hello, Laura," he said. "Are you all right? You're very pale. Come in, come in."

She came in. He asked her what was wrong.

"There's been a terrible accident," she said.

His look of concern deepened. "Dick or one of the kids? Do you need me to come? Sit down, Laura, you look ready to faint."

"All of mine are all right," she said. "It's . . . Charles, it's Patsy. And Morrie."

He set the big book carefully on a table in the hall. That was probably when she saw the title, and I'm not surprised that she remembered it; at such times one sees everything and remembers it all. I know from personal experience. I wish I did not.

"How badly are they hurt?" And before she could answer: "Are they at St. Stevie's? They must be, it's the closest. Can we take your station wagon?"

St. Stephen's Hospital was in Castle Rock, but of course that wasn't where they had been taken. "Charles, you must prepare yourself for a terrible shock."

He took her by the shoulders—gently, she said, not hard, but when he bent to look into her face, his eyes were blazing. *"How bad? Laura, how badly are they hurt?"*

My mother began to cry. "They're dead, Charles. I am so sorry."

He let go of her and his arms dropped to his sides. "No they're not," he said. It was the voice of a man stating a simple fact.

"I should have driven down," my mother said. "I should have brought the station wagon, yes. I wasn't thinking. I just came."

"They're not," he said again. He turned from her and put his forehead against the wall. "No." He banged his head hard enough to rattle a nearby picture of Jesus carrying a lamb. "No." He banged it again and the picture fell off its hook.

She took his arm. It was floppy and loose. "Charles, don't do that." And, as if he had been one of her children instead of a grown man: "Don't, honey."

"No." He banged his forehead again. "No!" Yet again. *"No!"*

This time she took hold of him with both hands and pulled him away from the wall. "Stop that! You stop it right now!"

He looked at her, dazed. A bright red mark dashed across his brow.

"Such a look," she told me years later, as she lay dying. "I couldn't bear it, but I had to. Once a thing like that is started, you have to finish it."

"Walk back to the house with me," she told him. "I'll give you a drink of Dick's whiskey, because you need something, and I know there's nothing like that here—"

He laughed. It was a shocking sound.

"—and then I'll drive you to Gates Falls. They're at Peabody's."

"Peabody's?"

She waited for it to sink in. He knew what Peabody's was as well as she did. By that time Reverend Jacobs had officiated at dozens of funerals.

"Patsy can't be dead," he said in a patient, instructional tone of voice. "It's Wednesday. Wednesday is Prince Spaghetti Day, that's what Morrie says."

"Come with me, Charles." She took him by the hand and tugged him first to the door and then into the gorgeous autumn sunshine. That morning he had awakened next to his wife, and had eaten breakfast across from his son. They talked about stuff, like people do. We never know. Any day could be the day we go down, and we never know.

When they reached Route 9—sunwashed and silent, empty of traffic as it almost always was—he cocked his head, doglike, toward the sound of sirens in the direction of Sirois Hill. On the horizon was a smudge of smoke. He looked at my mother.

"Morrie, too? You're sure?"

"Come on, Charlie." ("It was the only time I ever called him that," she told me.) "Come on, we're in the middle of the road."

They went to Gates Falls in our old Ford wagon, and they went by way of Castle Rock. It was at least twenty miles longer, but my mother was past the worst of her shock by then, and able to think clearly. She had no intention of driving past the scene of the crash, even if it meant going all the way around Robin Hood's barn.

Peabody's Funeral Home was on Grand Street. The gray Cadillac hearse was already in the driveway, and several vehicles were parked at the curb. One of them was Reggie Kelton's boat of a Buick. Another, she was enormously relieved to see, was a panel truck with MORTON FUEL OIL on the side.

Dad and Mr. Kelton came out the front door while Mom was leading Reverend Jacobs up the walk, by then as docile as a child. He was looking up, Mom said, as if to gauge how far the foliage had to go before it would reach peak color.

Dad hugged Jacobs, but Jacobs didn't hug back. He just stood there with his hands at his sides, looking up at the leaves.

"Charlie, I'm so sorry for your loss," Kelton rumbled. "We all are."

They escorted him into the oversweet smell of flowers. Organ music, low as a whisper and somehow awful, came from overhead speakers. Myra Harrington—Me-Maw to everyone in West Harlow—was already there, probably because she had been listening in on the party line when Doreen called my mother. Listening in was her hobby. She heaved her bulk from a sofa in the foyer and pulled Reverend Jacobs to her enormous bosom.

"Your dear sweet wife and your dear little boy!" she cried in her high, mewling voice. Mom looked at Dad, and they both winced. "Well, they're in heaven now! That's the consolation! Saved by the blood of the Lamb and rocked in the everlasting arms!" Tears poured down Me-Maw's cheeks, cutting through a thick layer of pink powder.

Reverend Jacobs allowed himself to be hugged and made of. After a minute or two ("Around the time I began to think she wouldn't stop until she suffocated him with those great tits of hers," my mother told me), he pushed her away. Not hard, but with firmness. He turned to my father and Mr. Kelton and said, "I'll see them now."

"Now, Charlie, not yet," Mr. Kelton said. "You need to hold on for a bit. Just until Mr. Peabody makes them presenta—"

Jacobs walked through the viewing parlor, where some old lady in a mahogany coffin was waiting for her final public appearance. He continued on down the hall toward the back. He knew where he was going; few better.

Dad and Mr. Kelton hurried after him. My mother sat down, and Me-Maw sat across from her, eyes alight under her cloud of white hair. She was old then, in her eighties, and when some of her score of grandchildren and great-grandchildren weren't visiting her, only tragedy and scandal brought her fully alive.

"How did he take it?" Me-Maw stage-whispered. "Did you get kneebound with him?"

"Not now, Myra," Mom said. "I'm done up. I only want to close my eyes and rest for a minute."

But there was no rest for her, because just then a scream rose from the back of the funeral home, where the prep rooms were.

"It sounded like the wind outside today, Jamie," she said, "only a hundred times worse." At last she looked away from the ceiling. I wish she hadn't, because I could see the darkness of death close behind the light in her eyes. "At first there were no words, just that banshee wailing. I almost wish it had stayed that way, but it didn't. '*Where's his face?*' he cried. '*Where's my little boy's face?*'"

Who would preach at the funeral? This was a question (like who cuts the barber's hair) that troubled me. I heard all about it later, but I wasn't there to see; my mother decreed that only she, Dad, Claire, and Con were to go to the funeral. It might be too upsetting for the rest of us (surely it was those chilling screams from Peabody's preparation room she was thinking of), and so Andy was left in charge of Terry and me. That wasn't a thing I relished, because Andy could be a boogersnot, especially when our parents weren't there. For an avowed Christian, he was awfully fond of Indian rope burns and head-noogies—hard ones that left you seeing stars.

There were no rope burns or head-noogies on the Saturday of Patsy and Morrie's double funeral. Andy said that if the folks weren't back by supper, he'd make Franco-American. In the meantime, we were just to watch TV and shut up. Then he went upstairs and didn't come back down. Grumpy and bossy though he could be, he had liked Tag-Along-Morrie as much as the rest of us, and of course he had a crush on Patsy (also like the rest of us . . . except for Con, who didn't care for girls then and never would). He might have gone upstairs to pray—go into your closet and lock your door, Saint Matthew advises—or maybe he just wanted to sit and think and try to make sense of it all. His faith wasn't broken by those two deaths—he remained a die-hard fundamentalist Christian until his death—but it must have been severely shaken. My own faith wasn't broken by the deaths, either. It was the Terrible Sermon that accomplished that.

Reverend David Thomas of the Gates Falls Congo gave the eulogy for Patsy and Morrie at our church, and that caused no raised eyebrows, since, as my Dad said, "There's not a dime's worth of difference between the Congregationalists and the Methodists."

What *did* raise eyebrows was Jacobs's choice of Stephen Givens to officiate at the Willow Grove Cemetery graveside services. Givens was the pastor (he did not call himself Reverend) of Shiloh Church, where at that time the congregants still held hard to the beliefs of Frank Weston Sandford, an apocalypse-monger who encouraged parents to whip their children for petty sins ("You must be schoolmasters of Christ," he advised them) and who insisted on thirty-six-hour fasts . . . even for infants.

Shiloh had changed a lot since Sandford's death (and is today little different from other Protestant church groups), but in 1965, a flock of old rumors—fueled by the odd dress of the members and their stated belief that the end of the world was coming soon, like maybe next week—persisted. Yet it turned out that our Charles Jacobs and their Stephen Givens had been meeting over coffee in Castle Rock for years, and were friends. After the Terrible Sermon, there were people in town who said that Reverend Jacobs had been "infected by Shilohism." Perhaps so, but according to Mom and Dad (also Con and Claire, whose testimony I trusted more), Givens was calm, comforting, and appropriate during the brief graveside ceremony.

"He didn't mention the end of the world once," Claire said. I remember how beautiful she looked that evening in her dark blue dress (the closest she had to black) and her grownup hose. I also remember she ate almost no supper, just pushed things around on her plate until it was all mixed together and looked like dog whoop.

"What scripture did Givens read?" Andy asked.

"First Corinthians," Mom said. "The one about how we see through a glass darkly?"

"Good choice," my older brother said sagely.

"How was he?" I asked Mom. "How was Reverend Jacobs?"

"He was . . . quiet," she said, looking troubled. "Meditating, I think."

"No, he wasn't," Claire said, pushing her plate away. "He was shell-shocked. Just sat there in a folding chair at the head of the grave, and when Mr. Givens asked him if he'd throw the first dirt and then join him in saying the benediction, he only went on sitting with his hands between his knees and his head hanging down." She began to cry. "It seems like a dream to me, a bad dream."

"But he *did* get up and toss the dirt," Dad said, putting an arm around her shoulders. "After awhile, he did. A handful on each coffin. Didn't he, Claire-Bear?"

"Yeah," she said, crying harder than ever. "After that Shiloh guy took his hands and practically pulled him up."

Con hadn't said anything, and I realized he wasn't at the table anymore. I saw him out in the backyard, standing by the elm from which our tire swing hung. He was leaning his head against the bark with his hands clasping the tree and his shoulders shaking.

Unlike Claire, though, he had eaten his dinner. I remember that. Ate up everything on his plate and asked for seconds in a strong, clear voice.

There were guest preachers, arranged for by the deacons, on the next three Sundays, but Pastor Givens wasn't one of them. In spite of being calm, comforting, and appropriate at Willow Grove, I expect he wasn't asked. As well as being reticent by nature and upbringing, Yankees also have a tendency to be comfortably prejudiced in matters of religion and race. Three years later, I heard one of my teachers at Gates Falls High School tell another, in tones of outraged wonder: "Now why would anyone want to shoot that Reverend King? Heaven sakes, he was a *good* nigger!"

MYF was canceled following the accident. I think all of us were glad—even Andy, also known as Emperor of Bible Drills. We were no more ready to face Reverend Jacobs than he was to face us. Toy Corner, where Claire and the other girls had entertained Morrie (and themselves), would have been awful to look at. And who would play the piano for Sing Time? I suppose someone in town could have done it, but Charles Jacobs was in no condition to ask, and it wouldn't have been the same, anyway, without Patsy's blond hair shifting from side to side as she swung the upbeat hymns, like

"We Are Marching to Zion." Her blond hair was underground now, growing brittle on a satin pillow in the dark.

One gray November afternoon while Terry and I were spray-stenciling turkeys and cornucopias on our windows, the telephone jangled one long and one short: our ring. Mom answered, spoke briefly, then put the phone down and smiled at Terry and me.

"That was Reverend Jacobs. He's going to be in the pulpit this coming Sunday to preach the Thanksgiving sermon. Won't that be nice?"

Years later—I was in high school and Claire was home on vacation from the University of Maine—I asked my sister why nobody had stopped him. We were out back, pushing the old tire swing. She didn't have to ask who I meant; that Sunday sermon had left a scar on all of us.

"Because he sounded so *reasonable*, I think. So *normal*. By the time people realized what he was actually saying, it was too late."

Maybe, but I remembered both Reggie Kelton and Roy Easterbrook interrupting him near the end, and I knew something was wrong even before he started, because he didn't follow that day's scriptural reading with the customary conclusion: *May God bless His holy word*. He never forgot that, not even on the day I met him, when he showed me the little electric Jesus walking across Peaceable Lake.

His scripture on the day of the Terrible Sermon was from the thirteenth chapter of First Corinthians, the same passage Pastor Givens read over the twin graves—one big, one small—at Willow Grove: "For we know in part, and we prophesy in part. But when that which is perfect is come, then that which is in part shall be done away. When I was a child, I spake as a child, I understood as a child, I thought as a child; but when I became a man, I put away childish things. For now we see through a glass, darkly; but then face to face: now I know in part; but then shall I know even as also I am known."

He closed the large Bible on the pulpit—not hard, but we all heard the thump. West Harlow Methodist was full on that Sunday, every pew taken, but it was dead quiet, not so much as a cough. I remember praying he'd get through it okay; that he wouldn't break down in tears.

Myra Harrington—Me-Maw—was in the front pew, and although her back was to me, I could imagine her eyes, half buried in their fatty, yellowish sockets and sparkling with avidity. My family was in the third pew, where we always sat. Mom's face was serene, but I could see her white-gloved hands clenched on her large softcover Bible with enough force to bend it into a **U**. Claire had nibbled off her lipstick. The silence between the conclusion of the scripture reading and the commencement of what was known in Harlow ever after as the Terrible Sermon could not have been much longer than five seconds, ten at most, but to me it seemed to stretch out forever. His head was bowed over the huge pulpit Bible with its bright gold edging. When he finally looked up and showed his calm, composed face, a faint sigh of relief rippled through the congregation.

"This has been a hard and troubled time for me," he said. "I hardly need to tell you that; this is a close-knit community, and we all know each other. You folks have reached out to me in every way you could, and I'll always be grateful. I want especially to thank Laura Morton, who brought me the news of my loss with such tenderness and gentle regard."

He nodded to her. She nodded back, smiled, then raised one white-gloved hand to brush away a tear.

"I have spent much of the time between the day of my loss and this Sunday morning in reflection and study. I would like to add *in prayer*, but although I have gotten on my knees time and again, I have not sensed the presence of God, and so reflection and study had to do."

Silence from the congregation. Every eye on him.

"I went to the Gates Falls Library in search of *The New York Times*, but all they have on file is the *Weekly Enterprise*, so I was directed to Castle Rock, where they have the *Times* on microfilm—'Seek and ye shall find,' Saint Matthew tells us, and how right he was."

A few low chuckles greeted this, but they died away quickly.

"I went day after day, I scrolled microfilm until my head ached, and I want to share some of the things I found."

From the pocket of his black suit coat he took a few file cards.

"In June of last year, three small tornadoes tore through the town of May, Oklahoma. Although there was property damage, no one was killed. The townsfolk flocked to the Baptist church to sing songs of praise and offer prayers of thanksgiving. While they were in there, a fourth tornado—a monster F5—swept down on May and demolished the church. Forty-one persons were killed. Thirty others were seriously injured, including children who lost arms and legs."

He shuffled that card to the bottom and looked at the next.

"Some of you may remember this one. In August of last year, a man and his two sons set out on Lake Winnipesaukee in a rowboat. They had the family dog with them. The dog fell overboard, and both boys jumped in to rescue him. When the father saw his sons were in danger of drowning, he jumped in himself, inadvertently overturning the boat. All three died. The dog swam to shore." He looked up and actually smiled for a moment—it was like the sun peeking through a scrim of clouds on a cold January day. "I tried to find out what happened to that dog—whether the woman who lost her husband and sons kept it or had it put down—but the information wasn't available."

I snuck a look at my brothers and sister. Terry and Con only looked puzzled, but Andy was white-faced with horror, anger, or both. His hands were clenched in his lap. Claire was crying silently.

Next file card.

"October of last year. A hurricane swept onshore near Wilmington, North Carolina, and killed seventeen. Six were children at a church day-care center. A seventh was reported missing. His body was found a week later, in a tree."

Next.

"This item concerns a missionary family ministering to the poor with food, medicine, and the gospel in what used to be the Belgian Congo and is now, I believe, Zaire. There were five of them. They were murdered. Although the article did not say—only the news that's fit to print in *The New York Times*, you know—the article implied that the killers may have been of a cannibalistic bent."

A disapproving mutter—Reggie Kelton was at the center of it—arose. Jacobs heard and raised one hand in what was almost a benedictory gesture.

"Perhaps I need not go into further details—the fires, the floods, the earthquakes, the riots, the assassinations—although I could. The world shudders with them. Yet reading these stories provided some comfort to me, because they prove that I am not alone in my suffering. The comfort is only small, however, because such deaths—like those of my wife and son—seem so cruel and capricious. Christ ascended into heaven in his body, we are told, but all too often we poor mortals here on earth are left with ugly heaps of maimed meat and that constant, reverberating question: Why? Why? *Why?*

"I have read scripture all my life—first at my mother's knee, then in Methodist Youth Fellowship, and then in divinity school—and I can tell you, my friends, that nowhere in scripture is that question directly addressed. The closest the Bible comes is this reading from Corinthians, where Saint Paul says, in effect, 'It's no good asking, my brethren, because you wouldn't understand, anyway.' When Job asked God Himself, he got an even more blunt response: 'Were you there when I made the world?' Which translates, in the language of our younger parishioners, to 'Buzz off, Bunky.'"

No chuckles this time.

He studied us, a faint smile touching the corners of his lips, the light from our stained glass window putting blue and red diamonds on his left cheek.

"Religion is supposed to be our comfort when the hard times come. God is our rod and our staff, the Great Psalm declares; He will be with us and bear us up when we take that inevitable walk through the Valley of the Shadow of Death. Another Psalm assures us that God is our refuge and our strength, although the people who were lost in that Oklahoma church might dispute the idea . . . if they still had mouths to dispute with. And the father and his two children, drowning because they tried to rescue the family pet—did they ask God what was going on? What the deal was? And did He answer, 'Tell you in a few minutes, guys,' as the water choked their lungs and death darkened their minds?

"Let us say plainly what Saint Paul meant when he spoke of that darkened glass. He meant we're supposed to take it all on faith. If our faith is strong, we'll go to heaven, and we'll understand the whole thing when we get there. As if life were a joke, and heaven the place where the cosmic punchline is finally explained to us."

There was soft feminine sobbing in the church now, and more pronounced masculine rumblings of discontent. But at that point, no one had walked out or stood up to tell Reverend Jacobs he should sit down because he was edging into blasphemy. They were still too stunned.

"When I tired of researching the seemingly whimsical and often terribly painful deaths of the innocent, I looked into the various branches of Christianity. Gosh, friends, I was surprised at how many there are! Such a Tower of Doctrine! The Catholics, the Episcopalians, the Methodists, the Baptists—both hardshell and softshell—the C of Es, the Anglicans, the Lutherans, the Presbyterians, the Unitarians, the Jehovah's Witnesses, the Seventh-day Adventists, the Quakers, the Shakers, Greek Orthodox, Oriental Orthodox, the Shilohites—mustn't forget them—and half a hundred more.

"Here in Harlow, we're all on party lines, and it seems to me that religion is the biggest party line of them all. Think how the lines to heaven must get jammed on Sunday mornings! And do you know what I find fascinating? Each and every church dedicated to Christ's teaching thinks it's the only one that actually has a *private* line to the Almighty. And good gosh, I haven't even mentioned the Muslims, or the Jews, or the theosophists, or the Buddhists, or those who worship America itself just as fervently as, for eight or a dozen nightmare years, the Germans worshipped Hitler."

Right then was when the walkouts started. First just a few at the back, heads down and shoulders hunched (as if they had been spanked), then more and more. Reverend Jacobs seemed to take no notice.

"Some of these various sects and denominations are peaceful, but the largest of them—the most *successful* of them—have been built on the blood, bones, and screams of those who have the effrontery not to bow to their idea of God. The Romans fed Christians to the lions; the Christians dismembered those they deemed to be heretics or sorcerers or witches; Hitler sacrificed the Jews in their millions to the false god of racial purity. Millions have been burned, shot, hung, racked, poisoned, electrocuted, and torn to pieces by dogs . . . all in God's name."

My mother was sobbing audibly, but I didn't look around at her. I couldn't. I was frozen in place. By horror, yes, of course. I was only nine. But there was also a wild, inchoate exultation, a feeling that at last someone was telling me the exact unvarnished truth. Part of me hoped he would stop; most of me wished fiercely that he would go on, and I got my wish.

"Christ taught us to turn the other cheek and to love our enemies. We pay the concept lip service, but when most of us are struck, we try to pay back double. Christ drove the moneychangers from the temple, but we all know those quick-buck artists never stay away for long; if you've ever sat yourself down to a rousing game of church bingo or heard a radio preacher begging for money, you know exactly what I mean. Isaiah prophesied that the day would come when we'd beat our swords into plowshares, but all they've been beaten into in our current dark age is atomic bombs and intercontinental ballistic missiles."

Reggie Kelton stood up. He was as red as my brother Andy was pale. "You need to sit down, Reverend. You're not yourself."

Reverend Jacobs did not sit down.

"And what do we get for our faith? For the centuries we've given this church or that one our gifts of blood and treasure? The assurance that heaven is waiting for us at the end of it all, and when we get there, the punchline will be explained and we'll say, 'Oh yeah! *Now* I get it.' That's the big payoff. It's dinned into our ears from our earliest days: heaven, heaven, heaven! We will see our lost children, our dear mothers will take us in their arms! That's the carrot. The stick we're beaten with is hell, hell, hell! A Sheol of eternal damnation and torment. We tell children as young as my dear lost son that they stand in danger of eternal fire if they steal a piece of penny candy or lie about how they got their new shoes wet.

"There's no proof of these after-life destinations; no backbone of science; there is only the bald assurance, coupled with our powerful need to believe *that it all makes sense*. But as I stood in the back room of Peabody's and looked down at the mangled remains of my boy, who wanted to go to Disneyland much more than he wanted to go to heaven, I had a revelation. Religion is the theological equivalent of a quick-buck insurance scam, where you pay in your premium year after year, and then, when you need the benefits you paid for so—pardon the pun—so religiously, you discover the company that took your money does not, in fact, exist."

That was when Roy Easterbrook stood up in the rapidly emptying church. He was an unshaven hulk of a man who lived in a rusty little trailer park on the east side of town, close to the Freeport line. As a rule, he only came at Christmas, but today he'd made an exception.

"Rev'run," he said. "I heard there was a bottle of hooch in the glovebox of your car. And Mert Peabody said when he bent over to work on your wife, she smelt like a barroom. So there's your reason. There's your sense of it. You ain't got the spine to accept the will of God? Fine. But leave these other ones alone." With that, Easterbrook turned and lumbered out.

It stopped Jacobs cold. He stood gripping the pulpit, eyes blazing in his white face, lips pressed together so tightly his mouth had disappeared.

My dad stood, then. "Charles, you need to step down."

Reverend Jacobs shook his head as if to clear it. "Yes," he said. "You're right, Dick. Nothing I say will make any difference, anyway."

But it did. To one little boy, it did.

He stepped back, glanced around as if he no longer knew where he was, and then stepped forward again, although there was now no one to hear him except for my family, the church deacons, and Me-Maw, still planted in the first row with her eyes bugging out.

"Just one more thing. We came from a mystery and it's to a mystery we go. Maybe there's something there, but I'm betting it's not God as any church understands Him. Look at the babble of conflicting beliefs and you'll know that. They cancel each other out and leave nothing. If you want truth, a power greater than yourselves, look to the lightning—a billion volts in each strike, and a hundred thousand amperes of current, and temperatures of *fifty thousand degrees Fahrenheit*. There's a higher power in that, I grant you. But here, in this building? No. Believe what you want, but I tell you this: behind Saint Paul's darkened glass, there is nothing but a lie."

He left the pulpit and walked through the side door. The Morton family sat in the kind of silence people must experience after a bomb blast.

When we got home, Mom went into the big back bedroom, said she did not want to be disturbed, and closed the door. She stayed there the rest of the day. Claire cooked supper, and we ate mostly in silence. At one point Andy began to quote some scriptural passage that completely disproved what the Reverend had said, but Dad told him to shut his piehole. Andy looked at our father's hands shoved deep into his pockets and zipped his lip.

After supper, Dad went out to the garage, where he was tinkering with Road Rocket II. For once Terry—usually his loyal assistant, almost his acolyte—did not join him, so I did . . . although not without hesitation.

"Daddy? Can I ask you a question?"

He was under the Rocket on a Crawligator, a caged light in one hand. Only his khaki-clad legs stuck out. "I suppose so, Jamie. Unless it's about that goddam mess this morning. If that's the case, you can also keep *your* piehole shut. I ain't going there tonight. Tomorrow'll be time enough. We'll have to petition the New England Methodist Conference to fire him, and *they'll* have to take it to Bishop Matthews in Boston. It's a fucking mess, and if you ever tell your mother I used that word around you, she'll beat me like a redheaded stepchild."

I didn't know if my question was about the Terrible Sermon or not, I only knew I had to ask it. "Was what Mr. Easterbrook said true? Was she drinking?"

The moving light beneath the car went still. Then he rolled himself out so he could look up at me. I was afraid he'd be mad, but he wasn't mad. Just unhappy. "People have been whispering about it, and I suppose it'll get around a lot faster now that that nummie Easterbrook went and said it right out loud, but you listen to me, Jamie: *it doesn't matter*. George Barton had an epileptic seizure and he was on the wrong side of the road and she come around a blind turn and pop goes the weasel. It doesn't matter if she was sober or head down and tail over the dashboard. Mario Andretti couldn't have avoided that crash. Reverend was right about one thing: people always want a reason for the bad things in life. Sometimes there ain't one."

He raised the hand not holding the caged light and pointed a grease-smeared finger at me. "All the rest was just the bullshit of a grief-struck man, and don't you forget it."

The Wednesday before Thanksgiving was a half day in our school district, but I had promised Mrs. Moran that I'd stay to wash the blackboards and neaten up our little library of tattered books. When I told Mom, she waved her hand in a distracted way and told me to just be home for supper. She was already putting a turkey in the oven, but I knew it couldn't be ours; it was way too small for seven.

As it turned out, Kathy Palmer (a teacher's pet wannabe if there ever was one) also stayed to help out, and the work was done in half an hour. I thought of going to Al's or Billy's house to play guns or something, but I knew they'd want to talk about the Terrible Sermon and how Mrs. Jacobs had gotten herself and Morrie killed because she was shitfaced drunk—a rumor that had indeed gained the credence of absolute fact—and I didn't want any part of that, so I went home. It was an unseasonably warm day, our windows were open, and I could hear my sister and my mother arguing.

"Why *can't* I come?" Claire asked. "I want him to know at least some people in this stupid town are still on his side!"

"Because your father and I think all you children should stay away from him," my mother said. They were in the kitchen, and by now I was lingering outside the window.

"I'm not a *child*, anymore, Mother, I'm seventeen!"

"Sorry, but at seventeen you're still a child, and a young girl visiting him wouldn't look right. You'll just have to take my word for that."

"But it's okay for you? You know Me-Maw'll see you, and it'll be all over the party line in twenty minutes! If you're going, let me go with you!"

"I said no, and that's final."

"He gave Con back his voice!" Claire stormed. "How can you be so mean?"

There was a long pause and then my mother said, "That's why I'm going to see him. Not to take him a meal for tomorrow but to let him know we're grateful in spite of those terrible things he said."

"You know why he said them! He just lost his wife and son and he was all messed up! Half crazy!"

"I *do* know that." Mom was speaking more quietly now, and I had to strain to hear because Claire was crying. "But it doesn't change how shocked people were. He went too far. *Much* too far. He's leaving next week, and that's for the best. When you know you're going to be fired, it's best to quit first. It allows you to keep a little self-respect."

"Fired by the deacons, I suppose," Claire almost sneered. "Which means Dad."

"Your father has no choice. When you're no longer a *child*, you may realize that, and have a little sympathy. This is tearing Dick apart."

"Go on, then," Claire said. "See if a few slices of turkey breast and some sweet potatoes make up for the way he's getting treated. I bet he won't even eat it."

"Claire . . . Claire-Bear—"

"*Don't call me that!*" she yelled, and I heard her pounding for the stairs. She'd sulk and cry in her bedroom for awhile, I supposed, and then get over it, the way she did a couple of years ago when Mom told her fifteen was absolutely too young to go to the drive-in with Donnie Cantwell.

I decided to hustle my butt into the backyard before Mom left with her special-made dinner. I sat in the tire swing, not exactly hiding but not exactly in full view, either. Ten minutes later, I heard the front door shut. I went to the corner of the house and saw Mom walking down the road with a foil-covered tray in her hands. The foil twinkled in the sun. I went in the house and up the stairs. I knocked on my sister's door, which was graced by a large Bob Dylan poster.

"Claire?"

"Go away!" she shouted. "I don't want to talk to you!" The record player went on: the Yardbirds, and at top volume.

Mom came back about an hour later—a pretty long visit just to drop off a gift of food—and although Terry and I were in the living room by then, watching TV and jostling each other for the best place on our old couch (in the middle, where the springs didn't poke your bum), she barely seemed to notice us. Con was upstairs playing the guitar he'd gotten for his birthday. And singing.

David Thomas of Gates Falls Congo was back for a return engagement on the Sunday after Thanksgiving. The church was once more full, maybe because people wanted to see if Reverend Jacobs would show up and try to say some more awful things. He didn't. If he had, I'm sure he would have been shut up before he got a running start, maybe even carried out bodily. Yankees take their religion seriously.

The next day, Monday, I ran the quarter mile from school instead of walking. I had an idea, and I wanted to be home before the schoolbus arrived. When it came, I grabbed Con and pulled him into the backyard.

"Who put a bug up your butt?" he asked.

"You need to come down to the parsonage with me," I said. "Reverend Jacobs is going away pretty soon, maybe even tomorrow, and we should see him before he goes. We should tell him we still like him."

Con drew away from me, brushing his hand down the front of his Ivy League shirt, as if he was afraid I'd left cooties on it. "Are you crazy? I'm not doing that. He said there's no God."

"He also electrified your throat and saved your voice."

Con shrugged uneasily. "It would have come back, anyway. Dr. Renault said so."

"He said it would come back in a week or two. That was in February. You still didn't have it back in April. *Two months later.*"

"So what? It took a little longer, that's all."

I couldn't believe what I was hearing. "What are you, chicken?"

"Say that again and I'll knock you down."

"Why won't you at least say thanks?"

He stared at me, mouth tight and cheeks red. "We're not supposed to see him, Mom and Dad said so. He's crazy, and probably a drunk like his wife."

I couldn't speak. My eyes shimmered with tears. They weren't of sorrow; those were tears of rage.

"Besides," Con said, "I have to fill the woodbox before Dad gets home or I'll get in dutch. So just shut up about it, Jamie."

He left me standing there. My brother, who became one of the world's most preeminent astronomers—in 2011 he discovered the fourth so-called "Goldilocks planet," where there might be life—left me standing there. And never mentioned Charles Jacobs again.

The next day, Tuesday, I ran up Route 9 again as soon as school let out. But I didn't go home.

There was a new car in the parsonage driveway. Well, not really new; it was a '58 Ford Fairlane with rust on the rocker panels and a crack in the passenger side window. The trunk was up, and when I peeped in, I saw two suitcases and a bulky electronic gadget Reverend Jacobs had demonstrated at MYF one Thursday night: an oscilloscope. Jacobs himself was in his shed workshop. I could hear stuff rattling around.

I stood by his new-old car, thinking of the Belvedere, which was now a burned-out wreck, and I almost turned tail and beat feet for home. I wonder how much of my life would have been different if I'd done that. I wonder if I'd be writing this now. There's no way of telling, is there? Saint Paul was all too right about that dark glass. We look through it all our days and see nothing but our own reflections.

Instead of running, I gathered my courage and went to the shed. He was putting electronic equipment into a wooden orange crate, using large sheets of crumpled-up brown paper for padding, and didn't see me at first. He was dressed in jeans and a plain white shirt. The notched collar was gone. Children aren't very observant about the changes in adults, as a rule, but even at nine I could see he'd lost weight. He was standing in a shaft of sunlight, and when he heard me come in, he looked up. There were new lines on his face, but when he saw me and smiled, the lines disappeared. That smile was so sad it put an arrow in my heart.

I didn't think, just ran to him. He opened his arms and lifted me up so he could kiss me on the cheek. "Jamie!" he cried. "Thou art Alpha and Omega!"

"Huh?"

"Revelation, chapter one, verse eight. 'I am Alpha and Omega, the beginning and the end.' You were the first kid I met when I came to Harlow, and you're the last. I'm so very, very glad you came."

I started to cry. I didn't want to but couldn't help it. "I'm sorry, Reverend Jacobs. I'm sorry for everything. You were right in church, it's not fair."

He kissed my other cheek and set me down. "I don't think I said that in so many words, but you certainly caught the gist of it. Not that you should take anything I said seriously; I was off my head. Your mother knew that. She told me so when she brought me that fine Thanksgiving feast. And she wished me all the best."

Hearing that made me feel a little better.

"She gave me some good advice, too—that I should go far from Harlow, Maine, and start over. She said I might find my faith again in some new place. I strongly doubt that, but she was right about leaving."

"I'll never see you again."

"Never say that, Jamie. Paths cross all the time in this world of ours, sometimes in the strangest places." He took his handkerchief from his back pocket and wiped the tears from my face. "In any case, I'll remember you. And I hope you'll think of me from time to time."

"I will." Then, remembering: "You betchum bobcats."

He went back to his worktable, now sadly bare, and finished packing up the last items—a couple of big square batteries he called "dry cells." He closed the lid of the crate and began tying it shut with two stout pieces of rope.

"Connie wanted to come with me to say thank you, but he's got . . . um . . . I think it's soccer practice today. Or something."

"That's okay. I doubt if I really did anything."

I was shocked. "You brought his voice back, for criminey sakes! You brought it back with your gadget!"

"Oh yes. My gadget." He knotted the second rope, and yanked it tight. His sleeves were rolled up, and I could see he had awesome muscles. I had never noticed them before. "The Electrical Nerve Stimulator."

"You ought to sell it, Reverend Jacobs! You could make a mint!"

He leaned an elbow on the crate, propped his chin on one hand, and gazed at me. "Do you think so?"

"Yes!"

"I doubt it very much. And I doubt if my ENS unit had anything to do with your brother's recovery. You see, I built it that very day." He laughed. "And powered it with a very small Japanese-made motor filched from Morrie's Roscoe Robot toy."

"Really?"

"Really. The *concept* is valid, I feel sure of that, but such prototypes—built on the fly, without any experiments to verify the steps in between—very rarely work. Yet I believed I had a chance, because I never doubted Dr. Renault's original diagnosis. It was a stretched nerve, no more than that."

"But—"

He hoisted the crate. The muscles in his arms bulged, veins standing out on them. "Come on, kiddo. Walk with me."

I followed him out to the car. He set the crate down beside the back fender, inspected the trunk, and said he'd have to move the suitcases to the backseat. "Can you take the small one, Jamie? It's not heavy. When you're traveling far, it's best to travel light."

"Where are you going?"

"No idea, but I think I'll know it when I get there. If this thing doesn't break down, that is. It burns enough oil to drain Texas."

We moved the suitcases to the back of the Ford. Reverend Jacobs hoisted the big crate into the trunk with a grunt of effort. He slammed it closed, then leaned against it, studying me.

"You have a wonderful family, Jamie, and wonderful parents who actually pay attention. If I asked them to describe you kids, I bet they'd say that Claire is the motherly one, Andy's the bossy one—"

"Boy, you're right about *that.*"

He grinned. "There's one in every family, boyo. They'd say Terry is the mechanical one and you're the dreamer. What would they say about Con?"

"The studying one. Or maybe the folk-singing one since he got his guitar."

"Perhaps, but I bet those wouldn't be the first things to pop into their minds. Ever notice Con's fingernails?"

I laughed. "He bites em like mad! Once my dad offered him a buck if he stopped for a week, but he couldn't!"

"Con is the nervy one, Jamie—that's what your folks would say if they were to be completely honest. The one who's apt to turn up with ulcers by the time he's forty. When he got hit in the neck with that ski pole and lost his voice, he started to worry that it would never come back. And when it didn't, he told himself it never would."

"Dr. Renault said—"

"Renault's a fine doctor. Conscientious. He turned up here Johnny-on-the-spot when Morrie had the measles and again when Patsy had . . . well, a female problem. Took care of both like a pro. But he doesn't have that air of confidence the best GPs have. That way of saying 'Bosh, this is nothing, you'll be fine in no time.'"

"He *did* say that!"

"Yes, but Conrad wasn't convinced because Renault isn't convincing. He's able to treat the body, but the mind? Not so much. And the mind is where half the healing takes place. Maybe more. Con thought, 'He's lying now so I can get used to having no voice. Later on he'll tell me the truth.' That's just the way your brother's built, Jamie. He lives on his nerve endings, and when people do that, their minds can turn against them."

"He wouldn't come with me today," I said. "I lied about that."

"Did you?" Jacobs didn't look very surprised.

"Yeah. I asked him, but he was scared."

"Never be angry with him for that," Jacobs said. "Frightened people live in their own special hell. You could say they make it themselves—like Con manufactured his muteness—but they can't help it. It's the way they're built. They deserve sympathy and compassion."

He turned to the parsonage, which already looked abandoned, and sighed. Then he turned back to me.

"Perhaps the ENS did *something*—I have every reason to believe the theory behind it is valid—but I really doubt it. Jamie, I believe I tricked your brother. Or, if you don't mind the pun, I *conned* him. It's a skill they try to teach in divinity school, although they call it kindling faith. I was always good at it, which has caused me to feel both shame and delight. I told your brother to expect a miracle, then I turned on the current and activated my glorified joy buzzer. As soon as I saw him twitching his mouth and blinking his eyes, I knew it was going to work."

"That's awesome!" I said.

"Yes indeed. Also rather vile."

"Huh?"

"Never mind. The important thing is you must never tell him. He probably wouldn't lose his voice again, but he might." He glanced at his watch. "You know what? I think that's all the powwow I have time for, if I'm going to make Portsmouth by tonight. And you better get home. Where your visit to me this afternoon will be another secret we'll keep between us, right?"

"Right."

"You didn't go past Me-Maw's, did you?"

I rolled my eyes, as if to ask if he was really that stupid, and Jacobs laughed some more. I loved that I could make him laugh in spite of everything that had happened. "I cut through Marstellar's field."

"Good lad."

I didn't want to go, and I didn't want *him* to go. "Can I ask you one more question?"

"Okay, but make it quick."

"When you were giving your . . . um . . ." I didn't want to use the word *sermon*, it seemed dangerous, somehow. "When you were talking in church, you said lightning was, like, fifty thousand degrees. Is that true?"

His face kindled as it only did when the subject of electricity came up. His hobbyhorse, Claire would have said. My dad would have called it his obsession.

"*Completely* true! Except maybe for earthquakes and tidal waves, lightning is the most powerful force in nature. More powerful than tornadoes and much more powerful than hurricanes. Have you ever seen a bolt strike the earth?"

I shook my head. "Only in the sky."

"It's beautiful. Beautiful and terrifying." He looked up, as if seeking one, but the sky that afternoon was blue, the only clouds little white puffs moving slowly southwest. "If you ever want to see one up close . . . you know Longmeadow, right?"

Of course I did. Halfway up the road leading to Goat Mountain Resort, there was a state-maintained public park. That was Longmeadow. From it you could look east for miles and miles. On a very clear day, you could see all the way to the Desert of Maine in Freeport. Sometimes even to the Atlantic Ocean beyond. The MYF had its summer cookout at Longmeadow every August.

He said, "If you go up the road from Longmeadow, you come to the Goat Mountain Resort gatehouse . . ."

". . . where they won't let you in unless you're a member or a guest."

"Right. The class system at work. But just before you get to the gatehouse, there's a gravel road that splits off to the left. Anyone can use it, because that's all state land. About three miles up, it ends at an outlook called Skytop. I never took you kids there, because it's dangerous—just a granite slope ending in a two-thousand-foot drop. There's no fence, just a sign warning people to keep back from the edge. At the Skytop summit there's an iron pole twenty feet high. It's driven deep into the rock. I have no idea who put it there, or why, but it's been there a long, long time. It should be rusty, but it's not. Do you know *why* it's not?"

I shook my head.

"Because it's been struck by lightning so many times. Skytop's a special place. It *draws* the lightning, and that iron rod is its focal point."

He was looking dreamily off toward Goat Mountain. It was certainly not big compared to the Rockies (or even the White Mountains of New Hampshire), but it dominated the rolling hills of western Maine.

"The thunder is louder there, Jamie, and the clouds are closer. The sight of those stormclouds rolling in makes a person feel very small, and when a person is beset by worries . . . or doubts . . . feeling small is not such a bad thing. You know when the lightning's going to come, because there's a breathless feeling in the air. A feeling of . . . I don't know . . . an unburned burning. Your hair stands on end and your chest gets heavy. You can feel your skin trembling. You wait, and when the thunder comes, it doesn't boom. It *cracks*, like when a branch loaded with ice finally gives way, only a hundred times louder. There's silence . . . and then a *click* in the air, sort of like the sound an old-fashioned light switch makes. The thunder rolls and the lightning comes. You have to squint, or the stroke will blind you and you won't see that iron pole go from black to purple-white and then to red, like a horseshoe in the forge."

"Wow," I said.

He blinked and came back. He kicked the tire of his new-old car. "Sorry, kiddo. Sometimes I get carried away."

"It sounds awesome."

"Oh, it's way beyond awesome. Go up there sometime when you're older and see for yourself. Just be careful around the pole. The lightning has chipped up all kinds of loose scree, and if you started to slide, you might not be able to stop. And now, Jamie, I really do have to get rolling."

"I wish you didn't have to go." I wanted to cry some more, but I wouldn't let myself.

"I appreciate that, and I'm touched by it, but you know what they say—if wishes were horses, beggars would ride." He opened his arms. "Now give me another hug."

I hugged him hard, breathing deep, trying to store up the smells of his soap and his hair tonic—Vitalis, the kind my dad used. And now Andy, as well.

"You were my favorite," he said into my ear. "That's another secret you should probably keep."

I just nodded. There was no need to tell him that Claire already knew.

"I left something for you in the parsonage basement," he said. "If you want it. Key's under the doormat."

He set me on my feet, kissed me on the forehead, then opened the driver's door. "This caa ain't much, chummy," he said, putting on a Yankee accent that made me smile in spite of how bad I felt. "Still, I reckon it'll get me down the road apiece."

"I love you," I said.

"I love you, too," he said. "But don't you cry on me again, Jamie. My heart is already as broken as I can stand."

I didn't cry again until he was gone. I stood there and watched him back down the driveway. I watched him until he was out of sight. Then I walked home. We still had a hand pump in our backyard in those days, and I washed my face in that freezing-cold water before I went inside. I didn't want my mother to see that I'd been crying, and ask me why.

It would be the job of the Ladies Auxiliary to give the parsonage a good stem-to-stern cleaning, removing all traces of the ill-fated Jacobs family and making it ready for the new preacher, but there was no hurry, Dad said; the wheels of the New England Methodist Bishopric moved slowly, and we would be lucky to have a new minister assigned to us by the following summer.

"Let it sit awhile," was Dad's advice, and the Auxiliary was happy enough to take it. They didn't get to work with their brooms and brushes and vacuums until after Christmas (Andy preached the lay sermon that year, and my parents almost burst with pride). Until then, the parsonage stood empty, and some of the kids at my school began to claim that it was haunted.

There was one visitor, though: me. I went on a Saturday afternoon, once more cutting through Dorrance Marstellar's cornfield to evade the watchful eye of Me-Maw Harrington. I used the key under the doormat and let myself in. It was scary. I had scoffed at the idea that the place might be haunted, but once I was inside, it was all too easy to imagine turning around and seeing Patsy and Tag-Along-Morrie standing there, hand in hand, goggle-eyed and rotting.

Don't be stupid, I told myself. *They've either gone on to some other place or just into black nothing, like Reverend Jacobs said. So stop being scared. Stop being a stupid fraidy-cat.*

But I couldn't stop being a stupid fraidy-cat any more than I could stop having a stomachache after eating too many hotdogs on Saturday night. I didn't run away, though. I wanted to see what he had left me. I *needed* to see what he had left me. So I went to the door that still had a poster on it (Jesus holding hands with a couple of kids who looked like Dick and Jane in my old first-grade reader), and the sign that said LET THE LITTLE CHILDREN COME UNTO ME.

I turned on the light and went down the stairs and looked at the folding chairs stacked against the wall, and the piano with the cover down, and Toy Corner, where the little table was now bare of dominos and coloring books and Crayolas. But Peaceable Lake was still there, and so was the little wooden box with Electric Jesus inside. That was what he had left me, and I was horribly disappointed. Nonetheless, I opened the box and took Electric Jesus out. I set him at the edge of the lake, where I knew the track was, and started to reach up under his robe to turn him on. Then the greatest rage of my young life swept through me. It was as sudden as one of those lightning strikes Reverend Jacobs had talked about seeing up on Skytop. I swung my arm and knocked Electric Jesus all the way to the far wall.

"*You're not real!*" I shouted. "*You're not real! It's all a bunch of tricks! Damn you, Jesus! Damn you, Jesus! Damn you, damn you, damn you, Jesus!*"

I ran up the stairs, crying so hard I could barely see.

We never did get another minister, as it turned out. Some of the local padres tried to take up the slack, but attendance dropped to almost nothing, and by my senior year of high school, our church was locked and shuttered. It didn't matter to me. My belief had ended. I have no idea what happened to Peaceable Lake and Electric Jesus. The next time I went into the downstairs MYF room in the parsonage—this was a great many years later—it was completely empty. As empty as heaven.

IV

Two Guitars. Chrome Roses. Skytop Lightning.

When we look back, we think our lives form patterns; every event starts to look logical, as if something—or Someone—has mapped out all our steps (and missteps). Take the foul-mouthed retiree who unknowingly ordained the job I worked at for twenty-five years. Do you call that fate or just happenstance? I don't know. How can I? I wasn't even there on the night when Hector the Barber went looking for his old Silvertone guitar. Once upon a time, I would have said we choose our paths at random: this happened, then that, hence the other. Now I know better.

There are forces.

In 1963, before the Beatles burst on the scene, a brief but powerful infatuation with folk music gripped America. The TV show that came along at the right time to capitalize on the craze was *Hootenanny*, featuring such Caucasian interpreters of the black experience as the Chad Mitchell Trio and the New Christy Minstrels. (Perceived *commie* Caucasians like Pete Seeger and Joan Baez were not invited to perform.) My brother Conrad was best friends with Billy Paquette's older brother, Ronnie, and they watched *The Hoot*, as they called it, every Saturday night at the Paquettes' house.

At that time, Ronnie and Billy's grandfather lived with the Paquettes. He was known as Hector the Barber because that had been his trade for almost fifty years, although it was hard to visualize him in the role; barbers, like bartenders, are supposed to be pleasantly chatty types, and Hector the Barber rarely said anything. He just sat in the living room, tipping capfuls of bourbon whiskey into his coffee and smoking Tiparillos. The smell of them permeated the whole house. When he did talk, his discourse was peppered with profanity.

He liked *Hootenanny*, though, and always watched it with Con and Ronnie. One night, after some white boy sang something about how his baby left him and he felt so sad, Hector the Barber snorted and said, "Shit, boys, that ain't the blues."

"What do you mean, Grampa?" Ronnie asked.

"Blues is *mean* music. That boy sounded like he just peed the bed and he's afraid his mama might find out."

The boys laughed at this, partly out of delight, partly in amazement that Hector was actually something of a music critic.

"You wait," he said, and slowly mounted the stairs, yanking himself along by the banister with one gnarled hand. He was gone so long the boys had almost forgotten about him when Hector came back down carrying a beat-up Silvertone guitar by the neck. Its body was scuffed and held together with a hank of frayed hayrope. The tuning keys were crooked. He sat down with a grunt and a fart, and hauled the guitar onto his bony knees.

"Shut that shit off," he said.

Ronnie did so—that week's hoot was almost over, anyway. "I didn't know you played, Grampa," he said.

"Ain't in years," Hector said. "Put it away when the arthritis started to bite. I don't know if I can even tune the bitch anymore."

"Language, Dad," Mrs. Paquette called from the kitchen.

Hector the Barber paid no attention to her; unless he needed her to pass the mashed potatoes, he rarely did. He tuned the guitar slowly, muttering curses under his breath, then played a chord that actually sounded a bit like music. "You could tell it was still off," Con said when he told me the story later, "but it was pretty cool, anyway."

"Wow!" Ronnie said. "Which chord is that, Grampa?"

"E. All this shit starts with E. But wait, you ain't heard nothing yet. Lemme see if I can remember how this whoremaster goes."

From the kitchen: "Language, Dad."

He paid no more mind this time, only began to strum the old guitar, using one horny, nicotine-yellowed fingernail as a pick. He was slow at first, muttering more unapproved language under his breath, but then he picked up a steady, chugging rhythm that made the boys glance at each other in amazement. His fingers slid up and down the fretboard, clumsily at first, then—as the old memory synapses guttered back to life—a little more smoothly: B to A to G and back home to E. It's a progression I've played a hundred thousand times, although in 1963 I wouldn't have known an E chord from a spinal cord.

In a high, wailing voice utterly unlike the one he spoke in (when he *did* speak), Ronnie's grandpa sang: "Why don't you drop down, darlin, let your daddy see . . . you got somethin, darlin, keep on *worryin* me . . ."

Mrs. Paquette came in from the kitchen, drying her hands on a dishtowel and looking as if she'd seen some exotic bird—an ostrich or an emu, say—strutting down the middle of Route 9. Billy and little Rhonda Paquette, who could have been no more than five, came halfway down the stairs, leaning over the railing and goggling at the old man.

"That *beat*," Con told me later. "It sure wasn't like anything they play on *Hootenanny*."

Hector the Barber was now thumping his foot in time and grinning. Con said he'd never seen the old man grin before, and it was a little scary, like he'd turned into some kind of singing vampire.

"My mama don't allow me to fool around all night long . . . she afraid some woman might . . . might . . ." He drew it out. "*Miiight* not treat me right!"

"Go, Grampa!" Ronnie shouted, laughing and clapping his hands.

Hector launched into the second verse, the one about how the jack of diamonds told the queen of spades to go on and start her *creepin* ways, but then a string broke: *TWANNG.*

"Oh, you dirty cunt," he said, and that was it for Hector the Barber's impromptu concert. Mrs. Paquette snatched away his guitar (the broken string flying dangerously close to her eye) and told him to go on outside and sit on the porch if he was going to talk that way.

Hector the Barber did not go out on the porch, but he did lapse back into his accustomed silence. The boys never heard him sing and play again. He died the following summer, and Charles Jacobs—still going strong in 1964, the Year of the Beatles—officiated at his funeral.

The day after that abbreviated version of Arthur "Big Boy" Crudup's "My Mama Don't Allow Me," Ronnie Paquette found the guitar in one of the swill barrels out back, deposited there by his outraged mom. Ronnie took it to school, where Mrs. Calhoun, the English teacher who doubled as the middle school music teacher, showed him how to put on a new string, and how to tune it by humming the first three notes of "Taps." She also gave Ronnie a copy of *Sing Out!*, a folk music magazine that had both lyrics and chord changes to songs like "Barb'ry Allen."

During the next couple of years (with a brief hiatus during the time when the Ski Pole of Destiny rendered Connie mute), the two boys learned folk song after folk song, trading the old guitar back and forth as they learned the same basic chords Leadbelly no doubt strummed during his prison years. Neither of them could play worth a tin shit, but Con had a pretty good voice—although too sweet to be convincing on the blues tunes he loved—and they performed in public a few times, as Con and Ron. (They flipped a coin to see whose name would come first.)

Con eventually got his own guitar, a Gibson acoustic with the cherry finish. It was a hell of a lot nicer than Hector the Barber's old Silvertone, and it was the one they used when they sang stuff like "Seventh Son" and "Sugarland" at the Eureka Grange on Talent Night. Our dad and mom were encouraging, and so were Ronnie's folks, but GIGO holds true for guitars as well as computers: garbage in, garbage out.

I paid little attention to Con and Ron's attempts to attain local stardom as a folk duo, and hardly noticed when my brother's interest in his Gibson guitar began to wither away. After Reverend Jacobs drove his new-old car out of Harlow, it felt to me as if there was a hole in my life. I had lost both God and my only grownup friend, and for a long time after I felt sad and vaguely frightened. Mom tried to cheer me up; so did Claire. Even my dad had a go. I tried to get happy again, and eventually succeeded, but as 1965 gave way to 1966 and then 1967, the cessation of badly rendered tunes like "Don't Think Twice" from upstairs wasn't even on my radar.

By then Con was all about high school athletics (he was a hell of a lot better at those than he ever was at playing the guitar), and as for me . . . a new girl had moved into town, Astrid Soderberg. She had silky blond hair, cornflower-blue eyes, and little sweater-nubbins that might in the future become actual breasts. During the first years we were in school together, I don't think I ever crossed her mind—unless she wanted to copy my homework, that was. I, on the other hand, thought of her constantly. I had an idea that if she allowed me to touch her hair, I might have a heart attack. One day I got the Webster's dictionary from the reference shelf, took it back to my desk, and carefully printed ASTRID across the definition of *kiss*, with my heart thumping and my skin prickling. *Crush* is a good word for that sort of infatuation, because crushed is how I felt.

Picking up Con's Gibson never occurred to me; if I wanted music I turned on the radio. But talent is a spooky thing, and has a way of announcing itself quietly but firmly when the right time comes. Like certain addictive drugs, it comes as a friend long before you realize it's a tyrant. I found that out for myself the year I turned thirteen.

First this, then that, hence the other thing.

My musical talent was far from huge, but much larger than Con's . . . or anyone else's in our family, for that matter. I discovered it was there on a boring, overcast Saturday in the fall of 1969. Everyone else in the family—even Claire, who was home from college for the weekend—had gone over to Gates Falls for the football game. Con was then a junior and a starting tailback for the Gates Falls Gators. I stayed home because I had a stomachache, although it wasn't as bad as I made out; I just wasn't much of a football fan, and besides, it looked like it was going to rain.

I watched TV for awhile, but there was more football on two

channels, and golf on the third—even worse. Claire's old bedroom was now Connie's, but some of her paperbacks were still stacked in the closet, and I thought I might try one of the Agatha Christies. Claire said they were easy to read, and it was fun to detect along with Miss Marple or Hercule Poirot. I walked in and saw Con's Gibson in the corner, surrounded by an untidy heap of old *Sing Out!* magazines. I looked at it, leaning there and long forgotten, and thought, *I wonder if I could play "Cherry, Cherry" on that.*

I remember that moment as clearly as my first kiss, because the thought was an exotic stranger, utterly unconnected to anything that had been on my mind when I walked into Con's room. I'd swear to it on a stack of Bibles. It wasn't even like a thought. It was like a voice.

I took the guitar and sat down on Con's bed. I didn't touch the strings at first, just thought about that song some more. I knew it would sound good on Connie's acoustic because "Cherry, Cherry" is built around an acoustic riff (not that I knew the word then). I listened to it in my head and was astounded to realize I could see the chord changes as well as hear them. I knew everything about them except where they were hiding on the fretboard.

I grabbed an issue of *Sing Out!* at random and looked for a blues, any blues. I found one called "Turn Your Money Green," saw how to make an E (*All this shit starts with E*, Hector the Barber had told Con and Ronnie), and played it on the guitar. The sound was muffled but true. The Gibson was a fine instrument that had stayed in tune even though it had been neglected. I pushed down harder with the first three fingers of my left hand. It hurt, but I didn't care. Because E was right. E was divine. It matched the sound in my head perfectly.

It took Con six months to learn "The House of the Rising Sun," and he was never able to go from the D to the F without a hesitation as he arranged his fingers. I learned the three-chord "Cherry, Cherry" riff—E to A to D and back to A—in ten minutes, then realized I could use the same three chords to play "Gloria," by Shadows of Knight, and "Louie, Louie," by the Kingsmen. I played until my fingertips were howling with pain and I could hardly unbend my left hand. When I finally stopped, it wasn't because I wanted to but because I had to. And I couldn't wait to start again. I didn't care about the New Christy Minstrels, or Ian and Sylvia, or any of those folk-singing assholes, but I could have played "Cherry, Cherry" all day: it had the way to move me.

If I could learn to play well enough, I thought, Astrid Soderberg might look at me as something other than just a homework source. Yet even that was a secondary consideration, because playing filled that hole in me. It was its own thing, an emotional truth. Playing made me feel like a real person again.

Three weeks later, on another Saturday afternoon, Con came home early after the football game instead of staying for the traditional post-game cookout put on by the boosters. I was sitting on the landing at the top of the stairs, scratching out "Wild Thing." I thought he'd go nuts and grab his guitar away from me, maybe accuse me of sacrilege for playing three-chord idiocy by the Troggs on an instrument meant for such sensitive songs of protest as "Blowin' in the Wind."

But Con had scored three TDs that day, he'd set a school record for yards gained rushing, and the Gators were headed for the Class C playoffs. All he said was, "That's just about the stupidest song to ever get on the radio."

"No," I said. "I think the prize goes to 'Surfin' Bird.' I can play that one, too, if you want to hear it."

"Jesus, no." He could curse because Mom was out in the garden, Dad and Terry were in the garage, working on Road Rocket III, and our religion-minded older brother no longer lived at home. Like Claire, Andy was now attending the University of Maine (which, he claimed, was full of "useless hippies").

"But you don't mind if I play it, Con?"

"Knock yourself out," he said, passing me on the stairs. There was a gaudy bruise on one cheek and he smelled of football sweat. "But if you break it, you're paying for it."

"I won't break it."

I didn't, either, but I busted a lot of strings. Rock and roll is tougher on strings than folk music.

In 1970, I started high school across the Androscoggin River in Gates Falls. Con, now a senior and a genuine Big Deal thanks to his athletic prowess and Honor Roll grades, took no notice of me. That was okay; that was fine. Unfortunately, neither did Astrid Soderberg, although she sat one row behind me in homeroom and right next to me in Freshman English. She wore her hair in a ponytail and her skirts at least two inches above the knee. Every time she crossed her legs I died. My crush was bigger than ever, but I had eavesdropped on her and her girlfriends as they sat together on the gym bleachers during lunch, and I knew the only boys they had eyes for were upperclassmen. I was just another extra in the grand epic of their newly minted high school lives.

Someone took notice of me, though—a lanky, long-haired senior who looked like one of Andy's useless hippies. He sought me out one day when I was eating my own lunch in the gym, two bleachers up from Astrid and her posse of gigglers.

"You Jamie Morton?" he asked.

I owned up to it cautiously. He was wearing baggy jeans with patches on the knees, and there were dark circles under his eyes, as if he was getting by on two or three hours' sleep a night. Or whacking off a lot.

"Come down to the Band Room," he said.

"Why?"

"Because I said so, freshie."

I followed him, weaving my way through the thronging students who were laughing, yelling, pushing, and banging their lockers. I hoped I wasn't going to get beaten up. I could imagine getting beaten up by a sophomore for some trifling reason—freshman hazing by sophomores was forbidden in principle but lavishly practiced in fact—but not by a senior. Seniors rarely noticed freshies were alive, my brother being a case in point.

The Band Room was empty. That was a relief. If this guy intended to tune up on me, at least he didn't have a bunch of friends to help him do it. Instead of beating me up, he held out his hand. I shook it. His fingers were limp and clammy. "Norm Irving."

"Nice to meet you." I didn't know if it was or not.

"I hear you play guitar, freshie."

"Who told you that?"

"Your brother. Mr. Football." Norm Irving opened a storage cabinet filled with cased guitars. He pulled one out, flicked the catches, and revealed a gorgeous dead-black electric Yamaha.

"SA 30," he said briefly. "Got it two years ago. Painted houses all summer with my dad. Turn on that amp. No, not the big one, the Bullnose right in front of you."

I went to the mini-amp, looked around for a switch or a button, and didn't see any.

"On the back, freshie."

"Oh." I found a rocker switch and flipped it. A red light came on, and there was a low hum. I liked that hum from the very first. It was the sound of power.

Norm scrounged a cord from the guitar cabinet and plugged in. His fingers brushed the strings, and a brief *BRONK* sound came from the little amp. It was atonal, unmusical, and completely beautiful. He held the guitar out to me.

"What?" I was both alarmed and excited.

"Your brother says you play rhythm. So play some rhythm."

I took the guitar, and that *BRONK* sound came again from the little Bullnose amp at my feet. The guitar was a lot heavier than my brother's acoustic. "I've never played an electric," I said.

"It's the same."

"What do you want me to play?"

"How about 'Green River.' Can you play that?" He reached into the watch pocket of his baggy jeans and held out a pick.

I managed to take it without dropping it. "Key of E?" As if I had to ask. All that shit starts with E.

"You decide, freshie."

I slipped the strap over my head and settled the pad on my shoulder. The Yammie hung way low—Norman Irving was a lot taller than I was—but I was too nervous to even think of adjusting it. I played an E chord and jumped at how loud it was in the closed Band Room. That made him grin, and the grin—which revealed teeth that were going to give him a lot of problems in the future if he didn't start taking care of them—made me feel better.

"Door's shut, freshie. Turn it up and jam out."

The volume was set at 5. I turned it up to 7, and the resulting *WHANGGG* was satisfyingly loud.

"I can't sing worth a crap," I said.

"You don't have to sing. I sing. You just have to play rhythm."

"Green River" has a basic rock-and-roll beat—not quite like

"Cherry, Cherry," but close. I hit E again, listening to the first phrase of the song in my head and deciding it was right. Norman began to sing. His voice was almost buried by the sound of the guitar, but I could hear enough to tell he had good pipes. "Take me back down where cool water flows, yeah . . ."

I switched to A, and he stopped.

"Stays E, doesn't it?" I said. "Sorry, sorry."

The first three lines were all in E, but when I switched to A again, where most basic rock goes, it was still wrong.

"Where?" I asked Norman.

He just looked at me, hands in his back pockets. I listened in my head, then began again. When I got to the fourth line, I went to C, and that was right. I had to start over once more, but after that it was a cinch. All we needed was drums, a bass . . . and some lead guitar, of course. John Fogerty of Creedence hammered that lead in a way I never could in my wildest dreams.

"Gimme the ax," Norman said.

I handed it over, disappointed to let it go. "Thanks for letting me play it," I said, and headed for the door.

"Wait a minute, Morton." It wasn't much of a change, but at least I had been promoted from freshie. "Audition's not over."

Audition?

From the storage cabinet he took a smaller case, opened it, and produced a scratched-up Kay semi-hollowbody—a 900G, if you're keeping score.

"Plug into the big amp, but turn it down to four. That Kay feeds back like a motherfucker."

I did as instructed. The Kay fit my body better than the Yammie; I wouldn't have to hunch over to play it. There was a pick threaded into the strings and I took it out.

"Ready?"

I nodded.

"One . . . two . . . one-two-three-and . . ."

I was nervous while I was working out the simple rhythm progression of "Green River," but if I'd known how well Norman could play, I don't think I could have played at all; I would simply have fled the room. He hit the Fogerty lead just right, playing the same licks as on that old Fantasy single. As it was, I was swept along.

"Louder!" he shouted at me. "Jack it and fuck the feedback!"

I turned the big amp up to 8 and kicked it back in. With both guitars playing and the amp feeding back like a police whistle, Norm's voice was lost in the sound. It didn't matter. I stuck the groove and let his lead carry me. It was like surfing a glassy wave that rolled on without breaking for two and a half minutes.

It ended and silence crashed back in. My ears were ringing. Norm stared up at the ceiling, considering, then nodded. "Not great, but not terrible. With a little practice, you might be better than Snuffy."

"Who's Snuffy?" I asked. My ears were ringing.

"A guy who's moving to Assachusetts," he said. "Let's try 'Needles and Pins.' You know, the Searchers?"

"E?"

"No, this one's D, but not straight D. You gotta diddle it." He demonstrated how I was supposed to hammer high E with my pinky, and I picked it up right away. It didn't sound exactly like the record, but it was in the ballpark. When we finished I was dripping with sweat.

"Okay," he said, unslinging the guitar. "Let's go out to the SA. I need a butt."

• • •

The smoking area was behind the vocational tech building. It was where the burns and hippies hung out, along with girls who wore tight skirts, dangly earrings, and too much makeup. Two guys were squatting at the far end of the metal shop. I'd seen them around, as I had Norman, but didn't know them. One had sandy blond hair and a lot of acne. The other had a kinky pad of red hair that stuck out in nine different directions. They looked like losers, but I didn't care. Norman Irving also looked like a loser, but he was the best guitar player I'd ever heard who wasn't on a record.

"How is he?" the sandy blond asked. This turned out to be Kenny Laughlin.

"Better than Snuffy," Norman said.

The one with the crazy red hair grinned. "That ain't sayin shit."

"Yeah, but we need someone, or we can't play the Grange on Saturday night." He produced a pack of Kools and tipped it my way. "Smoke?"

"I don't," I said. And then, feeling absurd but not able to help myself, "Sorry."

Norman ignored that and lit up with a Zippo that had a snake and DON'T TREAD ON ME engraved on the side. "This is Kenny Laughlin. Plays bass. The redhead is Paul Bouchard. Drums. This shrimp is Connie Morton's brother."

"Jamie," I said. I desperately wanted these guys to like me—to let me in—but I didn't want to start whatever relationship we might have as nothing more than Mr. Football's kid brother. "I'm Jamie." I held out my hand.

Their shakes were as limp as Norman's had been. I've gigged with hundreds of players since the day Norman Irving auditioned me in the GFHS Band Room, and almost every guy I ever worked with had the same dead-fish shake. It's as if rockers feel they have to save all their strength for work.

"So what do you say?" Norman asked. "Wanna be in a band?"

Did I? If he'd told me I had to eat my own shoelaces as an initiation rite, I would have pulled them from the eyelets immediately and started chewing.

"Sure, but I can't play in any places where they serve booze. I'm only fourteen."

They looked at each other, surprised, then laughed.

"We'll worry about playing the Holly and the Deuce-Four once we get a rep," Norman said, jetting smoke from his nostrils. "For now we're just playing teen dances. Like the one at the Eureka Grange. That's where you're from, right? Harlow?"

"How-Low," Kenny Laughlin said, snickering. "That's what we call it. As in How-Low can you shitkickers go?"

"Listen, you want to play, right?" Norm said. He lifted his leg so he could bogart his cigarette on one of his battered old Beatle boots. "Your brother says you're playing his Gibson, which doesn't have a pickup, but you can use the Kay."

"The Music Department won't care?"

"The Music Department won't know. Come to the Grange on Thursday afternoon. I'll bring the Kay. Just don't break the stupid feedbacky fucker. We'll set up and rehearse. Bring a notebook so you can write down the chords."

The bell rang. Kids butted their smokes and started drifting back toward the school. As one of the girls passed, she kissed Norman on the cheek and patted him on the butt of his sagging jeans. He seemed not to notice her, which struck me as incredibly sophisticated. My respect for him went up another notch.

None of my fellow bandmates showed any signs of heeding the bell, so I started off on my own. Then another thought crossed my mind, and I turned back.

"What's the name of the band?"

Norm said, "We used to call ourselves the Gunslingers, but people thought that was a little too, you know, militaristic. So now we're Chrome Roses. Kenny thought it up while we were stoned and watching a gardening show at my dad's place. Cool, huh?"

In the quarter century that followed, I played with the J-Tones, Robin and the Jays, and the Hey-Jays (all led by a snazzy guitarist named Jay Pederson). I played with the Heaters, the Stiffs, the Undertakers, Last Call, and the Andersonville Rockers. During the flowering of punk I played with Patsy Cline's Lipstick, the Test Tube Babies, Afterbirth, and The World Is Full of Bricks. I even played with a rockabilly group called Duzz Duzz Call the Fuzz. But there was never a better name for a band, in my opinion, than Chrome Roses.

"I don't know," Mom said. She didn't look mad, she looked like she was coming down with a headache. "You're only fourteen, Jamie. Conrad says those boys are *much* older." We were at the dinner table, which looked a lot bigger with Claire and Andy gone. "Do they smoke?"

"No," I said.

My mother turned to Con. "Do they?"

Con, who was passing the creamed corn to Terry, didn't miss a beat. "Nope."

I could have hugged him. We'd had our differences over the years, as all brothers do, but brothers also have a way of sticking together when the chips are down.

"It's not bars, or anything, Mom," I said . . . knowing in some intuitive way that it *would* be bars, and probably long before the most junior member of Chrome Roses turned twenty-one. "Just the Grange. We have rehearsal this Thursday."

"You'll need plenty," Terry said snidely. "Gimme another pork chop."

"Say please, Terence," my mother said distractedly.

"*Please* gimme another pork chop."

Dad passed the platter. He hadn't said anything. That could be good or bad.

"How will you get to rehearsal? For that matter, how will you get to these . . . these *gigs*?"

"Norm's got a VW microbus. Well, it's his dad's, but he let Norm paint the band's name on the side!"

"This Norm can't be more than eighteen," Mom said. She had stopped eating her food. "How do I know he's a safe driver?"

"Mom, they *need* me! Their rhythm guy moved to Massachusetts. With no rhythm guy, they'll lose the gig Saturday night!" A thought blazed across my mind like a meteor: Astrid Soderberg might be at that dance. "It's important! It's a big deal!"

"I don't like it." Now she was rubbing her temples.

My father spoke up at last. "Let him do it, Laura. I know you're worried, but it's what he's good at."

She sighed. "All right. I guess."

"Thanks, Mom! Thanks, Dad!"

My mother picked up her fork, then put it down. "Promise me that you won't smoke cigarettes or marijuana, and that you won't drink."

"I promise," I said, and that was a promise I kept for two years.

Or thereabouts.

What I remember best about that first gig at Eureka Grange No. 7 was the stench of my own sweat as the four of us trooped onto the bandstand. When it comes to sweat, nobody can beat an adolescent of fourteen. I had showered for twenty minutes before my maiden show—until the hot water ran out—but when I bent to pick up my borrowed guitar, I reeked of fear. The Kay seemed to weigh at least two hundred pounds when I slung it over my shoulder. I had good reason to be scared. Even taking the inherent simplicity of rock and roll into account, the task Norm Irving set me—learning thirty songs between Thursday afternoon and Saturday night—was impossible, and I told him so.

He shrugged and offered me the most useful advice I ever got as a musician: When in doubt, lay out. "Besides," he said, baring his decaying teeth in a fiendish grin, "I'm gonna be turned up so loud they won't hear what you're doing, anyway."

Paul rolled a short riff on his drums to get the crowd's attention, finishing with a cymbal-clang. There was a brief spatter of anticipatory applause. There were all those eyes (millions, it seemed to me) looking up at the little stage where we were crowded together under the lights. I remember feeling incredibly stupid in my rhinestone-studded vest (the vests were holdovers from the brief period when Chrome Roses had been the Gunslingers), and wondering if I was going to vomit. It hardly seemed possible, since I'd only picked at lunch and hadn't been able to eat any supper at all, but it sure felt that way. Then I thought, *Not vomit. Faint. That's what I'm going to do, faint.*

I really might have, but Norm didn't give me time. "We're Chrome Roses, okay? You guys get up and dance." Then, to us: "One . . . two . . . you-know-what-to-do."

Paul Bouchard laid down the tomtom drumbeat that opens "Hang On Sloopy," and we were off. Norm sang lead; except for a couple of songs when Kenny took over, he always did. Paul and I did backing vocals. I was terribly shy about that at first, but the feeling passed when I heard how different my amplified voice sounded—

how adult. Later on I realized that no one pays much attention to the backup singers anyway . . . although they'd miss those voices if they were gone.

I watched the couples move onto the floor and start to dance. It was what they'd come for, but in my deepest heart I hadn't believed they would—not to music I was a part of. When it became clear to me that we weren't going to be booed off the stage, I felt a rising euphoria that was close to ecstasy. I've taken enough drugs to sink a battleship since then, but not even the best of them could equal that first rush. *We* were playing. *They* were dancing.

We played from seven until ten thirty, with a twenty-minute break around nine, when Norm and Kenny dropped their instruments, turned off their amps, and dashed outside to smoke. For me those hours passed in a dream, so I wasn't surprised when during one of the slower numbers—I think it was "Who'll Stop the Rain"—my mother and father waltzed by.

Mom's head was on Dad's shoulder. Her eyes were closed and there was a dreamy little smile on her face. My dad's eyes were open, and he gave me a wink as they passed the bandstand. There was no need to be embarrassed by their presence; although the high school dances and the PAL hops at the Lewiston Roller Rink were strictly for kids, there were always a lot of adults when we played at the Eureka Grange, or the Elks and Amvets in Gates. The only thing wrong with that first gig was that, although some of Astrid's friends were there, she wasn't.

My folks left early, and Norm drove me home in the old microbus. We were all high on our success, laughing and reliving the show, and when Norm held out a ten-dollar bill to me, I didn't understand what it was for.

"Your cut," he said. "We got fifty for the gig. Twenty for me—because it's my 'bus and I play lead—ten for each of you guys."

I took it, still feeling like a boy in a dream, and slid open the side door with my aching left hand.

"Rehearsal this Thursday," Norm said. "Band Room after school this time. I can't take you home, though. My dad needs me to help paint a house over in Castle Rock."

I said that was okay. If Con couldn't give me a ride home, I'd hitch. Most of the people who used Route 9 between Gates Falls and Harlow knew me and would pick me up.

"You need to work on 'Brown-Eyed Girl.' You were way behind."

I said I would.

"And Jamie?"

I looked at him.

"Otherwise you did okay."

"Better than Snuffy," Paul said.

"*Way* better than that hoser," Kenny added.

That almost made up for Astrid's not being at the dance.

Dad had gone to bed, but Mom was sitting at the kitchen table with a cup of tea. She had changed into a flannel nightgown, but she still had her makeup on, and I thought she looked very pretty. When she smiled, I saw her eyes were full of tears.

"Mom? Are you okay?"

"Yes," she said. "I'm just happy for you, Jamie. And a little scared."

"Don't be," I said, and hugged her.

"You won't start smoking with those boys, will you? Promise me."

"I already promised, Mom."

"Promise me again."

I did. Making promises when you're fourteen is even easier than working up a sweat.

Upstairs, Con was lying on his bed, reading a science book. It was hard for me to believe anyone would read such books for pleasure (especially a big-shot football player), but Connie did. He put it down and said, "You were pretty good."

"How would you know?"

He smiled. "I peeked in. Just for a minute. You were playing that asshole song."

"Wild Thing." I didn't even have to ask.

We played at the Amvets the following Friday night, and the high school dance on Saturday. At that one, Norm changed the words to 'I Ain't Gonna Eat Out My Heart Anymore' to 'I Ain't Gonna Eat Out My Girl Anymore.' The chaperones didn't notice, they never noticed any of the lyrics, but the kids did, and loved it. The Gates gym was big enough to act as its own amplifier, and the sound we made, especially on really loud tunes like "Good Lovin'," was tremendous. If I may misquote Slade, us boyz made big noize. During the break, Kenny went along with Norm and Paul to the smoking area, so I did, too.

There were several girls there, including Hattie Greer, the one who'd patted Norm's butt on the day I auditioned. She put her arms around his neck and pressed her body against his. He put his hands in her back pockets to pull her closer. I tried not to stare.

A timid little voice came from behind me. "Jamie?"

I turned. It was Astrid. She was wearing a straight white skirt and a blue sleeveless blouse. Her hair had been released from its prim school ponytail and framed her face.

"Hi," I said. And because that didn't seem like enough: "Hi, Astrid. I didn't see you inside."

"I came late, because I had to ride with Bonnie and Bonnie's dad. You guys are really *good*."

"Thanks."

Norm and Hattie were kissing strenuously. Norm was a noisy kisser, and the sound was a bit like my Mom's Electrolux. There was other, quieter, making out going on as well, but Astrid didn't seem to notice. Those luminous eyes never left my face. She was wearing frog earrings. *Blue* frogs that matched her blouse. You notice everything at times like that.

Meanwhile, she seemed to be waiting for me to say something else, so I amplified my previous remark: "Thanks a lot."

"Are you going to have a cigarette?"

"Me?" It crossed my mind that she was spying for my mom. "I don't smoke."

"Walk me back, then?"

I walked her back. It was four hundred yards between the smoking area and the back door of the gym. I wished it had been four miles.

"Are you here with anybody?" I asked.

"Just Bonnie and Carla," she said. "Not a guy, or anything. Mom and Dad won't let me go out with guys until I'm fifteen."

Then, as if to show me what she thought of such a silly idea, she took my hand. When we got to the back door, she looked up at me. I almost kissed her then, but lost my courage.

Boys can be dopes.

When we were loading Paul's drumkit into the back of the microbus after the dance, Norm spoke to me in a stern, almost paternal voice. "After the break, you were off on everything. What was that about?"

"Dunno," I said. "Sorry. I'll do better next time."

"I hope so. If we're good, we get gigs. If we're not, we don't." He patted the rusty side of the microbus. "Betsy here don't run on air bubbles, and neither do I."

"It was that girl," Kenny said. "Pretty little blondie in a white skirt."

Norm looked enlightened. He put his hands on my shoulders and gave me a fatherly little shake to go with the fatherly voice. "Get with her, little buddy. Soon as you can. You'll play better."

Then he gave me fifteen dollars.

We played the Grange on New Year's Eve. It was snowing. Astrid was there. She was wearing a parka with a fur-lined hood. I led her under the fire escape and kissed her. She was wearing lipstick that tasted like strawberries. When I pulled back, she looked at me with those big eyes of hers.

"I thought you never would," she said, then giggled.

"Was it all right?"

"Do it again and I'll tell you."

We stood kissing under the fire escape until Norm tapped me on the shoulder. "Break it up, kids. Time to play some music."

Astrid pecked me on the cheek. "Do 'Wild Thing,' I love that one," she said, and ran toward the back door, slipping around in her dancing shoes.

Norm and I followed. "Blue balls much?" he asked.

"Huh?"

"Never mind. We're gonna play her song first. You know how it works, right?"

I did, because the band played plenty of requests. And I was happy to do it, because now I felt more confident when I had the Kay in front of me, an electric shield plugged in and ready to drive.

We walked onto the stand. Paul hit the customary drum-riff to signal that the band was back and ready to rock. Norm gave me a nod as he adjusted a guitar strap that didn't need adjusting. I stepped to the center mike and bellowed, "This one is for Astrid, by request, and because . . . *wild thing, I think I LOVE you*!" And although it was ordinarily Norm's job—his prerogative, as leader of the band—I counted the song off: One, two, you-know-what-to-do. On the floor, Astrid's friends were pummeling her and shrieking. Her cheeks were bright red. She blew me a kiss.

Astrid Soderberg blew me a kiss.

So the boys in Chrome Roses had girlfriends. Or maybe they were groupies. Or maybe they were both. When you're in a band, it's not always easy to tell where the line is. Norm had Hattie. Paul had Suzanne Fournier. Kenny had Carol Plummer. And I had Astrid.

Hattie, Suzanne, and Carol sometimes crammed into the microbus with us when we went to our gigs. Astrid wasn't allowed to do that, but when Suzanne was able to borrow her parents' car, Astrid was permitted to ride with the girls.

Sometimes they got out on the floor and danced with each other; mostly they just stood in their own tight little clique and watched. Astrid and I spent most of the breaks kissing, and I began to taste cigarettes on her breath. I didn't mind. When she saw that (girls have ways of knowing), she started to smoke around me, and a couple of times she'd blow a little into my mouth while we were kissing. It gave me a hard-on I could have broken concrete with.

A week after her fifteenth birthday, Astrid was allowed to go with us in the microbus to the PAL hop in Lewiston. We kissed all the way home, and when I slipped my hand inside her coat to cup a breast that was now quite a bit more than a nubbin, she didn't push it away as she always had before.

"That feels good," she whispered in my ear. "I know it's wrong, but it feels good."

"Maybe that's why," I said. Sometimes boys aren't dopes.

It was another month before she allowed my hand in her bra, and two before I was allowed to explore all the way up her skirt, but when I eventually got there, she admitted that also felt good. But beyond that she would not go.

"I know I'd get pregnant the first time," she whispered in my ear one night when we were parking and things had gotten especially hot.

"I can get something at the drugstore. I could go to Lewiston, where they don't know me."

"Carol says sometimes those things break. That's what happened one time when she was with Kenny, and she was scared for a month. She said she thought her period would never come. But there are other things we can do. She told me."

The other things were pretty good.

I got my license when I was sixteen, the only one of my siblings to succeed the first time I took the road test. I owed that partly to Driver's Ed and mostly to Cicero Irving. Norm lived with his mother, a goodhearted bottle blonde with a house in Gates Falls, but he spent most weekends with his dad, who lived in a scuzzy trailer park across the Harlow line in Motton.

If we had a gig on Saturday night, the band—along with our girlfriends—often got together at Cicero's trailer on Saturday afternoon for pizza. Joints were rolled and smoked, and after saying no for almost a year, I gave in and tried it. I found it hard to hold the smoke in at first, but—as many of my readers will know for themselves—it gets easier. I never smoked much dope in those days; just enough to get loose for the show. I played better when I had a little residual buzz on, and we always laughed a lot in that old trailer.

When I told Cicero I was going for my license the following week, he asked me if my appointment was in Castle Rock or up-the-city, meaning Lewiston-Auburn. When I said it was L-A, he nodded sagely. "That means you'll get Joe Cafferty. He's been doing that job for twenty years. I used to drink with him at the Mellow Tiger in Castle Rock, when I was a constable there. This was before the Rock got big enough to have a regular PD, you know."

It was hard to imagine Cicero Irving—grizzled, red-eyed, rail-thin, rarely dressed in anything but old khakis and strappy tee-shirts—being in the law enforcement biz, but people change; sometimes they go up the ladder and sometimes they go down. Those descending are frequently aided by various substances, such as the one he was so adept at rolling and sharing with his son's teenage compadres.

"Ole Joey hardly ever gives anyone their license first crack out of the basket," Cicero said. "As a rule, he don't believe in it."

This I knew; Claire, Andy, and Con had all fallen afoul of Joe Cafferty. Terry drew someone else (perhaps Officer Cafferty was sick that day), and although he was an excellent driver from the first time he got behind the wheel, Terry was a bundle of nerves that day and managed to back into a fire hydrant when he tried to parallel-park.

"Three things if you want to pass," Cicero said, handing the joint he had just rolled to Paul Bouchard. "Number one, stay off this shit until after your road test."

"Okay." That was actually something of a relief. I enjoyed the bud, but with every toke I remembered the promise I'd made to my mother and was now breaking . . . although I consoled myself with the fact that I still wasn't smoking cigarettes or drinking, which meant I was batting .666.

"Second, call him sir. Thank you sir when you get in the car and thank you sir when you get out. He likes that. Got it?"

"Got it."

"Third and most important, cut your fucking hair. Joe Cafferty hates hippies."

I didn't like that idea one bit. I had shot up three inches since joining the band, but when it came to hair, I was a slowpoke. It had taken me a year to get it almost down to my shoulders. There had also been a lot of hair arguments with my parents, who told me I looked like a bum. Andy's verdict was even blunter: "If you want to look like a girl, Jamie, why don't you put on a dress?" Gosh, there's nothing like reasoned Christian discourse, is there?

"Oh, man, if I cut my hair I'll look like a nerd!"

"You look like a nerd already," Kenny said, and everyone laughed. Even Astrid laughed (then put a hand on my thigh to take the sting out of it).

"Yeah," Cicero Irving said, "you'll look like a nerd with a driver's license. Paulie, are you going to fire up that joint or just sit there and admire it?"

I laid off the bud. I called Officer Cafferty sir. I got a Mr. Businessman haircut, which broke my heart and lifted my mother's. When I parallel-parked, I tapped the bumper of the car behind me, but Officer Cafferty gave me my license, anyway.

"I'm trusting you, son," he said.

"Thank you, sir," I said. "I won't let you down."

When I turned seventeen, there was a birthday party for me at our house, which now stood on a paved road—the march of progress. Astrid was invited, of course, and she gave me a sweater she had knitted herself. I pulled it on at once, although it was August and the day was hot.

Mom gave me a hardbound set of Kenneth Roberts historical novels (which I actually read). Andy gave me a leatherbound Bible (which I also read, mostly to spite him) with my name stamped in gold on the front. The inscription on the flyleaf was from Revelation 3: "Behold, I stand at the door and knock: if any man hear my voice, and open the door, I will come in to him." The implication—that I had Fallen Away—was not exactly unwarranted.

From Claire—now twenty-five and teaching school in New Hampshire—I got a spiffy sportcoat. Con, always something of a cheapie, gave me six sets of guitar strings. Oh well, at least they were Dollar Slicks.

Mom brought in the birthday cake, and everyone sang the traditional song. If Norm had been there, he probably would have blown the candles out with his rock-and-roll voice, but he wasn't, so I blew them out myself. As Mom was passing the plates around, I realized I hadn't gotten anything from Dad or Terry—not so much as a Flower Power tie.

After the cake and ice cream (van-choc-straw, of course), I saw Terry flash Dad a glance. Dad looked at Mom and she gave him a nervous little smile. It is only in retrospect that I realized how often I saw that nervous smile on my mother's face as her children grew up and went into the world.

"Come on out to the barn, Jamie," my dad said, standing up. "Terence and I have got a little something for you."

The "little something" turned out to be a 1966 Ford Galaxie. It was washed, waxed, and as white as moonlight on snow.

"Oh my God," I said in a faint voice, and everyone laughed.

"The body was good, but the engine needed some work," Terry

ms to her on several occasions after the first time, had far as to purchase a three-pack of Trojans (one kept in e other two secreted behind the baseboard in my bed-he was positive that the first one we tried would either . So . . . recess.

ad at me, aren't you?" Claire asked.

id. "Never mad at you, Claire-Bear." And I never was. was waiting for the monster she married, and it never

her and promised I would not get Astrid pregnant. It se I kept, although we got close before that day in the kytop.

ears I sometimes dreamed of Charles Jacobs—I'd see his fingers into my pretend mountain to make caves, or he Terrible Sermon with blue fire circling his head like diadem—but he pretty much slipped from my conscious one day in June of 1974. I was eighteen. So was Astrid. was out. Chrome Roses had gigs lined up all summer a couple in bars, where my parents had given me reluc-en permission to perform), and during the days I'd be the Marstellars' farmstand, as I had the year before. Mor-il was doing well, and my parents could afford tuition at rsity of Maine, but I was expected to do my share. I had ore reporting for farmstead duty, though, so Astrid and I f time together. Sometimes we went to my house; some-were at hers. On a lot of afternoons we cruised the back y Galaxie. We'd find a place to park and then . . . recess. ternoon we were in a disused gravel pit on Route 9, swap-int of not-very-good local grass back and forth. It was

said. "Me n Dad reground
new battery . . . the works.
"New tires," Dad said,
those are not recaps. Do yo
I hugged him. I hugged
"Just promise me and yo
the wheel if you've taken a
each other someday and say
hurt yourself or someone els
"I promise," I said.
Astrid—with whom I wo
when I took her home in my
make him keep it."
After driving down to Ha
trips so I could give everyone
tug on my hand. It was Clair
as she had on the day Revere
Stimulator to give Connie bac
"Mom wants another promi
too embarrassed to ask. So I sa
I waited.
"Astrid is a nice girl," Clair
on her breath, but that doesn't
good taste. Going with you for
I waited.
"She's a smart girl, too. She's
the promise, Jamie: don't you g
that car. Can you promise that?"
I almost smiled. If I had, it wo
and fifty percent pained. For the
had a code word: *recess*. It meant

tioned cond
even gone so
my wallet, t
room), but s
break or lea
"You're n
"No," I s
That anger
abated.
I hugged
was a prom
cabin near

In those y
him pokin
preaching
an electric
mind unti
School
(including
tant writt
working a
ton Fuel C
the Unive
a week be
had a lot
times we
roads in
That a
ping a j

tioned condoms to her on several occasions after the first time, had even gone so far as to purchase a three-pack of Trojans (one kept in my wallet, the other two secreted behind the baseboard in my bedroom), but she was positive that the first one we tried would either break or leak. So . . . recess.

"You're mad at me, aren't you?" Claire asked.

"No," I said. "Never mad at you, Claire-Bear." And I never was. That anger was waiting for the monster she married, and it never abated.

I hugged her and promised I would not get Astrid pregnant. It was a promise I kept, although we got close before that day in the cabin near Skytop.

In those years I sometimes dreamed of Charles Jacobs—I'd see him poking his fingers into my pretend mountain to make caves, or preaching the Terrible Sermon with blue fire circling his head like an electric diadem—but he pretty much slipped from my conscious mind until one day in June of 1974. I was eighteen. So was Astrid.

School was out. Chrome Roses had gigs lined up all summer (including a couple in bars, where my parents had given me reluctant written permission to perform), and during the days I'd be working at the Marstellars' farmstand, as I had the year before. Morton Fuel Oil was doing well, and my parents could afford tuition at the University of Maine, but I was expected to do my share. I had a week before reporting for farmstead duty, though, so Astrid and I had a lot of time together. Sometimes we went to my house; sometimes we were at hers. On a lot of afternoons we cruised the back roads in my Galaxie. We'd find a place to park and then . . . recess.

That afternoon we were in a disused gravel pit on Route 9, swapping a joint of not-very-good local grass back and forth. It was

said. "Me n Dad reground the valves, replaced the plugs, stuck in a new battery . . . the works."

"New tires," Dad said, pointing to them. "Just blackwalls, but those are not recaps. Do you like it, Son?"

I hugged him. I hugged them both.

"Just promise me and your mother that you'll never get behind the wheel if you've taken a drink. Don't make us have to look at each other someday and say we gave you something you used to hurt yourself or someone else."

"I promise," I said.

Astrid—with whom I would share the last inch or so of a joint when I took her home in my new car—squeezed my arm. "And I'll make him keep it."

After driving down to Harry's Pond twice (I had to make two trips so I could give everyone a ride), history repeated itself. I felt a tug on my hand. It was Claire. She led me into the mudroom just as she had on the day Reverend Jacobs used his Electrical Nerve Stimulator to give Connie back his voice.

"Mom wants another promise from you," she said, "but she was too embarrassed to ask. So I said I'd do it for her."

I waited.

"Astrid is a nice girl," Claire said. "She smokes, I can smell it on her breath, but that doesn't make her bad. And she's a girl with good taste. Going with you for three years proves that."

I waited.

"She's a smart girl, too. She's got college ahead of her. So here's the promise, Jamie: don't you get her pregnant in the backseat of that car. Can you promise that?"

I almost smiled. If I had, it would have been fifty percent amused and fifty percent pained. For the last two years, Astrid and I had had a code word: *recess*. It meant mutual masturbation. I had men-

sultry, and stormclouds were forming in the west. Thunder rumbled, and there must have been lightning. I didn't see it, but static crackled from the dashboard radio speaker, momentarily blotting out "Smokin' in the Boys' Room," a song the Roses played at every show that year.

That was when Reverend Jacobs returned to my mind like a long absent guest, and I started the car. "Snuff that jay," I said. "Let's go for a ride."

"Where?"

"A place someone told me about a long time ago. If it's still there."

Astrid put the remains of the joint in a Sucrets box and tucked it under the seat. I drove a mile or two down Route 9, then turned west on Goat Mountain Road. Here the trees bulked close on either side, and the last of that day's hazy sunshine disappeared as the stormclouds rolled in.

"If you're thinking about the resort, they won't let us in," Astrid said. "My folks gave up their membership. They said they had to economize if I'm going to college in Boston." She wrinkled her nose.

"Not the resort," I said.

We passed Longmeadow, where the MYF used to have its annual wienie-roast. People were throwing nervous glances at the sky as they gathered up their blankets and coolers and hurried to their cars. The thunder was louder now, loaded wagons rolling across the sky, and I saw a bolt of lightning hit somewhere on the other side of Skytop. I started to feel excited. *Beautiful*, Charles Jacobs had said that last day. *Beautiful and terrifying*.

We passed a sign reading GOAT MTN GATEHOUSE 1 MILE PLEASE SHOW MEMBERSHIP CARD.

"Jamie—"

"There's supposed to be a spur that goes to Skytop," I said. "Maybe it's gone, but . . ."

It wasn't gone, and it was still gravel. I turned into it a little too fast, and the Galaxie's rear end wagged first one way, then the other.

"I hope you know what you're doing," Astrid said. She didn't sound frightened to be driving straight toward a summer thunderstorm; she sounded interested and a little excited.

"I hope so, too."

The grade steepened. The Galaxie's rear end flirted on the loose gravel from time to time, but mostly it held steady. Two and a half miles beyond the turnoff, the trees pulled back and there was Skytop. Astrid gasped and sat up straight in her seat. I hit the brake and brought my car to a crunching stop.

On our right was an old cabin with a mossy, sagging roof and crashed-out windows. Graffiti, most of it too faded to be legible, danced in tangles across the gray, paintless sides. Ahead and above us was a great bulging forehead of granite. At the summit, just as Jacobs had told me half my life ago, was an iron pole jutting toward the clouds, which were now black and seemingly low enough to touch. To our left, where Astrid was looking, hills and fields and gray-green miles of woods stretched toward the ocean. In that direction the sun was still shining, making the world glow.

"Oh my God, was this here all the time? And you never took me?"

"I never took myself," I said. "My old minister told me—"

That was as far as I got. A brilliant bolt of lightning came down from the sky. Astrid screamed and put her hands over her head. For a moment—strange, terrible, wonderful—it seemed to me that the air had been replaced by electric oil. I felt the hair all over my body, even the fine ones in my nose and ears, go stiff. Then came the *click*, as if an invisible giant had snapped his fingers. A second bolt flashed down and hit the iron rod, turning it the same bright blue I had seen dancing around Charles Jacobs's head in my dreams. I had to shut my eyes to keep from going blind. When I opened them again, the pole was glowing cherry red. *Like a horseshoe in a forge*, he'd said, and that was just what it was like. Follow-thunder bellowed.

"*Do you want to get out of here?*" I was shouting. I had to, in order to hear myself over the ringing in my ears.

"*No!*" she shouted back. "*In there!*" And pointed at the slumping remains of the cabin.

I thought of telling her we'd be safer in the car—some vaguely remembered adage about how rubber tires could ground you and protect you from lightning—but there had been thousands of storms on Skytop, and the old cabin was still standing. As we ran toward it, hand in hand, I realized there was a good reason for that. The iron rod drew the lightning. At least it had so far.

It began to hail as we reached the open door, pebble-size chunks of ice that struck the granite with a rattling sound. "Ouch, ouch, *ouch*!" Astrid yelled . . . but she was laughing at the same time. She darted in. I followed just as the lightning flashed again, artillery on some apocalyptic battlefield. This time it was preceded by a *snap* instead of a *click*.

Astrid seized my shoulder. "*Look!*"

I'd missed the storm's second swipe at the iron rod, but I clearly saw what followed. Balls of St. Elmo's fire bounced and rolled down the scree-littered slope. There were half a dozen. One by one they popped out of existence.

Astrid hugged me, but that wasn't enough. She locked her hands around my neck and *climbed* me, her thighs locked around my hips. "*This is fantastic!*" she screamed.

The hail turned to rain, and it came in a deluge. Skytop was blotted out, but we never lost sight of the iron rod, because it was struck repeatedly. It would glow blue or purple, then red, then fade, only to be struck again.

Rain like that rarely lasts long. As it lessened, we saw that the granite slope below the iron rod had turned into a river. The thunder continued to rumble, but it was losing its fury and subsiding into sulks. We heard running water everywhere, as if the earth were whispering. The sun was still shining to the east, over Brunswick and Freeport and Jerusalem's Lot, where we saw not one or two rainbows but half a dozen, interlocking like Olympic rings.

Astrid turned me toward her. "I have to tell you something," she said. Her voice was low.

"What?" I was suddenly sure that she would destroy this transcendent moment by telling me we had to break up.

"Last month my mother took me to the doctor. She said she didn't want to know how serious we were about each other, that it wasn't her business, but she needed to know I was taking care of myself. That was how she put it. 'All you have to say is that you want it because your periods are painful and irregular,' she said. 'When he sees that I brought you myself, that will do.' "

I was a little slow, I guess, so she punched me in the chest.

"Birth control pills, dummy. Ovral. It's safe now, because I had a period since I started taking them. I've been waiting for the right time, and if this isn't it, there won't ever be one."

Those luminous eyes on mine. Then she dropped them, and began biting her lip.

"Just don't . . . don't get carried away, all right? Think of me and be gentle. Because I'm scared. Carol said her first time hurt like hell."

We undressed each other—all the way, at last—while the clouds unraveled overhead and the sun shone through and the whisper of running water began to die away. Her arms and legs were already tanned. The rest of her was as white as snow. Her pubic hair was fine gold, accentuating her sex rather than obscuring it. There was an old mattress in the corner, where the roof was still whole—we weren't the first to use that cabin for what it was used for that day.

She guided me in, then made me stop. I asked her if it was all right. She said it was, but that she wanted to do it herself. "Hold still, honey. Just hold still."

I held still. It was agony to hold still, but it was also wonderful to hold still. She raised her hips. I slid in a little deeper. She did it again and I slipped in a little more. I remember looking at the mattress and seeing its old faded pattern, and smudges of dirt, and a single trundling ant. That she raised her hips again. I slid in all the way and she gasped.

"Oh my God!"

"Does it hurt? Astrid, does it—"

"No, it's wonderful. I think . . . you can do it now."

I did. *We* did.

That was our summer of love. We made it in several places—once in Norm's bedroom in Cicero Irving's trailer, where we broke his bed and had to put it back together—but mostly we used the cabin at Skytop. It was our place, and we wrote our names on one of the walls, among half a hundred others. There was never another storm, though. Not that summer.

In the fall, I went to the University of Maine and Astrid went to Suffolk University in Boston. I assumed this would be a temporary separation—we'd see each other on vacations, and at some hazy point in the future, when we both had our degrees, we'd marry. One of the few things I've learned since then about the fundamental differences between the sexes is this: men make assumptions, but women rarely do.

On the day of the thunderstorm, as we were driving home, Astrid said, "I'm glad you were my first." I told her I was glad, too, not even thinking about what that implied.

There was no big breakup scene. We just drifted apart, and if there was an architect for that gradual withering, it was Delia Soderberg, Astrid's pretty, quiet mother, who was unfailingly pleasant but always looked at me the way a storekeeper studies a suspicious twenty-dollar bill. *Maybe it's all right*, the storekeeper thinks, *but there's just a little something . . . off about it.* If Astrid had gotten pregnant, my assumptions about our future might have proved correct. And hey, we might have been very happy: three kids, two-car garage, backyard swimming pool, all the rest. But I don't think so. I think the constant gigging—and the girls who always hang around rock bands—would have broken us up. Looking back, I have to think that Delia Soderberg's suspicions were justified. I *was* a counterfeit twenty. Good enough to pass in most places, maybe, but not in *her* store.

There was no big breakup scene with Chrome Roses, either. On my first weekend home from school in Orono, I played with the band at the Amvets on Friday night and at Scooter's Pub in North Conway on Saturday. We sounded as good as ever, and we were now hauling down a hundred and fifty a gig. I remember I sang lead on "Shake Your Moneymaker" and played a pretty good harp solo.

But when I came home for Thanksgiving, I discovered that Norm had hired a new rhythm guitarist and changed the name of the band to Norman's Knights. "Sorry, man," he said, shrugging. "The offers were piling up, and I can't work in a trio. Drums, bass, two guitars—that's rock and roll."

"It's okay," I said. "I get it." And I did, because he was right. Or almost. Drums, bass, two guitars, and everything starts in the key of E.

"We're playing the Ragged Pony in Winthrop tomorrow night, if you want to sit in. Guest artist kind of thing?"

"I'll pass," I said. I'd heard the new rhythm guitarist. He was a year younger than me, and already better; he could chickenscratch like a mad bastard. Besides, that meant I could spend Saturday night with Astrid. Which I did. I suspect she was already dating other guys by then—she was too pretty to stay home—but she was discreet. And loving. It was a good Thanksgiving. I didn't miss Chrome Roses (or Norman's Knights, a name I would never have to get used to, which suited me fine) at all.

Well. You know.

Hardly at all.

One day not long before Christmas break, I dropped by the Bear's Den in the University of Maine Memorial Union for a burger and a Coke. On the way out, I stopped to look at the bulletin board. Among the litter of file cards advertising textbooks for sale, cars for sale, and rides wanted to various destinations, I found this:

> GOOD NEWS! The Cumberlands are reuniting! BAD NEWS! We're short a rhythm guitarist! We are a LOUD AND PROUD COVER BAND! If you can play Beatles, Stones, Badfinger, McCoys, Barbarians, Standells, Byrds, etc., come to Room 421, Cumberland Hall, and bring your ax. If you like Emerson, Lake, & Palmer, or Blood, Sweat, & Tears, stay the f**k away.

By then I had a bright red Gibson SG, and that afternoon, after class, I toted it over to Cumberland Hall, where I met Jay Pederson.

Because of noise restrictions during study hours, we played tennis-racket style in his room. Later that night we plugged in down in the dorm's rec area. We rocked the place for half an hour, and I got the gig. He was a lot better than me, but I was used to that; I had, after all, started my rock-and-roll career with Norm Irving.

"I'm thinking of changing the name of the band to the Heaters," Jay said. "What do you think?"

"As long as I get time to study during the week and you split fair, I don't care if you call it Assholes from Hell."

"Good name, right up there with Doug and the Hot Nuts, but I don't think we'd get many high school dances." He offered me his hand, I clasped it, and we gave each other that dead-fish shake. "Welcome aboard, Jamie. Rehearsal Wednesday night. Be there or be square."

I was many things, but square wasn't one of them. I was there. For almost two decades, in a dozen bands and a hundred cities, I was there. A rhythm guitarist can always find work, even if he's so stoned he can barely stand. Basically, it all comes down to two things: you have to show up, and you have to be able to play a bar E.

My problems started when I stopped showing up.

V

The Fluid Passage of Time. Portraits in Lightning. My Drug Problem.

When I graduated from the University of Maine (2.9 cume, missed the Dean's List by a coat of paint), I was twenty-two. When I met Charles Jacobs for the second time, I was thirty-six. He looked younger than his age, perhaps because when I saw him last he had been thinned and made haggard by grief. By 1992, I looked much older than mine.

I've always been a movie fan. During the 1980s I saw a lot of them, mostly on my own. I dozed off on occasion (*Heathers*, for instance—that one was a nodder for sure), but mostly I'd make it through no matter how stoned I was, surfing on noise and color and impossibly beautiful women in scanty clothing. Books are good, and I read my share, and TV's okay if you're stuck in a motel room during a rainstorm, but for Jamie Morton, there was nothing like a movie up there on the big screen. Just me, my popcorn, and my super-sized Coke. Plus my heroin, of course. I'd take an extra straw from the concession stand, bite it in half, and use it to snort the powder off the back of my hand. I didn't get to the needle until 1990 or '91, but I got there eventually. Most of us do. Trust me on this.

The thing I find most charming about the movies is the fluid way time passes. You might start off with this nerdy teenager—no friends, no money, lousy parents—and all at once he turns into Brad Pitt in his prime. The only thing separating the nerd from the god is a title card that says 14 YEARS LATER.

"It's wicked to wish time away," my mother used to lecture us kids—usually when we were pining for summer vacation in the depths of February, or waiting for Halloween to hurry up and come—and probably she was right, but I can't help thinking that such temporal jumps might be a good thing for people living bad lives, and between the advent of the Reagan administration in 1980 and the Tulsa State Fair in 1992, I was living a very bad life. There were blackouts, but no title cards. I had to live every day of those years, and when I couldn't get high, some of the days were a hundred hours long.

The fade-in goes like this: The Cumberlands became the Heaters, and the Heaters became the J-Tones. Our last gig as a college band was the huge and hilarious Graduation Dance '78 in Memorial Gym. We played from eight until two in the morning. Shortly thereafter, Jay Pederson hired a locally popular chick vocalist who could also play both tenor and alto sax like nobody's business. Her name was Robin Storrs. She turned out to be a perfect fit for us, and by August the J-Tones had become Robin and the Jays. We turned into one of Maine's premier party bands. We had all the gigs we could play, and life was good.

Now here comes the dissolve.

Fourteen years later, Jamie Morton woke up in Tulsa. Not in a good hotel, not even in a so-so chain motel; this was a roachpit called the Fairgrounds Inn. Such places were Kelly Van Dorn's idea of economy. It was eleven in the morning, and the bed was wet. I wasn't surprised. When you crash for nineteen hours, assisted by Madame H., wetting your bed is almost inevitable. I suppose you'd even do it if you died in that drug-assisted slumber, although look at the bright side: in that case you'd never wake up in pee-soaked Jockeys again.

I did the zombie walk to the bathroom, sniffling and watering at the eyes, shucking my skivvies on the way. I made my shaving kit the first stop . . . but not to clear the stubble. My works were still there, along with a taped-down sandwich bag containing a couple of grams. No reason to think anyone would break in to steal such a paltry stash, but checking is second nature to a junkie.

With that taken care of, I addressed the bowl and rid myself of the urine that had accumulated since my nighttime accident. As I was standing there, I realized that something of importance had slipped my mind. I was currently playing with a country crossover band, and we had been scheduled to open for Sawyer Brown the night before, on the big Oklahoma Stage at the Tulsa State Fair. A primo gig, especially for a not-ready-for Nashville band like White Lightning.

"Sound check at five o'clock," Kelly Van Dorn had told me. "You'll be there, right?"

"Sure," I'd said. "Don't worry about me."

Oops.

Coming out of the bathroom, I saw a folded note poking under the door. I had a pretty good idea what it said, but I picked it up and read it, just to be sure. It was short and not sweet.

I called the Union High Music Department and lucked into a kid who could play just enough rhythm and slide guitar to get us through. He was happy to pocket your $600. By the time you get this, we'll be *on the way to Wildwood Green. Don't even think about following us. You're fired. Sorry as hell to do it, but enough is enough.*

Kelly

PS: I guess you probably won't pay attention to this, Jamie, but if you don't clean up your act, you'll be in prison a year from now. That's if you're lucky. Dead if you're not.

I tried to stick the note in my back pocket and it fell on the balding green carpet instead—I'd forgotten that I wasn't wearing anything. I picked it up, tossed it in the wastebasket, and peeked out the window. The courtyard parking lot was totally empty except for an old Ford and some farmer's broke-ass pickup. Both the Explorer the band rode in and the equipment van that our sound guy drove were gone. Kelly hadn't been kidding. The out-of-tune nutbags had left me. Which was probably all for the best. I sometimes thought if I had to play one more drinkin-n-cheatin song, I'd lose what little mind I had left.

I decided to make re-upping the room my first priority. I had no desire to spend another night in Tulsa, especially with the State Fair going full blast down the street, but I'd need some time to think about my next career move. I needed to score, too, and if you can't find someone to sell you dope at a state fair, you're not trying.

I kicked the damp skivvies into the corner—*a tip for the chambermaid*, I thought snidely—and unzipped my duffel. Nothing in there but dirty clothes (I had meant to find a Laundromat yesterday, another thing that had slipped my mind), but at least they were *dry* dirty clothes. I dressed and trekked across the cracked asphalt of the courtyard to the motel office, my zombie walk slowly perking up to the zombie shuffle. My throat hurt every time I swallowed. Just a little extra something to add to the fun.

The lady on the desk was a hard-faced country girl of about fifty, currently living her life under a volcano of teased red hair. A talk show host was on her little television, chatting up a storm with Nicole Kidman. Above the TV was a framed picture of Jesus bringing a boy and girl a puppy. I was in no way surprised. In flyover country, they have a way of getting Christ and Santa all mixed up.

"Your group has already checked out," she said, after finding my name in her register book. She had the local accent, which sounds like a badly tuned banjo. "Left a couple of hours ago. Said they were driving all the way to North Cah'lina."

"I'm aware," I said. "I'm no longer with the band."

She raised an eyebrow.

"Creative differences," I said.

The eyebrow climbed higher.

"I'll be staying another night."

"Uh-huh, okay. Cash or credit card?"

I had two hundred or so in cash, but most of that liquidity was earmarked for the dope purchase I hoped to make at the fair, so I gave her my BankAmericard. She called it in and waited, phone cocked between her ear and one meaty shoulder, now watching an ad for paper towels that could apparently drink up spills the size of Lake Michigan. I watched with her. When the talk show returned, Nicole Kidman was joined by Tom Selleck, and the country girl was still on hold. She didn't seem to mind, but I did. The itches had started, and my bad leg was starting to throb. Just as another ad came on, the country girl perked up. She swiveled around in her chair, looked out her window at a blazing blue Oklahoma sky, and chatted briefly. Then she hung up and handed back my credit card.

"Declined. Which makes me dubious about taking cash. Supposing you have it."

That was mean, but I gave her my best smile, just the same. "The card's good. They made a mistake. It happens all the time."

"Then you'll be able to rectify it at some other motel," she said. (*Rectify!* Such a big word for a country girl!) "There's four more down the block, but they ain't much."

Unlike this roadside Ritz-Carlton, I thought, but what I said was, "Try the card again."

"Honey," she said, "I look at you and I don't have to."

I sneezed, turning my head to catch it on the short sleeve of my Charlie Daniels Band tee. Which was okay since it hadn't been washed lately. Or even not so lately. "What's that supposed to mean?"

"It means I left my first husband when him and both his brothers took to smokin the rock. No offense, but I know what I'm lookin at. Last night's paid for—on the band's credit card—but now that you're what they call a solo artist, checkout time's one o'clock."

"On the door it says three."

She leveled a chipped nail at a sign to the left of the calendar featuring Puppy-Giving Jesus: DURING STATE FAIR, SEPTEMBER 25 TO OCTOBER 4, CHECOUT TIME WILL BE 1 PM.

"*Checkout* is spelled wrong," I said. "You should rectify that."

She glanced at the sign, then turned back to me. "So 'tis, but the one PM part needs no rectifyin." She glanced at her watch. "That gives you an hour and a half. Don't make me call the police, hon. At state fair time, they're thicker'n flies on a fresh dog turd, and they'd be here in a jiff."

"This is such bullshit," I said.

That was a blurry time for me, but I remember her reply as clearly as if she had spoken it in my ear two minutes ago: "Uh-uh, honey, this is reality."

Then she turned back to the television, where some fool was tap-dancing.

• • •

I wasn't going to try scoring dope in the daytime, not even at the state fair, so I stayed at the Fairgrounds Inn until one thirty (just to spite the country girl). Then I grabbed my duffel in one hand and my guitar case in the other, and set out walking. I made a stop at a Texaco station around where North Detroit Avenue becomes South Detroit. By then my walk had become a portside limp and my hip was throbbing with my heartbeat. In the men's room I cooked up and delivered half my goods into the hollow of my left shoulder. Mellowness ensued. Both my sore throat and the ache in my leg began to recede.

My good left leg became my bad left leg on a sunny summer day in 1984. I was on a Kawasaki; the elderly asshole coming the other way was piloting a Chevrolet the size of a cabin cruiser. He wandered into my lane, leaving me a choice: either the soft shoulder or a head-on collision. I picked the obvious choice and made it past the asshole okay. The mistake was trying to swerve back onto the road at forty. Advice to all you novice riders out there: swerving on gravel at forty is a terrible idea. I dumped the bike and broke the leg in five places. I also shattered my hip. Shortly thereafter, I discovered the Joy of Morphine.

With my leg feeling better and the itches and twitches at bay, I was able to move on from the gas station with a bit more vigor, and by the time I got to the Greyhound terminal, I was asking myself why I'd stuck with Kelly Van Dorn and his screwed-up country band as long as I had. Playing weepy ballads (in the key of C, for God's sake) was not what I was cut out for. I was a rocker, not a shitkicker.

I purchased a ticket on the following day's noon bus to Chicago, which also bought me the right to stash my duffel and my Gibson SG—the only valuable possession I had left—in the baggage room. The ticket cost me twenty-nine dollars. I counted the rest sitting in a bathroom stall. It came to a hundred and fifty-nine bucks, about what I had expected. The future was looking brighter. I would score at the fair, find a place to crash—maybe at a local homeless shelter, maybe outside—and tomorrow I'd ride the big gray dog to Shytown. There was a musicians' exchange there, as there is in most big cities, with players sitting around, telling jokes, swapping gossip, and looking for gigs. For some this wasn't easy (accordion players, for instance), but bands were always looking for competent rhythm guitar players, and I was a smidge more than that. By 1992 I could even play a little lead, if called upon to do so. And if I wasn't too wrecked. The important thing was to get to Chicago and get a gig before Kelly Van Dorn put out the word that I was unreliable, and the pisshead just might.

With at least six hours to kill until dark, I cooked up the rest of my shit and put it where it would do the most good. Once that was taken care of, I bought a paperback western at the newsstand, sat on a bench with it opened to someplace in the middle, and nodded off. When I woke myself up with a volley of sneezes, it was seven o'clock, and time for the former rhythm guitarist of White Lightning to hunt up some of the good stuff.

By the time I got to the fair, sunset was just a bitter orange line in the west. Although I wanted to save most of my money for a buy, I splurged on a taxi to get there, because I wasn't feeling good at all. It wasn't just the usual coming-down twitches and aches, either. The sore throat was back. There was a high, sour humming in my ears, and I felt hot all over. I told myself that last was normal, because it was one hot bitchkitty of a night. As for the rest, I was sure six or seven hours of sleep would put me right. I could catch it on the bus. I wanted to be all I could be before I re-enlisted in the Rock and Roll Army.

I bypassed the main entrance to the fair, because only an idiot would attempt to buy heroin at a craft exhibit or livestock exhibition. Beyond it was the entrance to Bell's Amusement Park. That adjunct to the Tulsa State Fair is gone now, but in September of 1992, Bell's was blasting away full force. Both roller coasters—the wooden Zingo and the more modern Wildcat—were whirling and twirling, trailing happy screams behind each hairpin turn and suicidal plunge. There were long lines at the water slides, the Himalaya, and the Phantasmagoria dark ride.

I ignored these and idled my way down the midway past the food concessions, where the smells of fried dough and sausages—usually enticing—made me feel a little sick to my stomach. There was a guy with the right look hanging around the Pitch Til U Win shy, and I almost approached him, but caught a narc vibe when I got close. The shirt he was wearing (COCAINE! BREAKFAST OF CHAMPIONS!) was just a little too on-the-nose. I kept moving, past the shooting gallery, the wooden milkbottle shy, the Skeeball, the Wheel of Fortune. I was feeling worse all the time, my skin hotter and that humming in my ears louder. My throat was so sore I winced with every swallow.

Up ahead was an elaborate mini-golf layout. It was mostly filled with laughing teenagers, and I thought I had arrived at Ground Zero. Wherever there are teenagers out for a night of fun, there are dealers in the vicinity who are happy to help them maximize said fun. And oh yeah, I could see a couple of fellows who had just the right look. By their shifty eyes and unwashed hair shalt thou know them.

The midway ended at a **T** junction beyond the mini-golf, one way leading back to the fairgrounds, the other to the racetrack. I had no desire to go to either place, but I'd been hearing a strange electric crackle off to the right, followed by applause, laughter, and cries of amazement. Now, as I drew closer to the junction, I could see that each crackle was accompanied by a bright blue flash that reminded me of lightning. The lightning on Skytop, to be perfectly specific. I hadn't thought of that in years. Whatever the gaff was, it had drawn a big crowd. I decided the sharpies hanging around the golf course could wait a few minutes. Guys like that never go away until they shut off the neon, and I wanted to see who was making lightning on this hot and clear Oklahoma night.

An amplified voice cried, "Now that you have seen the power of my Lightning Maker—the only one in the world, I assure you—I'll give an actual demonstration of the wonderful portrait that one portrait of Alexander Hamilton from your wallet or purse will buy you; one *amazing* demonstration before I open my Electric Studio and offer you the chance to sit for the photographic representation of a lifetime! But I'll need a volunteer so you'll see *exactly* what you'll be getting for the best ten dollars you ever spent! Volunteer? May I have a volunteer? It's perfectly safe, I assure you! Come on, folks, I always heard Sooners were famous in the Lower Forty-eight for their bravery!"

There was a good-size crowd, fifty or sixty, in front of a raised stage. The canvas backdrop was six feet wide and at least twenty feet high. On it was a photograph almost as big as a movie screen image. It featured a beautiful young woman on what appeared to be a ballroom floor. Her black hair was piled atop her head in a series of complicated twirls and tucks that must have taken hours to create. Her strapless evening gown was cut low, the tops of her breasts curving sweetly above it. She was wearing diamond earrings and bloodred lipstick.

Facing the giant ballroom girl was an old-fashioned camera, the nineteenth-century kind that stands on a tripod and has a black drape the photographer can throw over his head. Placed as it was, you would have said it could only snap the ballroom girl from the knees down. Next to it was a flash-powder tray on a post. The black-suited, top-hatted gaffmeister had one loosely curled hand on the camera, and I knew him at once.

All that is clear, but my memory of what happened next is untrustworthy—I freely admit it. I was a longtime junkie who had graduated to the needle two years previous, first just skin-popping, but more and more frequently aiming for the vein. I was malnourished and severely underweight. On top of that, I was running a temperature. It was the flu, and it had come on fast. Getting up that morning, I'd thought I just had the usual case of heroin sniffles, a cold at worst, but by the time I saw Charles Jacobs standing beside an old-fashioned tripod camera and in front of a canvas backdrop with PORTRAITS IN LIGHTNING written over a giant girl, I felt like I was living in a dream. It didn't surprise me to see my old minister, now with touches of gray at his temples and lines (faint ones) bracketing his mouth. It wouldn't have surprised me if my late mother and sister had joined him onstage, dressed as Playboy Bunnies.

A couple of men raised their hands in response to Jacobs's call for volunteers, but he laughed and pointed at the beautiful girl looming over his shoulder. "I'm sure you guys are brave as the devil on Saturday night, but none of you would look good in a strapless."

Good-natured laughter greeted this.

"I want a *gal*," said the fellow who showed me Peaceable Lake when I was but a tyke in short pants. "I want a *pretty* gal! A pretty little *Sooner* gal! How 'bout you folks? You down with that?"

They clapped their hands to show how down with it they were.

And Jacobs, who had surely already picked out his mark, pointed his cordless mike toward someone in the front of the crowd. "How about you, miss? You're about as pretty a gal as anyone could want!"

I was at the back of the tip, but the crowd seemed to part before me as if I were possessed of some magical repelling force. Probably I just elbowed my way forward, but I don't remember it that way, and if anyone elbowed me back, I don't remember that, either. I seemed to float forward. All the colors were brighter now, the tootling of the carousel calliope and the screams from the Zingo louder. The humming in my ears had escalated to a tuneful ringing: G^7, I think. I moved through an aromatic atmosphere of perfume, aftershave, and discount store hairspray.

The pretty Sooner gal was protesting, but her friends were having none of that. They pushed her forward, and she mounted the steps on the left side of the stage, tanned thighs flashing beneath the frayed hem of her short denim skirt. Above the skirt was a green smock that was high at the neck but left a flirty inch of midriff revealed. Her hair was blond and long. A few men whistled.

"Every pretty girl carries her own positive charge!" Jacobs told the crowd, and swept off his tophat. I saw him clench the hand holding it. For just a moment I felt sensations I hadn't since that day at Skytop: gooseflesh on my arms, hair standing to attention on the nape of my neck, the air too heavy in my lungs. Then the tray beside the camera exploded with something that was certainly not flash powder, and the canvas backdrop lit up in a dazzling blue glare. The face of the girl in the evening gown was blotted out. As the dazzle faded I saw in her place—or thought I saw—the fifty-something country girl who had kicked me out of the Fairgrounds Inn some nine hours earlier. Then the girl in the low-cut spangly gown was back.

It wowed the crowd and it wowed me, too . . . but it didn't completely surprise me. Reverend Jacobs up to his old tricks, that was all. Nor did it surprise me when he put his arm around the girl, turned her to face us, and for an instant I thought it was Astrid Soderberg, once more sixteen years old and worried about getting pregnant. Astrid who sometimes used to blow smoke from her Virginia Slims into my mouth, giving me a hard-on for the ages.

Then she was just a pretty little Sooner gal again, in from the farm and ready for a night of fun.

Jacobs's assistant, a kid with zits and a bad haircut, trotted out with an ordinary wooden chair. He put it in front of the camera, then made a comic business of dusting off Jacobs's old-fashioned frock coat. "Sit down, honey," Jacobs said, ushering the girl to the chair. "I promise you a *shockingly* good time."

He waggled his eyebrows and his young assistant did a little electric jitter. The audience yukked it up. Jacobs's eyes found me, now in the first row, passed on, then came back. After a second's consideration, they moved on again.

"Will it hurt?" the girl asked, and now I saw she didn't look much like Astrid, after all. Of course not. She was much younger than my first girlfriend would be now . . . and wherever Astrid might be, her last name was almost surely no longer Soderberg.

"Not a bit," Jacobs assured her. "And unlike any other lady who dares to step forward, your portrait will be . . ."

He looked away from her, back at the crowd, this time directly at me.

". . . absolutely free."

He seated her in the chair, continuing with the patter, but he seemed a little hesitant now, as if he had lost the thread. He kept glancing at me as his assistant fastened a white silk blindfold over the girl's eyes. If he was distracted, the crowd didn't notice; a petite pretty girl was about to be photographed at the feet of a giant beautiful girl—while blindfolded, no less—and all that was very interesting. So was the fact that the live girl was showing a lot of leg and the one on the backdrop was showing a lot of cleavage.

"Who wants"—the pretty girl began, and Jacobs promptly put his microphone in front of her mouth so she could share her question with the whole crowd—"a picture of me wearin a blindfold?"

"*The rest of you sure ain't blindfolded, hon!*" someone yelled, and the crowd cheered good-naturedly. The girl in the chair pressed her knees tightly together, but she was smiling a little, too. The old I'm-being-a-good-sport smile.

"My dear, I think you'll be surprised," Jacobs said. Then he turned to address the crowd. "Electricity! Although we take it for granted, it's the greatest natural wonder of our world! The Great Pyramid of Giza is only an anthill in comparison! It's the foundation of our modern civilization! Some claim to understand it, ladies and gentlemen, but none understand the *secret* electricity, that power which binds the very universe into one harmonic whole. Do *I* understand it? No, I do not. Not fully. Yet I know its power to destroy, to heal, and to create magical beauty! What's your name, miss?"

"Cathy Morse."

"Cathy, there's an old saying that beauty is in the eye of the beholder. You and I and everyone here is going to witness the truth of that saying tonight, and when you walk away, you'll have a portrait you can show your grandchildren. A portrait they'll show to *their* grandchildren! And if those as-yet-unborn ancestors don't marvel over it, my name's not Dan Jacobs."

But it isn't, I thought.

I was swaying back and forth now, as if to the music of the calliope and the music I was hearing in my ears. I tried to stop and found I couldn't. My legs had a strangely meaty feel, as if the bones were being extracted, inch by inch.

You're Charles, not Dan—do you think I don't know the man who gave my brother back his voice?

"Now, ladies and gentlemen, you may want to shield your eyes!"

The assistant theatrically covered his own. Jacobs whirled, puffed up the black cloth on the back of the camera, and disappeared beneath it. "Close your eyes, Cathy!" he called. "Even beneath the blindfold, an electrical pulse this powerful can be dazzling! I'll count to three! One . . . and . . . two . . . and . . . *three*!"

Once again I felt that strange thickening of the air, and I wasn't alone; the crowd shuffled back a step or two. Next came a hard *click*, as if someone had snapped his fingers beside my right ear. The world lit up in a blue burst of light.

Aaaahhh, went the crowd. And when they could see again and realized what had become of the backdrop: *AAAAAAHHHHHHH!*

The evening gown was the same—low-cut spangled silver. The inviting curve of bosom was the same, as was the complicated hairdo. But the breasts were now smaller and the hair was blond instead of black. The face had changed, too. It was Cathy Morse standing there on the ballroom floor. Then I blinked, and the pretty little Sooner gal was gone. It was Astrid again, Astrid as she had been at sixteen, the love of my days and the eventually requited lust of my nights.

The crowd exhaled a low gust of astonishment, and I had an idea that was both crazy and persuasive: they were also seeing people from their own back pages, those either gone or changed by the fluid passage of time.

Then it was just Cathy Morse, but that was astounding enough: Cathy Morse standing twenty feet high in the sort of expensive gown she would never own in real life. The diamond earrings were there, and although the lipstick of the girl in the chair was candy pink, that of the giant Cathy behind her was bright red.

No sign of a blindfold, either.

Same old Reverend Jacobs, I thought, *but he's learned some tricks a lot flashier than Electric Jesus walking across Peaceable Lake or a cloth belt with a toy motor inside it.*

He popped out from beneath the black cloth, tossed it back, and pulled a plate from the back of his camera. He showed it to the audience, and they went *AAAAHHHHH* again. Jacobs bowed, then turned to Cathy, who was looking mighty puzzled. He held the plate out to her and said, "You may take off the blindfold, Cathy. It's safe now."

She slipped it down and saw the picture on the plate: an Oklahoma girl somehow transformed into a costly French courtesan of the demimonde. Her hands went to her mouth, but Jacobs had the mike right there and everyone heard her *Oh my God.*

"Now turn around!" Jacobs cried.

She stood, turned, looked, and reeled back at the sight of herself, twenty feet high and tricked out in high-class glitter. Jacobs put an arm around her waist to steady her. His mike hand, which was also concealing some sort of control device, clenched again, and this time the crowd did more than gasp. There were a few screams, as well.

The giant Cathy Morse did a slow fashion-model turn, revealing the back of the gown, which was cut much lower than the front. She looked over her shoulder . . . and winked.

Jacobs did not neglect the mike—he was clearly an old hand at this—and the tip heard the real Cathy's follow-up exclamation as clearly as they had the first: "*Oh my fuckin God!*"

They laughed. They cheered. And when they saw her bright crimson blush, they cheered even harder. Above Jacobs and the girl, the giant Cathy was changing. The blond hair grew muddy. The features faded, although the red lipstick remained bright, like the grin of the Cheshire Cat in *Alice*.

Then it was the original girl again. The image of Cathy Morse had faded out of existence.

"But *this* version will never fade," Jacobs said, holding up the old-fashioned plate again. "My assistant will print it and frame it and you can pick it up before you go home tonight."

"Watch out there, Slick!" someone in the front row yelled out. "Girl's gonna faint!"

But she didn't. She only swayed a little on her feet.

I was the one who fainted.

When I next opened my eyes, I was in a queen-size bed. A blanket was pulled up to my chin. When I looked to my right, I saw a wall done in fake wood paneling. When I looked to my left, I saw a nice kitchen area: fridge, sink, microwave oven. Beyond it was a couch, a dinette with four chairs, even an easy chair in the living area facing the built-in TV. I couldn't crane my neck far enough to see the driving compartment, but as an itinerant musician who had traveled tens of thousands of miles in similar rigs (although few as squared away as this one), I knew where I was, anyway: a large RV, probably a Bounder. Someone's home away from home.

I was hot, burning up. My mouth was dry as road dust. I was also jonesing like a motherfucker. I pushed the blanket down and immediately started shivering. A shadow fell over me. It was Jacobs, holding out a beautiful thing: orange juice in a tall glass with a bendy straw sticking out of it. The only thing better would have been a loaded hypo, but one thing at a time. I held my hand out for the glass.

He pulled the blanket back up first, then took a knee beside the bed. "Slow, Jamie. You're one sick American, I'm afraid."

I drank. It was wonderful on my throat. I tried to take the glass and chug it down, but he held it away from me. "Slow, I said."

I dropped my hand and he gave me another sip. It went down fine, but on the third one, my belly clenched and the shivers came back. That wasn't the flu.

"I need to score," I said. This was hardly the way I wanted to re-introduce myself to my former minister and first adult friend, but a junkie in need has no shame. Besides, he might have a skeleton or two in his own closet. Why else would he be going under the name Dan Jacobs instead of Charles?

"Yes," he said. "I saw the tracks. And I intend to maintain you, at least until you've beaten whatever bug you've got running around in your system. Otherwise you'll start throwing up whatever I try to feed you, and we can't have that, can we? Not when you look to be at least fifty pounds underweight as it is."

From his pocket he brought a brown gram bottle. It had a small spoon attached to the cap. I reached for it. He shook his head and held it away from me.

"Same deal. I do the driving."

He unscrewed the cap, dipped out a tiny spoonful of grimy white powder, and held it under my nose. I snorted it up my right nostril. He dipped again, and I treated the left nostril. It wasn't what I needed—not *enough* of what I needed, to be exact—but the shakes began to subside, and I stopped feeling like I might hurl up that nice cold orange juice.

"Now you can doze," he said. "Or nod off, if that's what you call it. I'm going to make you some chicken soup. Just Campbell's, not like your mother used to make, but it's what I've got."

"I don't know if I can hold it down," I said, but it turned out I could. When I'd finished the mug he held for me, I asked for more dope. He administered two very stingy snorts.

"Where'd you get it?" I asked as he tucked the bottle back into a front pocket of the jeans he was now wearing.

He smiled. It lit up his face and made him twenty-five again, with a wife he loved and a young son he adored. "Jamie," he said, "I've been working amusement parks and the carny circuit for a long time now. If I couldn't find drugs, I'd be either blind or an idiot."

"I need more. I need a shot."

"No, a shot's what you *want*, and you're not going to get it from me. I have no interest in helping you get high. I just don't want you to go into convulsions and die in my boondocker. Go to sleep now. It's nearly midnight. If you're better in the morning, we'll discuss many things, including how to detach the monkey currently riding on your back. If you're not better, I'm taking you to either St. Francis or the OSU Medical Center."

"Good luck getting them to take me," I said. "I'm two steps from broke and my medical plan is convenience store Tylenol."

"In the words of Scarlett O'Hara, we'll worry about that tomorrow, for tomorrow is another day."

"Fiddle-de-dee," I croaked.

"If you say so."

"Give me a little more." The short snorts he'd doled out were about as useful to me as a Marlboro Light to a guy who's been chain-smoking Chesterfield Kings all his life, but even short snorts were better than nothing.

He considered, then parceled out two more hits. Even stingier than the last pair.

"Giving heroin to a man with a bad case of the flu," he said, and chuckled. "I must be crazy."

I peeked under the blanket and saw he'd undressed me down to my skivvies. "Where are my clothes?"

"In the closet. I segregated them from mine, I'm afraid. They smelled a trifle gamy."

"My wallet's in the front pocket of my jeans. There's a claim check for my duffel bag and my guitar. The clothes don't matter, but the guitar does."

"Bus station or train station?"

"Bus." The dope might only have been powder, and administered in medicinal quantities, but either it was very good stuff or it was hitting my depleted body especially hard. The soup was warm in my belly, and my eyelids felt like sashweights.

"Sleep, Jamie," he said, and gave my shoulder a little squeeze. "If you're going to beat the bug, you have to sleep."

I lay back on the pillow. It was much softer than the one in my Fairgrounds Inn room. "Why are you calling yourself Dan?"

"Because it's my name. Charles Daniel Jacobs. Now go to sleep."

I was going to, but there was one other thing I had to ask. Adults change, sure, but if they haven't been struck by some debilitating disease or disfigured by an accident, you can usually recognize them. Children, on the other hand . . .

"You knew me. I could see it. How?"

"Because your mother lives in your face, Jamie. I hope Laura's well."

"She's dead. Her and Claire both."

I don't know how he took it. I closed my eyes, and ten seconds later I was out.

When I woke up I felt cooler, but the shakes were back big-time. Jacobs put a drugstore fever strip on my forehead, held it there for a minute or so, then nodded. "You might live," he said, and gave me two more teensy snorts from the brown bottle. "Can you get up and eat some scrambled eggs?"

"Bathroom first."

He pointed, and I made my way into the small cubicle, holding onto things. I only had to pee, but I was too weak to stand up, so I sat down and did it girly-style. When I came out, he was scrambling eggs and whistling. My stomach rumbled. I tried to recall when I'd last eaten something more substantial than canned soup. Cold cuts backstage before the gig two nights ago came to mind. If I'd eaten anything after that, I couldn't remember it.

"Ingest slowly," he said, setting the plate on the dinette table. "You don't want to bark it right back up again, do you?"

I ate slowly, and cleaned the plate. He sat across from me, drinking coffee. When I asked for some, he gave me half a cup, heavy on the half-and-half.

"The trick with the picture," I said. "How did you do that?"

"Trick? You wound me. The image on the backdrop is coated with a phosphorescent substance. The camera is also an electrical generator—"

"That much I got."

"The flash is very powerful and very . . . special. It projects the image of the subject onto that of the girl in the evening dress. It doesn't hold for long; the area is too large. The pictures I sell, on the other hand, last much longer."

"Long enough so she can show it to her grandchildren? Really?"

"Well," he said, "no."

"How long?"

"Two years. Give or take."

"By which time you're long gone."

"Indeed. And the pictures that matter . . ." He tapped his temple. "Up here. For all of us. Don't you agree?"

"But . . . Reverend Jacobs . . ."

I saw a momentary flicker of the man who had preached the Terrible Sermon back when LBJ was president. "Please don't call me that. Plain old Dan will do. That's who I am now. Dan the Lightning Portraits Man. Or Charlie, if that's more comfortable for you."

"But she turned around. The girl on your background did a complete three-sixty."

"A simple trick of motion picture projection." But he glanced away as he said it. Then he looked back at me. "Do you want to get better, Jamie?"

"I *am* better. Must have been one of those twenty-four-hour things."

"It's not a twenty-four-hour thing, it's the flu, and if you try leaving here for the bus station, it'll be back full blast by noon. Stay here and yes, I think you'll probably be better in a few days. But it's not the flu I'm talking about."

"I'm okay," I said, but now it was my turn to look away. What brought my eyes back front and center was the little brown bottle. He was holding it by the spoon and swinging it on its little silver chain like a hypnotist's amulet. I reached for it. He held it away.

"How long have you been using?"

"Heroin? About three years." It had been six. "I had a motorcycle accident. Smashed the hell out of my hip and leg. They gave me morphine—"

"Of course they did."

"—and then stepped me down to codeine. That sucked, so I started chugging cough syrup to go with the pills. Terpin hydrate. Ever heard of it?"

"Are you kidding? On the circuit they call it GI Gin."

"My leg healed, but it never healed right. Then—I was in a band called the Andersonville Rockers, or maybe they'd changed the name to the Georgia Giants by then—this guy introduced me to Tussionex. That was a big step in the right direction, as far as pain control went. Listen, do you really want to hear this?"

"Absolutely."

I shrugged as if it didn't matter much to me one way or the other, but it was a relief to spill it out. Before that day in Jacobs's Bounder, I never had. In the bands I played with, everyone just shrugged and looked the other way. As long as you kept showing up, that was, and remembered the chords to "In the Midnight Hour"—which, believe me, ain't rocket science.

"It's another cough syrup. More powerful than terpin hydrate, but only if you knew how to get at the good stuff. To do that, you tied a string around the neck of the bottle and twirled it like a mad bastard. The centrifugal force separated the syrup into three levels. The good stuff—the hydrocodone—was in the middle. You used a straw to suck it up."

"Fascinating."

Not very, I thought. "After awhile, when I was still having pain, I started scoring morphine again. Then I discovered heroin worked as well, and at half the price." I smiled. "There's a kind of drug stock market, you know. When everybody started using rock cocaine, horse took a nosedive."

"Your leg looks fine to me," he said mildly. "There's a bad scar, and there's obviously been some muscle loss, but not that much. Some doctor did a fine job on you."

"I can walk, yeah. But you try standing on a leg that's full of metal clips and screws for three hours a night, under hot lights and with a nine-pound guitar strapped on. Lecture all you want, you picked me up when I was down and I guess I owe you that, but don't tell me about pain. Nobody knows unless they're on the inside."

He nodded. "As someone who's suffered . . . losses . . . I can relate to that. But here's something I bet you already know, deep down. It's your *brain* that's hurting, and blaming it on your leg. Brains are crafty that way."

He put the bottle back in his pocket (I watched it go with deep regret) and leaned forward, his eyes locked on mine. "But I believe I can take care of you with an electrical treatment. No guarantees, and the treatment might not cure your mental craving forever, but I believe I can give you what the football players call running room."

"Cure me the way you did Connie, I suppose. When that kid clotheslined him with a ski pole."

He looked surprised, then laughed. "You remember that."

"Of course! How could I forget it?" I also remembered how Con had refused to go with me to see Jacobs after the Terrible Sermon. It wasn't exactly like Peter denying Jesus, but it was in the same ballpark.

"A dubious cure at best, Jamie. More likely the placebo effect. I'm offering you an *actual* cure, one that will—or so I believe—short-circuit the painful withdrawal process."

"Well of course you'd *say* that, wouldn't you?"

"You're judging me by my carny persona. But that's all it is, Jamie—a persona. When I'm not wearing my show suit and making a living, I try to tell the truth. In fact, I mostly tell the truth when I'm working. That picture *will* amaze Miss Cathy Morse's friends."

"Yeah," I said. "For two years, anyway. Give or take."

"Stop dodging and answer my question. Do you want to get better?"

What came to mind was the PS of the note Kelly Van Dorn had slid under my door. In prison a year from now if I didn't clean up my act, he'd written. And that was if I struck lucky.

"I got straight three years ago." Sort of true, although I *had* been on the Marijuana Maintenance Program. "Did it righteous, went through the shakes and sweats and the Hershey squirts. My leg was so bad I could barely hobble. It's some kind of nerve damage."

"I believe I can take care of that, too."

"What are you, some kind of miracle worker? Is that what you want me to believe?"

He had been sitting on the carpet beside the bed. Now he got up. "That's enough for now. You need to sleep. You're still quite a long way from well."

"Then give me something that will help me."

He did so without argument, and it helped me. It just didn't help enough. By 1992, real help came in the needle. There was nothing else. You don't just wave a magic wand over that shit and make it gone.

Or so I believed.

I stayed in his Bounder for the best part of a week, living on soup, sandwiches, and nasally administered doses of heroin that were just enough to keep the worst of the shakes at bay. He brought my guitar and duffel. I kept a spare set of works in the duffel, but when I looked (it was the second night, and he was working the crowds at his Portraits in Lightning shy), the kit was gone. I begged him to give it back, along with enough heroin so I could cook and shoot up.

"No," he said. "If you want to mainline—"

"I've only been skin-popping!"

He gave me an *Oh, please* look. "If you want that, you'll have to find the proper equipment yourself. If you're not well enough to do it tonight, you will be by tomorrow, and around this place I'm sure it wouldn't take you long. Just don't come back here."

"When do I get this so-called miracle cure?"

"When you're well enough to withstand a small application of electricity to your frontal lobe."

I felt cold at that. I swung my legs out of his bed (he was sleeping on the pullout couch) and watched him take off his show clothes, hanging them up carefully and replacing them with a pair of plain white pajamas that looked like something inmate extras might wear in a horror movie set in an insane asylum. Sometimes I wondered if he might not belong in an asylum, and not because he was running what was essentially a carny wonder-show. Sometimes—especially when he talked about the curative powers of electricity—he got a look in his eyes that didn't seem sane. It was not unlike the way he'd looked when he preached himself out of a job in Harlow.

"Charlie . . ." This was what I called him now. "Are you talking about shock treatment?"

He looked at me soberly, buttoning the top of his white inmate pajamas. "Yes and no. Certainly not in the conventional sense, because I don't intend to treat you with conventional electricity. My spiel sounds unbelievable, because it's what the customers want. They don't come here for reality, Jamie, they come for fantasy. But there really is a secret electricity, and its uses are manifold. I just haven't discovered all of them yet, and that includes the one that interests me most."

"Want to share?"

"No. I gave several exhausting performances, and I need sleep. I hope you'll still be here in the morning, but if you're not, that's your choice."

"Once upon a time you would have said there are no real choices, only God's will."

"That was a different man. A young fellow with naïve beliefs. Will you wish me goodnight?"

I did, then lay in the bed he had given up so I could use it. He was no longer a preacher, but still of the Good Samaritan stripe in so many ways. I hadn't been naked, like the man who had been set upon by robbers on his way to Jericho, but heroin had robbed me of plenty for sure. He had fed me, and given me shelter, and propped me up with just enough horse to keep me from going out of my fucking mind. The question now was whether or not I wanted to give him a chance to blast my brainwaves flat. Or outright kill me by shooting megavolts of "special electricity" into my head.

Five times, maybe ten or a dozen, I thought I would get up and drag the midway until I found somebody who'd sell me what I needed. That need was like a drillbit in my head, boring in deeper and deeper. Nasally administered sips of H didn't cut it. I needed a big blast direct to the central nervous system. Once I actually swung my legs out of bed and reached for my shirt, determined to do it and get it done, but then I lay back down again, shaking and sweating and twitching.

Finally I began to drift off. I let myself go, thinking *Tomorrow. I'll leave tomorrow.* But I stayed. And on my fifth morning—I think it was the fifth—Jacobs slipped behind the wheel of his Bounder, keyed the engine, and said, "Let's take a ride."

I had no choice about it, unless I wanted to open the door and jump out, because we were already rolling.

VI

The Electrical Treatment. A Nighttime Excursion. One Pissed-Off Okie. A Ticket on the Mountain Express.

Jacobs's electrical workshop was in West Tulsa. I don't know what that part of town is like now, but in 1992 it was a forlorn industrial zone where a lot of the industries seemed to be dead or dying. He pulled into the parking lot of an all-but-destitute strip mall on Olympia Avenue and parked in front of Wilson Auto Body.

"It was standing empty for a long time, that's what the Realtor told me," Jacobs said. He was dressed in faded jeans and a blue golf shirt, his hair washed and combed, his eyes sparkling with excitement. Just looking at him made me nervous. "I had to take a year's lease, but it was still dirt cheap. Come on in."

"You ought to take down the sign and put up your own," I said. I framed it with hands that were only shaking a little. "'Portraits in Lightning, C. D. Jacobs, Proprietor.' It would look good."

"I won't be in Tulsa that long," he said, "and the portraits are really just a way of supporting myself while I conduct my experiments. I've come a long way since my pastoral days, but I've still got a long way to go. You have no idea. Come in, Jamie. Come in."

He unlocked a door and led me through an office that was empty of furniture, although I could still see square clean patches on the grimy linoleum, where the legs of a desk had once stood. On the wall was a curling calendar with April 1989 showing.

The garage had a corrugated metal roof and I expected it to be baking under the September sun, but it was wonderfully cool. I could hear the whisper of air conditioners. When he flicked a bank of switches—recently modified, judging from the makeshift way the wires stuck out of the uncovered holes where the plates had been—a dozen brilliant lights came on. If not for the oil-darkened concrete and the rectangular caverns where two lifts had once been, you would have thought it was an operating theater.

"It must cost a fortune to air-condition this place," I said. "Especially when you've got all those lights blazing."

"Dirt cheap. The air conditioners are my own design. They draw very little power, and most of that I generate myself. I could generate all of it, but I wouldn't want Tulsa Power and Light down here, snooping around to find out if I was volt-jacking, somehow. As for the lights . . . you could wrap a hand around one of the bulbs without burning yourself. Or even heating your skin, for that matter."

Our footfalls echoed in all that empty space. So did our voices. It was like being in the company of phantoms. *It just feels that way because I'm strung out*, I told myself.

"Listen, Charlie—you're not messing with anything radioactive, are you?"

He grimaced and shook his head. "Nuclear's the last thing I'm interested in. It's energy for idiots. A dead end."

"So how do you generate the juice?"

"Electricity breeds electricity, if you know what you're doing. Leave it at that. Step over here, Jamie."

There were three or four long tables at the end of the room with electrical stuff on them. I recognized an oscilloscope, a spectrometer, and a couple of things that resembled Marshall amps but could have been batteries of some kind. There was a control board that looked mostly torn apart, and several stacked consoles with darkened dials. Thick electrical cords snaked every whichway. Some disappeared into closed metal containers that could have been Craftsman tool chests; others just looped back to the dark equipment.

This could all be a fantasy, I thought. *Equipment that only comes alive in his imagination*. But the Portraits in Lightning weren't make-believe. I had no idea how he was making those, his explanation had been vague at best, but he *was* making them. And although I was standing directly beneath one of those brilliant lights, it really did not seem to be throwing any heat.

"There doesn't seem to be much here," I said doubtfully. "I expected more."

"Flashing lights! Chrome-plated knife-switches sticking out of science fiction control panels! *Star Trek* telescreens! Possibly a teleportation chamber, or a hologram of Noah's Ark in a cloud chamber!" He laughed cheerily.

"Nothing like that," I said, although he had pretty much hit the nail on the head. "It just seems kind of . . . sparse."

"It is. I've gone about as far as I can for the time being. I've sold some of my equipment. Other stuff—more controversial stuff—I've dismantled and put in storage. I've done good work in Tulsa, especially considering how little spare time I have. Keeping body and soul together is an annoying business, as I suppose you know."

I certainly did.

"But yes, I made some progress toward my ultimate goal. Now I need to think, and I don't believe I can do that when I'm turning half a dozen tips a night."

"Your ultimate goal being what?"

He ignored the question this time, too. "Step over here, Jamie. Would you like a small pick-me-up before we begin?"

I wasn't sure I *wanted* to begin, but I wanted a pick-me-up, all right. Not for the first time, I considered just snatching the little brown bottle and running. Only he'd probably catch me and wrest it away. I was younger, and almost over the flu, but he was still in better shape. He hadn't suffered a shattered hip and leg in a motorcycle accident, for one thing.

He grabbed a paint-spattered wooden chair and set it in front of one of the black boxes that looked like a Marshall amp. "Sit here."

But I didn't, not right away. There was a picture on one of the tables, the kind with a little wedge on the back to prop it up. He saw me reach for it and made a move as if to stop me. Then he just stood there.

A song on the radio can bring back the past with fierce (if mercifully transitory) immediacy: a first kiss, a good time with your buddies, or an unhappy life-passage. I can never hear Fleetwood Mac's "Go Your Own Way" without thinking of my mother's last painful weeks; that spring it seemed to be on the radio every time I turned it on. A picture can have the same effect. I looked at this one and all at once I was eight again. My sister was helping Morrie set up dominos in Toy Corner while Patsy Jacobs played "Bringing in the Sheaves," swaying on the piano bench, her smooth blond hair shifting from side to side.

It was a studio portrait. Patsy was wearing the sort of billowy, shin-length dress that went out of fashion years ago, but it looked good on her. The kid was on her lap, wearing short pants and a sweater vest. A cowlick I remembered well stuck up at the back of his head.

"We used to call him Tag-Along-Morrie," I said, running my fingers lightly over the glass.

"Did you?"

I didn't look up. His unsteady voice made me afraid of what I might see in his eyes. "Yeah. And all of us boys were in love with your wife. Claire was, too. I think Mrs. Jacobs was what she wanted to be."

At the thought of my sister, my own eyes began to fill up. I could tell you it was just because I was physically low and full of craving, and it would be the truth, but not the whole truth.

I swiped an arm across my face and set the picture down. When I looked up, he was fiddling with a voltage regulator that didn't look like it needed fiddling with. "You never remarried?"

"No," he said. "Never even close. Patsy and Morrie were all I wanted. Needed. There's not a day when I don't think of them, not a month when I don't have a dream that they're okay. It was the accident that was the dream, I think. Then I wake up. Tell me something, Jamie. Your mother and your sister. Do you ever wonder where they are? *If* they are?"

"No." Any scraps of belief that survived the Terrible Sermon had withered away in high school and college.

"Ah. I see." He dropped the regulator and turned on the thing that looked like a Marshall amp—the kind of amp the bands I played with could rarely afford. It hummed, but not like a Marshall. This sound was lower, and almost musical. "Well, let's get on with it, shall we?"

I looked at the chair, but didn't sit on it. "You were going to give me a little hit first."

"So I was." He produced the brown bottle, considered it, then handed it to me. "Since we can hope this will be your last, why don't you do the honors?"

He didn't have to ask twice. I took two heaping snorts, and would have doubled down if he hadn't snatched the small bottle away. Nevertheless, a window on a tropic beach opened in my head. A mellow breeze wafted in, and I suddenly no longer cared about what might become of my brainwaves. I sat down in the chair.

He opened one of several wall cabinets and brought out a pair of battered, taped-up headphones with crisscrosses of metal mesh over the earpads. He plugged them into the amp-like device and held them out to me.

"If I hear 'In-A-Gadda-Da-Vida,' I'm taillights," I said.

He smiled and said nothing.

I put the headphones on. The mesh was cool against my ears. "Have you tried this on anyone?" I asked. "Will it hurt?"

"It won't hurt," he said, not answering the first question at all. As if to contradict this, he gave me a mouthguard of the type basketball players sometimes wear, then smiled at my expression. "Just a precaution. Pop it on in."

I popped it on in.

From his pocket he took a white plastic box no bigger than a doorbell. "I think you'll—" But then he pressed a button on the little box, and I lost the rest.

There was no blackout, no sense of time passing, no discontinuity at all. Just a *click*, very loud, as if Jacobs had snapped his fingers beside my ears, although he was standing at least five feet away. Yet all at once he was bending over me instead of standing beside the thing that wasn't a Marshall amp. The little white control box was nowhere to be seen, and my brain had gone wrong. It was stuck.

"Something," I said. "Something, something, something. Happened. Happened. Something happened. Something happened, happened, something happened. Happened. Something."

"Stop that. You're all right." But he didn't sound sure. He sounded scared.

The headphones were gone. I tried to get up and shot one hand into the air instead, like a second-grader who knows the right answer and is dying to give it.

"Something. Something. Something. Happened. Happened, happened. Something happened."

He slapped me, and hard. I jerked backward and would have fallen over if the chair hadn't been placed almost directly against the metal side of his workshop.

I lowered my hand, stopped repeating, and just looked at him.

"What's your name?"

I'll say it's something happened, I thought. *First name Something, last name Happened.*

But I didn't. "Jamie Morton."

"Middle name?"

"Edward."

"My name?"

"Charles Jacobs. Charles *Daniel* Jacobs."

He produced the little bottle of heroin and gave it to me. I looked at it, then handed it back. "I'm good for now. You just gave me some."

"Did I?" He showed me his wristwatch. We had arrived at midmorning. It was now quarter past two in the afternoon.

"That's impossible."

He looked interested. "Why's that?"

"Because no time passed. Except . . . I guess it did. Didn't it?"

"Yes. We spoke at great length."

"What did we talk about?"

"Your father. Your brothers. Your mother's passing. And Claire's."

"What did I say about Claire?"

"That she married an abusive man and kept quiet about it for three years because she was ashamed. She finally opened up to your brother Andy, and—"

"His name was Paul Overton," I said. "He taught English at a fancy prep school in New Hampshire. Andy drove down there and waited in the parking lot and when Overton showed up, Andy beat the living shit out of him. We all loved Claire—everybody did, I suppose even Paul Overton did in his way—but she and Andy were the oldest, and they were especially close. Is that what I told you?"

"Almost word for word. Andy said, 'If you touch her again, I'll kill you.'"

"Tell me what else I said."

"That Claire moved out, got a protection order, and sued for divorce. She moved to North Conway and got another teaching job. Six months after the divorce became final, Overton drove up there and shot her dead in her classroom while she was correcting papers after school. Then he killed himself."

Yes. Claire dead. Her funeral had been the last time what remained of my big, brawling, usually happy family was together. A sunny day in October. When it was over, I drove to Florida just because I had never been there. A month later I was playing with Patsy Cline's Lipstick in Jacksonville. Gas prices were high, the climate was usually warm, and I traded my car for a Kawasaki. Not a good decision, as it turned out.

In one corner of the room was a small fridge. He opened it and brought me a bottle of apple juice. I drank it down in five long gulps.

"See if you can stand up."

I rose from the chair and staggered. Jacobs caught me by the elbow and steadied me.

"Good so far. Now walk across the room."

I did, at first weaving like a drunk, but when I came back, I was okay. Steady Eddie.

"Good," he said. "Not a sign of a limp. Let's go back to the fairgrounds. You need to rest."

"Something *did* happen," I said. "What?"

"A minor restructuring of your brainwaves, I believe."

"You believe."

"Yes."

"But you don't *know*?"

He considered this for what seemed like a long time, although it might only have been seconds; it was a week before anything like a real sense of time returned to me. At last he said, "I've found certain important books very difficult to obtain, and I have a long way to go in my studies as a result. Sometimes that means taking small risks. Acceptable ones only. You're fine, aren't you?"

I thought it was too early to tell, but didn't say so. After all, the thing was done.

"Come on, Jamie. I've got a long night's work ahead of me, and I need rest myself."

When we got to his Bounder, I tried to reach for the door and once more stuck my hand straight up in the air instead. The elbow locked; it was as if the joint had turned to iron. For one terrifying moment I thought it would never come down, that I was just going to spend the rest of my life with one hand raised in that *Teacher, teacher, call on me* gesture. Then it let go. I lowered my arm, opened the door, and got in.

"That will pass," he said.

"How can you know, if you don't know exactly what you did?"

"Because I've seen it before."

When he was parked in his usual spot at the fairgrounds, he showed me the little bottle of heroin again. "You can have this if you want it."

But I didn't. I felt like a man looking at a banana split minutes after polishing off a nine-course Thanksgiving dinner. You know that sugar-loaded treat is good, and you know that under certain circumstances you would gobble it greedily, but not after a heavy meal. After a heavy meal, a banana split is not an object of desire but just an object.

"Later, maybe," I said, but later hasn't come yet. Now, as a going-on-elderly man with a touch of arthritis writes of those old days, I know it never will. He cured me, but it was a dangerous cure, and he knew it—when one speaks of acceptable risks, the question is always *acceptable to whom?* Charlie Jacobs was a Good Samaritan. He was also a half-mad scientist, and that day in the abandoned auto body shop I was his latest guinea pig. He could have killed me, and sometimes—many times, actually—I wish he had.

I slept the remainder of the afternoon. When I woke up, I felt like an earlier version of Jamie Morton, clearheaded and full of pep. I swung my legs over the side of his bed and watched him put on his show clothes. "Tell me something," I said.

"If it's about our little adventure in West Tulsa, I'd rather not discuss it. Why don't we just wait and see if you remain as you are now, or if you relapse into craving . . . damn this tie, I can never get it right and Briscoe is utterly useless."

Briscoe was his assistant, the fellow who mugged and distracted the audience when it needed distracting.

"Hold still," I said. "You're making a mess of that. Let me."

I stood behind him, reached over his shoulders, and tied the tie. With the shakes gone from my hands, it was easy. Like my walk once the brain shot had worn off, they were Steady Eddie.

"Where did you learn to do that?"

"After my accident, when I could stand up and play for a couple of hours without falling down, I worked with a group called the Undertakers." It hadn't been much of a group. Any band where I was the best player wasn't. "We wore frock coats, stovepipe hats, and string ties. The drummer and the bass player got into a fight over a girl and the group broke up, but I came out of it with a new skill."

"Well . . . thank you. What did you want to ask me?"

"About the Portraits in Lightning gig. You only take pictures of women. It seems to me that you're losing fifty percent of your business that way."

He grinned his boyish grin, the one he'd worn when he was leading the games in the parsonage basement. "When I invented the portrait camera—which is actually a combined generator and projector, as I'm sure you know—I *did* attempt to do both men and women. This was at a little seaside amusement park in North Carolina called Joyland. Out of business now, but it was a lovely place, Jamie. I enjoyed it greatly. During my time on the midway—which was called Joyland Avenue—there was a Rogues' Gallery next to Mysterio's Mirror Mansion. It featured life-size cardboard figures with cutouts where the faces belonged. There was a pirate, a gangster with an automatic, a tough Jane with a tommygun, the Joker and Catwoman from the Batman comics. People would put their faces in and the park's traveling photographers—Hollywood Girls, they were called—would snap their pictures."

"That gave you the idea?"

"Yes. At the time I was styling myself Mr. Electrico—an homage to Ray Bradbury, but I doubt if any of the rubes knew it—and although I had invented a crude version of my current projector, it had never crossed my mind to feature it in the show. Mostly I used the Tesla coil and a spark generator called Jacob's Ladder. I demonstrated a small Jacob's Ladder to you kids when I was your minister, Jamie. I used chemicals to make the rising sparks change color. Do you remember?"

I did.

"The Rogues' Gallery made me aware of the possibilities inherent in my projector, and I created Portraits in Lightning. Just another gaff, you'd say . . . but it also helped me to advance my studies, and still does. During my stint at Joyland, I used a backdrop featuring a man in expensive black tie as well as the beautiful girl in the ball gown. Some men took me up on it, but surprisingly few. I believe their shitkicker friends laughed at them when they saw them dressed to the nines like that. Women never laugh, because women *love* dressing to the nines. To the tens, if possible. And when they see the demonstration, they line up."

"How long have you been gigging?"

He calculated, one eye squinted shut. Then he opened them both wide in an expression of surprise. "It's almost fifteen years now."

I shook my head, smiling. "You went from preaching to huckstering."

As soon as it was out of my mouth I realized it was a mean thing to say, but the idea of my old minister turning tips still boggled my mind. He wasn't offended, though. He just gave his perfectly knotted tie a final admiring look in the mirror, and tipped me a wink.

"No difference," he said. "They're both just a matter of convincing the rubes. Now please excuse me while I go and sell some lightning."

He left the heroin on the little table in the middle of the Bounder. I glanced at it from time to time, even picked it up once, but I had no urge to use any. To tell you the truth, I couldn't understand why I'd trashed so much of my life over it in the first place. All that crazy need seemed like a dream to me. I wondered if everyone felt that way when their compulsions passed. I didn't know.

I still don't.

Briscoe lit out for the territories, as gazoonies so often do, and when I asked Jacobs if I could have the job, he agreed at once. There really wasn't much to it, but it spared him the task of finding some local yokel to tote the camera on and offstage, hand him his tophat, and pretend to get electrocuted. He even suggested that I play some chords on my Gibson during the demonstrations. "Something suspenseful," he instructed. "Something that will put it in the rubes' heads that the girl might actually get fried."

This was easy enough. Switching between A minor and E (the foundation chords of "House of the Rising Sun" and "The Springhill Mining Disaster," if you're interested) always suggests impending doom. I enjoyed it, although I thought that a big slow drumbeat would have added something.

"Don't get too wedded to the job," Charlie Jacobs advised me. "I intend to move on. When the fair closes down, attendance at Bell's goes into the toilet."

"Move on where?"

"I'm not sure, but I've gotten used to traveling alone." He clapped me on the shoulder. "Just so you know."

I already did. After the deaths of his wife and child, Charlie Jacobs was strictly a solo act.

The visits he made to his workshop grew shorter and shorter. He began bringing some equipment back and stowing it in the small trailer he'd tow behind the Bounder when he resumed his rambling. The amplifiers that weren't amplifiers didn't come; neither did two of the four long metal boxes. I got the idea he meant to start fresh, wherever he ended up. As if he'd gone as far down one road as he could, and meant to try another.

I had no idea what I wanted to do with my own life, now drug-free (and limp-free; that, too), but traveling on with the King of High Voltage wasn't it. I was grateful to him, but since I could no longer really recall the horrors of heroin addiction (any more, I suppose, than a woman who's had a baby can recall the pain of childbirth), not as grateful as you might think. Also, he scared me. So did his secret electricity. He talked about it in extravagant terms—*secret of the universe, path to ultimate knowledge*—but he had no more idea of what it really was than a toddler has of a gun he finds in Daddy's closet.

And, speaking of closets . . . I snooped, okay? And what I found was a photograph album filled with pictures of Patsy, Morrie, and the three of them together. The pages were well thumbed, and the binding was loose. It didn't take Sam Spade to know he looked at those pictures a lot, but I never saw him do it. The album was a secret.

Like his electricity.

In the early-morning hours of October third, shortly before the Tulsa State Fair shut up shop for another year, I suffered another aftereffect of the brain-blast Jacobs had given me. Jacobs was paying me for my services (quite a bit more than the services actually merited), and I had rented a room by the week about four blocks from the fairgrounds. It was clear he wanted to be alone, no matter how much he liked me (if he did like me), and I felt it was high time he got his own bed back.

I turned in at midnight, about an hour after we wrapped the last show of the evening, and went to sleep at once. I almost always did. With the dope out of my system, I slept well. Only that morning I woke up two hours later, in the weedy backyard of the rooming house. An icy rind of moon hung overhead. Beneath it stood Jamie Morton, naked save for one sock and with a piece of rubber tubing wrapped around his biceps. I have no idea where I got it, but above it, the blood vessels—any one of them perfect for shooting up—bulged. Below it, my forearm was white and cold and fast asleep.

"Something happened," I said. I had a fork in one hand (God knows where that came from, too), and I was poking my swollen upper arm with it over and over again. Blood was beading up from at least a dozen pricks. "Something. Happened. Something happened. Oh Mother, something happened. Something, something."

I told myself to stop, but at first I couldn't. I wasn't out of control, exactly, but I was out of *my* control. I thought of Electric Jesus trundling across Peaceable Lake on a hidden rail. I was like that.

"Something."

Stab.

"Something happened."

Stab-stab.

"Something—"

I stuck out my tongue and bit it. The *click* came again, not beside my ears but buried deep inside my head. The compulsion to speak and stab was gone, just like that. The fork tumbled from my hand. I unwrapped the makeshift tourniquet, and my forearm began to prickle as the blood rushed back into it.

I looked up at the moon, shivering and wondering who, or what, had been controlling me. Because I *had* been controlled. When I got back to my room (grateful not to be seen with my wingwang dangling in the breeze), I saw I had stepped on some broken glass and cut my foot quite badly. It should have awakened me, but hadn't. Why? Because I hadn't been asleep. I was sure of it. Something had moved me out of myself and taken over, driving my body like a car.

I washed my foot and got back into bed. I never told Jacobs about that experience—what good would it have done? He would have suggested that a gashed foot suffered on a little midnight stroll was a small price to pay for a miracle cure from heroin addiction, and he would have been right. Still:

Something happened.

Closing Day at the Tulsa State Fair that year was October tenth. I arrived at Jacobs's Bounder around five thirty that afternoon, in plenty of time to tune my guitar and tie his tie—a thing that had become a tradition. While I was doing it, there was a knock at the door. Charlie went to answer it, frowning. He had six shows to do that night, including the final one at midnight, and he didn't like being interrupted beforehand.

He opened the door, saying, "If it's not important, I wish you'd come back la—" and then a farmer in bib overalls and a Case cap (a pissed-off Okie if ever an Okie there was) punched him in the mouth. Jacobs went staggering back, got tangled in his own feet, and went down, narrowly avoiding giving his head a good whap on the dinette table, which might have knocked him unconscious.

Our visitor barged in, bent down, seized Jacobs by the lapels. He was about Jacobs's age, but a lot bigger. And he was in a rage. This could be trouble, I thought. Of course it was already, but I was thinking of the kind that ends with an extended stay in the hospital.

"You're the reason she got took in by the police!" he shouted. "Goddam you, she'll have a record that'll follow her around for the rest of her life! Like a tin can tied to a puppydog's tail!"

I didn't think, just seized an empty pot from the sink and bonked him briskly on the side of the head. It wasn't a hard blow, but the Okie let go of Jacobs and looked at me in astonishment. Tears began leaking down the grooves on either side of his considerable beak.

Charlie scooted away, propped on his hands and propelling himself with his feet. Blood was pouring from his lower lip, which was split in two places.

"Why don't you pick on someone your own size?" I asked. Hardly reasoned discourse, I know, but when we find ourselves in that sort of confrontation, how the schoolyard comes back.

"She got to go to court!" he shouted at me in that out-of-tune banjo Okie accent. "And it's that sucka's fault! That sucka rahchair, scuttlin like a dadburn *crab*!"

He said dadburn. He really did.

I put the pot on the stove and showed him my empty hands. I spoke in my most soothing voice. "I don't know who you're talking about, and I'm sure"—I almost said *Charles*—"I'm sure Dan doesn't, either."

"My dotta! My dotta Cathy! Cathy Morse! He told her the pitcher was free—because she got up onstage—but it wa'nt free! That pitcher has costed her plenty! Rooned her dadburned life is what that pitcher did!"

I put a cautious arm around his shoulders. I thought he might clobber me, but now that his initial fury had been vented, he only looked sad and bewildered. "Come on outside," I said. "We'll find a bench in the shade and you can tell me all about it."

"Who're you?"

I was going to say *Mr. Jacobs's assistant*, but that sounded like pretty weak tea. My years as a musician came to my rescue. "His agent."

"Yeah? Can you gi' me compensation? Because I want it. The lawyer's fees alone are 'bout to half kill me." He pointed a finger at Jacobs. "On account of you! Your dadgum fault!"

"I . . . I have no idea . . ." Charlie wiped a palmful of blood off his chin. "I have no idea what you're talking about, Mr. Morse, I assure you."

I had gotten Morse as far as the door, and I didn't want to lose the ground I had gained. "Let's discuss this out in the fresh air."

He let me lead him out. There was a refreshment stand at the edge of the employees' parking lot, with rusty tables shaded by tattered canvas umbrellas. I bought him a large Coke and handed it to him. He slopped the first inch out on the table, then drank half of the paper cup in big swallows. He set it down and pressed the heel of his palm to his forehead.

"I never learn not to take a colddrink like that," he said. "Puts a nail in your head, don't it?"

"Yes," I said, and thought of standing naked in scant moonlight, poking the tines of a fork into my blood-engorged upper arm. *Something happened.* To me, and, it seemed, to Cathy Morse, as well.

"Tell me what the problem seems to be."

"That pitcher he give her, that's the goddarn problem. She walked around with it damn near ever'where. Her friends commenced on to makin fun of her, but she didn't care. She tole people 'That's how I *really* look.' I tried to shake the notion out of her one night and Mother tole me to stop, said it would pass on its own. And it seemed to. She left the pitcher in her room, I dunno, two days or three. Went on down to the hairdressin school without it. We thought it was over."

It wasn't. On October seventh, three days previous, she had walked into J. David Jewelry in Broken Arrow, a town southeast of Tulsa. She was carrying a shopping bag. Both salesmen recognized her, because she had been in several times since her star turn at Jacobs's midway pitch. One of them asked if he could help her. Cathy blew past him without a word and went to the display case where the most expensive geegaws were kept. From her shopping bag she produced a hammer, which she used to shatter the glass top of the case. Ignoring the bray of the alarm and two cuts serious enough to warrant stitches ("And them will leave scars," her father mourned), she reached in and took out a pair of diamond earrings.

"These are mine," she said. "They go with my dress."

Morse had no more than finished his story when two wide boys with SECURITY printed on their black tee-shirts showed up. "Is there a problem here?" one of them asked.

"No," I said, and there wasn't. Telling the story had finished venting his rage, which was good. It had also shriveled him somehow, and that wasn't so good. "Mr. Morse was just leaving."

He got up, clutching the remains of his Coke. Charlie Jacobs's blood was drying on his knuckles. He looked at it as if he didn't know where it had come from.

"Siccin the cops on him wouldn't do no good, would it?" he asked. "All he did was take her pitcher, they'd say. Hell, it was even free."

"Come on, sir," one of the security guys said. "If you'd like to visit the fair, I'd be happy to stamp your hand."

"Nosir," he said. "My family's had enough of this fair. I'm goin home." He started off, then turned back. "Has he done it before, mister? Has he knocked other ones for a loop the way he knocked my Cathy?"

Something happened, I thought. *Something, something, something.*

"No," I said. "Not at all."

"Like you'd say, even if he did. You bein his agent and all."

Then he went away, head lowered, not looking back.

In the Bounder, Jacobs had changed his blood-spotted shirt and had a dishtowel filled with ice on his fattening lower lip. He listened while I told him what Morse had told me, then said, "Tie my tie for me again, will you? We're already late."

"Whoa," I said. "Whoa, whoa, whoa. You need to fix her up. The way you fixed me up. With the headphones."

He gave me a look that was perilously close to contempt. "Do you think Daddy Dearest would let me within a mile of her? Besides, what's wrong with her . . . her compulsion . . . will wear off on its own. She'll be fine, and any lawyer worth his salt will be able to convince the judge that she wasn't herself. She'll get off with a slap on the wrist."

"None of this is exactly new to you, is it?"

He shrugged, still looking in my direction but no longer quite meeting my eyes. "There have been aftereffects from time to time, yes, although nothing quite so spectacular as Miss Morse's attempted smash-and-grab."

"You're self-teaching, aren't you? All your customers are actually guinea pigs. They just don't know it. *I* was a guinea pig."

"Are you better now, or not?"

"Yes." Except for the occasional early-morning stab-a-thon, that was.

"Then please tie my tie."

I almost didn't. I was angry with him—on top of everything else, he'd snuck out the back way and yelled for security—but I owed him. He had saved my life, which was good. I was now living a *straight* life, and that was even better.

So I tied his tie. We did the show. In fact, we did six of them. The crowd *aaaahhh*ed when the close-of-fair fireworks went off, but never so loud as they did when Dan the Lightning Portraits Man worked his magic. And as each girl stared dreamily up at herself on the backdrop while I switched between A minor and E, I wondered which among them would discover that she had lost a little piece of her mind.

An envelope sticking under my door. Déjà vu all over again, Yogi would have said. Only this time I hadn't peed in my bed, my surgically mended leg didn't ache, I wasn't coming down with the flu, and I wasn't jitter-jiving with the need to score. I bent, picked it up, and tore it open.

My fifth business wasn't one for gooey goodbyes, I'll give him that. The envelope contained an Amtrak ticket envelope with a sheet of notepaper paper-clipped to it. Written there were a name and an address in the town of Nederland, Colorado. Below, Jacobs had scrawled three sentences. *This man will give you a job, if you want it. He owes me. Thanks for tying my tie. CDJ.*

I opened the Amtrak envelope and found a one-way ticket on the *Mountain Express* from Tulsa to Denver. I looked at it for a long time, thinking that maybe I could turn it in and get a cash refund. Or use it and make the musicians' exchange in Denver my first stop. Only it would take awhile to get that groove-thing going again. My fingers had gone soft and my chops were rusty. There was also the dope thing to consider. When you're on the road, dope is everywhere. The magic wore off the Portraits in Lightning after two years or so, Jacobs had said. How did I know it wouldn't be the same with cures for addiction? How *could* I know, when he didn't know himself?

That afternoon I took a cab to the auto body shop he'd rented in West Tulsa. It was abandoned and bare to the walls. There wasn't so much as a single snip of wire on the grease-darkened floor.

Something happened to me here, I thought. The question was whether or not I'd put on those modified headphones again, given the chance to do it over. I decided I would, and in some fashion I didn't quite understand, that helped me make up my mind about the ticket. I used it, and when I got to Denver, I took the bus to Nederland, high up on the Western Slope of the Rockies. There I met Hugh Yates, and began my life for the third time.

VII

A Homecoming. Wolfjaw Ranch. God Heals Like Lightning. Deaf in Detroit. Prismatics.

My father died in 2003, having outlived his wife and two of his five children. Claire Morton Overton wasn't yet thirty when her estranged husband took her life. Both my mother and my eldest brother died at the age of fifty-one.

Question: Death, where is thy sting?

Answer: Every-fucking-where.

I went home to Harlow for Dad's memorial service. Most of the roads were paved now, not just ours and Route 9. There was a housing development where we used to go swimming, and a Big Apple convenience store half a mile from Shiloh Church. Yet the town was in many essential ways the same. Our church still stood just down the road from Myra Harrington's house (although Me-Maw herself had gone to that great party line in the sky), and the tire swing still hung from the tree in our backyard. I suppose Terry's children had used it, although they'd all be too old for such things now; the rope was frayed and dark with age.

Maybe I'll replace that, I thought . . . but why? For whom? Not my children, certainly, for I had none, and this place was no longer my place.

The only car in the driveway was a battered '51 Ford. It looked like the original Road Rocket, but of course that was impossible—Duane Robichaud had wrecked Road Rocket I at Castle Rock Speedway in the first lap of its only race. Yet there was the Delco Batteries sticker on the trunk, and the number *19* on the side, in paint as red as blood. A crow came down and roosted on the hood. I remembered how our dad had taught all us kids to poke the sign of the evil eye at crows (*Nothing in it, but it doesn't hurt to be sure*, he said), and I thought: *I don't like this. Something is wrong here.*

I could understand Con not having arrived, Hawaii was a lot farther away than Colorado, but where was Terry? He and his wife, Annabelle, still *lived* here. And what about the Bowies? The Clukeys? The Paquettes? The DeWitts? What about the crew from Morton Fuel Oil? Dad had been getting up there, but surely he hadn't outlived all of the home folks.

I parked, got out of my car, and saw it was no longer the Ford Focus I'd driven off the Hertz lot in Portland. It was the '66 Galaxie my father and brother had given me for my seventeenth birthday. On the passenger seat was the set of hardbound Kenneth Roberts novels my mother had given me: *Oliver Wiswell* and *Arundel* and all the rest.

This is a dream, I thought. *It's one I've had before.*

There was no relief in the realization, only increased dread.

A crow landed on the roof of the house I'd grown up in. Another alighted on the branch supporting the tire swing, the one with all the bark rubbed off so it stuck out like a bone.

I didn't want to go in the house, because I knew what I'd find there. My feet carried me forward, nonetheless. I mounted the steps, and although Terry had sent me a photo of the rebuilt porch eight years before (or maybe it was ten), the same old board, second from the top, gave out the same old ill-tempered squawk when I stepped on it.

They were waiting for me in the dining room. Not the whole family; just the dead ones. My mother was little more than a mummy, as she had been as she lay dying during that cold February. My father was pale and wizened, much as he'd appeared in the Christmas card photo Terry had sent me not long before his final heart attack. Andy was corpulent—my skinny brother had put on a great deal of meat in middle age—but his hypertensive flush had faded to the waxy pallor of the grave. Claire was the worst. Her crazed ex-husband hadn't been content just to kill her; she'd had the temerity to leave him, and only complete obliteration would do. He shot her in the face three times, the last two as she lay dead on her classroom floor, before putting a bullet in his own brain.

"Andy," I said. "What happened to you?"

"Prostate," he said. "I should have listened, baby brother."

Sitting on the table was mold-covered birthday cake. As I watched, the frosting humped up, broke apart, and a black ant the size of a pepper-shaker crawled out. It trundled up my dead brother's arm, across his shoulder, and then onto his face. My mother turned her head. I could hear the dry tendons creak, the sound like a rusty spring holding an old kitchen door.

"Happy birthday, Jamie," she said. Her voice was grating, expressionless.

"Happy birthday, Son." My dad.

"Happy birthday, kiddo." Andy.

Then Claire turned to look at me, although she had only a single raw socket to look out of. *Don't speak*, I thought. *If you speak, it will drive me insane.*

But she did, the words coming from a clotted hole filled with broken teeth.

"Don't you get her pregnant in the backseat of that car."

And my mother nodding like a ventriloquist's dummy while more huge ants crawled out of the ancient cake.

I tried to cover my eyes, but my hands were too heavy. They hung limply at my sides. Behind me, I heard that porch board give out its ill-tempered squeal. Not once but twice. Two new arrivals, and I knew who they were.

"No," I said. "No more. Please, no more."

But then Patsy Jacobs's hand fell on my shoulder, and those of Tag-Along-Morrie circled my leg just above the knee.

"Something happened," Patsy said in my ear. Hair tickled my cheek, and I knew it was hanging from her scalp, torn off her head in the crash.

"Something happened," Morrie agreed, hugging my leg tighter.

Then they all began to sing. The tune was "Happy Birthday," but the lyrics had changed.

"*Something happened . . . TO YOU! Something happened . . . TO YOU! Something happened, dear Jamie, something happened TO YOU!*"

That was when I began to scream.

I had this dream for the first time on the train that took me to Denver, although—fortunately for the people riding in the same car with me—my screams emerged in the real world as a series of guttural grunts deep in my throat. Over the next twenty years I had it perhaps two dozen times. I always awoke with the same panic-stricken thought: *Something happened.*

At that time, Andy was still alive and well. I began calling him and telling him to get his prostate checked. At first he just laughed at me, then he grew annoyed, pointing out that our father was still as healthy as a horse, and looked good to go for another twenty years or so.

"Maybe," I told him, "but Mom died of cancer, and she died young. So did her mom."

"In case you didn't notice, neither of them had a prostate."

"I don't think that matters to the gods of heredity," I said. "They just send the Big C wherever it's most welcome. For Christ's sake, what's the big deal? It's a finger up your ass, it's over in ten seconds, and as long as you don't feel both of the doctor's hands on your shoulders, you don't even have to worry about your backdoor virginity."

"I'll get it done when I'm fifty," he said. "That's the recommendation, that's what I'm going to do, and that's the end of it. I'm glad you cleaned up your act, Jamie. I'm glad you're holding down what passes for a grownup job in the music business. But none of that gives you the right to oversee my life. God does that for me."

Fifty will be too late, I thought. *By the time you're fifty, it will already have taken hold.*

Because I loved my brother (even though he had in my humble opinion grown up to become a moderately annoying God-botherer), I made an end run and went to Francine, his wife. To her I could say what I knew Andy would scoff at—I'd had a premonition, and it was a strong one. Please, Francie, *please* have him get that prostate exam.

He compromised ("Just to shut you both up") by getting a PSA screening shortly after his forty-seventh birthday, grumbling that the damn test was unreliable. Perhaps, but it was hard for even my scripture-quoting, doctorphobic brother to argue with the result: a perfect Bo Derek ten. A trip to a Lewiston urologist followed, then an operation. He was pronounced cancer-free three years later.

A year after that—at fifty-one—he suffered a stroke while watering the lawn, and was in the arms of Jesus before the ambulance got him to the hospital. This was in upstate New York, where the funeral was held. There was no memorial service in Harlow. I was glad. I went home all too often in my dreams, which were a long-term result of Jacobs's treatment for drug addiction. Of that I had no doubt.

I awoke from this dream again on a bright Monday in June of 2008, and lay in bed for ten minutes, getting myself under control. My breathing eventually slowed, and I got past the idea that if I opened my mouth, nothing would come out except *Something happened*, over and over again. I reminded myself that I was clean and sober, and that was still the biggest thing in my life, the thing which had changed that life for the better. The dream came less often now, and it had been at least four years since I had awakened to find myself poking at my skin (the last time with a spatula, which had done zero damage). *It's no worse than a small surgical scar*, I told myself, and usually I could think of it that way. It was only in the immediate aftermath that I felt something lurking *behind* the dream, something malevolent. And female. I was sure of that, even then.

By the time I was showered and dressed, the dream had receded to a faint mist. Soon it would burn off entirely. I knew this from experience.

I had a second-floor apartment on Boulder Canyon Drive in Nederland. By 2008 I could have afforded a house, but it would have meant a mortgage, and I didn't want that. Being single, the apartment did me fine. The bed was a queen, like the one in Jacobs's boondocker, and there had been no shortage of princesses to share it with me over the years. They were fewer and farther between these days, but that was to be expected, I supposed. I would soon turn fifty-two, the age, give or take a few years, when smooth Lotharios begin their inevitable transformation into shaggy old goats.

Besides, I liked to see my savings account slowly fatten. I wasn't a miser by any means, but money was not an unimportant consideration to me, either. The memory of waking up in the Fairgrounds Inn, sick and broke, had never left me. Nor had the face of the red-haired country girl when she handed back my maxed-out credit card. *Try the card again*, I'd told her. *Honey*, she had replied, *I look at you and I don't have to.*

Yeah, but look at me now, sweetbritches, I thought as I drove my 4Runner west on Caribou Road. I had added forty pounds since the night I met Charles Jacobs in Tulsa, but at six-one, a hundred and ninety looked good on me. Okay, so my belly wasn't quite flat, and my last cholesterol count had been iffy, but back then I'd looked like a Dachau survivor. I wasn't ever going to play Carnegie Hall, or arenas with the E Street Band, but I did still play—plenty—and had work I liked and was good at. If a man or woman wants more, I often told myself, that man or woman is tempting the gods. So don't tempt them, Jamie. And if you should happen to hear Peggy Lee singing that rueful old Leiber and Stoller classic—"Is That All There Is?"—change the station and get some good old stompin music.

Four miles along Caribou Road, just as it starts to climb more steeply into the mountains, I turned off at the sign reading WOLF-JAW RANCH, 2 MILES. I punched my code into the gate keypad and parked in the gravel lot marked EMPLOYEES AND TALENT. The only time I'd seen that lot full was when Rihanna recorded an EP at Wolfjaw. And that day there were more cars parked on the access road, almost down to the gate. The chick had a serious entourage.

Pagan Starshine (real name: Hillary Katz) would have fed the horses two hours ago, but I went down the double line of stalls anyway, giving them apple slices and pieces of carrots. Most were big and beautiful—I sometimes thought of them as Cadillac limos on four feet. My favorite, however, was more of a beat-up Chevrolet. Bartleby, a dapple gray with no bloodline to speak of, had been at Wolfjaw when I arrived with nothing but a guitar, a duffel bag, and a bad case of nerves, and he hadn't been young then. Most of his teeth had gone the way of the blue suede shoe years ago, but he chewed his apple slice with the few he had left, jaws ruminating lazily from side to side. His mild dark eyes never left my face.

"You good business, Bart," I said, stroking his muzzle. "And I just love good business."

He nodded as if to say he knew it.

Pagan Starshine—Paig, to her friends—was feeding the chickens out of her apron. She couldn't wave, so she gave me a big rusty halloo, followed by the first two lines of "Mashed Potato Time." I joined her on the next two: it's the latest, it's the greatest, etc., etc. Pagan used to sing backup, and when she was in her prime, she sounded like one of the Pointer Sisters. She also smoked like a chimney, and by the age of forty, she sounded more like Joe Cocker at Woodstock.

Studio 1 was closed and dark. I lit it up and checked the bulletin board for that day's sessions. There were four: one at ten, one at two, one at six, and one at nine that would probably go on until past midnight. Studio 2 would be just as stacked. Nederland is a tiny burg nestled up on the Western Slope where the air is rare—less than fifteen hundred full-time residents—but it has a vital musical presence out of all proportion to its size; the bumper stickers reading NEDERLAND! WHERE NASHVILLE GETS HIGH! aren't a total exaggeration. Joe Walsh recorded his first album in Wolfjaw 1, when Hugh Yates's father ran the place, and John Denver recorded his last in Wolfjaw 2. Hugh once played me outtakes of Denver talking to his band about an experimental plane he'd just bought, something called a Long-EZ. Listening to it gave me the creeps.

There were nine downtown bars where you could hear live music any night of the week, and three recording operations besides ours. Wolfjaw Ranch was the biggest and best, though. On the day I stepped timidly into Hugh's office and told him Charles Jacobs had sent me, there were at least two dozen pictures on his walls, including Eddie Van Halen, Lynyrd Skynyrd, Axl Rose (in his prime), and U2. Yet the one he was proudest of—and the only one he was in himself—was of the Staples Singers. "Mavis Staples is a goddess," he told me. "The best woman singer in America. No one else even comes close."

I had recorded on my share of cheap singles and bad indie albums during my dues-paying years on the road, but never heard myself on a major label until I filled in at a Neil Diamond session for a rhythm guitarist who had come down with mono. I was terrified that day—sure I would just lean over and puke on my SG—but since then I'd played on lots of sessions, mostly as a fill-in but sometimes by request. The money wasn't great, but it was far from terrible. Weekends I played with the house band at a local bar called Comstock Lode, and had been known to filch gigs on the side in Denver. I also gave music lessons to aspiring high school players at a summer program Hugh inaugurated after his father died. It was called Rock-Atomic.

"I can't do that," I protested to Hugh when he suggested adding this to my duties. "I can't read music!"

"You can't read *notes* is what you mean," he said. "You can read tablature just fine, and that's all these kids want. Fortunately for us and them, it's all most of them need. You ain't going to find Segovia up here in the hills, my man."

He was right about that, and once my fright wore off, I enjoyed the lessons. They brought back memories of Chrome Roses, for one thing. For another . . . maybe I should be ashamed to say this, but the pleasure I felt working with the Rock-Atomic teenagers was similar to the pleasure I got from feeding Bartleby his morning apple slice and stroking his nose. Those kids just wanted to *rock*, and most of them discovered they could . . . once they mastered a bar E, that was.

Studio 2 was also dark, but Mookie McDonald had left the soundboard on. I shut everything down and made a note to talk to him about it. He was a good board guy, but forty years of smoking rope had made him forgetful. My Gibson SG was propped up with the rest of the instruments, because later that day I was going to play on a demo with a local rockabilly combo called Gotta Wanna. I sat on a stool and played tennis-racket style for ten minutes or so, stuff like "Hi-Heel Sneakers" and "Got My Mojo Working," just limbering up. I was better now than in my years on the road, much better, but I was still never going to be Clapton.

The phone rang—although in the studios, it didn't actually ring, just lit up blue around the edges. I put my guitar down and answered it. "Studio Two, Curtis Mayfield speaking."

"How's the afterlife, Curtis?" Hugh Yates asked.

"Dark. The good side is that I'm no longer paralyzed."

"Glad to hear it. Come on up here to the big house. I have something you should see."

"Jeez, man, we've got somebody recording a half an hour from now. I think that c&w chick with the long legs."

"Mookie will get her set up."

"No, he won't. He's not here yet. Also, he left the board on in Two. Again."

Hugh sighed. "I'll talk to him. Just come on up."

"Okay, but Hugh? *I'll* talk to the Mookster. My job, right?"

He laughed. "I sometimes wonder what happened to the wouldn't-say-shit-if-he-had-a-mouthful sad sack I hired," he said. "Come on. This'll blow your mind."

The big house was a sprawling ranch with Hugh's vintage Continental parked in the turnaround. The man was a fool for anything that slurped hi-test, and he could afford the indulgence. Although Wolfjaw did only a little better than break-even, there was a lot of elderly Yates family dough in blue chip investments, and Hugh—twice divorced, prenups in both, no children from either—was the last sprig on the Yates family tree. He kept horses, chickens, sheep, and a few pigs, but that was little more than a hobby. The same was true of his cars and collection of big-engine pickup trucks. What he cared about was music, and about that he cared deeply. He claimed to have once been a player himself, although I'd never seen him pick up a horn or a guitar.

"Music matters," he told me once. "Pop fiction goes away, TV shows go away, and I defy you to tell me what you saw at the movies two years ago. But music lasts, even pop music. *Especially* pop music. Sneer at 'Raindrops Keep Fallin' on My Head' if you want to, but people will still be listening to that silly piece of shit fifty years from now."

It was easy enough to remember the day I met him, because Wolfjaw looked the same, right down to the midnight-blue Connie with the opera windows parked in front. Only I had changed. He met me at the door on that day in the fall of 1992, shook my hand, and showed me into his office. There he plopped into a high-backed chair behind a desk that looked big enough to land a Piper Cub on. I was nervous following him in; when I saw all those famous faces looking down from the walls, what little saliva remaining in my mouth dried up entirely.

He looked me up and down—a visitor wearing a dirty AC/DC tee and even dirtier jeans—and said, "Charlie Jacobs called me. I've owed the Rev a large favor for quite a few years now. It's larger than I could ever repay, but he tells me you square it."

I stood there in front of the desk, tongue-tied. I knew how to audition for a band, but this was something different.

"He said you used to be a doper."

"Yes," I said. No point denying it.

"He said it was Big H."

"Yes."

"But now you're clean?"

"Yes."

I thought he'd ask me for how long, but he didn't. "Sit down, for God's sake. You want a Coke? A beer? Lemonade? Iced tea, maybe?"

I sat, but couldn't seem to relax against the back of my seat. "Iced tea sounds good."

He used the intercom on his desk. "Georgia? Two iced teas, honey." Then, to me: "This is a working ranch, Jamie, but the livestock I care about are the animals who show up with instruments."

I tried a smile, but it made me feel moronic and I gave up on it.

He seemed not to notice. "Rock bands, country bands, solo artists. They're our bread and butter, but we also do commercial jingles for the Denver radio stations and twenty or thirty recorded books each year. Michael Douglas recorded a Faulkner novel at Wolfjaw, and Georgia 'bout peed her pants. He's got that easygoing public persona, but whoo, what a perfectionist in the studio."

I couldn't think of a reply to this, so kept silent and rooted for the iced tea. My mouth was as dry as a desert.

He leaned forward. "Do you know what every working ranch needs more than anything else?"

I shook my head, but before he could elucidate further, a pretty young black woman came in with two tall, ice-choked glasses of iced tea on a silver tray. There was a sprig of mint in each. I squeezed two lemon slices into my tea, but left the sugar bowl alone. During my heroin years I had been a bear for sugar, but since that day with the headphones in the auto body shop, any sweetness seemed cloying to me. I had bought a Hershey bar in the dining car shortly after leaving Tulsa, and found I couldn't eat it. Just smelling it made me feel like gagging.

"Thank you, Georgia," Yates said.

"Very welcome. Don't forget visiting hours. They start at two and Les will be expecting you."

"I'll remember." She went out, closing the door softly behind her, and he turned back to me. "What every working ranch needs is a foreman. The one who takes care of the ranching and farming side here at Wolfjaw is Rupert Hall. He's fine and well, but my *music* foreman is recuperating in Boulder Community Hospital. Les Calloway. Don't suppose the name means anything to you."

I shook my head.

"What about the Excellent Board Brothers?"

That rang a bell. "Instrumental group, weren't they? Surf sound, kind of like Dick Dale and His Del-Tones?"

"Yeah, that was them. Kind of weird, seeing as how they all

hailed from Colorado, which is about as far from both oceans as you can get. Had one top forty hit—'Aloona Ana Kaya.' Which is very bad Hawaiian for 'Let's have sex.'"

"Sure, I remember that." Of course I did; my sister played it about a billion times. "It's the one with the girl laughing all the way through it."

Yates grinned. "That laugh was their ticket to one-hit-wonderdom, and I'm the daddy-o who put it on the record. No more than an afterthought, really. This was when my father ran the place. And the girl who's laughing her ass off also works here. Hillary Katz, although these days she calls herself Pagan Starshine. She's sober now, but on that day she was so stoned on nitrous she couldn't *stop* laughing. I recorded her right there in the booth—she had no idea. It made that record, and they cut her in for seven grand."

I nodded. The annals of rock are full of similar lucky accidents.

"Anyway, the Excellent Board Brothers had one tour, then did the two brokes. You know those?"

I certainly did, and from personal experience. "Went broke and broke up."

"Uh-huh. Les came home and went to work for me. He produces better than he ever played, and he's been my chief ramrod on the music side for going on fifteen years now. When Charlie Jacobs called me, my idea was to make you Les's understudy, thinking you could earn while you learn, play some gigs on the side, all the usual shit. That's still the idea, but your learning curve better be goddam steep, son, because Les had a heart attack last week. He's gonna be okay—so I'm told—but he's got to lose a bunch of weight and take a bunch of pills and he's talking about retiring in a year or so. Which will give me plenty of time to see if you're gonna work out."

I felt something close to panic. "Mr. Yates—"

"Hugh."

"Hugh, I know next to nothing about A&R. The only recording studios I've ever been in are the ones where the group I was playing with paid for time by the hour."

"Mostly with the lead guitarist's doting parents footing the bill," he said. "Or the drummer's wife, waitressing eight hours a day and hustling tips on sore feet."

Yes, that was pretty much how it went. Until wifey wised up, that was, and put him out of doors.

He leaned forward, hands clasped. "You'll either learn or you won't. The Rev says you will. That's good enough for me. Got to be. I owe him. For now, all you have to do is light up the studios, keep track of AH—you know what that is, don't you?"

"Artists' hours."

"Uh-huh, and lock up at night. I've got a guy who can show you the ropes until Les gets back. Mookie McDonald's his name. If you pay as much attention to what Mookie does wrong as to what he does right, you'll learn a lot. Don't let him keep the log, whatever you do. And one more thing. If you smoke some rope, that's your business as long as you show up for work on time and don't start a grassfire. But if I hear you're riding the pink horse again . . ."

I made myself look him in the eye. "I'm not going back to that."

"A brave statement, and one I've heard many times, in a few cases from people who are now dead. Sometimes, though, it turns out to be true. I hope it will be in your case. But just so we're clear: you use and you're gone, favor owed or no favor owed. Are we clear on that?"

We were. Crystal.

Georgia Donlin was just as beautiful in 2008 as in 1992, but she'd put on a few pounds, there were streaks of silver in her dark hair, and she was wearing bifocals. "You don't happen to know what's got him all fired up this morning, do you?" she asked me.

"No clue."

"He started cussing, then he laughed a little, then he started cussing again. Said he fucking knew it, said that son of a bitch, then threw something, it sounded like. All I want to know is if somebody's gonna get fired. If that's the case, I'm taking a sick day. I can't deal with confrontation."

"Says the woman who threw a pot at the meat delivery man last winter."

"That was different. That four-oh-four son of a bitch tried to caress my butt."

"A four-oh-four with good taste," I remarked, and when she gave me the stinkeye: "Just sayin."

"Huh. Last few minutes it's been all quiet in there. I hope he didn't give himself a heart attack."

"Maybe it was something he saw on TV. Or read in the paper?"

"TV went off fifteen minutes after I came in, and as for the *Camera* and the *Post*, he stopped takin em two months ago. Says he gets everything from the Internet. I tell him, 'Hugh, all that Internet news is written by boys not old enough to shave and girls hardly out of their training bras. It's not to be trusted.' He thinks I'm just a clueless old lady. He doesn't say it, but I can see it in his eyes. Like I don't have a daughter who's taking computer courses at CU. *Bree*'s the one who told me not to trust that bloggish crap. Go on, now. But if he's sittin in his chair dead of vapor lock, don't call me to give him CPR."

She moved away, tall and regal, the gliding walk no different from that of the young woman who had brought the iced tea into Hugh's office sixteen years before.

I tapped a knuckle on the door. Hugh wasn't dead, but he was slumped behind his oversize desk, rubbing his temples like a man with a migraine. His laptop was open in front of him.

"Are you going to fire someone?" I asked.

He looked up. "Huh?"

"Georgia says if you're going to fire someone, she's taking a sick day."

"I'm not going to fire anyone. That's ridiculous."

"She says you threw something."

"Bullshit." He paused. "I *did* kick the wastebasket when I saw the shit about the holy rings."

"Tell *me* about the holy rings. Then I'll give the wastebasket another ritual kick and go to work. I've got sixteen billion things to do today, including learning two tunes for that Gotta Wanna session. A wastebasket field goal might be just the thing to get me jump-started."

Hugh went back to rubbing his temples. "I thought this might happen, I knew he had it in him, but I never expected anything quite this . . . this *grand*. But you know what they say—go big or go home."

"No fucking clue what you're talking about."

"You will, Jamie, you will."

I parked my butt on the corner of his desk.

"Every morning I watch the six AM news while I do my crunches and pedal the stationary bike, okay? Mostly because watching the weather chick has its own aerobic benefits. And this morning I saw an ad for something besides magic wrinkle creams and Time-Warner golden oldie collections. I couldn't believe it. Couldn't, fucking, believe it. At the same time I could." He laughed then, not a *this-is-funny* laugh but an *I-can't-fucking-believe-it* laugh. "So I turn off the idiot box and investigate further on the Internet."

I started around his desk but he held up a hand to stop me. "First I have to ask you if you'll go on a man-date with me, Jamie. To see someone who has—after a couple of false starts—finally realized his destiny."

"Sure, I guess so. As long as it isn't a Justin Bieber concert. I'm a little long in the tooth for the Bieb."

"Oh, this is much better than the Bieb. Take a look. Just don't let it burn your eyes."

I walked around the desk and met my fifth business for the third time. The first thing I noticed was the hokey hypnotist's stare. His hands were spread to either side of his face, and he was wearing a thick gold band on the third finger of each.

It was a poster on a website headed PASTOR C. DANNY JACOBS HEALING REVIVAL TOUR 2008.

OLD-TIME TENT REVIVAL!

JUNE 13–15
NORRIS COUNTY FAIRGROUNDS
20 Miles East of Denver

FEATURING FORMER "SOUL SINGER" AL STAMPER

FEATURING THE GOSPEL ROBINS, WITH DEVINA ROBINSON

AND

EVANGELIST C. DANNY JACOBS

AS SEEN ON THE DANNY JACOBS HOUR OF HEALING GOSPEL POWER

REVIVAL

RENEW YOUR SOUL THROUGH SONG
REFRESH YOUR FAITH THROUGH HEALING
THRILL TO THE STORY OF THE HOLY RINGS,
TOLD AS ONLY PASTOR DANNY CAN!

"Bring hither the poor, and the maimed, and the halt, and the blind; compel them to come in, that my house may be filled." Luke 14:21 and 23.

WITNESS GOD'S POWER TO CHANGE YOUR LIFE!

FRIDAY 13TH: 7 PM
SATURDAY 14TH: 2 PM and 7 PM
SUNDAY 15TH: 2 PM and 7 PM

GOD SPEAKS SOFTLY (1 KINGS 19:12)
GOD HEALS LIKE LIGHTNING (MATTHEW 24:27)

COME ONE!

COME ALL!

BE RENEWED!

At the bottom was a photo of a boy throwing away his crutches while a congregation stood watching with expressions of joyous awe. The caption below the photo read *Robert Rivard, healed of MUSCULAR DYSTROPHY 5/30/07, St. Louis, Mo.*

I was stunned, the way a person would be, I suppose, if he caught sight of an old friend who has been reported dead or arrested for committing a serious crime. Yet part of me—the changed part, the healed part—wasn't surprised. That part of me had been waiting for this all along.

Hugh laughed and said, "Man, you look like a bird flew into your mouth and you swallowed it." Then he spoke aloud the only coherent thought I had in my brain at that moment. "Looks like the Rev's up to his old tricks."

"Yes," I said, then pointed at the reference to the Book of Matthew. "But that verse isn't about healing."

He raised his eyebrows. "I never knew you were a Bible scholar."

"There's a lot you don't know," I said, "because we never talk about him. But I knew Charlie Jacobs long before Tulsa. When I was a little boy, he was the minister at our church. It was his first pastoral job, and I would have guessed it was his last. Until now."

His smile went away. "You're shitting me! How old was he, eighteen?"

"I think around twenty-five. I was six or seven."

"Was he healing people back then?"

"Not at all." Except for my brother Con, that was. "In those days he was straight-up Methodist—you know, Welch's grape juice at communion instead of wine. Everyone liked him." At least until the Terrible Sermon. "He quit after he lost his wife and son in a road accident."

"The Rev was married? He had a kid?"

"Yes."

Hugh considered. "So he's actually got a right to at least one of those wedding rings—if they *are* wedding rings. Which I doubt. Look at this."

He went to the band at the top of the website page, put the cursor on MIRACLE TESTIMONY, and clicked. The screen now showed a line of YouTube videos. There were at least a dozen.

"Hugh, if you want to go see Charlie Jacobs, I'm happy to tag along, but I really don't have time to discuss him this morning."

He regarded me closely. "You *don't* look like someone who swallowed a bird. You look like somebody gave you a hard punch to the gut. Look at this one vid, and I'll let you go."

Halfway down was the boy from the poster. When Hugh clicked on it, I saw the clip, which was only a little over a minute long, had racked up better than a hundred thousand views. Not quite viral, but close.

When the picture started to move, someone shoved a microphone with KSDK on it into Robert Rivard's face. An unseen woman said, "Describe what happened when this so-called healing took place, Bobby."

"Well, ma'am," Bobby said, "when he grabbed on my head, I could feel the holy wedding rings on the sides, right here." He indicated his temples. "I heard a snap, like a stick of kin'lin wood. I might have passed out for a second or two. Then this . . . I don't know . . . *warmth* went down my legs . . . and . . ." The boy began to weep. "And I could stand on em. I could walk! I was healed! God bless Pastor Danny!"

Hugh sat back. "I haven't watched all the other testimonials, but the ones I *have* watched are pretty much the same. Remind you of anything?"

"Maybe," I said. Cautiously. "What about you?"

We had never discussed the favor "the Rev" had done for Hugh—a favor big enough to cause the boss of the Wolfjaw Ranch to hire a barely straight heroin addict on the basis of a phone call.

"Not while you're pressed for time. What are you doing for lunch?"

"Ordering in pizza. After the c&w chick exits, there's a guy from Longmont . . . sheet says he's 'a baritone interpreter of popular song' . . ."

Hugh looked blank for a moment, then slapped his forehead with the heel of his hand. "Oh my God, is it George Damon?"

"Yeah, that's the name."

"Christ, I thought that sucker was dead. It's been years—before your time. The first record he made with us was *Damon Does Gershwin*. Long before CDs this was, although eight-tracks might have been around. Every song, and I mean *every fucking song*, sounded like Kate Smith singing 'God Bless America.' Let Mookie handle him. They go back. If the Mookster screws up, you can fix it in the mix."

"You sure?"

"Yes. If we're going to see the Rev's fine and holy shit-show, I want to hear what you know about him first. Probably we should have had this conversation years ago."

I thought that over. "Okay . . . but if you want to get, you have to give. A full and fair exchange of information."

He laced his hands together on the not inconsiderable middle of his western-style shirt and rocked back in his chair. "It's nothing I'm ashamed of, if that's what you're thinking. It's just so . . . unbelievable."

"I'll believe it," I said.

"Maybe so. Before you leave, tell me what that verse in Matthew says, and how you know it."

"I can't quote it exactly after so many years, but it's something like, 'As the lightning flashes from east to west, covering the sky, so shall be the coming of Jesus.' It's not about healing, it's about the apocalypse. And I remember it because it was one of Reverend Jacobs's favorites."

I glanced at the clock. The long-legged country girl—Mandy something-or-other—was a chronic early bird, she was probably already sitting on the steps outside Studio 1 with her guitar propped up beside her, but there was one thing I had to know right then. "What did you mean when you said you doubted they were wedding rings?"

"Didn't use the rings on you, huh? When he took care of your little drug problem?"

I thought of the abandoned auto body shop. "Nope. Headphones."

"This was in what? 1992?"

"Yes."

"My experience with the Rev was in 1983. He must have updated his MO in the time between. He probably went back to the rings because they seem more religious than headphones. But I bet he's moved ahead with his work since my time . . . *and* yours. That's the Rev, wouldn't you say? Always trying to take it to the next level?"

"You call him the Rev. Was he preaching when you met him?"

"Yes and no. It's complicated. Go on, get out of here, your girl will be waiting. Maybe she'll be wearing a miniskirt. That'll take your mind off Pastor Danny."

As a matter of fact, she *was* wearing a mini, and those legs were definitely spectacular. I hardly noticed them, though, and I couldn't tell you a thing she sang that day without checking the log. My mind was on Charles Daniel Jacobs, aka the Rev. Now known as Pastor Danny.

Mookie McDonald bore his scolding about the soundboard quietly, head down, nodding, at the end promising he would do better. He would, too. For awhile. Then, a week or two from now, I'd come in and find the board on again in 1, 2, or both. I think the idea of putting people in jail for smoking the rope is ludicrous, but there's no doubt in my mind that long-term daily use is a recipe for CRS, also known as Can't Remember Shit.

He brightened up when I told him he'd be recording George Damon. "I always loved that guy!" the Mookster exclaimed. "Everything he sang sounded like—"

"Kate Smith singing 'God Bless America.' I know. Have a good time."

There was a pretty little picnic area in a grove of alders behind the big house. Georgia and a couple of the office girls were having their lunch there. Hugh led me to a table well away from theirs and took a couple of wrapped sandwiches and two cans of Dr Pepper from his capacious manpurse. "Got chicken salad and tuna salad from Tubby's. You choose."

I chose tuna. We ate in silence for awhile, there in the shadow of the big mountains, and then Hugh said, "I also used to play rhythm, you know, and I was quite a bit better than you."

"Many are."

"At the end of my career I was in a band out of Michigan called Johnson Cats."

"From the seventies? The guys who wore those Army shirts and sounded like the Eagles?"

"It was actually the early eighties when we broke through, but yeah, that was us. Had four hit singles, all off the first album. And do you want to know what got that album noticed in the first place? The title and the jacket, both my idea. It was called *Your Uncle Jack Plays All the Monster Hits*, and it had my very own Uncle Jack Yates on the cover, sitting in his living room and strumming his ukulele. Inside, lots of heaviness and monster fuzz-tone. No wonder it didn't win Best Album at the Grammys. That was the era of Toto. Fucking 'Africa,' what a piece of crap that was."

He brooded.

"Anyway, I was in the Cats, had been for two years, and that's me on the breakout record. Played the first two tour dates, then got let go."

"Why?" Thinking, *It must have been drugs. Back then it always was.* But he surprised me.

"I went deaf."

The Johnson Cats tour started in Bloomington—Circus One—then moved on to the Congress Theater in Oak Park. Small venues, warmup gigs with local ax-whackers to open. Then to Detroit, where the big stuff was scheduled to start: thirty cities, with Johnson Cats as the opening act for Bob Seger and the Silver Bullet Band. Arena rock, the real deal. What you dream of.

The ringing in Hugh's ears started in Bloomington. At first he dismissed it as just part of the price you paid when you sold your soul for rock and roll—what self-respecting player didn't suffer tinnitus from time to time? Look at Pete Townshend. Eric Clapton, Neil Young. Then, in Oak Park, the vertigo and nausea started. Halfway through their set, Hugh reeled offstage and hurled into a bucket filled with sand.

"I still remember the sign on the post above it," he told me. "USE FOR SMALL FIRES ONLY."

He finished the gig—somehow—took his bows, and reeled offstage.

"What's wrong with you?" Felix Granby asked. He was the lead guitarist and lead vocalist, which meant to the public at large—the portion of it that rocked, at least—he *was* Johnson Cats. "Are you drunk?"

"Stomach flu," Hugh said. "It's getting better."

He thought it was true; with the amps off, the tinnitus did seem to be ebbing. But the next morning it was back, and other than the hellish ringing, he could hear almost nothing.

Two members of Johnson Cats fully grasped looming disaster:

Felix Granby and Hugh himself. Only three days ahead was the Silverdome, in Pontiac. Capacity ninety thousand. With Detroit favorite Bob Seger headlining, it would be almost full. The JC was on the cusp of fame, and in rock and roll, such chances rarely come around a second time. So Felix Granby had done to Hugh what Kelly Van Dorn of White Lightning had done to me.

"I bore him no grudge," Hugh said. "If our positions had been reversed, I might have done the same. He hired a session player out of L'Amour Studio in Detroit, and it was that guy who went onstage with them that night at the Dome."

Granby did the firing in person, not by talking but by writing notes and holding them up for Hugh to read. He pointed out that while the other members of the JC came from middle-class families, Hugh was from real money. He could fly back to Colorado in a comfy seat at the front of the plane, and consult all the best doctors. Granby's last note, written in capital letters, read: U WILL BE BACK WITH US BEFORE U KNOW IT.

"As if," Hugh said as we sat in the shade, eating our sandwiches from Tubby's.

"You still miss it, don't you?" I asked.

"No." Long pause. "Yes."

He did not go back to Colorado.

"If I had've, I sure wouldn't have flown. I had an idea my head might explode once we got above twenty thousand feet. Besides, home wasn't what I wanted. All I wanted to do was lick my wounds, which were still bleeding, and Detroit was as good a lickin place as any. That's the story I told myself, anyway."

The symptoms did not abate: vertigo, nausea ranging from moderate to severe, and always that hellish ringing, sometimes soft, sometimes so loud he thought his head would split open. On occasion all these symptoms would draw back like a tide going out, and then he would sleep for ten or even twelve hours at a stretch.

Although he could have afforded better, he was living in a fleabag hotel on Grand Avenue. For two weeks he put off going to a doctor, terrified that he would be told he had a malignant and inoperable brain tumor. When he finally did force himself into a doc-in-the-box on Inkster Road, a Hindu medic who looked about seventeen listened, nodded, did a few tests, and urged Hugh to check himself into a hospital for more tests, plus experimental antinausea medications he himself could not prescribe, so sorry.

Instead of going to the hospital, Hugh began taking long and pointless safaris (when the vertigo permitted it, that was) up and down the fabled stretch of Detroit road known as 8-Mile. One day he passed a storefront with radios, guitars, record players, tape decks, amplifiers, and TVs in the dusty window. According to the sign, this was Jacobs New & Used Electronics . . . although to Hugh Yates, most of it looked beat to shit and none of it looked new.

"I can't tell you exactly why I went in. Maybe it was some creeped-out nostalgia for all that audio candy. Maybe it was self-flagellation. Maybe I just thought the place would be air-conditioned, and I could get out of the heat—boy, was I ever wrong about that. Or maybe it was the sign over the door."

"What did it say?" I asked.

Hugh smiled at me. "*You Can Trust the Rev.*"

He was the only customer. The shelves were packed with equipment a lot more exotic than the wares in the window. Some stuff he knew: meters, oscilloscopes, voltometers and voltage regulators, amplitude regulators, rectifiers, power inverters. Other stuff he didn't recognize. Electric cords snaked across the floor and wires were strung everywhere.

The proprietor came out through a door framed in blinking Christmas lights ("Probably a bell jingled when I came in, but I sure didn't hear it," Hugh said). My old fifth business was dressed in faded jeans and a plain white shirt buttoned to the collar. His mouth moved in *Hello* and something that might have been *Can I help you*. Hugh tipped him a wave, shook his head, and browsed along the shelves. He picked up a Stratocaster and gave it a strum, wondering if it was in tune.

Jacobs watched him with interest but no detectable concern, although Hugh's rock-dog 'do now hung in unwashed clumps to his shoulders and his clothes were equally dirty. After five minutes or so, just as he was losing interest and getting ready to walk back to the fleabag where he now hung his hat, the vertigo hit. He reeled, putting out one hand and knocking over a disassembled stereo speaker. He almost recovered, but he hadn't been eating much, and the world turned gray. Before he hit the shop's dusty wooden floor, it had turned black. It was my story all over again. Only the location was different.

When he woke up, he was in Jacobs's office with a cold cloth on his forehead. Hugh apologized and said he would pay for anything he might have broken. Jacobs drew back, blinking in surprise. This was a reaction Hugh had seen often in the last weeks.

"Sorry if I'm talking too loud," Hugh said. "I can't hear myself. I'm deaf."

Jacobs rummaged a notepad from the top drawer of his cluttered desk (I could imagine that desk, littered with snips of wire and batteries). He jotted and held the pad up.

Recent? I saw you w/ guitar.

"Recent," Hugh agreed. "I have something called Ménière's disease. I'm a musician." He considered that and laughed . . . soundlessly to his own ears, although Jacobs responded with a smile. "*Used* to be, anyhow."

Jacobs turned a page in his notebook, wrote briefly, and held it up: *If it's Ménière's, I might be able to do something for you.*

"Obviously he did," I said.

Lunch hour was over; the girls had gone back inside. There was stuff I could be doing—plenty—but I had no intention of leaving until I heard the rest of Hugh's story.

"We sat in his office for a long time—conversation's slow when one person has to write his side of it. I asked him how he thought he could help me. He wrote that just lately he'd been experimenting with transcutaneous electrical nerve stimulation, TENS for short. He said the idea of using electricity to stimulate damaged nerves went back thousands of years, that it was invented by some old Roman—"

A dusty door far back in my memory opened. "An old Roman named Scribonius. He discovered that if a guy with a bad leg stepped on an electric eel, the pain sometimes went away. And that 'just lately' stuff was crap, Hugh. Your Rev was playing around with TENS before it was officially invented."

He stared at me, eyebrows up.

"Go on," I said.

"Okay, but we'll come back to this, right?"

I nodded. "You show me yours, I show you mine. That was the deal. I'll give you a hint: there's a fainting spell in my story, too."

"Well . . . I told him that Ménière's disease was a mystery—doctors didn't know if it had to do with the nerves, or if it was a virus causing a chronic buildup of fluid in the middle ear, or some kind of bacterial thing, or maybe genetic. He wrote, *All diseases are electrical in nature.* I said that was crazy. He just smiled, turned to a new page in his pad, and wrote for a longer time. Then he handed it across to me. I can't quote it exactly—it's been a long time—but I'll never forget the first sentence: *Electricity is the basis of all life.*"

That was Jacobs, all right. The line was better than a fingerprint.

"The rest said something like, *Take your heart. It runs on microvolts. This current is provided by potassium, an electrolyte. Your body converts potassium into ions—electrically charged particles—and uses them to regulate not just your heart but your brain and EVERYTHING ELSE.*

"Those last words were in capitals. He put a circle around them. When I handed his pad back, he drew something on it, very quick, then pointed to my eyes, my ears, my chest, my stomach, and my legs. Then he showed me what he'd drawn. It was a lightning bolt."

Sure it was.

"Cut to the chase, Hugh."

"Well . . ."

Hugh said he'd have to think it over. What he didn't say (but was certainly thinking) was that he didn't know Jacobs from Adam; the guy could be one of the crazybirds that flap around every big city.

Jacobs wrote that he understood Hugh's hesitation, and felt plenty of his own. "I'm going out on a limb to even make the offer. After all, I don't know you any more than you know me."

"Is it dangerous?" Hugh asked in a voice that was already losing tone and inflection, becoming robotic.

The Rev shrugged and wrote.

Won't kid you, there is some risk involved in applying electricity directly through the ears. But LOW VOLTAGE, OK? I'd guess the worst side effect you'd suffer might be peeing your pants.

"This is crazy," Hugh said. "We're insane just to be having this discussion."

The Rev shrugged again, but this time didn't write. Only looked.

Hugh sat in the office, the cloth (still damp but now warm) clutched in one hand, seriously considering Jacobs's proposal, and a large part of his mind found serious consideration, even on such short acquaintance, perfectly normal. He was a musician who had gone deaf and been cast aside by a band he'd helped to found, one now on the verge of national success. Other players and at least one great composer—Beethoven—had lived with deafness, but hearing loss wasn't where Hugh's woes ended. There was the vertigo, the trembling, the periodic loss of vision. There was nausea, vomiting, diarrhea, galloping pulse. Worst of all was the almost constant tinnitus. He had always thought deafness meant silence. This was not true, at least not in his case. Hugh Yates had a constantly braying burglar alarm in the middle of his head.

There was another factor, too. A truth not acknowledged until then, but glimpsed from time to time, as if in the corner of the eye. He had remained in Detroit because he was working up his courage. There were many pawnshops on 8-Mile, and all of them sold barrel-iron. Was what this guy was offering any worse than the muzzle of a thirdhand .38 socked between his teeth and pointing at the roof of his mouth?

In his too-loud robot's voice, he said, "What the fuck. Go ahead."

Hugh gazed at the mountains while he told the rest, his right hand stroking his right ear as he spoke. I don't think he knew he was doing it.

"He put a CLOSED sign in the window, locked the door, and dropped the blinds. Then he sat me down in a kitchen chair by the cash register and put a steel case the size of a footlocker on the counter. Inside it were two metal rings wrapped in what looked like gold mesh. They were about the size of those big dangly earrings Georgia wears when she's stylin. You know the ones I mean?"

"Sure."

"There was a rubber widget on the bottom of each, with a wire coming out of it. The wires ran into a control box no bigger than a doorbell. He opened the bottom of the box and showed me what looked like a single triple-A battery. I relaxed. That *can't do much damage*, I thought, but I didn't feel quite so comfortable when he put on rubber gloves—you know, like the kind women wear when they're washing dishes—and picked up the rings with tongs."

"I think Charlie's triple-A batteries are different from the ones you buy in the store," I said. "A lot more powerful. Didn't he ever talk to you about the secret electricity?"

"Oh God, many times. It was his hobbyhorse. But that was later, and I never made head or tail of it. I'm not sure he did, either. He'd get a look in his eyes . . ."

"Puzzled," I said. "Puzzled, worried, and excited, all at the same time."

"Yeah, like that. He put the rings against my ears—using the tongs, you know—and then asked me to push the button on the control unit, since his own hands were full. I almost didn't, but I flashed on the pistols in all those pawnshop windows, and I did it."

"Then blacked out." I didn't ask it as a question, because I was sure of it. But he surprised me.

"There were blackouts, all right, and what I called prismatics, but they came later. Right then there was just an almighty *snapping* sound in the middle of my head. My legs shot out and my hands went up over my head like a schoolkid who's just desperate to tell the teacher he knows the right answer."

That brought back memories.

"Also, there was a taste in my mouth. Like I'd been sucking on pennies. I asked Jacobs if I could have a drink of water, and *heard* myself asking, and broke into tears. I cried for quite awhile. He held me." At last Hugh turned from the mountains and looked at me. "After that I would have done anything for him, Jamie. *Anything*."

"I know the feeling."

"When I had control of myself again, he took me back out into the shop and put a pair of Koss headphones on me. He plugged into an FM station and kept turning the music down and asking me if I could hear it. I did until he got all the way to zero, and I could almost swear I even heard it then. He not only brought my hearing back, it was more acute than it had been since I was fourteen, and playing with my first jam-band."

Hugh asked how he could repay Jacobs. The Rev, only a scruffy guy in need of a haircut and a bath, considered this.

"Tell you what," he said at last. "There's little in the way of business here, and some of the people who do wander in are pretty sketchy. I'm going to transport all this stuff to a storage facility on the North Side while I think about what to do next. You could help me."

"I can do better than that," Hugh said, still relishing the sound of his own voice. "I'll rent the storage space myself, and hire a crew to move everything. I don't look like I can afford it, but I can. Really."

Jacobs seemed horrified at the idea. "Absolutely not! The goods

I have for sale are mostly junk, but my equipment is valuable, and much of it in the back area—my lab—is delicate, as well. Your help would be more than enough repayment. Although first you need to rest a little. And eat. Put on a few pounds. You've been through a difficult time. Would you be interested in becoming my assistant, Mr. Yates?"

"If that's what you want," Hugh said. "Mr. Jacobs, I still can't believe you're talking and I'm hearing you."

"In a week, you'll take it for granted," he said dismissively. "That's the way it works with miracles. No use railing against it; it's plain old human nature. But since we *have* shared a miracle in this overlooked corner of the Motor City, I can't have you calling me Mr. Jacobs. To you, let me be the Rev."

"As in Reverend?"

"Exactly," he said, and grinned. "Reverend Charles D. Jacobs, currently chief prelate in the First Church of Electricity. And I promise not to work you too hard. There's no hurry; we'll take our time."

"I'll bet you did," I said.

"What's that supposed to mean?"

"He didn't want you to buy him a moving crew, and he didn't want your money. He wanted your time. I think he was studying you. Looking for aftereffects. What did *you* think?"

"Then? Nothing. I was riding a mighty cloud of joy. If the Rev had asked me to rob First of Detroit, I might have given it a shot. Looking back on it, though, you could be right. There wasn't much to the work, after all, because when you came right down to it, he had very little to sell. There was more in his back room, but with a big enough U-Haul, we could have moved the whole kit and caboodle off the 8-Mile in two days. But he strung it out over a week." He considered. "Yeah, okay. He was watching me."

"*Studying*. Looking for aftereffects." I peeked at my watch. I had to be in the studio in fifteen minutes, and if I lingered longer in the picnic area I was going to be late. "Walk with me down to Studio One. Tell me what they were."

We walked, and Hugh told me about the blackouts that had followed Jacobs's electrical treatment for deafness. They were brief but frequent in the first couple of days, and there was no actual sense of unconsciousness. He would just find himself in a different place and discover that five minutes had gone by. Or ten. On two occasions it happened while he and Jacobs were loading equipment and secondhand sales goods into an old plumbing-supply panel truck Jacobs had borrowed from someone (maybe from another of his miracle cures, although if that was the case, Hugh never found out—the Rev was closemouthed about such things).

"I asked him what happened during those times, and he said nothing, that we just went on moving stuff and conversing like normal."

"Did you believe him?"

"I did at the time. Now I don't know."

One night, Hugh said—this would have been five or six days post-treatment—he was sitting in his fleabag hotel room's one chair, reading a book, and suddenly found himself standing in the corner, facing the wall.

"Were you saying anything?" I asked, thinking, *Something happened. Something, something, something.*

"No," he said. "But . . ."

"But what?"

He shook his head at the memory. "I'd taken off my pants, then put my sneakers back on. I was just standing there in my Jockey shorts and Reeboks. Crazy, huh?"

"*Muy loco,*" I said. "How long did these mini-lapses go on?"

"The second week there were only a couple. By the third week they were gone. But there was something else that lasted longer. Something with my eyes. These . . . events. The prismatics. I don't know what else to call them. They happened maybe a dozen times over the next five years. Nothing at all since then."

We had reached the studio. Mookie was waiting for us, his Broncos gimme cap turned around backward, making him look like the world's oldest skateboarder. "The band's in there. They're practicing." He lowered his voice. "Dudes, they're fucking horrible."

"Tell them we'll be starting late," I said. "We'll give them extra time on the other end to make up for it."

Mookie looked from Hugh to me and then back to Hugh—taking the emotional temperature. "Hey, nobody's gonna get fired, are they?"

"Not unless you leave the soundboard on again," Hugh said. "Now get in there and let the adults talk."

Mookie saluted and went inside.

Hugh turned back to me. "The prismatics were much weirder than the blackouts. I don't really know how to describe them. Like the man said, you had to be there."

"Try."

"I always knew when it was going to happen. I'd be going along through my day, you know, business as usual, and then my vision would seem to *sharpen.*"

"Like your hearing after the treatment?"

He shook his head. "No, that was real. My ears are still better now than they were before the Rev's treatment, and I know a hearing test would prove it, although I've never bothered to get one. No, the vision thing was . . . you know how epileptics can tell a seizure is coming by a tingling in their wrists, or some phantom smell?"

"Precursors."

"Right. That sense I got of my vision sharpening was a precursor. What happened after was . . . color."

"Color."

"The world filled with reds, blues, and greens at the edges of things. The colors would shift back and forth. It was like looking through a prism, but one that magnified things at the same time it was shattering them into pieces." He patted his forehead, a gentle gesture of frustration. "That's as close as I can get. And during the thirty or forty seconds it was happening, it was as if I could almost look through the world, and there was another world right behind it. A *realer* world."

He looked at me soberly.

"Those were the prismatics. I've never talked about them to anyone until today. They scared the hell out of me."

"You never even told the Rev?"

"I would've, but he was already gone the first time it happened. No big goodbyes, just a note saying he had a business opportunity in Joplin. This was six months or so after the miracle cure, and I was back in here in Nederland. The prismatics . . . they were beautiful in a way I could never describe, but I hope they never come back. Because if that other world is really there, I don't want to see it. And if it's in my mind, I want it to stay there."

Mookie came out. "They're hot to go, Jamie. I'll roll some sound, if you want. I sure can't fuck it up, because these guys make the Dead Milkmen sound like the Beatles."

That might be, but they had paid cash for their session. "No, I'll be right in. Tell them two more minutes."

He disappeared.

"So," Hugh said. "You got mine, but I didn't get yours. And I still want it."

"I've got an hour around nine tonight. I'll come up to the big house and tell you then. It won't take long. My story is basically the same as yours: treatment, cure, aftereffects that attenuated, then passed completely." Not quite true, but I had a session to record.

"No prismatics?"

"Nope. Other stuff. Tourette's without the swearing, for one thing." I decided I'd keep the dreams of dead family members to myself, at least for the time being. Maybe they were *my* glimpses of Hugh's other world.

"We ought to go see him." Hugh gripped my arm. "We really ought to."

"I think you're right."

"But no big reunion dinner, okay? I don't even want to talk to him, just observe."

"Fine," I said, and looked down at his hand. "Now let go of me before you leave a bruise. I have to record some music."

He let go. I went into the studio, and the sound of some local punk band playing leather-jacket-and-safety-pin stuff the Ramones did a lot better back in the '70s. When I looked back over my shoulder, Hugh was still standing there, looking at the mountains.

The world beyond the world, I thought, then put it out of my mind—or tried to—and went to work.

I didn't break down and get a laptop of my own for another year, but there was plenty of computing power in Studios 1 and 2—by 2008 we were recording almost everything with Mac programs—and when I got a break around five, I googled C. Danny Jacobs and found thousands of references. Apparently I'd missed quite a lot since "C. Danny" first appeared on the national scene ten years before, but I didn't blame myself. I'm not much of a TV watcher, my interest in popular culture revolved around music, and my churchgoing days were long over. No wonder I had missed the preacher his Wikipedia entry called "the twenty-first-century Oral Roberts."

He had no megachurch, but his weekly *Hour of Healing Gospel Power* was telecast from coast to coast on high cable channels where the buy-in price was low and the return in "love offerings" was presumably high. The shows were taped at his Old-Time Tent Revivals, which crisscrossed most of the country (steering clear of the East Coast, where people were presumably a bit less credulous). In pictures taken over the years, I watched Jacobs grow older and grayer, but the look in his eyes never changed: fanatical and somehow wounded.

A week or so before Hugh and I made our trip to see Jacobs in his native environment, I called Georgia Donlin and asked if I could have her daughter's number—the one who was studying computers at Colorado University. The daughter's name was Brianna.

Bree and I had an extremely interesting conversation.

VIII

Tent Show.

It was seventy miles from Nederland to the Norris County Fairgrounds, which gave Hugh and me plenty of time to talk, but we said almost nothing until we were east of Denver; just sat and looked at the scenery. Except for the ever-present smog line over Arvada, it was a perfect late summer day.

Then Hugh snapped off the radio, which had been playing a steady stream of oldies on KXKL, and said: "Did your brother Conrad have any lingering effects after the Rev fixed up his laryngitis, or whatever it was?"

"No, but that's not surprising. Jacobs said the cure was bogus, a placebo, and I always thought he was telling the truth. Probably he was. That was early days for him, remember, when his idea of a big project was getting better TV reception. Con's mind just needed permission to get better."

"Belief is powerful," Hugh agreed. "So is faith. Look at all the groups and solo acts we have lining up to make CDs, even though hardly anybody buys them anymore. Have you done any research on C. Danny Jacobs?"

"Plenty. Georgia's daughter is helping me with that."

"I've done some myself, and I'll bet plenty of his cures are like your brother's. People with psychosomatic illnesses who decide they're healed when Pastor Danny touches them with his magic God-rings."

That might be true, but after watching Jacobs operate at the Tulsa fairgrounds, I was sure he had learned the real secret of building a tip: you had to give the rubes at least a little steak to go with the sizzle. Women declaring their migraines were gone and men exclaiming their sciatica had departed were all very well, but stuff like that wasn't very visual. They weren't Portraits in Lightning, you might say.

There were at least two dozen debunking websites about him, including one called C. DANNY JACOBS: FAITH'S FRAUD. Hundreds of people had posted to these sites, claiming the "cancerous tumors" Pastor Danny removed were pig's livers or goat guts. Although cameras carried by audience members were forbidden at C. Danny's services, and the film was confiscated if one of the "ushers" glimpsed someone taking snaps, plenty of photos had leaked out just the same. Many of them seemed to actually complement the official videos posted on C. Danny's website. In others, however, the glistening goop in Pastor Danny's hands certainly did look like goat guts. My guess was that the tumors *were* fake—that part of the show just smelled too carny-from-carny to be anything else. But it didn't mean everything Jacobs was doing was fake. Here were two men in a boat-size Lincoln Continental who could testify to that.

"You had sleepwalking and involuntary movements," Hugh said. "Which, according to WebMD, is called myoclonus. Transient, in your case. Also the need to poke things into yourself, as if down deep you still wanted to be riding the needle."

"All true."

"I had blackouts where I talked and moved around—like booze blackouts, only without the booze."

"And the prismatics," I said.

"Uh-huh. Then there's the girl from Tulsa you told me about. The one who stole the earrings. World's ballsiest smash-and-grab."

"She thought they belonged to her because they were in the picture he took of her. I bet she was rolling around boutiques in Tulsa looking for the dress, too."

"Did she remember breaking into the display case?"

I shook my head. I was long gone from Tulsa by the time Cathy Morse came up for trial, but Brianna Donlin had found a brief item about her online. The Morse girl claimed to remember nothing, and the judge believed her. He ordered a psychological evaluation and released her into the custody of her parents. After that she dropped out of sight.

Hugh was quiet for awhile. So was I. We watched the road unroll. Now that we were out of the mountains, it ran straight as a string all the way to the horizon. At last he said, "What's it for, Jamie? Money? He works the funnel cake circuit for a few years, then one day says, 'Aha, this is chickenfeed, why don't I start a healing ministry and go for the really big bucks?'"

"Maybe, but I never got the idea that Charlie Jacobs cared about the big bucks. He doesn't care about God anymore, either, unless he's done a three-sixty from when he blew up his ministry in my little town, and I didn't see any sign of religious feeling when I was in Tulsa. He cared about his wife and son—that book of photographs I found in his RV was so well thumbed it was just about falling apart—and I'm sure he still cares about his experiments. When it comes to his secret electricity, he's like Mr. Toad with his motorcar."

"I don't follow."

"Obsessed. If I had to guess, I'd say he needs money to keep moving forward with his various experiments. More than he could make running a midway shy."

"So healing's not the end point? That's not the goal?"

I couldn't be sure, but I didn't think healing *was* the goal. Running a revival biz was undoubtedly a cynical jape at the religion he had rejected as well as a way to turn a great many fast bucks via "love offerings," but Jacobs hadn't healed me for money; that had been a plain old Christian hand up from a guy who had been able to reject the label but not the two basic tenets of Jesus's ministry: charity and mercy.

"I don't know where he's headed," I said.

"Do you think *he* does?"

"I do, actually."

"This secret electricity. I wonder if he even knows what it is."

I wondered if he even cared. Which was a scary thought.

The Norris County Fair ran during the last half of September; I had been there with a lady friend a couple of years before, and it was a big one. This being June, the fairgrounds were deserted except for a single huge canvas tent. Fittingly enough, it was where the cheesiest end of the midway would be when the fair was up and running—the rigged gambling shys and the tittie shows. The large parking lots were filled with cars and pickup trucks, many of them old beaters with bumper stickers saying things like JESUS DIED FOR ME, I LIVE FOR HIM. Crowning the tent, probably bolted to the centerpole, was a huge electric cross in rising barber pole stripes of red, white, and blue. From inside came the sound of an electrified gospel combo and the rhythmic clapping of the audience. People were still streaming in. The majority were graying, but there were plenty of younger folks, too.

"They sound like they're having a good time," Hugh said.

"Yeah. Brother Love's Traveling Salvation Show."

With a cool wind blowing in from the plains, it was a comfortable sixty-five outside the tent, but it had to be twenty degrees warmer inside. I saw farmers in bib overalls and elderly wives with flushed, happy faces. I saw men in suits and women in dressy dresses, as if they had come here directly from their office jobs in Denver. There was a contingent of Chicano ranch hands in jeans and workshirts, some displaying what looked like prison tats below their rolled-up sleeves. I even saw a few inked teardrops. Down front was the Wheelchair Brigade. The six-piece band was swaying and laying down hot licks. In front of them, stepping exuberantly from side to side in voluminous burgundy choir robes, were half a dozen hefty chicks: Devina Robinson and the Gospel Robins. They flashed white teeth in brown faces and clapped their hands over their heads.

Devina herself danced forward, cordless mike in hand, gave out a musical cry that sounded like Aretha in her prime, and launched into song.

"I got Jesus in my heart,
Yes I do, yes I do,
I'm goin up to Glory, so can you!
I could go today
Cause he washed my sins away,
I got Jesus in my heart, yes I do!"

She urged the faithful to join in, which they did with a will. Hugh and I took our places at the back, because by now the tent, which probably held upwards of a thousand, was SRO. Hugh leaned toward me and shouted in my ear, "Dig the pipes! She's great!"

I nodded and began clapping along. There were five verses with plenty of *yes I do*s, and by the time Devina finished, sweat was rolling down her face and even the Wheelchair People were into it. She climaxed with another Aretha-style ululation, mike held high. The organist and lead guitarist held that last chord for dear life.

When they finally let go, she shouted, "*Gimme hallelujah, you beautiful people!*"

They did.

"*Now give it to me like you know God's love!*"

They gave it to her like they knew God's love.

Satisfied on that score, she asked if they were ready for some Al Stamper. They let her know they were more than ready.

The band brought it down to something slow and slinky. The audience took their seats in rows of folding chairs. A bald black man strode briskly onstage, carrying his three hundred–plus pounds with delicious ease.

Hugh leaned close, able to speak more quietly now. "He used to be with the Vo-Lites, in the seventies. Skinny as a rail back then and had an Afro big enough to hide a coffee table in. I thought he was fuckin dead. All the coke he snorted, he should be."

Stamper immediately confirmed this. "I was a big sinner," he confided to the audience. "Now, praise God, I'm just a big eater."

They laughed. He laughed with them, then grew serious again.

"I was saved by the grace of Jesus and healed of my addictions by Pastor Danny Jacobs. Some of you might remember the secular songs I did with the Vo-Lites, and some *fewer* of you might remember the ones I did when I went out on my own. I'm singin different tunes these days, all those God-sent tunes I once rejected—"

"Praise Jesus!" someone shouted from the audience.

"That's right, brother, praise his name, and that's what I'm gonna do right now."

He launched into "Let the Lower Lights Be Burning," a hymn I remembered well from my childhood, in a voice so deep and true it made my throat ache. By the time he finished, most of the faithful were singing along, their eyes shining.

He did two more songs (the melody and backbeat of the second sounding suspiciously like Al Green's "Let's Stay Together"), then re-introduced the Gospel Robins. They sang; he sang with them; they made a joyous noise unto the Lord and whipped that congregation into a good-God come-to-Jesus frenzy. As the crowd stood, clapping themselves red-handed, the lights in the tent went down, except for a bright white spot at stage left, which was where C. Danny Jacobs entered. It was my Charlie, all right, and Hugh's Rev, but how he had changed since I saw him last.

His voluminous black coat—similar to the one Johnny Cash wore onstage—partially concealed how thin he'd grown, but his gaunt face tattled the truth. There were other truths there, as well. I think most people who have suffered great losses in their lives—great tragedies—come to a crossroads. Maybe not right then, but when the shock wears off. It may be months later; it may be years. They either expand as a result of their experience, or they contract. If that sounds New Age-y—and I suppose it does—I don't apologize. I know what I'm talking about.

Charles Jacobs had contracted. His mouth was a pale line. His blue eyes blazed, but they were caught in nets of wrinkles and looked smaller. Shielded, somehow. The cheerful young man who had helped me make caves in Skull Mountain when I was six, the man who had listened with such kindliness when I told him how Con had gone mute . . . that man now looked like an old-time New England schoolmaster about to birch a recalcitrant pupil.

Then he smiled, and I could at least hope the young guy who had befriended me was still somewhere inside this carny-show gospel shouter. That smile lit up his whole face. The crowd applauded. Partly out of relief, I think. He raised his hands, then lowered them with the palms down. "Sit, brothers and sisters. Sit, boys and girls. Let us take fellowship, one with the other."

They sat in a great rustling swoosh. The tent grew quiet. Every eye was upon him.

"I bring you good news that you have heard before: God loves you. Yes, every one of you. Those who've lived upright lives and those who are neck-deep in sin. He so loved you that he gave His only begotten son—John three: sixteen. On the eve of his crucifixion, His son prayed that you should be kept from evil—John seventeen: fifteen. When God corrects, when He gives us burdens and afflictions, he does so in love—Acts seventeen: eleven. And can he not lift those burdens and afflictions in that same spirit of love?"

"*Yes, praise God!*" came an exultant shout from Wheelchair Row.

"I stand before you, a wanderer on the face of America, and a vessel of God's love. Will you accept me, as I accept you?"

They shouted they would. Sweat was rolling down my face, and Hugh's, and the faces of those on either side of us, but Jacobs's face was dry and shining, although the spotlight he stood in had to make the air around him even hotter. Add to that the black coat.

"Once I was married, and had a little boy," he said. "There was a terrible accident, and they drowned."

It was like a splash of cold water in my face. Here was a lie when there was no reason to lie, at least none that I could see.

The audience murmured—almost moaned. Many of the women were crying, and a few of the men, as well.

"I turned my face from God then, and cursed Him in my heart. I wandered in the wilderness. Oh, it was New York, and Chicago, and Tulsa, and Joplin, and Dallas, and Tijuana; it was Portland Maine and Portland Oregon, but it was all the same, all the wilderness. I wandered from God, but I never wandered from the memory of my wife and my little boy. I put off the teachings of Jesus, but I never put off this."

He raised his left hand, displaying a gold band that seemed too wide and thick to be an ordinary wedding ring.

"I was tempted by women—of course I was, I'm a man, and Potiphar's wife is always among us—but I stayed true."

"Praise God!" a woman shouted. One who probably thought she'd know a Potiphar's wife if she ever saw that hotbox harlot in matron's clothing.

"And then one day, after refusing such a temptation that was unusually severe . . . unusually *seductive* . . . I had a revelation from God even as did Saul, on the road to Damascus."

"*God's word!*" a man shouted, lifting his hands heavenward (top-of-the-tentward, at least).

"God told me I had work, and that my work would be to lift the burdens and afflictions of others. He came to me in a dream and told me to put on *another* ring, one that would signify my marriage to the teachings of God through His Holy Word and the teachings of His son, Jesus Christ. I was in Phoenix then, working in a godless carnival show, and God told me to walk into the desert without food and water, like any Old Testament pilgrim on the face of the land. He told me that in the wilderness I would find the ring of my second and final marriage. He told me if I remained true to that marriage, I would do great good, and be reunited with my wife and son in heaven, and our true marriage would be re-consecrated by His holy throne, and in His holy light."

There were more cries and ejaculations. A woman in a trim business suit, tan hose, and stylish low heels fell into the aisle and began to testify in a language that seemed solely comprised of vowels. The man with her—husband or boyfriend—knelt beside her, pillowing her head with his hands, smiling tenderly, urging her on.

"He doesn't believe a word of it," I said. I was astounded. "Every word is a lie. They must see that."

But they didn't, and Hugh didn't hear me. He was staring, transfixed. The tent was a tumult of gladness, Jacobs's voice rising above it, pounding through the hosannas by the grace of electricity (and a cordless mike).

"All day I walked. I found food someone had left in a trashbin at a rest area, and ate it. I found half a bottle of Co'cola beside the trail, and drank it. Then God told me to leave the path, and although it was coming on to dark by then, and better trailhands than me have died in that desert, I did as he said."

Must have been all the way out in the suburbs by then, I thought. *Maybe all the way to North Scottsdale, where the rich folks live.*

"The night was dark with clouds, not a star to be seen. But just after midnight, those clouds parted and a ray of moonlight shone down on a pile of rocks. I went to them, and beneath it, I found . . . this."

He held up his right hand. On the third finger was another thick gold band. The audience burst into applause and hallelujahs. I kept trying to make sense of it, and kept coming up short. Here were people who routinely used their computers to stay in touch with their friends and get the news of the day, people who took weather satellites and lung transplants for granted, people who expected to live lives thirty and forty years longer than those of their great-grandparents. Here they were, falling for a story that made Santa and the Tooth Fairy look like gritty realism. He was feeding them shit and they were loving it. I had the dismaying idea that he was loving it, too, and that was worse. This was not the man I'd known in Harlow, or the one who had taken me in that night in Tulsa. Although when I thought of how he had treated Cathy Morse's bewildered and brokenhearted farmer father, I had to admit this man had been on the way even then.

I don't know if he hates these people, I thought, *but he holds them in contempt.*

Or maybe not. Maybe he just didn't care. Except for what was in the collection basket at the end of the show, that was.

Meanwhile, he was continuing his testimony. The band had begun to play as he spoke, whipping the crowd up even further. The Gospel Robins were swaying and clapping, and the audience joined in.

Jacobs talked about his first hesitant healings with the rings of his two marriages—the secular and the sacred. About his realization that God wanted him to bring His message of love and healing to a wider audience. His repeated declarations—kneebound and agonized—that he wasn't worthy. God replying that He never would have endowed him with the rings if that were true. Jacobs made it sound as if he and God had had long conversations about these matters in some celestial smoking room, perhaps puffing pipes and looking out at the rolling hills of heaven.

I hated the way he looked now—that narrow schoolmaster's face and the blue glare of his eyes. I hated the black coat, too. Carnies call that kind of coat a gag-jacket. I had learned as much working Jacobs's Portraits in Lightning gaff at Bell's Amusement Park.

"Join me in prayer, won't you?" Jacobs asked, and fell to his knees with what looked like a brief squint of pain. Rheumatism? Arthritis? *Pastor Danny, heal thyself*, I thought.

The congregation went to its knees in another vast swoosh of clothes and exalted murmurs. Those of us standing at the back of the tent did likewise. I almost resisted—even to a lapsed Methodist like me, this deal reeked of showbiz blasphemy—but the last thing I wanted was to attract his notice, as I had in Tulsa.

He saved your life, I thought. *You don't want to forget that.*

True. And the years since had been good years. I closed my eyes, not in prayer but confusion. I wished I hadn't come, but there had really been no choice. Not for the first time, I wished I hadn't asked Georgia Donlin to put me in touch with her computer-savvy daughter.

Too late now.

Pastor Danny prayed for those present. He prayed for the shut-ins who wanted to be here with them but could not be. He prayed for the men and women of goodwill. He prayed for the United States of America, and that God would imbue her leaders with His wisdom. Then he got down to business, praying for God to work healing through his hands and holy rings, as it accorded with His will.

And the band played on.

"Are there those among you who would be healed?" he asked, struggling to his feet with another grimace. Al Stamper started to come forward to assist him, but Jacobs waved the ex–soul singer back. "Are there those among you with heavy burdens that they would lay down, and afflictions they would be free of?"

The congregation agreed—and loudly—that these things were so. The Wheelchair People and the chronics in the first two rows were staring raptly. So were those in the rows behind, many of them haggard and looking sick unto death. There were bandages, and disfigurements, and oxygen masks, and withered limbs, and braces. There were those who twitched and rocked helplessly as their CP-impaired brains did pissed-off jigs inside their skulls.

Devina and the Gospel Robins began to sing "Jesus Says Come Forth" as softly as a spring wind blowing off the desert. Ushers in pressed jeans, white shirts, and green vests appeared like magic. Some began organizing a line down the center aisle of those hoping to be healed. Other green-vests—*many* others—circulated in the crowd with wicker collection baskets so big they looked like panniers. I heard the clink of coins, but it was scattered and sporadic; most of these people were tossing in folding green—what carnies call "the kick." The woman who had been speaking in tongues was being helped back to her folding chair by her boyfriend or husband. Her hair hung loose around her flushed, exalted face and her suit jacket was smeared with dirt.

I felt smeared with dirt myself, but now we'd gotten to what I really wanted to see. From my pocket I pulled a notebook and a Bic. It already held several entries, some from my own research, more courtesy of Brianna Donlin.

"What are you doing?" Hugh asked in a low voice.

I shook my head. The healing was about to begin, and I had watched enough videos on Pastor Danny's website to know how it went. *This is old-school*, Bree had said after watching several of the videos herself.

A woman in a wheelchair rolled forward. Jacobs asked for her name and held the microphone to her lips. In a trembling voice she declared herself to be Rowena Mintour, a schoolteacher who had come all the way from Des Moines. She had terrible arthritis and could no longer walk.

I wrote her name in my notebook beneath that of Mabel Jergens, healed of a spinal cord injury a month ago, in Albuquerque.

Jacobs dropped the mike into an outside pocket of his gag-jacket and grasped her head in his hands, pressing the rings to her temples and her face to his chest. He closed his eyes. His lips moved in silent prayer . . . or the words to "Here We Go Round the Mulberry Bush," for all I knew. Suddenly she jerked. Her hands flew up to either side and flapped like white birds. She stared into Jacobs's face, her eyes wide either with astonishment or the aftermath of a jolt of electricity.

Then she stood up.

The crowd bellowed hallelujahs. As she embraced Jacobs and covered his cheeks with kisses, several men tossed their hats in the air, a thing I had seen in movies but never in real life. Jacobs grasped her shoulders, turned her toward the audience—all of them agog, not excluding me—and dipped for his microphone with the practiced smoothness of an old midway showie.

"Walk to your husband, Rowena!" Jacobs thundered into the mike. "Walk to him, and praise Jesus with every step! Praise God with every step! Praise His holy name!"

She tottered to her husband, holding her arms out to keep her balance, and weeping. An usher in a green vest pushed her wheelchair close behind her in case her legs gave way . . . but they didn't.

It went on for an hour. The music never stopped, nor did the ushers with the deep offering baskets. Jacobs didn't heal everybody, but I can tell you that his collection crew stripped those rubes right down to their no doubt maxed-out credit cards. Many of the Wheelchair Brigade were unable to rise after being touched by the holy rings, but half a dozen of them did. I wrote down all the names, crossing out those who seemed as fucked over after Jacobs's healing touch as before.

There was a woman with cataracts who declared she could see, and under the bright lights, the milky glaze really did appear to have left her eyes. A crooked arm was made straight. A wailing baby with some sort of heart defect stopped crying as if a switch had been turned off. A man who approached on Canadian crutches, his head bent, tore off the neck brace he was wearing and cast the crutches aside. A woman suffering from advanced COPD dropped her oxygen mask. She declared that she could breathe freely and the weight on her chest was gone.

Many of the cures were impossible to quantify, and it was very possible some were plants. The man with ulcers who declared his stomach pain was gone for the first time in three years, for instance. Or the woman with diabetes—one leg amputated below the knee—who said she could feel her hands and remaining toes again. A couple of chronic migraine sufferers who testified that their pain was gone, praise God, all gone.

I wrote the names down, anyway, and—when they gave them—the towns and states they hailed from. Bree Donlin was good, she had gotten interested in the project, and I wanted to give her as much to work with as possible.

Jacobs only removed one tumor that night, and that fellow's name I didn't even consider writing down, because I saw one of Jacobs's hands dart into the gag-jacket before he applied his magic rings. What he displayed to the gasping, rapturous audience looked suspiciously like supermarket calves' liver to me. He gave it to one of the green-vests, who popped it into a jar and hustled it out of sight posthaste.

At last Jacobs declared the healing touch exhausted for the night. I don't know about that, but *he* certainly looked exhausted. Done to death, in fact. His face was still dry, but the front of his shirt was sticking to his chest. When he stepped back from the reluctantly dispersing faithful who hadn't gotten a chance (many would undoubtedly follow him to his next revival meeting), he stumbled. Al Stamper was there to grab him, and this time Jacobs accepted the help.

"Let us pray," Jacobs said. He was having a hard time catching his breath, and I couldn't help worrying that he might faint or go into cardiac arrest right there. "Let us offer our thanks to God, as we offer our burdens to Him. After that, brothers and sisters, Al and Devina and the Gospel Robins will see us out in song."

This time he didn't attempt kneeling, but the congregation did, including a few who had probably never expected to kneel again in their earthly lives. There was that airy swoosh of clothes, and it almost covered the gagging noises from beside me. I turned just in time to see the back of Hugh's plaid shirt disappearing between the flaps at the entrance to the tent.

I found him standing beneath a pole light fifteen feet away, bent double and grasping his knees. The night had cooled considerably, and the puddle between his feet was steaming lightly. As I approached, his body heaved and the puddle grew larger. When I touched his arm, he jerked and stumbled, almost falling into his own vomit, which would have made for a fragrant ride home.

The panicky gaze he turned on me was that of an animal caught in a forest fire. Then he relaxed and straightened up, pulling an old-fashioned rancher's bandanna from his back pocket. He wiped his mouth with it. His hand was trembling. His face was dead white. Some of that was undoubtedly because of the harsh glare thrown by the pole light, but not all.

"Sorry, Jamie. You startled me."

"I noticed."

"It was the heat, I guess. Let's get out of here, what do you say? Beat the crowd."

He started walking toward the Lincoln. I touched his elbow. He pulled away. Except that's not quite right. He *shied* away.

"What was it really?"

He didn't answer at first, just kept walking toward the far side of the lot, where his Detroit cabin cruiser was parked. I walked beside him. He reached the car and put his hand on the dew-misted hood, as if for comfort.

"It was a prismatic. The first one in a long, long time. I felt it coming on while he was healing that last one—the guy who said he was paralyzed from the waist down in a car accident. When he got up from his chair, everything went *sharp*. Everything went *clear*. You know?"

I didn't, but nodded as if I did. From behind us the congregation was clapping joyously and singing "How I Love My Jesus" at the top of its lungs.

"Then . . . when the Rev started to pray . . . the colors." He looked at me, his mouth trembling. He looked twenty years older. "They were ever so much brighter. They shattered everything."

He reached out and grasped my shirt hard enough to tear off two of the buttons. It was the grip of a drowning man. His eyes were huge and horrified.

"Then . . . then all those fragments came together again, but the colors didn't go away. They danced and twisted like the aurora borealis on a winter night. And the people . . . they weren't people anymore."

"What were they, Hugh?"

"Ants," he whispered. "Huge ants, the kind that must only live in tropical forests. Brown ones and black ones and red ones. They were looking at him with dead eyes and that poison they use, formic acid, was dripping from their mouths." He drew a long, ragged breath. "If I ever see anything like that again, I'll kill myself."

"It's gone, though, right?"

"Yes. Gone. Thank God."

He dragged his keys from his pocket and dropped them in the dirt. I picked them up. "I'll drive us back."

"Sure. You do that." He started toward the passenger seat, then looked at me. "You too, Jamie. I turned to you and I was standing next to a huge ant. You turned . . . you looked at me . . ."

"Hugh, I didn't. I barely saw you going out."

He seemed not to hear. "You turned . . . you looked at me . . .

and I think you tried to *smile*. There were colors all around you, but your eyes were dead, like all the rest. And your mouth was full of poison."

He said nothing more until we arrived back at the big wooden gate leading to Wolfjaw. It was closed and I started to get out of the car to open it.

"Jamie."

I turned to look at him. He'd gotten some of his color back, but only a little.

"Never mention his name to me again. *Never*. If you do, you're done here. Are we clear on that?"

We were. But that didn't mean I was going to let it go.

IX

Reading Obituaries in Bed. Cathy Morse Again. The Latches.

Brianna Donlin and I were scanning obituaries in bed on a Sunday morning in early August of 2009. Thanks to the sort of computer hocus-pocus only true geeks can manage, Bree was able to collate death notices from a dozen major American newspapers and view them as an alphabetical list.

It wasn't the first time we'd done this in such pleasurable circumstances, but we both understood we were getting closer and closer to the last time. In September she'd be leaving for New York to interview for I-T jobs with the sort of firms that paid upwards of six figures at the entry level—she had appointments with four already penciled into her calendar—and I had my own plans. But our time together had been good for me in all sorts of ways, and I had no reason not to believe her when she said it had been good for her, too.

I wasn't the first man to enjoy a dalliance with a woman less than half his age, and if you said there's no fool like an old fool and no goat like an old goat, I wouldn't argue with you, but sometimes such liaisons are okay, at least in the short term. Neither of us was attached, and neither of us had any illusions about the long term. It had just happened, and Brianna had made the first move. This was about three months after the Norris County tent revival and four into our computer-sleuthing. I hadn't been a particularly tough sell, especially after she slipped out of her blouse and skirt one evening in my apartment.

"Are you sure you want to do this?" I had asked.

"Absolutely." She flashed a grin. "Soon I'll be in the big wide world, and I think I better work out my daddy issues first."

"Was your daddy a white ex–guitar player, then?"

That made her laugh. "All cats are gray in the dark, Jamie. Now are we going to get it on or not?"

We got it on, and it was terrific. I'd be lying if I said her youth didn't excite me—she was twenty-four—and I'd also be lying if I said I could always keep up with her. Stretched out next to her that first night and pretty much exhausted after the second go, I asked her what Georgia would say.

"She's not going to find out from me. Is she from you?"

"Nope, but Nederland's a small town."

"That's true, and in small towns, discretion only goes so far, I guess. If she *should* speak to me, I'd just remind her that she once did more for Hugh Yates than keep his books."

"Are you serious?"

She giggled. "You white boys can be so *dumb*."

Now, with coffee on her side of the bed and tea on mine, we sat propped up on pillows with her laptop between us. Summer sunshine—morning sunshine, always the best—made an oblong on the floor. Bree was wearing one of my tee-shirts and nothing else. Her hair, kept short, was a curly black cap.

"You could continue without me just fine," she said. "You pretend to be computer illiterate—mostly so you can keep me where you can nudge me in the night, I think—but running search engines ain't rocket science. And I think you've got enough already, don't you?"

As a matter of fact, I did. We had started with three names from the Miracle Testimony page of C. Danny Jacobs's website. Robert Rivard, the boy cured of muscular dystrophy in St. Louis, led the list. To these three Bree had added the ones I was sure of from the Norris County revival meeting—ones like Rowena Mintour, whose sudden recovery was hard to argue with. If that tottery, weeping walk to her husband had been a put-up job, she deserved an Academy Award for it.

Bree had tracked the Pastor Danny Jacobs Healing Revival Tour from Colorado to California, ten stops in all. Together we had watched the new YouTube vids added to the website's Miracle Testimony page with the avidity of marine biologists studying some newly discovered species of fish. We debated the validity of each (first in my living room, later in this same bed), eventually putting them into four categories: *utter bullshit*, *probable bullshit*, *impossible to be sure*, and *hard not to believe*.

By this process, a master list had slowly emerged. On that sunny August morning in the bedroom of my second-floor apartment, there were fifteen names on it. These were cures we felt ninety-eight percent sure of, culled down from a roster of almost seven hundred and fifty possibles. Robert Rivard was on that list; Mabel Jergens from Albuquerque was on it; so was Rowena Mintour and Ben Hicks, the man in the Norris County Fairgrounds tent who had torn off his neck brace and tossed his crutches aside.

Hicks was an interesting case. Both he and his wife had confirmed the authenticity of the cure in a *Denver Post* article published a couple of weeks after Jacobs's traveling show moved on. He was a history prof at the Community College of Denver with an impeccable reputation. He termed himself a religious skeptic and described his attendance at the Norris County revival as "a last resort." His wife confirmed this. "We are amazed and thankful," she said. She added that they had started going to church again.

Rivard, Jergens, Mintour, Hicks, and everyone else on our master list had been touched by Jacobs's "holy rings" between May of 2007 and December of 2008, when the Healing Revival Tour had concluded in San Diego.

Bree had begun the follow-up work with a light heart, but by October of 2008, her attitude had darkened. That was when she had found a story about Robert Rivard—no more than a squib, really—in the Monroe County *Weekly Telegram*. It said the "miracle boy" had been admitted to St. Louis Children's Hospital "for reasons unrelated to his former muscular dystrophy."

Bree made enquiries, both by computer and telephone. Rivard's parents refused to speak to her, but a nurse at Children's finally did when Bree told her she was trying to expose C. Danny Jacobs as a fraud. This was not what we were doing, exactly, but it worked. After being assured by Bree that she would never be named in any article or book, the nurse said Bobby Rivard had been admitted suffering what she called "chain headaches," and was given a battery of tests to rule out a brain tumor. Which they did. Eventually the boy had been transferred to Gad's Ridge, in Oakville, Missouri.

"What kind of hospital is that?" Bree had asked.

"Mental," the nurse said. And while Bree was digesting this: "Most people who go into Gad's, they never come out."

Bree's efforts to find out more were met by a stone wall at Gad's Ridge. Because I considered Rivard our Patient Zero, I flew to St. Louis, rented a car, and drove to Oakville. After several afternoons spent in the bar nearest to the hospital, I found an orderly who would talk for the small emolument of sixty dollars. Robert Rivard was still walking fine, the orderly said, but never walked any farther than the corner of his room. When he did, he would simply stand there, like a child being punished for misbehavior, until someone led him back to his bed or the nearest chair. On good days he ate; during his bad stretches, which were far more common, he had to be tube-fed. He was classed semicatatonic. A gork, in the orderly's words.

"Is he still suffering from chain headaches?" I asked him.

The orderly shrugged meaty shoulders. "Who knows?"

Who, indeed.

So far as we could tell, nine of the people on our master list were fine. This included Rowena Mintour, who had resumed teaching, and Ben Hicks, whom I interviewed myself in November of 2008, five months after his cure. I didn't tell him everything (for one thing, I never mentioned electricity of either the ordinary or the special type), but I shared enough to establish my bona fides: heroin addiction cured by Jacobs in the early nineties, followed by troubling aftereffects that eventually diminished and then disappeared. What I wanted to know was if *he* had suffered any aftereffects—blackouts, flashing lights, sleepwalking, perhaps lapses into Tourette's-like speech.

No to all, he said. He was fine as could be.

"I don't know if it was God working through him or not," Hicks told me over coffee in his office. "My wife does, and that's fine, but I don't care. I'm pain-free and walking two miles a day. In another two months I expect to be cleared to play tennis, as long as it's doubles, where I only have to run a few steps. *Those* are the things I care about. If he did for you what you say he did, you'll know what I mean."

I did, but I also knew more.

That Robert Rivard was enjoying his cure in a mental institution, sipping glucose via IV rather than Cokes with his friends.

That Patricia Farmingdale, cured of peripheral neuropathy in Cheyenne, Wyoming, had poured salt into her eyes in an apparent effort to blind herself. She had no memory of doing it, let alone why.

That Stefan Drew of Salt Lake City had gone on walking binges after being cured of a supposed brain tumor. These walks, some of them fifteen-mile marathons, did not occur during blackouts; the urge just came on him, he said, and he had to go.

That Veronica Freemont of Anaheim had suffered what she called "interruptions of vision." One had resulted in a low-speed collision with another driver. She tested negative for drugs and alcohol, but turned in her license just the same, afraid it would happen again.

That in San Diego, Emil Klein's miracle cure of a neck injury was followed by a periodic compulsion to go out into his backyard and eat dirt.

And there was Blake Gilmore of Las Vegas, who claimed C. Danny Jacobs had cured him of lymphoma during the late summer of 2008. A month later he lost his job as a blackjack dealer when he began to spew profanity at the customers—stuff like "Take a hit, take a fucking hit, you chickenshit asshole." When he began shouting similar things at his three kids, his wife threw him out. He moved to a no-tell motel north of Fashion Show Drive. Two weeks later he was found dead on the bathroom floor with a bottle of Krazy Glue in one hand. He had used it to plug his nostrils and seal his mouth shut. His wasn't the only obit coupled to Jacobs that Bree had found with her search engine, but it was the only one we felt sure was connected.

Until Cathy Morse, that was.

• • •

I was feeling sleepy again in spite of an infusion of black breakfast tea. I blamed it on the auto-scroll feature of Bree's laptop. It was helpful, I said, but also hypnotic.

"Honey, if I may misquote Al Jolson, you ain't seen nothing yet," she said. "Next year Apple's going to release a pad-style computer that'll revolutionize—" There was a *bing* before she could finish, and the auto-scroll came to a halt. She peered at the screen, where a line was highlighted in red. "Uh-oh. That's one of the names you gave me when we started."

"What?" Meaning *who*. I'd only been able to give her a few back then, and one had been that of my brother Con. Jacobs had *claimed* that one was just a placebo, but—

"Hold your water and let me click the link."

I leaned over to look. My first feeling was relief: not Con, of course not. My second was a species of dismal horror.

The obituary, from the Tulsa *World*, was for one Catherine Anne Morse, age thirty-eight. Died suddenly, the obit said. And this: *Cathy's grieving parents ask that in lieu of flowers, mourners send contributions to the Suicide Prevention Action Network. These contributions are tax deductible.*

"Bree," I said. "Go to last week's—"

"I know what to do, so let me do it." Then, taking a second look at my face: "Are you okay?"

"Yes," I said, but I didn't know if I was or not. I kept remembering how Cathy Morse had looked mounting to the Portraits in Lightning stage all those years ago, a pretty little Sooner gal with tanned legs flashing beneath a denim skirt with a frayed hem. *Every pretty girl carries her own positive charge*, Jacobs had said, but somewhere along the way, Cathy's charge had turned negative. No mention of a husband, although a girl that good-looking must not have lacked for suitors. No mention of children, either.

Maybe she liked girls, I thought, but that was pretty lame.

"Here you go, sugar," Bree said. She turned the laptop so I could see it more easily. "Same newspaper."

WOMAN IN DEATH JUMP FROM CYRUS AVERY MEMORIAL BRIDGE, the headline read. Cathy Morse had left no explanatory note behind, and her grieving parents were mystified. "I wonder if it wasn't somebody pushed her," Mrs. Morse said . . . but according to the article, foul play had been ruled out, although it didn't say how.

Has he done it before, mister? Mr. Morse had asked me back in 1992. This after punching my old fifth business in the face and splitting his lip. *Has he knocked other ones for a loop the way he knocked my Cathy?*

Yes, sir, I thought now. *Yes, sir, I believe he has.*

"Jamie, you don't know for sure," Bree said, touching my shoulder. "Sixteen years is a long time. It could have been something else entirely. She might have found out she had a bad cancer, or some other fatal disease. Fatal and painful."

"It was him," I said. "I know it, and by now I think you do, too. Most of his subjects are fine afterwards, but some go away with time bombs in their heads. Cathy Morse did, and it went off. How many others are going to go off in the next ten or twenty years?"

I was thinking I could be one of them, and Bree surely knew that, too. She didn't know about Hugh, because that wasn't my story to tell. He hadn't had a recurrence of his prismatics since the night at the tent revival—and that one was probably brought on by stress—but it could happen again, and although we didn't talk about it, I'm sure he knew it as well as I did.

Time bombs.

"So now you're going to find him."

"You bet." The obituary of Catherine Anne Morse was the last piece of evidence I needed, the one that made the decision final.

"And persuade him to stop."

"If I can."

"If he won't?"

"Then I don't know."

"I'll go with you, if you want."

But *she* didn't want. It was all over her face. She had started the assignment with an intelligent young woman's zest for pure research, and there had been the lovemaking to add extra spice, but now the research was no longer pure and she had seen enough to scare her badly.

"You're not going anywhere near him," I said. "But he's been off the road for eight months now and his weekly TV show's into reruns. I need you to find out where he's hanging his hat these days."

"I can do that." She set her laptop aside and reached under the sheet. "But I'd like to do something else first, if you're of a mind."

I was.

Shortly before Labor Day, Bree Donlin and I said our goodbyes in that same bed. They were very physical ones for the most part, satisfying to both of us, but also sad. For me more than her, I think. She was looking forward to life as a pretty, unattached career girl in New York; I was looking forward to the dreaded double-nickel in less than two years. I thought there would be no more lively young women for me, and on that score I have been proven absolutely correct.

She slipped out of bed, long-legged and beautifully naked. "I found what you wanted," she said, and began rummaging through her purse on the dresser. "It was harder than I expected, because he's currently going under the name of Daniel Charles."

"That's my boy. Not exactly an alias, but close."

"More of a precaution, I think. The way celebrities will check into a hotel under a fake name—or a variation of their real one—to fool the autograph hounds. He leased the place where he's living as Daniel Charles, which is legal as long as he's got a bank account and the checks don't bounce, but sometimes a fella just has to use his real name if he's going to stay on the right side of the law."

"What sometimes would you be talking about in this case?"

"He bought a car last year in Poughkeepsie, New York—not a fancy one, just a plain-vanilla Ford Taurus—and registered it under his real name." She got back into bed and handed me a slip of paper. "Here you go, handsome."

Written on it was *Daniel Charles (aka Charles Jacobs, aka C. Danny Jacobs), The Latches, Latchmore, New York 12561.*

"What's The Latches when it's at home with its feet up?"

"The house he's renting. Actually an estate. A *gated* estate, so be aware. Latchmore is a little north of New Paltz—same zip code. It's in the Catskills, where Rip Van Winkle bowled with the dwarfs back in the day. Except then—umm, your hands are nice and warm—the game was called ninepins."

She snuggled closer, and I said what men of my age find themselves saying more and more frequently: I appreciated the offer, but didn't feel myself capable of taking her up on it just then. In retrospect, I sure wish I'd tried a little harder. One last time would have been nice.

"That's okay, hon. Just hold me."

I held her. I think we drowsed, because when I became aware again, the sun had moved from the bed to the floor. Bree jumped up and began to dress. "Got to shake. A thousand things to do today."

She hooked her bra, then looked at me in the mirror. "When are you going to see him?"

"Probably not until October. Hugh's got a guy coming in from Minnesota to sub for me, but he can't get here until then."

"You have to stay in touch with me. Email *and* phone. If I don't hear from you every day you're out there, I'll get worried. I might even have to drive up and make sure you're okay."

"Don't do that," I said.

"You just stay in touch, white boy, and I won't have to."

Dressed, she came and sat on the side of the bed.

"You might not need to go at all. Has that idea crossed your mind? There's no tour scheduled, his website's gone stagnant, and there's nothing but reruns on his TV show. I came across a blog post the other day titled *Where in the World Is Pastor Danny?* The discussion thread went on for pages."

"Your point being?"

She took my hand, twined her fingers in mine. "We know—well, not *know*, but we're pretty sure—that he's hurt some people along the way while he was helping others. Okay, that's done and can't be undone. But if he's stopped healing, he won't be hurting anyone else. In that case, what would be the point of confronting him?"

"If he's stopped healing, it's because he's made enough money to move on."

"To what?"

"I don't know, but judging from his track record, it could be dangerous. And Bree . . . listen." I sat up and took her other hand. "Everything else aside, someone needs to call him to account for what he's done."

She lifted my hands to her mouth, where she kissed first one and then the other. "But should that someone be you, honey? After all, you were one of his successes."

"I think that's why. Also, Charlie and I . . . we go back. We go way back."

I didn't see her off at Denver International—that was her mother's job—but she called me when she landed, frothing with a combination of nerves and excitement. Looking forward, not back. I was glad for her. When my phone rang twenty minutes later, I thought it would be her again. It wasn't. It was her mother. Georgia asked if we could talk. Maybe over lunch.

Uh-oh, I thought.

We ate at McGee's—a pleasant meal, with pleasant conversation, mostly about the music business. When we had said no to dessert and yes to coffee, Georgia leaned her considerable bosom on the table and got down to business. "So, Jamie. Are you two done with each other?"

"I . . . um . . . Georgia . . ."

"Goodness, don't mumble and stumble. You know perfectly well what I mean, and I'm not going to bite your head off. If I had a mind to do that, I would have done it last year, when she first hopped in the sack with you." She saw my expression and smiled. "Nah, she didn't tell me and I didn't ask. Didn't need to. I can read her like a book. I bet she even told you I got up to some of the same doins with Hugh, back in the day. True?"

I made a zipping motion across my lips. It turned her smile into a laugh.

"Oh, that's good. I like that. And I like *you*, Jamie. I did almost from the first, when you were skinny as a rail and still getting over whatever junk you were putting into your system. You looked like Billy Idol, only dragged through the gutter. I don't have anything against mixed-race sweeties, either. Or the age thing. Do you know what my father gave me when I got old enough for a driver's license?"

I shook my head.

"A 1960 Plymouth with half the grille gone, bald tires, rusty rocker panels, and an engine that gobbled recycled oil by the quart. He called it a field-bomber. Said every new driver should have an old wreck to start with, before he or she stepped up to a car that would actually take an inspection sticker. Are you getting my point?"

I absolutely was. Bree wasn't a nun, she'd had her share of sexual adventures before I came along, but I had been her first long-term relationship. In New York, she would move up—if not to a man of her own race, then certainly to one a little closer to her own age.

"I just wanted that out front before I said what I really came here to say." She leaned forward even more, the rolling tide of her bosom endangering her coffee cup and water glass. "She wouldn't tell me much about the research she's been doing for you, but I know it scared her, and the one time I tried to ask Hugh, he about bit my head off."

Ants, I thought. *To him, the whole congregation looked like ants.*

"It's about that preacherman. I know that much."

I kept quiet.

"Cat got your tongue?"

"You could say so, I guess."

She nodded and sat back. "That's all right. That's fine. Just from now on, I want you to leave Brianna out of it. Will you do that? If only because I never suggested that you'd have done better to keep your elderly prick away from my daughter's underpants?"

"She's out of it. We agreed on that."

She gave a businesslike nod. Then: "Hugh says you're taking a vacation."

"Yes."

"Going to see the preacherman?"

I kept quiet. Which was the same as saying yes, and she knew it.

"Be careful." She reached across the table and interlaced her fingers in mine, as her daughter had been wont to do. "Whatever it was you and Bree were looking into, it upset her terribly."

I flew into Stewart Airport in Newburgh on a day in early October. The trees were turning color, and the ride to the town of Latchmore was beautiful. By the time I got there, the afternoon was waning and I checked into the local Motel 6. There was no dial-up, let alone WiFi, which made my laptop unable to touch the world outside my room, but I didn't need WiFi to find The Latches; Bree had done that for me. It was four miles east of downtown Latchmore, on Route 27, an estate home once owned by an old-money family named Vander Zanden. Around the turn of the twentieth century the old money had apparently run out, because The Latches had been sold and turned into a high-priced sanitarium for overweight ladies and soused gentlemen. That had lasted almost until the turn of the twenty-first century. Since then it had been for sale or lease.

I thought I would have a hard time sleeping, but I went under almost immediately, in the midst of trying to plan what I'd say to Jacobs when I saw him. *If* I saw him. When I woke early on another bright fall day, I decided that playing it by ear might be for the best. If I hadn't laid down tracks to run on, I reasoned (perhaps fallaciously), I couldn't be derailed.

I got in my rental car at nine, drove the four miles, found nothing. A mile or so farther on I stopped at a farmstand loaded with the season's last produce. The potatoes looked mighty paltry to my country boy's eye, but the pumpkins were wowsers. The stand was being presided over by a couple of teenagers. The resemblance said they were brother and sister. Their expressions said they were bored brainless. I asked for directions to The Latches.

"You passed it," the girl said. She was the older.

"I figured that much. I just don't know how I managed. I thought I had good directions, and it's supposed to be pretty big."

"There used to be a sign," the boy said, "but the guy who's renting the place took it down. Pa says he must like to keep himself to himself. Ma says he's probably stuck up."

"Shut up, Willy. Mister, you gonna buy anything? Pa says we can't shut down for the day until we get thirty dollars' worth of custom."

"I'll buy a pumpkin. *If* you can give me some decent directions."

She gave a theatrical sigh. "One pumpkin. A buck-fifty. Big whoop."

"How about one pumpkin for five dollars?"

Willy and his sister exchanged a look, then she smiled. "That'll work."

My expensive pumpkin sat in the backseat like an orange moonlet as I drove back the way I had come. The girl had told me to watch for a big slab of rock with METALLICA RULES sprayed on it. I spotted it and slowed to ten miles an hour. Two tenths of a mile after the big rock, I came to the turnoff I'd missed before. It was paved, but the entrance was badly overgrown and heaped with fallen autumn leaves. It looked like camouflage to me. When I'd asked the farmstand kids if they knew what the new occupant did, they had simply shrugged.

"Pa says he probably made his money in the stock market," the girl said. "He must have a lot of it, to live in a place like that. Ma says it must have fifty rooms."

"Why you goin to see him?" This was the boy.

His sister threw him an elbow. "That's rude, Willy."

I said, "If he's who I think he is, I knew him a long time ago. And thanks to you guys, I can bring him a present." I hefted the pumpkin.

"Make a lot of pies with that, f'sure," the boy said.

Or a jack-o'-lantern, I thought as I turned into the lane leading to The Latches. Branches brushed the sides of my car. *One with a bright little electric light inside instead of a candle. Right behind the eyes.*

The road—that's what it was once you got past the intersection with the highway, wide and well-paved—climbed in a series of **S**-turns. Twice I had to stop while deer lolloped across ahead of me. They looked at my car without concern. I guessed no one had hunted these woods in a long, long time.

Four miles up, I came to a closed wrought-iron gate flanked by signs: PRIVATE PROPERTY on the left and NO TRESPASSING on the right. There was an intercom box on a fieldstone post with a video camera above it, cocked down to look at callers. I pressed the button on the intercom. My heart was beating hard, and I was sweating. "Hello? Is anybody there?"

Nothing at first. At last: "How may I help you?" The resolution was much better than most intercom systems provide—terrific, in fact—but given Jacobs's interests, that didn't surprise me. The voice wasn't his, but it was familiar.

"I'm here to see Daniel Charles."

"Mr. Charles doesn't see callers without an appointment," the intercom informed me.

I considered this, then pushed the TALK button again. "What about Dan Jacobs? That's the name he was going under in Tulsa, where he was running a carny shy called Portraits in Lightning."

The voice from the box said, "I have no idea what you're talking about, and I'm sure Mr. Charles wouldn't, either."

The penny dropped, and I knew who went with that rolling tenor voice. "Tell him it's Jamie Morton, Mr. Stamper. And remind him I was there when he did his first miracle."

There was a long, long pause. I thought the conversation might be over, which would leave me up the creek without a paddle. Unless I wanted to try crashing the gate with my rented economy car, that was, and in such a conflict I was pretty sure the gate would win.

Just as I was about to turn away, Al Stamper said, "What was this miracle?"

"My brother Conrad lost his voice. Reverend Jacobs brought it back."

"Look up at the camera."

I did so. After several seconds, a new voice came through the intercom. "Come on up, Jamie," Charles Jacobs said. "It's wonderful to see you."

An electric motor began to purr, and the gate opened on a hidden track. *Like Jesus walking across Peaceable Lake*, I thought as I got into my car and started rolling. There was another of those tight curves fifty yards or so further up, and before I was around it, I saw the gate shutting. The association that came to me—the original residents of Eden turned out for eating the wrong apple—wasn't surprising; I had grown up with the Bible, after all.

The Latches was a vast sprawl that might have started life as a Victorian but had become a mishmash of architectural experiments. There were four stories, many gables, and a rounded, glassed-in addition on the west end that looked out on the valleys, dells, and ponds of the Hudson Valley. Route 27 was a dark thread running through a landscape that shone with color. The main building was barnboard trimmed in white, and several large outbuildings matched it. I wondered which one housed Jacobs's lab. One of them did, of that I was sure. Beyond the buildings, the land sloped up ever more steeply and woods took over.

Parked under the portico, where bellmen had once unloaded the fancy cars of incoming spa-goers and alkies, was the unassuming Ford Taurus Jacobs had registered under his own name. I parked behind it and mounted the steps to a porch that looked as long as a football field. I reached for the bell, but before I could ring it, the door opened. Al Stamper stood there in seventies-style bell-bottom trousers and a strappy tie-dyed tee-shirt. He'd put on even more weight since I'd last seen him in the revival tent, and looked approximately the size of a moving van.

"Hello, Mr. Stamper. Jamie Morton. I'm a big fan of your early work." I held out my hand.

He didn't shake it. "I don't know what you want, but Mr. Jacobs doesn't need anyone disturbing him. He's got a lot of work to do, and he hasn't been well."

"Don't you mean Pastor Danny?" I asked. (Well . . . sort of teased.)

"Come on in the kitchen." It was the warm and rolling Soul Brother Number One voice, but the face said, *The kitchen'll be good enough for the likes of you.*

I was willing, it *was* good enough for the likes of me, but before he could lead me there, another voice, one I knew well, exclaimed, "Jamie Morton! You *do* turn up at the most opportune times!"

He came down the hall, limping slightly and listing to starboard. His hair, now almost completely white, had continued to draw back from his temples, exposing arcs of shining scalp. The blue eyes, however, were as sharp as ever. His lips were drawn back in a smile that looked (to my eye, at least) rather predatory. He passed Stamper as if the big man wasn't there, his right hand held out. Today that one was ringless, although there was one on his left: a simple gold band, thin and scratched. I was sure the mate to it was buried beneath the soil of a Harlow cemetery, on a finger that was now little more than a bone.

I shook with him. "We're a long way from Tulsa, Charlie, wouldn't you say?"

He nodded, pumping my hand like a politician hoping for a vote. "Long, *long* way. How old are you now, Jamie?"

"Fifty-three."

"And your family? Are they well?"

"I don't see them much, but Terry is still in Harlow, running the oil business. He's got three kids, two boys and a girl. Pretty well grown now. Con's still stargazing in Hawaii. Andy passed away a few years ago. It was a stroke."

"Very sorry to hear it. But you look great. In the pink."

"So do you." This was a baldfaced lie. I thought briefly of the three ages of the Great American Male—youth, middle age, and you look fuckin terrific. "You must be . . . what? Seventy?"

"Close enough." He was still pumping my hand. It was a good strong grip, but I could feel a faint shake, just the same, lurking beneath the skin. "What about Hugh Yates? Are you still working for him?"

"Yes, and he's fine. Can hear a pin drop in the next room."

"Lovely. *Lovely.*" He let go of my hand at last. "Al, Jamie and I have a lot to talk about. Would you bring us a couple of lemonades? We'll be in the library."

"Now, you're not going to overdo it, are you?" Stamper was looking at me with distrust and dislike. *He's jealous*, I thought. *He's had Jacobs all to himself since the last tour ended, and that's just the way he likes it.* "You need your strength for your work."

"I'll be fine. There's no tonic like an old friend. Follow me, Jamie."

He led me down the main hall, past a dining room as long as a Pullman car on the left, and one-two-three living rooms on the right, the one in the middle graced by a huge chandelier that looked like a leftover prop from James Cameron's *Titanic* movie. We walked through a rotunda where polished wood gave way to polished marble, our footfalls picking up an echo. It was a warm day but the house was comfy. I could hear the silky whisper of air conditioners, and wondered how much it cost to cool this place in August, when the temperature would be a lot more than warmish. Remembering the workshop in Tulsa, my guess was very little.

The library was the circular room at the far end of the house. There were thousands of books on the curving shelves, but I had no idea how anyone could possibly read in here, given the view. The west wall was entirely made of glass, and I could look out over leagues and leagues of the Hudson Valley, complete with cobalt river shining in the distance.

"Healing pays well." I thought again of Goat Mountain, that rich people's playground that was gated to keep hicks like the Morton family out. Some views only money can buy.

"In all sorts of ways," he said. "I don't need to ask if you're still off the drugs; I can see it in your complexion. And in your eyes." Thus having reminded me of the debt I owed him, he asked me to sit down.

Now that I was actually here and in the presence, I hardly knew how or where to begin. Nor did I want to with Al Stamper—now serving as assistant-cum-butler—due with lemonades. It turned out not to be a problem. Before I could find some meaningless chit-chat to pass the time, the ex–lead singer of the Vo-Lites came in, looking grumpier than ever. He set a tray down on a cherrywood table between us.

"Thank you, Al," Jacobs said.

"Very welcome." Speaking to the boss and ignoring me.

"Nice pants," I said. "Takes me back to the days when the Bee Gees quit the transcendental stuff and went disco. Now you need some vintage platform shoes to go with."

He gave me a look that wasn't very soulful (or very Christian, for that matter), and left. It would not be a stretch to say Stamper stamped out.

Jacobs picked up his lemonade and sipped. From the bits of pulp floating on the surface, I deduced it was homemade. And from the way the ice cubes clittered together when he set it back down, I deduced I hadn't been wrong about the palsy. Sherlock had nothing on me that day.

"That was rude, Jamie," Jacobs said, but he sounded amused. "Especially for a guest, and an uninvited one, at that. Laura would be ashamed."

I let the reference to my mother—calculated, I'm sure—pass. "Uninvited or not, you seemed glad to see me."

"Of course. Why wouldn't I be? Try your lemonade. You look hot. Also, if I may be frank, a bit uncomfortable."

I was, but at least I wasn't frightened anymore. Angry is what I was. Here I sat in a gigantic house surrounded by a gigantic swatch of ground that no doubt included a gigantic swimming pool and a golf course—perhaps now too overgrown to be playable, but still part of the estate. A luxurious home for Charles Jacobs's electrical experiments in his later years. Somewhere else, Robert Rivard was standing in a corner, probably wearing a diaper, because bathroom functions were the least of his concerns these days. Veronica Freemont was taking the bus to work because she no longer dared to drive, and Emil Klein might still be snacking on dirt. Then there was Cathy Morse, a pretty little Sooner gal who was now in a coffin.

Easy, white boy, I heard Bree counsel. *Easy does it.*

I tasted my lemonade, then set it back down on the tray. Wouldn't want to mar the expensive cherrywood finish of the table; goddam thing was probably an antique. And okay, maybe I was still a little scared, but at least the ice cubes didn't clink in *my* glass. Jacobs, meanwhile, crossed his right leg over his left, and I noted he had to use his hands to help it along.

"Arthritis?"

"Yes, but not bad."

"I'm surprised you don't heal it with the holy rings. Or would that qualify as self-abuse?"

He gazed out at the spectacular view without replying. Shaggy iron-gray eyebrows—a unibrow, actually—drew together over the fierce blue eyes.

"Or maybe you're afraid of the aftereffects. Is that it?"

He raised a hand in a *stop* gesture. "Enough insinuations. You don't need to make them with me, Jamie. Our destinies are too entwined for that."

"I don't believe in destiny any more than you believe in God."

He turned to me, once more giving me that smile that was all teeth and no warmth. "I repeat: enough. You tell me why you came, and I'll tell you why I'm glad to see you."

There was really no way to say it but to say it. "I came to tell you that you have to stop the healing."

He sipped more lemonade. "And why would I do that, Jamie, when it's done so much good for so many?"

You know why I came, I thought. Then I had an even more uncomfortable thought: *You've been waiting for me.*

I shook the idea off.

"It's not so good for some of them." I had our master list in my back pocket, but there was no need to bring it out. I had memorized the names and the aftereffects. I began with Hugh and his prismatic interludes, and how he had suffered one at the Norris County revival.

Jacobs shrugged it off. "Stress of the moment. Has he had any since?"

"Not that he's told me."

"I think he would have, since you were there when he had the last one. Hugh's fine, I'm sure. What about you, Jamie? Any current aftereffects?"

"Bad dreams."

He made a polite scoffing sound. "Everyone has those from time to time, and that includes me. But the blackouts you suffered are gone, yes? No more compulsive talking, myoclonic movements, or poking at your skin?"

"No."

"So. You see? No worse than a sore arm after a vaccination."

"Oh, I think the aftereffects some of your followers have suffered are a little worse than that. Robert Rivard, for instance. Do you remember him?"

"The name rings a faint bell, but I've healed so many."

"From Missouri? Muscular dystrophy? His video was on your website."

"Oh, yes, now I remember. His parents made a very generous love offering."

"His MD's gone, but so is his mind. He's in the sort of hospital sometimes referred to as a vegetable patch."

"I'm very sorry to hear that," Jacobs said, and returned his attention to the view—midstate New York burning toward winter.

I went through the others, although it was clear he already knew a good deal of what I was telling him. I really surprised him only once, at the end, when I told him about Cathy Morse.

"Christ," he said. "The girl with the angry father."

"I think the angry father would do more than just punch you in the mouth this time. If he could find you, that is."

"Perhaps, but Jamie, you're not looking at the big picture." He leaned forward, hands clasped between his bony knees, his eyes on mine. "I've healed a great many poor souls. Some—the ones with psychosomatic problems—actually do the healing themselves, as I'm sure you know. But others *have* been healed by virtue of the secret electricity. Although God gets the credit, of course."

His teeth showed briefly in a cheerless spasm of a smile.

"Let me pose you a hypothetical situation. Suppose I were a neurosurgeon and you came to me with a malignant brain tumor, one not impossible to operate on but very difficult. Very risky. Suppose I told you that your chances of dying on the table were . . . mmm . . . let's say twenty-five percent. Wouldn't you still go ahead, knowing that the alternative was a period of misery followed by certain death? Of course you would. You'd beg me to operate."

I said nothing, because the logic was inarguable.

"Tell me, how many people do you think I've actually healed through electrical intervention?"

"I don't know. My assistant and I only listed the ones we felt we could be sure of. It was pretty short."

He nodded. "Good research technique."

"Glad you approve."

"I have my own list, and it's much longer. Because I *know* when it happens, you see. When it works. There is never any doubt. And based on my follow-up tracking, only a few suffer adverse effects later on. Three percent, perhaps five. Compared to the brain tumor example I just set you, I'd call those terrific odds."

I was a turn back, on the phrase *follow-up tracking*. I'd only had

Brianna. He had hundreds or even thousands of followers who would be happy to keep an eye on his cures; all he had to do was ask. "Except for Cathy Morse, you knew about every case I just cited, didn't you?"

He didn't reply. Only watched me. There was no doubt in his face, only rock solid certainty.

"Of course you did. Because you keep tabs. To you they're lab rats, and who cares if a few rats get sick? Or die?"

"That's terribly unfair."

"I don't believe it is. You put on the religious act, because if you did your stuff in the lab I'm sure you've got right here at The Latches, the government would arrest you for experimenting on human subjects . . . and killing some of them." I leaned forward, my eyes on his. "The newspapers would call you Josef Mengele."

"Does anyone call a neurosurgeon Josef Mengele just because he loses some of his patients?"

"They're not coming to you with brain tumors."

"Some have, and many of those are living and enjoying their lives today instead of lying in the ground. Did I sometimes display fake tumors when I was on the circuit? Yes, and I'm not proud of it, but it was *necessary*. Because you can't display something that's just gone." He considered. "It's true that most of the people who came to my revivals weren't suffering *terminal* illnesses, but in a way such nonfatal physical failings are worse. Those are the ones that allow folks to live long lives filled with pain. Agony, in some cases. And you sit there in judgment." He shook his head sorrowfully, but his eyes weren't sorrowful. They were furious.

"Cathy Morse wasn't in pain, and she didn't volunteer. You picked her out of the crowd because she was foxy. Eye candy for the rubes."

As Bree had, Jacobs pointed out that there might have been some other reason for Morse's suicide. Sixteen years was a long time. A lot could happen.

"You know better," I said.

He drank from his glass and set it down with a hand that was now visibly shaking. "This conversation is pointless."

"Because you won't stop?"

"Because I have. C. Danny Jacobs will never spread another revival tent. Right now there's a certain amount of discussion and speculation about that fellow on the Internet, but attention spans are short. Soon enough he'll fade from the public mind."

If that were so, I'd come to batter down a door only to discover it was unlocked. Instead of soothing me, the idea increased my unease.

"In six months, perhaps a year, the website will announce that Pastor Jacobs has retired due to ill health. After that it will go dark."

"Why? Because your research is finished?" Only, I didn't believe Charlie Jacobs's researches would ever be finished.

He turned to contemplate the view again. At last he uncrossed his legs and stood, pushing on the arms of his chair to accomplish it. "Come out back with me, Jamie. I want to show you something."

Al Stamper was at the kitchen table, a mountain of fat in '70s disco pants. He was sorting mail. In front of him was a stack of toaster waffles dripping with butter and syrup. Beside him was a liquor carton. On the floor next to his chair were three plastic USPS bins piled high with more letters and packages. As I watched, Stamper tore open a manila envelope. He shook out a scrawled letter, a photo of a boy in a wheelchair, and a ten-dollar bill. He put the ten-spot in the gin carton and scanned the letter, chomping a waffle as he did so. Standing beside him made Jacobs look thinner than ever. This time it wasn't Adam and Eve I thought of, but Jack Sprat and his wife.

"The tent may be folded," I said, "but I see the love offerings are still coming in."

Stamper gave me a look of malevolent indifference—if there is such a thing—then turned back to his opening and sorting. Not to mention his waffles.

"We read every letter," Jacobs said. "Don't we, Al?"

"Yes."

"Do you reply to every letter?" I asked.

"We ought to," Stamper said. "*I* think so, anyway. And we could, if I had help. One person would be enough, along with a computer to replace the one Pastor Danny carted out to his workshop."

"We've discussed that, Al," Jacobs said. "Once we started corresponding with supplicants . . ."

"We'd never finish, I know. I just wonder what happened to the Lord's work."

"You're doing it," Jacobs said. His voice was gentle. His eyes, however, were amused: the eyes of a man watching a dog do a trick.

Stamper made no reply, just opened the next envelope. No picture in this one, just a letter and a five-spot.

"Come on, Jamie," Jacobs said. "Let's leave him to it."

From the driveway, the outbuildings had looked trim and spruce, but closer up I could see that the boards were splintering in places and the trim needed a touch-up. The Bermuda grass we walked through, undoubtedly a hefty expense when the estate was last landscaped, needed to be cut. If it didn't happen soon, the two-acre expanse of back lawn would revert to meadow.

Jacobs stopped. "Which building do you think is my lab?"

I pointed to the barn. It was the largest, about the size of the rented auto body shop in Tulsa.

He smiled. "Did you know that the staff involved in the Manhattan Project shrank steadily before the first A-bomb test at White Sands?"

I shook my head.

"By the time the bomb went off, several of the prefab dormitories built to house the workers were empty. Here's a little-known rule about scientific research: as one progresses toward one's ultimate goal, support requirements tend to shrink."

He led me toward what looked like a humble toolshed, produced a key ring, and opened the door. I expected it to be hot inside, but it was as cool as the big house. There was a worktable running down the lefthand side with nothing on it but a few notebooks and a Macintosh computer, currently showing a screen saver of endlessly galloping horses. In front of the Mac was a chair that looked ergonomic and expensive.

On the right side of the shed were shelves stacked with boxes that looked like silver-plated cigarette cartons . . . only cigarette cartons don't hum like amplifiers on standby. On the floor was another box, this one painted green and about the size of a hotel mini-fridge. On top of it was a TV monitor. Jacobs clapped his hands softly and the monitor's screen lit up, showing a series of columns—red, blue, and green—that rose and fell in a way that suggested respiration. In terms of entertainment value I didn't think it would ever replace *Big Brother*.

"This is where you work?"

"Yes."

"Where's the equipment? The instruments?"

He pointed to the Mac, then to the monitor. "There and there. But the most important part . . ." He pointed to his own temple, like a man miming suicide. "Up here. You happen to be standing in the world's most advanced electronics research facility. The things I have discovered in this room make Edison's Menlo Park discoveries pale into insignificance. They are things that could change the world."

But would the change be for the better, I wondered. I didn't like the dreamy, proprietary expression on his face as he gazed around at what looked to me like almost nothing. Yet I couldn't dismiss his claim as delusion. There was a sense of sleeping power in the silver cartons and the green fridge-size box. Being in that shed was like standing too close to a power plant working at full bore, close enough to feel the stray volts zinging the metal fillings in your mouth.

"I'm currently generating electricity by geothermal means." He patted the green box. "This is a geosynchronous generator. Below it is a well pipe no bigger than the kind that might serve a medium-size country dairy farm. Yet at half power, this gennie could create enough superheated steam to power not just The Latches, but the entire Hudson Valley. At full power it could boil the entire aquifer like water in a teapot. Which might defeat the purpose." He laughed heartily.

"Not possible," I said. But of course, neither was curing brain tumors and severed spinal cords with holy rings.

"I assure you it is, Jamie. With a slightly bigger generator, which I could build with parts easily available by mail order, I could light up the whole East Coast." He said this calmly, not boasting but only stating a fact. "I'm not doing it because energy creation doesn't interest me. Let the world strangle in its own effluent; as far as I'm concerned, it deserves no better. And for my purposes, I'm afraid geothermal energy is a dead end. It's not enough." He looked broodingly at the horses galloping across the face of his computer.

"I expected better from this place, especially in summer, when . . . but never mind."

"And none of this runs on electricity as it's now understood?"

He gave me a look of amused contempt. "Of course not."

"It runs on the *secret* electricity."

"Yes. That's what I call it."

"A kind of electricity that nobody else has discovered in all the years since Scribonius. Until you came along. A minister who used to build battery-driven toys as a hobby."

"Oh, it's known. Or was. In *De Vermis Mysteriis*, written in the late fifteenth century, Ludvig Prinn mentions it. He calls it *potestas magnum universum*, the force that powers the universe. Prinn actually quotes Scribonius. In the years since I left Harlow, *potestas universum*—the search for it, the quest to harness it—has become my whole life."

I wanted to believe he was delusional, but the cures and the strange three-dimensional portraits I'd seen him create in Tulsa argued against that. Maybe it didn't matter. Maybe all that mattered was whether or not he was telling the truth about mothballing C. Danny Jacobs. If he was done with miracle cures, my mission was accomplished. Wasn't it?

He adopted a lecturely tone. "To understand how I've progressed so far and discovered so much on my own, you have to realize that science is in many ways as faddish as the fashion industry. The Trinity explosion at White Sands happened in 1945. The Russians exploded their first A-bomb in Semipalatinsk, four years later. Electricity was first generated by nuclear fission in Arco, Idaho, in 1951. In the half century since, electricity has become the ugly bridesmaid; nuclear power is the beautiful bride everyone sighs over. Soon fission will be demoted to ugly bridesmaid and fusion will become the beautiful bride. When it comes to research into electrical theory, grants and subsidies have dried up. More importantly, *interest* has dried up. Electricity is now seen as antique, even though *every* modern power source must be converted to amps and volts!"

Less lecture now, and more outrage.

"In spite of its vast power to kill and cure, in spite of the way it's reshaped the lives of every person on the planet, *and in spite of the fact that it is still not understood*, scientific research in this field is viewed with good-natured contempt! Neutrons are sexy! Electricity is dull, the equivalent of a dusty storage room from which all the valuable items have been taken, leaving only worthless junk. But the room isn't empty. There's an unfound door at the back, leading to chambers few people have ever seen, ones filled with objects of unearthly beauty. And there's no end to those chambers."

"You're starting to make me feel nervous, Charlie." I intended it to sound light, but it came out dead serious.

He paid no notice, only began to limp up and down between the worktable and the shelves, staring at the floor, touching the green box each time he passed it, as if to assure himself it was still there.

"Yes, others have visited those chambers. I'm not the first. Scribonius for one. Prinn for another. But most have kept their discoveries to themselves, just as I have. Because the power is enormous. Unknowable, really. Nuclear power? Pah! It's a joke!" He touched the green box. "What's in here could, if connected to a source powerful enough, make nuclear energy as insignificant as a child's cap pistol."

I wished I'd brought my lemonade with me, because my throat was dry. I had to clear it before I could speak. "Charlie, let's say everything you're telling me is true. Do you understand what you're dealing with? How it works?"

"A fair question. Let me pose one in return. Do *you* understand what happens when you flick a wall switch? Could you list the sequence of events that ends with light banishing the shadows in a dark room?"

"No."

"Do you even know if that flick of your finger closes a circuit or opens one?"

"No idea."

"Yet that never stopped you from turning on a light, did it? Or powering up your electric guitar when it was time to play?"

"True, but I never plugged into an amp powerful enough to light the whole East Coast."

He gave me a look of suspicion so dark it seemed close to paranoia. "If you have a point, I'm afraid I'm not taking it."

I believed he was telling the truth about that, which might have been the scariest thing of all.

"Never mind." I took him by the shoulders to stop his pacing and waited until he looked at me. Only even with his wide eyes fixed on my face, it was more like he was looking through me.

"Charlie—if you're done curing people, and if you don't want to end the energy crunch, what *do* you want?"

At first he didn't reply. He seemed to be in a trance. Then he pulled away from me and began pacing again, reverting to the lecture-hall prof.

"The transfer devices—the ones I use on human beings—have undergone a number of iterations. When I cured Hugh Yates of his deafness, I was using large rings coated in gold and palladium. They seem hilariously old-fashioned to me now, videocassettes in the age of computer downloads. The headphones I used on you were smaller and more powerful. By the time you appeared with your heroin problem, I had replaced palladium with osmium. Osmium is less expensive—a plus for a man on a budget, as I was then—and the headphones were effective, but they'd hardly look good at a revival meeting, would they? Did Jesus wear headphones?"

"Probably not," I said, "but I doubt if he wore wedding rings, either, being a bachelor."

He paid no attention. He paced back and forth like a man in a cell. Or the paranoids who circulate in any big city, the ones who want to talk about the CIA and the international Jewish conspiracy and the secrets of the Rosicrucians. "So I went back to the rings, and created a story that would make them . . . palatable . . . to my congregants."

"A pitch, in other words."

That brought him back to the here and now. He grinned, and for a moment I was with the Reverend Jacobs I remembered from my childhood. "Yes, okay, a pitch. By then I was using a ruthenium and gold alloy, and consequently the rings were much smaller. And even more powerful. Shall we leave, Jamie? You're looking a bit unsettled."

"I am. I may not understand your juice, but I can feel it. Almost like it's putting bubbles in my blood."

He laughed. "Yes! You could say the atmosphere in here is *electric*! Ha! I enjoy it, but then, I'm used to it. Come, let's step outside and get some fresh air."

The outside world never smelled sweeter than it did as we strolled back toward the house.

"I have one more question, Charlie. If you don't mind?"

He sighed, but didn't look displeased. Once out of that claustrophobia-inducing little room, he seemed sane again. "Glad to answer if I can."

"You tell the rubes your wife and son drowned. Why do you lie? I don't see what purpose it can serve."

He stopped and lowered his head. When he lifted it, I saw that serene normality had taken a hike, if it had ever been there at all. On his face was a rage so deep and black that I involuntarily fell back a step. The breeze had tumbled his thinning hair over his lined brow. He swept it back and then pressed his palms to his temples, like a man suffering a monster headache. Yet when he spoke, his voice was toneless and low. If not for the look on his face, I might have mistaken it for reasonableness.

"They don't deserve the truth. You called them rubes, and how right you are. They have set aside what brains they have—and many of them have quite a lot—and put their faith in that gigantic and fraudulent insurance company called religion. It promises them an eternity of joy in the next life if they live according to the rules in this one, and many of them try, but even that's not enough. When the pain comes, they want miracles. To them I'm nothing but a witch doctor who touches them with magic rings instead of shaking a bone rattle over them."

"Haven't any of them found out the truth?" My researches with Bree had convinced me that Fox Mulder was right about one thing: the truth is out there, and anyone in our current age, where almost everyone is living in a glass house, can find it with a computer and an Internet connection.

"Aren't you listening to me? They don't deserve the truth, and that's okay, because they don't *want* it." He smiled, and his teeth appeared, the upper and lower sets locked together. "They don't want the Beatitudes of the Song of Solomon, either. They only want to be healed."

• • •

Stamper didn't glance up as we crossed the kitchen. Two of the mail bins had been emptied and he was working on the third. The liquor box now looked about half full. There were some checks, but mostly it was crumpled currency. I thought of what Jacobs had said about witch doctors. In Sierra Leone, his customers would be lined up outside the door, bearing produce and chickens with freshly wrung necks. Same thing, really; all of it's just the kick. The grab. The take.

Back in the library, Jacobs seated himself with a grimace and drank the rest of his lemonade. "I'll have to piss all afternoon," he said. "It's the curse of growing old. The reason I was glad to see you, Jamie, is because I want to hire you."

"You want to *what?*"

"You heard me. Al will be leaving soon. I'm not sure he knows it yet, but I do. He wants no part of my scientific work; even though he knows it's the basis of my cures, he thinks it's an abomination."

I almost said, *What if he's right?*

"You can do his job—open each day's mail, catalogue the correspondents' names and complaints, put aside the love offerings, once a week drive down to Latchmore and deposit the checks. You'll vet gate-callers—their numbers are drying up, but there are still at least a dozen a week—and turn them away."

He turned to face me directly.

"You can also do what Al refuses to do—help me along the final steps to my goal. I'm very close, but I'm not strong. An assistant would be invaluable, and we've worked well before. I don't know how much Hugh is paying you, but I'll double—no, triple it. What do you say?"

At first I could say nothing. I was stunned.

"Jamie? I'm waiting."

I picked up the lemonade, and this time the melting remnants of the ice cubes *did* click together. I drank, then put it down again.

"You speak of a goal. Tell me what it is."

He considered. Or appeared to. "Not yet. Come to work for me and get to understand the power and beauty of the secret electricity a little better. Perhaps then."

I stood and held out my hand. "It's been nice to see you again." Another of those things you just say, a bit of grease to keep the wheels turning, but this lie was a lot bigger than telling him he looked great. "Take care of yourself. And be careful."

He stood, but didn't take my hand. "I'm disappointed in you. And, I confess, rather angry. You came a long way to scold a tired old man who once saved your life."

"Charlie, what if this secret electricity of yours gets out of your control?"

"It won't."

"I'll bet the people in charge at Chernobyl felt that way, too."

"That's beyond low. I allowed you into my home because I expected gratitude and understanding. I see I was wrong on both counts. Al will show you out. I need to lie down. I'm very tired."

"Charlie, I *do* feel gratitude. I appreciate what you've done for me. But—"

"But." His face was stony and gray. "Always a but."

"Secret electricity aside, I can't work for a man who's taking revenge on broken people because he can't take revenge on God for killing his wife and son."

His face went from gray to white. "How dare you? How *dare* you?"

"You may be curing some of them," I said, "but you're pissing on all of them. I'll leave now. I don't need Mr. Stamper to show me out."

I started back toward the front door. I was crossing the rotunda, my heels clacking on the marble, when he called after me, his voice amplified by all that open space.

"We're not done, Jamie. I promise you that. Not even close to done."

I didn't need Stamper to open the gate, either; it rolled back automatically as my car approached. At the foot of the access road I stopped, saw that I had bars on my cell, and called Bree. She answered on the first ring, and asked if I was all right before I could even open my mouth. I said I was, and then told her that Jacobs had offered me a job.

"Are you serious?"

"Yes. I told him no—"

"Well, damn, of *course* you did!"

"That's not the important part, though. He says he's done with the revival tours, and done healing. From the disgruntled demeanor of Mr. Al Stamper, formerly of the Vo-Lites and now Charlie's personal assistant, I believe him."

"So it's over?"

"As the Lone Ranger used to say to his faithful Indian sidekick, 'Tonto, our work here is done.'" *As long as he doesn't blow up the world with his secret electricity.*

"Call me when you get back to Colorado."

"I'll do that, Swee' Pea. How's New York?"

"It's great!" The enthusiasm I heard in her voice made me feel a lot older than fifty-three.

We talked about her new life in the big city for awhile, then I put my car in drive and turned onto the highway, heading back to the airport. A few miles down the road I looked into my rearview and saw an orange moonlet in the backseat.

I'd forgotten to give Charlie his pumpkin.

X

Wedding Bells. How to Boil a Frog. The Homecoming Party. "You Will Want to Read This."

Although I talked to Bree many times over the next two years, I didn't actually see her again until June 19th of 2011, when, in a church on Long Island, she became Brianna Donlin-Hughes. Many of the calls were about Charles Jacobs and his troubling cures—we found half a dozen more who were suffering probable aftereffects—but as time passed, our conversations focused more and more on her job and George Hughes, whom she had met at a party and with whom she was soon sharing accommodations. He was a high-powered corporate lawyer, he was African American, and he had just turned thirty. I was sure Bree's mother was satisfied on all counts . . . or as satisfied as the single mother of an only child can be.

Meanwhile, Pastor Danny's website had gone dark and Internet chatter about him had thinned to a trickle. There were speculations that he was either dead or in a private institution somewhere, probably under an assumed name and suffering from Alzheimer's. By late 2010, I had gleaned only two pieces of hard intelligence, both interesting but neither illuminating. Al Stamper had released a gospel CD called *Thank You Jesus* (guest artists included Hugh Yates's idol, Mavis Staples), and The Latches was once more available for lease to "qualified individuals or organizations."

Charles Daniel Jacobs had dropped off the radar.

Hugh Yates chartered a Gulfstream for the nuptials, and packed everyone from the Wolfjaw Ranch on board. Mookie McDonald represented the sixties admirably at the wedding, turning up in a paisley shirt with billowy sleeves, pipestem trousers, suede Beatle boots, and a psychedelic headscarf. The mother of the bride was just short of eye-popping in a vintage Ann Lowe dress she'd gotten on consignment, and as the vows were exchanged, she watered her corsage with copious tears. The groom could have stepped out of a Nora Roberts novel: tall, dark, and handsome. He and I had a friendly conversation at the reception, before the party began its inevitable journey from tipsy conversation to drunk-ass dancing. I had no sense that Bree had told him I was the jalopy with the rusty rocker panels on which she had learned, although I was sure that someday she would—in bed after particularly good sex, likely as not. That was fine with me, because I wouldn't have to be there for the inevitable masculine eye-roll.

The Nederland group went back to Colorado via American Airlines, because Hugh's gift to the newlyweds was use of the Gulfstream, which would fly them to their Hawaiian honeymoon retreat. When he announced this during the toasts, Bree squealed like a nine-year-old, jumped up, and hugged him. I'm sure Charles Jacobs was the furthest thing from her mind at that moment, which was just as it should have been. But he never left mine, not completely.

As the hour grew late, I saw Mookie whispering to the leader of the band, a very decent rock-and-blues combo with a strong lead singer and a good backlog of oldies at their command. The bandleader nodded and asked if I'd like to come up and play guitar with the band for a set or two. I was tempted, but my better angels won the day and I begged off. You may never be too old to rock and roll, but skills fade as the years stack up, and the chances of making a fool of oneself in public grow better.

I didn't exactly consider myself retired, but I hadn't played in front of a live audience in over a year, and had only sat in on three or four recording sessions, all cases of dire emergency. I did not acquit myself well in any of them. During the playback of one, I caught the drummer grimacing, as if he'd bitten into something sour. He saw me looking at him and said the bass had fallen out of tune. It hadn't, and we both knew it. If it's ridiculous for a man in his fifties to be playing bedroom games with a woman young enough to be his daughter, it's just as ridiculous for him to be playing a Strat and high-stepping to "Dirty Water." Still, I watched those guys kick out the jams with some longing and quite a lot of nostalgia.

Someone took my hand and I looked around to see Georgia Donlin. "How much do you miss it, Jamie?"

"Not as much as I respect it," I said, "which is why I'm sitting here. Those guys are good."

"And you're not anymore?"

I found myself remembering the day I had walked into my brother Con's bedroom and heard his acoustic Gibson whispering to me. Telling me I could play "Cherry, Cherry."

"Jamie?" She snapped her fingers in front of my eyes. "Come back, Jamie."

"I'm good enough to amuse myself," I said, "but my days of getting up in front of a crowd with a guitar are over."

Turned out I was wrong about that.

• • •

In 2012, I turned fifty-six. Hugh and his longtime girlfriend took me out to dinner. On the way home I remembered a bit of old folklore—probably you've heard it—about how to boil a frog. You put it in cold water, then start turning up the heat. If you do it gradually, the frog is too stupid to jump out. I don't know if it's true or not, but I decided it was an excellent metaphor for growing old.

When I was a teenager, I looked at over-fifties with pity and unease: they walked too slow, they talked too slow, they watched TV instead of going out to movies and concerts, their idea of a great party was hotpot with the neighbors and tucked into bed after the eleven o'clock news. But—like most other fifty-, sixty-, and seventysomethings who are in relative good health—I didn't mind it so much when my turn came. Because the *brain* doesn't age, although its ideas about the world may harden and there's a greater tendency to run off at the mouth about how things were in the good old days. (I was spared that, at least, because most of my so-called good old days had been spent as a full-bore, straight-on-for-Texas drug addict.) I think for most people, life's deceptive deliriums begin to fall away after fifty. The days speed up, the aches multiply, and your gait slows down, but there are compensations. In calmness comes appreciation, and—in my case—a determination to be as much of a do-right-daddy as possible in the time I had left. That meant ladling out soup once a week at a homeless shelter in Boulder, and working for three or four political candidates with the radical idea that Colorado should not be paved over.

I still dated the occasional lady. I still played tennis twice a week and rode my bike at least six miles a day, which kept my stomach flat and my endorphins flowing. Sure, I saw a few more lines around my mouth and eyes when I shaved, but on the whole, I thought I looked about the same as ever. That, of course, is the benign illusion of one's later years. It took going back to Harlow in the summer of 2013 for me to understand the truth: I was just another frog in a pot. The good news was that so far the temperature had only been turned up to medium. The bad was that the process wouldn't be stopping anytime soon. The three true ages of man are youth, middle age, and how the fuck did I get old so soon?

On June 19th of 2013, two years to the day after Bree's marriage to George Hughes and a year after the birth of their first child, I arrived home from a less-than-stellar recording session to find an envelope gaily decorated with balloons in my mailbox. The return address was familiar: RFD #2, Methodist Road, Harlow, Maine. I opened it and found myself looking at a photograph of my brother Terry's family with this caption: *TWO ARE BETTER THAN ONE! PLEASE COME TO OUR PARTY!*

I paused before opening it, noting Terry's white hair, Annabelle's expanding paunch, and the three young adults who were their children. The little girl who had once run giggling through the lawn sprinkler in nothing but a saggy pair of Smurfette underpants was now a good-looking young woman with a baby—my grand-niece, Cara Lynne—in her arms. One of my nephews, the skinny one, looked like Con. The husky one looked eerily like our father . . . and a little like me, poor guy.

I flipped the invitation open.

HELP US CELEBRATE TWO BIG DAYS
ON AUGUST 31, 2013!

THE 35TH WEDDING ANNIVERSARY OF
TERENCE AND ANNABELLE!
THE 1ST BIRTHDAY OF CARA LYNNE!

TIME: 12 NOON to ?
PLACE: OUR HOUSE TO START, THEN EUREKA GRANGE
FOOD: PLENTY!
BAND: THE CASTLE ROCK ALL-STARS
BYOB: DON'T YOU DARE! BEER & WINE WILL FLOW!

Below this was a note from my brother. Although only months from his sixtieth birthday, Terry wrote in the same grade-school scrawl that had caused one of his teachers to send him home with a note reading *Terence MUST improve his penmanship!* paperclipped to his rank card.

Hey Jamie! Please come to the party, okay? No excuses accepted when you've got 2 mos to arrange your schedule. If Connie can come from Hawaii you can manage the trip from Colo! We miss you, little bro!

I dropped the invitation into the wicker basket on the back of the kitchen door. I called this the Sometime Basket, because it was full of correspondence that I vaguely believed I'd answer sometime . . . which actually meant never, as you probably know. I told myself I had no desire to go back to Harlow, and this may have been true, but the pull of family was still there. Springsteen might have had something when he wrote that line about nothing feeling better than blood on blood.

I had a cleaning lady named Darlene who came by once a week

to vacuum and dust and change the bed (a chore I still felt guilty about delegating, having been taught to do myself, back in the day). She was a morose old thing, and I made it my business to be out when she was in. On one of Darlene's days, I came back to find she had fished the invitation out of the Sometime Basket and propped it open on the kitchen table. She had never done such a thing before, and I took it as an omen. That night I sat down at my computer, sighed, and sent Terry a three-word email: *Count me in*.

That was quite a Labor Day weekend. I enjoyed the hell out of myself, and could hardly believe I'd come close to saying no . . . or saying nothing, which probably would have severed my already frayed family ties for good.

It was hot in New England, and the descent into Portland Jetport on Friday afternoon was unusually bumpy in the unstable air. The drive north to Castle County was slow, but not because of traffic. I had to look at every old landmark—the farms, the rock walls, Brownie's Store, now closed and dark—and marvel over them. It was as if my childhood were still here, barely visible under a piece of plastic that had become scratched and dusty and semi-opaque with the passage of time.

It was past six in the evening when I got to the home place, where an addition had been built on, nearly doubling its original size. There was a red Mazda in the driveway that screamed airport rental (like my Ford Eclipse), and a Morton Fuel Oil truck parked on the lawn. The truck was garlanded with enough crepe paper and flowers to make it look like a parade float. A big sign propped against the front wheels read THE SCORE IS TERRY AND ANNABELLE 35, CARA LYNNE 1! BOTH WINNERS!!

YOU FOUND THE PARTY! COME ON IN! I parked, walked up the steps, raised my fist to knock, thought what the hell, I grew up here, and just strolled in.

For a moment I felt as if I had flipped back in time to the years when I could tell my age with a single number. My family was crowded around the dining room table just as they had been in the sixties, all talking at once, laughing and squabbling, passing pork chops, mashed potatoes, and a platter covered with a damp dish-towel: corn on the cob, kept warm just as my mother used to do it.

At first I didn't recognize the distinguished gray-haired man at the living room end of the table, and I certainly didn't know the dark-haired hunk of handsome sitting next to him. Then the professor-emeritus type caught sight of me and rose to his feet, his face lighting up, and I realized it was my brother Con.

"*JAMIE!*" he shouted, and buttonhooked around the table, almost knocking Annabelle out of her chair. He grabbed me in a bearhug and covered my face with kisses. I laughed and pounded him on the back. Then Terry was there as well, grabbing both of us, and the three brothers did a kind of clumsy *mitzvah tantz*, making the floor shake. I saw that Con was crying, and I felt a little bit like crying myself.

"Stop it, you guys!" Terry said, although he was still jumping himself. "We'll wind up in the basement!"

For awhile we went on jumping. It seemed to me that we had to. And that was all right. That was good.

Con introduced the hunk, who was probably twenty years his junior, as "my good friend from the University of Hawaii Botany Department." I shook hands with him, wondering if they had bothered to take two rooms at the Castle Rock Inn. In this day and age, probably not. I can't remember when I first realized that Con was gay; probably while he was in grad school and I was still playing "Land of 1000 Dances" with the Cumberlands at the University of Maine. I'm sure our parents knew much earlier. They didn't make a big deal of it, and so none of us did, either. Children learn much more by mute example than by spoken rules, or so it seems to me.

I only heard Dad allude to his second son's sexual orientation once, during the late eighties. It must have made a big impression on me, because those were my blackout years, and I called home as seldom as possible. I wanted my dad to know I was still alive, but I was always afraid he might hear my oncoming death, which I had pretty much accepted, in my voice.

"I pray for Connie every night," he said during that call. "This damn AIDS thing. It's like they're letting it spread on purpose."

Con had avoided that and looked awesomely healthy now, but there was no disguising the fact that he was getting on, especially sitting next to his friend from the Botany Department. I had a flash memory of Con and Ronnie Paquette sitting shoulder to shoulder on the living room couch, singing "House of the Rising Sun" and trying to harmonize . . . an exercise in futility if there ever was one.

Some of this must have shown on my face, because Con grinned as he wiped his eyes. "Been a long time since we were arguing over whose turn it was to bring in Ma's laundry off the line, huh?"

"Long time," I agreed, and thought again of a frog too dumb to realize the water in his stovetop pond was growing ever warmer.

Terry and Annabelle's daughter, Dawn, joined us with Cara Lynne in her arms. The baby's eyes were that shade our mother used to call Morton Blue. "Hi, Uncle Jamie. Here's your grand-niece. She's one tomorrow, and she's getting a new tooth to celebrate."

"She's beautiful. Can I hold her?"

Dawn smiled shyly at the stranger she'd last seen when she was still in braces. "You can try, but she usually bawls her head off when it's someone she doesn't know."

I took the baby, ready to hand her back the second the yowls started. Only they didn't. Cara Lynne examined me, reached out a hand, and tweaked my nose. Then she laughed. My family cheered and applauded. The baby looked around, startled, then looked back at me with what I could have sworn were my mother's eyes.

And laughed again.

The actual party the next day had much the same cast, only with more supporting characters. Some I recognized at once; others looked vaguely familiar, and I realized several were children of people who had worked for my father long ago and now worked for Terry, whose empire had grown: as well as the fuel oil business, he owned a New England–wide chain of convenience stores called Morton's Fast-Shops. Bad handwriting had been no bar to success.

A catering crew from Castle Rock presided over four grills, dealing out hamburgers and hotdogs to go with a mind-boggling array of salads and desserts. Beer flowed from steel kegs and wine from wooden ones. As I chowed down on a bacon-loaded calorie-bomb in the backyard, one of Terry's salesmen—drunk, cheerful, and voluble—told me Terry also owned Splash City in Fryeburg and Littleton Raceway in New Hampshire. "That track don't make a cent of money," the salesman said, "but you know Terry—he always loved the stocks and bombers."

I remembered him working with my father on various incarnations of the Road Rocket in the garage, both of them dressed in greasy tee-shirts and saggy-butt coveralls, and suddenly realized that my hometown, country-mouse brother was well-to-do. Perhaps even rich.

Every time Dawn brought Cara Lynne near, the little girl held her arms out to me. I ended up toting her around for most of the afternoon, and she finally fell asleep on my shoulder. Seeing this, her dad relieved me of my burden. "I'm amazed," he said as he laid her on a blanket in the shade of the backyard's biggest tree. "She never takes to folks like that."

"I'm flattered," I said, and kissed the sleeping baby's teething-flushed cheek.

There was a lot of talk about old days and old times, the kind of chatter that's fabulously interesting to those who were there and stupendously boring to those who weren't. I steered clear of the beer and wine, so when the party moved four miles down the road to the Eureka Grange, I was one of the designated drivers, trying to find my way through the gears of a monster King Cab pickup that belonged to the oil company. I hadn't driven a standard in thirty years, and my inebriated passengers—there must have been a dozen, counting the seven or so in the truck bed—howled with laughter each time I popped the clutch and the truck lurched. It was a wonder none of them tumbled out the back.

The catering crew had arrived ahead of us, and there were already food tables set up along the sides of a dance floor that I remembered well. I stood there looking at that expanse of polished wood until Con squeezed my shoulder.

"Bring back memories, baby brother?"

I thought of walking onto the bandstand for the first time, scared to death and smelling the sweat that came roasting up from my armpits in waves. And later, Mom and Dad waltzing by as we played "Who'll Stop the Rain?"

"More than you'll ever know," I said.

"I think I do," he said, and hugged me. In my ear he whispered it again: "I think I do."

• • •

There were maybe seventy people at the home place for the noon meal; by seven o'clock, there were twice that many at Eureka Grange No. 7, and the place could have used some of Charlie Jacobs's magic air-conditioning to augment the lackadaisical ceiling fans. I grabbed the sort of dessert that was still a Harlow specialty—lime Jell-O with bits of canned fruit suspended in it—and took it outside. I walked around the corner of the building, nibbling away with a plastic spoon, and there was the fire escape beneath which I had kissed Astrid Soderberg for the first time. I remembered how the fur parka she had been wearing framed the perfect oval of her face. I remembered the taste of her strawberry lipstick.

Was it all right? I had asked. And she had replied, *Do it again and I'll tell you.*

"Hey, freshie." From right behind me, making me jump. "Want to play some music tonight?"

At first I didn't recognize him. The lanky, long-haired teenager who had recruited me to play rhythm guitar in Chrome Roses was now bald on top, gray on the sides, and sporting a gut that hung over his tight-cinched trousers. I stared at him, my little paper bowl of Jell-O drooping in one hand.

"Norm? Norm Irving?"

He grinned widely enough to flash gold teeth at the back of his mouth. I dropped my Jell-O and hugged him. He laughed and hugged me back. We told each other that we looked great. We told each other it had been too long. And of course we talked about the old days. Norm said he'd gotten Hattie Greer pregnant and married her. It only lasted a few years, but after a period of post-divorce acrimony, they had decided to put the past aside and be friends.

Their daughter, Denise, was now pushing forty, and owned her own hair salon in Westbrook.

"Free and clear, too, bank all paid off. I got two boys by my second wife, but between you and me, Deenie's my darlin. Hattie's got one by her second husband." He leaned closer, smiling grimly. "In and out of jail. Kid's not worth the powder to blow him to hell."

"What about Kenny and Paul?"

Kenny Laughlin, our bass player, had also married his Chrome Roses sweetie, and they were still married. "He owns an insurance agency in Lewiston. Doin good. He's here tonight. You didn't see him?"

"No." Although maybe I had, and just hadn't recognized him. And maybe he hadn't recognized me.

"As for Paul Bouchard . . ." Norm shook his head. "He was climbing in Acadia State Park and took a fall. Lived two days, then passed away. 1990, that was. Probably a mercy. Docs said he would have been paralyzed from the neck down, if he'd lived. What they call a quad."

For a moment I imagined our old drummer pulling through. Lying in bed with a machine to help him breathe and watching Pastor Danny on TV. I shook the thought away. "What about Astrid? Do you know where she is?"

"Downeast somewhere. Castine? Rockland?" He shook his head. "Don't remember. I know she dropped out of college to get married, and her folks were pissed at her. Probably double pissed when she got divorced. I think she runs a restaurant, one of those lobster shack things, but don't quote me. You guys had it bad, didn't you?"

"Yes," I said. "We sure did."

He nodded. "Young love. Nothin on earth like it. Not sure I'd want to see her these days, because the old Soda Burger was steppin dynamite back then. Steppin *nitro.* Wasn't she?"

"Yes," I said, thinking of the ruined cabin next to Skytop. And the iron rod. How it glowed red when the lightning struck it. "Yes, she was."

For a moment we said nothing, then he clapped me on the shoulder. "Anyway, what do you think? Gonna gig with us? You better say yes, because the band's gonna be fuckin lame if you say no."

"*You're* in the band? The Castle Rock All-Stars? Kenny too?"

"Sure. We don't play much anymore—not like the old days—but no way we could turn this one down."

"Did my brother Terry put you up to this?"

"He might've thought you'd come up for a tune or two, but no. He just wanted a band from the old days, and me and Kenny are about the only ones from back then who are still alive, still hanging around this shit-all neck of the woods, and still playing. Our rhythm guy's a carpenter from Lisbon Falls, and last Wednesday he fell off a roof and broke both legs."

"Ouch," I said.

"His ouch is my gain," Norm Irving said. "We were gonna play as a trio, which, as you know, sucks the bird. Three out of four Chrome Roses ain't bad, considering we played our last gig at the PAL hop up-the-city over thirty-five years ago. So come on. Reunion tour, and all that."

"Norm, I don't have a guitar."

"I got three in the truck," he said. "You can take your pick. Just remember, we still start with 'Hang On Sloopy.'"

We trooped onstage to enthusiastic, alcohol-fueled applause. Kenny Laughlin, as thin as ever but now sporting several less than lovely moles on his face, looked up from adjusting the strap on his Fender P-Bass and dapped me. I wasn't nervous, as I had been the first time I stood on this stage with a guitar in my hands, but I did feel as if I were having a particularly vivid dream.

Norm adjusted his mike one-handed, just as he always had, and addressed the audience waiting to bust a few of their old-time rock-and-roll moves. "It says Castle Rock All-Stars on the drumkit, folks, but tonight we've got a special guest on rhythm, and for the next couple of hours, we're Chrome Roses again. Kick it in, Jamie."

I thought of kissing Astrid under the fire escape. I thought of Norm's rusty microbus and of his father, Cicero, sitting on the busted-down sofa in his old trailer, rolling dope in Zig-Zag papers and telling me if I wanted to get my license first crack out of the basket, I'd better cut my fucking hair. I thought of playing teen dances at the Auburn RolloDrome, and how we never stopped when the inevitable fights broke out between the kids from Edward Little and Lisbon High, or those from Lewiston High and St. Dom's; we just turned it up louder. I thought of how life had been before I realized I was a frog in a pot.

I shouted: "*One, two, you-know-what-to-do!*"

We kicked it in.

Key of E.

All that shit starts in E.

In the seventies, we might have played until one-o'clock curfew, but this was no longer the seventies, and by eleven o'clock we were dripping sweat and exhausted. That was okay; on Terry's orders, the beer and wine had been whisked away at ten, and with no more firewater, the crowd thinned out fast. Most of those remaining had resumed their seats, content to listen but too exhausted to dance.

"You're a hell of a lot better than you used to be, freshie," Norm said as we racked our instruments.

"So are you." Which was as much a lie as *you look great*. At fourteen I never would have believed the day would come when I'd be a better rock guitarist than Norman Irving, but that day had come. He gave me a smile to say he knew what was better left unspoken. Kenny joined us, and the three remaining members of Chrome Roses huddled in a hug we would have called "faggot stuff" when we were in high school.

Terry joined us, along with Terry Jr., his eldest son. My brother looked tired, but he also looked supremely happy. "Listen, Con and his friend took a bunch of folks who were too loaded to drive back to Castle Rock. Will you haul a bunch of Harlow folks in the King Cab, if I lend you Terry Jr. to copilot?"

I said I'd be happy to, and after a final so-long to Norm and Kenny (accompanied by those weird limp-fish handshakes peculiar to musicians), I gathered up my load of drunkies and set off. For awhile my nephew gave me instructions I hardly needed, even in the dark, but by the time I offloaded the last two or three couples out on Stackpole Road, he had ceased. I looked over and saw the kid was leaning against the passenger window, fast asleep. I woke him when we got back to the home place on Methodist Road. He kissed my cheek (which touched me more deeply than he could know), and stumbled into the house, where he would probably sleep until noon on Sunday, as adolescents are prone to do. I wondered if he would do so in my old room, and decided probably not; he'd be quartered in the new addition. Time changes everything, and maybe that's okay.

I hung the King Cab's keys on the rack in the hall, headed out to my rental car, and spied lights in the barn. I walked over, peeped in, and there was Terry. He had changed out of his party duds and into a coverall. His newest toy, a Chevy SS from the late sixties or early seventies, gleamed under the hanging lights like a blue jewel. He was Simonizing it.

He looked up when I came in. "Can't sleep just yet. Too much excitement. I'll buff on this baby for awhile, then toddle off to bed."

I ran my hand up the hood. "It's beautiful."

"*Now* it is, but you should have seen it when I picked it up at auction down in Portsmouth. Looked like junk to most of the buyers there, but I thought I could bring it back."

"Revive it," I said. Not really talking to Terry.

He gave me a thoughtful look, then shrugged. "You could call it that, I guess, and once I drop a new tranny in er, it'll be most of the way there. Not much like the old Road Rockets, is it?"

I laughed. "You remember when the first one went ass over teapot at the Speedway?"

Terry rolled his eyes. "First lap. Fucking Duane Robichaud. I think he got his license at Sears and Roebuck."

"Is he still around?"

"Nah, dead ten years. Ten at least. Brain cancer. By the time they found it, poor bastard never had a chance."

Suppose I were a neurosurgeon, Jacobs had said that day at The Latches. *Suppose I told you your chances of dying were twenty-five percent. Wouldn't you still go ahead?*

"That's tough."

He nodded. "Remember what we used to say when we were kids? 'What's tough? Life. What's *Life*? A magazine. How much does it cost? Fifteen cents. I only got a dime. That's tough. What's tough? Life.' Around and around it went."

"I remember. Back then we thought it was a joke." I hesitated. "Do you think of Claire very much, Terry?"

He tossed his polishing rag into a bucket and went to the sink to wash his hands. There had been nothing but one faucet back in the day—just cold—but now there were two. He turned them on, grabbed a cake of Lava, and began to soap up. All the way to the elbows, just as Dad had taught us.

"Every damn day. I think of Andy, too, but less often. That was what you call the natural order of things, I guess, although he might have lived a little longer if he hadn't been so fond of his knife and fork. What happened to Claire, though . . . that was just fucking *wrong*. You know?"

"Yes."

He leaned against the hood of the SS, looking at nothing in particular. "Remember how beautiful she was?" He shook his head slowly. "Our beautiful sister. That bastard—that *beast*—cheated her out of all the years she still had coming, then took the coward's way out." He swiped a hand across his face. "We shouldn't talk about Claire. It makes me emotional."

It made me emotional, too. Claire, who had been just enough older for me to see her as a kind of backup Mom. Claire, our beautiful sister, who never hurt anyone.

We walked across the dooryard, listening to the crickets sing in the high grass. They always sing the loudest in late August and early September, as if they know summer is ending.

Terry stopped at the foot of the steps, and I saw his eyes were still wet. He'd had a good day, but a long and stressful one, just the same. I had been wrong to bring up Claire at the end of it.

"Stay the night, little bro. The couch is a pullout."

"No," I said. "I promised Connie I'd have breakfast with him and his partner at the Inn in the morning."

"*Partner*," he said, and rolled his eyes. "Right."

"Now, now, Terence. Don't go all twentieth century on me. These days they could get married in a dozen states, if they wanted. Including this one."

"Oh, I don't mind that, who marries who ain't none of mine, but *partner* ain't what that guy is, no matter what Connie may think. I know a freeloader when I see one. Christ, he's half Con's age."

That made me think of Brianna, who was *less* than half my age.

I gave Terry a hug and a peck on the cheek. "I'll see you tomorrow. Lunch, before I head back to the airport."

"You got it. And Jamie? You played the spots off that guitar tonight."

I thanked him and walked to my car. I was opening the door when he spoke my name. I turned back.

"Do you remember Reverend Jacobs's last Sunday in the pulpit? When he gave what we used to call the Terrible Sermon?"

"Yes," I said. "Very well."

"We were all so shocked at the time, and we chalked it up to the grief he was feeling over the loss of his wife and son. But you know what? When I think of Claire, I think I'd like to find him and shake his hand." Terry's arms—brawny, like our father's—were folded over his coverall. "Because what I think now is that he was brave to say those things. What I think now is that every word was right."

Terry might have gotten rich, but he was still thrifty, and we ate catered leftovers for Sunday lunch. For most of it, I held Cara Lynne on my lap, feeding her tiny bits of things. When it was time for me to go and I handed her back to Dawn, the baby held her arms out to me.

"No, honey," I said, kissing that incredibly smooth forehead. "I have to go."

She only had a dozen words or so—one of them was now my name—but I've read that their understanding is much greater, and she knew what I was telling her. The little face wrinkled up, she held her arms out again, and tears filled those blue eyes that were the same shade as my mother's and my dead sister's.

"Go quick," Con said, "or you'll have to adopt her."

So I went. Back to my rental car, back to Portland Jetport, back to Denver International, back to Nederland. But I kept thinking of those chubby outstretched arms, and those tear-filled Morton Blue eyes. She was just a year old, but she had wanted me to stay longer. That's how you know you're home, I think, no matter how far you've gone from it or how long you've been in some other place.

Home is where they want you to stay longer.

During March of 2014, after most of the ski-bunnies had left Vail, Aspen, Steamboat Springs, and our own Eldora Mountain—came news of a monster blizzard approaching. Our piece of the famed Polar Vortex had dropped four feet on Greeley already.

I hung in at Wolfjaw for most of the day, helping Hugh and Mookie batten down the studios and the big house. I stayed until the wind began to pick up and the first flurries started to scatter down from the leaden skies. Then Georgia came out, dressed in a barncoat, earmuffs, and a Wolfjaw Ranch gimme cap. She was in full scold-mode.

"You send those guys home," she told Hugh. "Unless you want them stuck side o' the road somewhere until June."

"Like the Donner Party," I said. "But I'd never eat Mookie. Too tough."

"Go on, you two, scat," Hugh said. "Just double-check the studio doors on your way down to the road."

We did so, and checked the barn for good measure. I even took the time to dole out apple slices, although Bartleby, my favorite, had died three years ago. By the time I dropped Mookie off at his rooming house, it was snowing hard and the wind was blowing thirty or more. Downtown Nederland was deserted, the traffic lights swinging and drifts already piling up in the doorways of shops that had closed early for the day.

"Get home fast!" Mookie shouted to be heard over the wind. He had knotted his bandanna over his mouth and nose, making him look like an elderly outlaw.

I did as he said, the wind shouldering at my car like a bad-tempered bully the whole way. It pushed me even harder as I made my way up the walk, clutching my collar to my face, which was clean-shaven and unprepared for what Colorado winter felt like when it decided to get serious. I had to use both hands to yank the foyer door shut once I was inside.

I checked my mailbox and saw a single letter. I pulled it out, and one glance was enough to tell me who it was from. Jacobs's handwriting had grown shaky and spidery, but was still recognizable. The only surprise was the return address: *General Delivery, Motton, Maine.* Not quite my hometown, but right next door. Too close for comfort, in my opinion.

I tapped the envelope against my palm and almost obeyed my first impulse, which was to rip it to pieces, open the door, and scatter the shreds to the wind. I still imagine doing that—every day, sometimes every hour—and wonder what might have changed if I'd done so. Instead, I turned it over. There, written in the same unsteady hand, was a single sentence: *You will want to read this.*

I didn't, but tore it open, anyway. I pulled out a single sheet of paper wrapped around a smaller envelope. Written on the face of this second envelope was *Read my letter before opening this one.* So I did.

God help me, so I did.

March 4, 2014

Dear Jamie,

I have obtained both of your e-mail addresses, business and personal (as you know, I have my methods), but I am an old man now, with an old man's ways, and believe that important personal business should be conducted by letter and, when possible, by hand. As you can see, "by hand" is still possible for me, although for how much longer I do not know. I had a minor stroke in the fall of 2012, and another one, rather more serious, last summer. I hope you will excuse the execrable state of my handwriting.

I have another reason for reaching out to you by letter. It's all too easy to delete e-mails, a bit more difficult to destroy a letter someone has labored over with pen and ink. I will add a line to the back of the envelope to increase the chances of your reading this. If I get no reply, I will have to send an emissary, and that I do not want to do, as time is short.

An emissary. I didn't like the sound of that.

When we last met, I asked you to serve as my assistant. You refused. I am asking again, and this time I am confident you will agree. You must agree, as my work is now in its final stage. All that remains is one last experiment. I am sure it will succeed, but I dare not proceed alone. I need help, and, just as important, I need a witness. Believe me when I say that you have a stake in this experiment almost as great as my own.

You think you will say no, but I know you quite well, my old friend, and I believe that after you read the enclosed letter, you will change your mind.

All best regards,
Charles D. Jacobs

The wind howled; the sound of snow hitting the panes of the door was like fine sand. The road to Boulder would be closed soon, if it wasn't already. I held the smaller envelope, thinking *something happened*. I didn't want to know what, but it felt too late to turn back now. I sat on the stairs leading to my apartment and opened the enclosure as a particularly savage gust of wind shook the building. The handwriting was as shaky as Jacobs's, sloping down the page, but I knew it at once. Of course I did; I had received love letters, some of them quite hot, in this same hand. My stomach went soft, and for a moment I thought I might pass out. I lowered my head, the hand not holding the letter covering my eyes and squeezing my temples. When the faintness passed, I was almost sorry.

I read the letter.

Feb. 25, 2014

Dear Pastor Jacobs,

You are my last hope.

I feel crazy writing that, but it's true. I'm trying to reach you because my friend Jenny Knowlton urges me to do so. She is an RN and says she never believed in miracle cures (although she does believe in God). Several years ago she went to one of your healing revivals in Providence, RI, and you cured her arthritis, which was so bad she could hardly open and close her hands and she was "hooked" on OxyContin. She said to me, "I told myself I only went to hear Al Stamper sing, because I had all his old records with the Vo-Lites, but down deep I must have known why I was really there, because when he asked if there were any who would be healed, I got in the line." She said not only did the pain in her hands and arms disappear when you touched her temples with your rings, so did the need to take the Oxy. I found that even harder to believe than the arthritis being cured, because where I live a lot of people use that stuff and I know it is very hard to "kick the habit."

Pastor Jacobs, I have lung cancer. I lost my hair during the radiation treatments and the chemo made me throw up all the time (I have lost 60 lbs), but at the end of those hellish treatments, the cancer was still there. Now my doctor wants me to have an operation to take out one of my lungs, but my friend Jenny sat me down and said, "I am going to tell you a hard truth, honey. Mostly when they do that it's already too late, and they know it but do it anyway because it's all they have left."

I turned the paper over, my head thudding. For the first time in years, I wished I were high. Being high would make it possible to look at the signature waiting for me below without wanting to scream.

Jenny says she has looked up your cures online and many more than hers appear to be valid. I know you are no longer touring the country. You may be retired, you may be sick, you may even be dead (although I pray not, for your sake as well as my own). Even if you are alive and well, you may no longer read your mail. So I know this is like putting a message in a bottle and throwing it overboard, but something—not just Jenny—urges me to try. After all, sometimes one of those bottles washes up on shore, and someone reads the message inside.

I have refused the operation. You really are my last hope. I know how thin that hope is, and probably foolish, but the Bible says, "With faith, all things are possible." I will wait to hear . . . or not. Either way, may God bless and keep you.

Yours in hope,

Astrid Soderberg
17 Morgan Pitch Road
Mt. Desert Island, Maine 04660
(207) 555-6454

Astrid. Dear God.

Astrid again, after all these years. I closed my eyes and saw her standing beneath the fire escape, her face young and beautiful, framed in the hood of her parka.

I opened my eyes and read the note Jacobs had added below her address.

> *I have seen her charts and latest scans. You may trust me on this; as I said in my covering letter, I have my methods. Radiation and chemotherapy shrank the tumor in her left lung, but did not eradicate it, and more spots have shown up on her right lung. Her condition is grave, but I can save her. You may trust me on this, too, but such cancers are like a fire in dry brush—they move fast. Her time is short, and you must decide at once.*

If it's so goddam short, I wondered, *why didn't you call, or at least send your devil's bargain by Express Mail?*

But I knew. He *wanted* time to be short, because it wasn't Astrid he cared about. Astrid was a pawn. I, on the other hand, was one of the pieces in the back row. I had no idea why, but I knew it was so.

The letter shook in my hand as I read the last lines.

> *If you agree to assist me while I finish my work this coming summer, your old friend (and, perhaps, your lover) will be saved, the cancer expelled from her body. If you refuse, I will let her die. Of course this sounds cruel to you, even monstrous, but if you knew the tremendous import of my work, you would feel differently. Yes, even you! My numbers, both landline and cell, are below. Beside me as I write this is Miss Soderberg's number. If you call me—with a favorable answer, of course—I will call her.*
>
> *The choice is yours, Jamie.*

I sat on the stairs for two minutes, taking deep breaths and willing my heart to slow. I kept thinking of her hips tilted against mine, my cock throbbing and as hard as a length of rebar, one of her hands caressing the nape of my neck as she blew cigarette smoke into my mouth.

At last I got up and climbed to my apartment, the two letters dangling from my hand. The stairs weren't long or steep, and I was in good shape from all the bike-riding, but I still had to stop and rest twice to catch my breath before I got to the top, and my hand was shaking so badly I had to steady it with the other before I could get my key into the slot.

The day was dark and my apartment was full of shadows, but I didn't bother to turn on any lights. What I had to do was best done quickly. I took my phone off my belt, dropped onto the couch, and dialed Jacobs's cell. It rang a single time.

"Hello, Jamie," he said.

"You bastard," I said. "You fucking bastard."

"Glad to hear from you, too. What's your decision?"

How much did he know about us? Had I ever told him anything? Had Astrid? If not, how much had he dug up? I didn't know and it didn't matter. I could tell from the tone of his voice that he was only asking for form's sake.

I told him I'd be there ASAP.

"If you want to come, of course. Delighted to have you, although I don't actually need you until July. If you'd rather not see her . . . as she is now, I mean—"

"I'll be on a plane as soon as the weather clears. If you can do your thing before I get there . . . fix her . . . heal her . . . then go ahead. But you will not let her leave wherever you are until I see her. No matter what."

"You don't trust me, do you?" He sounded as if this made him terribly sad, but I didn't put much stock in that. He was a master at projecting emotion.

"Why would I, Charlie? I've seen you in operation."

He sighed. The wind gusted, shaking the building and howling along the eaves.

"Where in Motton are you?" I asked . . . but, like Jacobs, only for form's sake. Life is a wheel, and it always comes back around to where it started.

XI

Goat Mountain. She Waits. Bad News from Missouri.

And so, little more than six months after the brief reincarnation of Chrome Roses, I once more touched down at the Portland Jetport and once more journeyed north to Castle County. Not to Harlow this time, though. Still five miles from the home place, I turned off Route 9 and onto Goat Mountain Road. It was a warm day, but Maine had gotten belted with its own spring blizzard a few days before, and the musical sounds of melting and runoff were everywhere. Pines and spruces still crowded close to the road, their branches sagging under the weight of snow, but the road itself had been plowed and shone wetly in the afternoon sun.

I paused for a couple of minutes at Longmeadow, site of all those childhood MYF picnics, and longer at the spur leading to Skytop. I had no time to revisit the crumbling cabin where Astrid and I had lost our virginity, and couldn't have even if there had been. The gravel was now paved, and this road had also been plowed, but the way was barred by a stout wooden gate with a padlock the size of an orc's fist threaded through the latch. If that didn't make the point, there was a large sign reading ABSOLUTELY NO TRESPASSING and VIOLATORS WILL BE PROSECUTED TO THE FULL EXTENT OF THE LAW.

A mile further up, I came to the Goat Mountain gatehouse. The way wasn't barred, but there was a security guard wearing a light jacket over his brown uniform. The jacket was unbuttoned, maybe because the day was warm, maybe to give anyone stopping by a good view of the holstered gun on his hip. It looked like a big one.

I powered down my window, but before the guard could ask for my name, the gatehouse door opened and Charlie Jacobs came out. The bulky parka he wore couldn't disguise how little was left of him. The last time we'd met, he had been thin. Now he was gaunt. My old fifth business was limping more severely than ever, and although he might have thought his smile of greeting warm and welcoming, it barely lifted the left side of his face, resulting in something closer to a sneer. *The stroke*, I thought.

"Jamie, good to see you!" He held out his hand and I shook it . . . although not without reservations. "I didn't really expect you until tomorrow."

"In Colorado they get the airports open fast after storms."

"I'm sure, I'm sure. May I ride back up with you?" He nodded in the direction of the security guard. "Sam brought me down in a golf cart, and there's a space heater in the guardhouse, but I chill very easily now, even on a day as springlike as this one. Do you remember what we used to call spring snow, Jamie?"

"Poor man's fertilizer," I said. "Come on, get in."

He limped around the front of the car, and when Sam tried to take his arm, Jacobs shook him off briskly. His face didn't work right, and the limp was actually closer to a lurch, but he was pretty spry, just the same. *A man on a mission*, I thought.

He got in with a grunt of relief, turned up the heater, and rubbed his gnarled hands in front of the passenger-side vent like a man warming himself over an open fire. "Hope you don't mind."

"Knock yourself out."

"Does this remind you of the approach to The Latches?" he asked, still rubbing his hands. They made an unpleasant papery sound. "It does me."

"Well . . . except for that." I pointed to the left, where there had once been an intermediate-level ski run called Smoky Trail. Or maybe it had been Smoky Twist. Now one of the lift cables had come down, and a couple of the chairs lay half-buried in a drift that would probably be there for another five weeks, unless the weather stayed warm.

"Messy," he agreed, "but there's no point fixing it. I'm going to have all the lifts taken out once the snow's gone. I'd say my skiing days are over, wouldn't you? Were you ever here when you were a child, Jamie?"

I had been, on half a dozen occasions, tagging along with Con and Terry and their flatlander friends, but I had no more stomach for small talk. "Is she here?"

"Yes, arrived around noon. Her friend Jenny Knowlton brought her. They had hoped to get here yesterday, but the storm was much worse Downeast. And before you ask your follow-up question, no, I haven't treated her. The poor woman is exhausted. Tomorrow will be time enough for that, and time enough for her to see you. Although you may see *her* today, if you like, when she eats what little dinner she can manage. The restaurant is equipped with closed-circuit television cameras."

I started to tell him what I thought of that, but he held up a hand.

"Peace, my friend. I didn't put them in; they were here when I bought the place. I believe the management must have used them to make sure the service staff was performing up to expectations."

His one-sided smile looked sneerier than ever. Maybe that was just me, but I didn't think so.

"Are you gloating?" I asked. "Is that what you're doing, now that you've got me here?"

"Of course not." He half turned to regard the melting snowbanks rolling past us on either side. Then he turned back to me. "Well. Perhaps. Just a little. You were so high and mighty the last time we met. So *haughty*."

I didn't feel high and mighty now, and I certainly didn't feel haughty. I felt caught in a trap. I was here, after all, because of a girl I hadn't seen in over forty years. One who had bought her own doom, pack by pack, at the nearest convenience store. Or at the pharmacy in Castle Rock, where you could buy cigarettes at the counter right up front. If you needed actual medicine, you had to walk all the way to the back. One of life's ironies. I imagined dropping Jacobs off at the lodge and just driving away. The idea had a nasty attraction.

"Would you really let her die?"

"Yes." He was still warming his hands in front of the vent. Now what I imagined was grabbing one of them and snapping those gnarled fingers like breadsticks.

"Why? Why am I so goddamned important to you?"

"Because you're my destiny. I think I knew it the first time I saw you, down on your knees in your dooryard and grubbing in the dirt." He spoke with the patience of a true believer. Or a lunatic. Maybe there's really no difference. "I knew for sure when you showed up in Tulsa."

"What are you doing, Charlie? What is it you want me for this summer?" It wasn't the first time I'd asked him, but there were other questions I didn't dare ask. *How dangerous is it? Do you know? Do you care?*

He seemed to be thinking about whether or not to tell me . . . but I never knew what he was thinking, not really. Then Goat Mountain Resort hove into view—even bigger than The Latches, but ugly and full of modern angles; Frank Lloyd Wright gone bad. Probably it had looked modern, even futuristic, to the wealthy people who had come here to play in the sixties. Now it looked like a cubist dinosaur with glass eyes.

"Ah!" he said. "Here we are. You'll want to freshen up and rest a bit. I know *I* want to rest a bit. It's very exciting having you here, Jamie, but also tiring. I've put you in the Snowe Suite on the third floor. Rudy will show you the way."

Rudy Kelly was a mountain of a man in faded jeans, a loose gray smock top, and white crepe-soled nurse's shoes. He *was* a nurse, he said, as well as Mr. Jacobs's personal assistant. Judging by his size, I thought he might also be Jacobs's bodyguard. His handshake was certainly no limp-fish musician's howdy.

I had been in the resort's lobby as a kid, had once even eaten lunch here with Con and the family of one of Con's friends (terrified the whole time of using the wrong fork or dribbling down my shirt), but I had never been on any of the upper floors. The elevator was a clanky bucket, the kind of antique conveyance that in scary novels always stalls between floors, and I resolved to take the stairs for however long I had to be here.

The place was well heated (by virtue of Charlie Jacobs's secret electricity, I had no doubt), and I could see some repairs had been made, but they felt haphazard. All the lights worked and the floorboards didn't creak, but the air of desertion was hard to miss. The Snowe Suite was at the end of the corridor, and the view from the spacious living room was almost as good as that from Skytop, but the wallpaper was waterstained in places, and in here a vague aroma of mold had replaced the lobby's smell of floor wax and fresh paint.

"Mr. Jacobs would like you to join him for dinner in his apartment at six," Rudy said. His voice was soft and deferential, but he looked like an inmate in a prison flick—not the guy who plans the breakout, but the death-row enforcer who kills any guards who try to stop the escapees. "Will that work for you?"

"It's fine," I said, and when he left, I locked the door.

I took a shower—the hot water was abundant, and came at once—then laid out fresh clothes. With that done and time to kill, I lay down on the coverlet of the queen-size bed. I hadn't slept well the night before, and I can never sleep on planes, so a nap would have been good, but I couldn't drift off. I kept thinking about Astrid—both as she'd been then, and as she must be now. Astrid, who was in this same building with me, three floors down.

When Rudy knocked softly on the door at two minutes to six, I was up and dressed. At my suggestion that we take the stairs, he flashed a smile that said he knew a wimp when he saw one. "The elevator is totally safe, sir. Mr. Jacobs oversaw certain repairs himself, and that old slidebox was high on the list."

I didn't protest. I was thinking about how my old fifth business was no longer a reverend, no longer a rev, no longer a pastor. At this end of his life, he was back to plain old mister, and getting his blood pressure taken by a guy who looked like Vin Diesel after a face-lift gone bad.

Jacobs's apartment was on the first floor in the west wing. He had changed into a dark suit and white shirt open at the collar. He rose to greet me, smiling that one-sided smile. "Thank you, Rudy. Will you tell Norma that we'll be ready to eat in fifteen minutes?"

Rudy nodded and left. Jacobs turned to me, still smiling and once more producing that unpleasant papery sound as he rubbed his hands together. Outside the window, a ski slope with no lights to illuminate it and no skiers to groove the spring snow descended into darkness, a highway to nowhere. "It will only be soup and salad, I'm afraid. I gave up meat two years ago. It creates fatty deposits in the brain."

"Soup and salad is fine."

"There's also bread, Norma's sourdough. It's excellent."

"Sounds delicious. I'd like to see Astrid, Charlie."

"Norma will serve her and her friend Jenny Knowlton around seven. Once they've eaten, Miss Knowlton will give Astrid her pain medication, and help her make her evening toilet. I told Miss Knowlton that Rudy could assist with these tasks, but she won't hear of it. Alas, Jenny Knowlton no longer seems to trust me."

I thought back to Astrid's letter. "Even though you cured her of her arthritis?"

"Ah, but then I was Pastor Danny. Now that I've eschewed all those religious trappings—I told them so, felt I had to—Miss Knowlton is suspicious. That's what the truth does, Jamie. It makes people suspicious."

"Is Jenny Knowlton suffering aftereffects?"

"Not at all. She's just uncomfortable without all her miracle mumbo-jumbo to fall back on. But since you brought up the subject of aftereffects, step into my study. I want to show you something, and there's just time before our evening repast appears."

The study was an alcove off the suite's parlor. His computer was on, the extra-large screen showing those endlessly galloping horses. He sat down, grimacing with discomfort, and tapped a key. The horses gave way to a plain blue desktop with only two folders on it. They were labeled **A** and **B**.

He clicked **A**, revealing a list of names and addresses in alphabetical order. He pressed a button, and the list began to scroll at medium speed. "Do you know what these are?"

"Cures, I'd assume."

"*Verified* cures, all affected by administration of electrical current to the brain—although not the sort of current any electrician would recognize. Over thirty-one hundred in all. Take my word for it?"

"Yes."

He turned to look at me, although the movement clearly pained him. "You mean it?"

"Yes."

Looking gratified, he closed file **A** and opened **B**. More names and addresses, also in alphabetical order, and this time the scroll was slow enough to pick out several names I recognized. Stefan Drew, the compulsive walker; Emil Klein, the dirt eater; Patricia Farmingdale, who had poured salt in her eyes. This list was much shorter than the first one. Before it ended, I saw Robert Rivard go sliding by.

"These are the ones who have suffered significant post-cure aftereffects. Eighty-seven in all. As I believe I told you the last time we met, it amounts to less than three percent of the total. Once there were over a hundred and seventy names in File B, but many have stopped having problems—in medical parlance, they have resolved. As you have. I stopped following my cures eight months ago, but if I'd kept on, I'm sure this list would be even shorter. The ability of the human body to recover from trauma is extraordinary. With the proper application of this new electricity to the cortex and the nerve tree, that ability is effectively unlimited."

"Who are you trying to convince? Me or you?"

He blew his breath out in a disgusted *pah* sound. "What I'm *trying* to do is set your mind at rest. I'd rather have a willing assistant than a reluctant one."

"I'm here. I'll do what I promised . . . if you can cure Astrid. Let that be enough."

There was a soft knock at the door.

"Come," Jacobs said.

The woman who entered had the plump, matronly figure of the Good Gramma in a children's story and the beady eyes of a dick in a department store. She set a tray down on the table in the parlor, then stood with her hands clasped primly in front of her plain black dress. Jacobs rose with another grimace, then tottered. In my first act as his assistant—in this new stage of our lives, at least—I caught his elbow and steadied him. He thanked me and led me out of the study.

"Norma, I'd like you to meet Jamie Morton. He'll be with us at least through breakfast tomorrow, and back for a longer stay this summer."

"Pleased," she said, and held out her hand. I shook it.

"You don't know what a victory that handshake represents for Norma," Jacobs said. "Since childhood, she's had a deep aversion to touching people. Haven't you, dear? Not a physical problem, you'll notice, but a psychological one. Nevertheless, she's been cured. I think that's interesting, don't you?"

I told Norma it was nice to meet her, holding her hand a moment longer than necessary. I saw her mounting unease, and let loose. Cured, but perhaps not *completely* cured. That was interesting, too.

"Miss Knowlton says she'll bring your patient to dinner a bit early tonight, Mr. Jacobs."

"All right, Norma. Thank you."

She left. We ate. It was light fare, but sat heavily in my stomach, just the same. My nerves felt all on the outside, sizzling my skin. Jacobs ate slowly—as if to taunt me—but at last he set aside his empty soup bowl. He seemed about to reach for another slice of bread, then looked at his watch and pushed back from the table instead.

"Come with me," he said. "I think it's time you saw your old friend."

The door across the hall was marked RESORT PERSONNEL ONLY. Jacobs led me through a large outer office furnished with bare desks and empty shelves. The door to the inner office was locked.

He said, "Other than the security company that supplies twenty-four-seven gate guards, my staff consists of just Rudy and Norma. And while I trust them both, I see no need to put temptation in their way. And the temptation to peek at the unsuspecting is a strong one, wouldn't you say?"

I didn't answer. I wasn't sure I could have. My mouth was as dry as old carpet. There were a dozen monitors in all, stacked in three rows of four. Jacobs pushed the power button on RESTAURANT CAMERA 3. "I believe this is the one we want." Cheerful. Like a cross between Pastor Danny and a game show host.

It seemed to take forever before a black-and-white picture swam into view. The restaurant was large, with at least fifty tables, but only one was occupied. Two women were sitting there, but at first I could only see Jenny Knowlton, because Norma blocked the other one out as she bent to serve them their bowls of soup. Jenny was pretty, dark-haired, mid-fifties. I saw her mouth move in a silent *thank you*. Norma nodded, straightened up, stepped away from the table, and I saw what remained of the first girl I ever loved.

If this were a romance, I might say something like, "Although necessarily changed by the passage of years and somewhat wasted by the depredations of disease, her essential beauty remained." I wish I could, but if I begin lying now, everything I have told so far becomes worthless.

Astrid was a crone in a wheelchair, her face a pallid pouch of flesh from which dark eyes stared listlessly down at food she obviously had no interest in. Her companion had put a large knitted cap—a kind of tam-o'-shanter—on her head, but it had slipped to one side, revealing a bald skull fuzzed with white stubble.

She picked up her spoon with a scrawny hand that was all tendons, then put it down again. The dark-haired woman exhorted her. The pallid creature nodded. Her tam fell off when she did, but Astrid appeared not to notice. She dipped into her soup and raised the spoon slowly to her mouth. Most of its cargo fell off during the trip. She sipped what was left, pooching her lips out in a way that reminded me of how the late Bartleby would take a slice of apple from my hand.

My knees unhinged. If there hadn't been a chair in front of the bank of monitors, I would have gone straight to the floor. Jacobs stood beside me, gnarled hands clasped behind his back, rocking to and fro with a slight smile on his face.

And since this is to be a true account rather than a romance, I must add that I felt a sneaking relief. I would never have to keep my half of our devil's bargain, because there was no way the woman in the wheelchair was coming back. Cancer is the pitbull of diseases, and it had her in its jaws, biting and rending. It would not stop until it had torn her to pieces.

"Turn it off," I whispered.

Jacobs leaned toward me. "I beg your pardon? My ears aren't as good as they used to be these da—"

"You heard me perfectly well, Charlie. *Turn it off.*"

He did.

• • •

We were kissing beneath the fire escape of Eureka Grange No. 7 as the snow swirled down. Astrid was blowing cigarette smoke into my mouth while the tip of her tongue slipped back and forth, first along my upper lip and then inside it, lightly caressing the line of my gum. My hand was squeezing her breast, although there wasn't much to feel because of the heavy parka she was wearing.

Kiss me forever, I thought. *Kiss me forever so I don't have to see where the years have taken us and what you've become.*

But no kiss goes on forever. She pulled back and I saw the ashen face inside the fur of her hood, the dusty eyes, the slack mouth. The tongue that had been inside my mouth was black and peeling. I had been kissing a corpse.

Or maybe not, because the lips rose in a grin.

"Something happened," Astrid said. "Didn't it, Jamie? Something happened, and Mother will be here soon."

I jerked awake with a gasp. I had gone to bed in my skivvies, but now I was naked and standing in the corner. I had the pen from the bedside table curled in my right hand and was using it to jab at my left forearm, where there was a small but growing constellation of blue dots. I dropped it on the floor and staggered backward.

Stress, I thought. *It was stress that brought on Hugh's prismatics at the Norris County revival, and it was stress tonight. Besides, it's not like you poured salt in your eyes. Or came around to find yourself outside gobbling dirt.*

It was quarter past four, that deadly time of morning when it's too late to go back to sleep and still too early to rise and shine. I pulled a book from the smaller of my two bags, sat down by the window, and opened it. My eyes took in the words just as my mouth had taken in Norma's soup and salad: without tasting. Eventually

I stopped trying and just looked out into the darkness, waiting for dawn.

It was a long time coming.

I took breakfast in Jacobs's suite . . . if you can call a single piece of toast and half a cup of tea breakfast. Charlie, on the other hand, worked his way through a fruit cup, scrambled eggs, and a goodly heap of homefries. Skinny as he was, it was hard to tell where he put it. On the table by the door was a mahogany box. In it, he told me, were his healing instruments.

"I no longer use rings. No need of them, now that my performing career is over."

"When are you going to start? I want to get it over with and get out of here."

"Very soon. Your old friend dozes through her days, but doesn't sleep much at night. Last night will have been a particularly difficult one for her, because I told Miss Knowlton to withhold her midnight pain meds—they depress the brainwaves. We'll do our business in the East Room. It's my favorite at this time of day. If you and I didn't know God is a profitable and self-sustaining construct of the worlds' churches, the morning light would be almost enough to make us believers again."

He leaned forward, looking at me earnestly.

"There's no need for you to be a part of this, you know. I saw how upset you were last night. I'll need your help this summer, but this morning either Rudy or Miss Knowlton can assist me. Why don't you come back tomorrow? Pop over to Harlow. Visit your brother and his family. I think that, were you to do that, you'd see an entirely different Astrid Soderberg on your return."

In a way, that was exactly what I was afraid of, because since leaving Harlow, Charlie Jacobs had made a career of trickery. As Pastor Danny, he had displayed pigs' livers and declared them to be extracted tumors. It was not a résumé that inspired trust. Could I be absolutely sure the haggard woman in the wheelchair actually *was* Astrid Soderberg?

My heart said she was; my head told my heart to be careful and trust nothing. The Knowlton woman could be an accomplice—a shill, in carny terms. The next half hour was going to be an ordeal, but I had no intention of ducking out and allowing Jacobs to affect a sham cure. Of course he would need the real Astrid to pull it off, but many lucrative years on the revival circuit made that a possibility, especially if my long-ago girlfriend found herself hard up financially in her old age.

An unlikely scenario, to be sure. What it came down to was the responsibility I felt to see this through to what was certain to be a bitter end.

"I'll stick around."

"As you like." He smiled, and although the bad side of his mouth still wouldn't cooperate, there was nothing sneery about this one. "It will be nice to work with you again. Like the old days in Tulsa."

A soft knock came at the door. It was Rudy. "The women are in the East Room, Mr. Jacobs. Miss Knowlton says they're ready when you are. She says the sooner the better, because Miss Soderberg is in a lot of discomfort."

I walked side by side with Jacobs down the hall, carrying the mahogany box under my arm, until we got to the East Wing. There my nerve temporarily failed me, and I let Jacobs go in while I stood in the doorway.

He didn't notice. All his attention—and considerable charisma—

was focused on the women. "Jenny and Astrid!" he said heartily. "My two favorite ladies!"

Jenny Knowlton gave his outstretched hand a token touch—enough for me to see that her fingers were straight and seemingly untouched by arthritis. Astrid made no attempt to raise her own hand. She was hunched in her wheelchair, peering up at him. There was an oxygen mask over the lower half of her face, and a tank on a wheelie-cart beside her.

Jenny said something to Jacobs, too low to hear, and he nodded vigorously. "Yes, we must waste no time. Jamie, would you—" He looked around, saw I wasn't there, and beckoned to me impatiently.

It was no more than a dozen steps to the center of the room, which was filled with brilliant early light, but those steps seemed to take a very long time. It was as if I were walking underwater.

Astrid glanced at me with the disinterested eyes of one expending all her energy to cope with her pain. She showed no recognition, only looked down at her lap again, and I had a moment's relief. Then her head jerked up. Her mouth fell open inside the transparent mask. She covered her face with her hands, knocking the mask aside. It was only part incredulity, I think. Most of it was horror, that I should see her in such a state.

She might have hidden behind her hands longer, but she didn't have the strength for it and they dropped into her lap. She was crying. The tears washed her eyes and made them young again. Any doubts I might have had about her identity passed away. It was Astrid, all right. Still the young girl I'd loved, now living inside the failing wreck of a sick old woman's body.

"Jamie?" Her voice was as hoarse as a jackdaw's.

I got on one knee, like a swain about to propose. "Yeah, honey. It's me." I took one of her hands, turned it over, and kissed the palm. The skin was cold.

"You should go away. I don't want you to . . ." There was a whistling sound as she drew in breath. ". . . to see me like this. I don't want *anyone* to see me like this."

"It's all right." *Because Charlie's going to make you better*, I wanted to add, but didn't. Because Astrid was beyond help.

Jacobs had drawn Jenny away and was conversing with her, giving us our moment of privacy. The hell of being with Charlie was that sometimes he could be tender.

"Cigarettes," she said in that hoarse jackdaw voice. "What a stupid way to kill yourself. And I knew better, which makes it even stupider. *Everybody* knows better. Do you want to know something funny? I still want them." She laughed, and that turned into a harsh chain of coughs that clearly hurt her. "Smuggled in three packs. Jenny found them and took them away. As if it would make any difference now."

"Hush," I said.

"I stopped. For seven months, I stopped. If the baby had lived, I might have stopped for good. Something . . ." She drew a deep, wheezing breath. "Something tricks us. That's what I believe."

"It's wonderful to see you."

"You're a beautiful liar, Jamie. What's he got on you?"

I said nothing.

"Well, never mind." Her hand had strayed to the back of my head, just as it used to when we were making out, and for one horrible moment I thought she might try to kiss me with that dying mouth. "You kept your hair. It's lovely and thick. I lost mine. Chemo."

"It'll grow back."

"No it won't. This . . ." She looked around. Her breath whistled like a child's toy. "A fool's errand. And I'm the fool."

Jacobs led Jenny back. "It's time to do this thing." Then, to Astrid: "It won't take long, my dear, and there will be no pain. I expect you'll pass out, but most people have no awareness of that."

"I'm looking forward to passing out for good," Astrid told him, and smiled wanly.

"Now, now, none of that. I never make absolute guarantees, but I believe that in a short time, you're going to feel much better. Let's begin, Jamie. Open the box."

I did so. Inside, each item nestled in its own velvet-lined depression, were two stubby steel rods tipped with black plastic, and a white control box with a slide switch on top. It looked exactly like the one Jacobs had used the day Claire and I had brought Con to him. It crossed my mind that, of the four people in the room, three were idiots and one was crazy.

Jacobs plucked the rods from their nesting places and touched the black plastic tips together. "Jamie, take the control and move that slide switch the tiniest bit. Just a nudge. You'll hear a click."

When I did, he pulled the tips apart. There was a brilliant blue spark, and a brief but powerful *mmmm* sound. It didn't come from the rods but from the far side of the room, like some weird electrical ventriloquism.

"Excellent," Jacobs said. "We're good to go. Jenny, you need to place your hands on Astrid's shoulders. She'll spasm, and we don't want her to come around on the floor, do we?"

"Where are your holy rings?" Jenny asked. She was looking and sounding more doubtful by the second.

"These are better than the rings. Much more powerful. More *holy*, if you like. Hands on her shoulders, please."

"Don't you electrocute her!"

In her harsh jackdaw's voice, Astrid said, "The least of my worries, Jen."

"Won't happen," Jacobs said, adopting his lecture-hall voice. "*Can't*. In ECT therapy—shock treatments, to use the layman's term—doctors employ up to a hundred and fifty volts, thus provoking a grand mal seizure. But *these* . . ." He tapped the rods together. "Even at full power, they would barely budge the needle of an electrician's ammeter. The energy I intend to tap—energy present in this room, all around us at this very moment—can't be measured by ordinary instruments. It is essentially unknowable."

Unknowable was not a word I wanted to hear.

"Please just do it," Astrid said. "I'm very tired, and there's a rat in my chest. One that's on fire."

Jacobs looked at Jenny. She hesitated. "It wasn't like this at the revival. Not at *all.*"

"Perhaps not," Jacobs said, "but this *is* revival. You'll see. Put your hands on her shoulders, Jenny. Be prepared to press down hard. You won't hurt her."

She did as she was told.

Jacobs turned his attention to me. "When I place the tips of the rods on Astrid's temples, slide the switch. Count the clicks as it advances. When you feel the fourth one, stop and wait for any further instructions. Ready? Here we go."

He put the tips of the rods in the hollows at the sides of her head, where delicate blue veins pulsed. In a prim little voice, Astrid said, "So nice to see you again, Jamie." Then she closed her eyes.

"She may be frisky, so be ready to bear down," Jacobs told Jenny. Then: "All right, Jamie."

I pushed the slide switch. Click . . . and click . . . and click . . . and *click.*

Nothing happened.

All an old man's delusion, I thought. *Whatever he might have done in the past, he can't do it any long—*

"Advance two more clicks, if you please." His voice was dry and confident.

I did so. Still nothing. With Jenny's hands on her shoulders, Astrid was more hunched over than ever. Her whistling respiration was painful to listen to.

"One more," Jacobs said.

"Charlie, I'm almost at the end of the—"

"Did you not hear me? *One more!*"

I pushed the slide. There was another click, and this time the hum on the other side of the room was much louder, not *mmmm* but *MMMOWWW*. There was no flash of light that I saw (or that I remember, at least), but for a moment I was dazzled, anyway. It was as if a depth charge had gone off far down in my brain. I think Jenny Knowlton cried out. I dimly saw Astrid jerk in the wheelchair, a spasm so powerful that it flung Jenny—no lightweight—backward and almost off her feet. Astrid's wasted legs shot out, relaxed, then shot out again. A security alarm began to bray.

Rudy came running into the room, closely followed by Norma.

"I told you to turn that blasted thing off before we started!" Jacobs shouted at Rudy.

Astrid pistoned her arms up, one right in front of Jenny's face as she came back to put her hands on Astrid's shoulders again.

"Sorry, Mr. Jacobs—"

"Shut it OFF, you idiot!"

Charlie snatched the control box out of my hands and slid the switch back to the off position. Now Astrid was making a series of gagging sounds.

"Pastor Danny, she's choking!" Jenny cried.

"Don't be stupid!" Jacobs snapped. His cheeks were flushed, his eyes bright. He looked twenty years younger. "Norma! Call the gate! Tell them the alarm was an accident!"

"Should I—"

"Go! *Go!* Goddammit, *GO!*"

She went.

Astrid's eyes opened, only there *were* no eyes, just bulging whites. She gave another of those myoclonic jerks, then slid forward, legs kicking and jerking. Her arms flailed like those of a drowning swimmer. The alarm brayed and brayed. I grabbed her by the hips and shoved her back in her chair before she could land on the floor. The crotch of her slacks was dark, and I could smell strong urine. When I looked up, I saw foam drizzling from one side of her mouth. It fell from her chin to the collar of her blouse, darkening that, too.

The alarm quit.

"Thank God for small favors," Jacobs said. He was bent forward, hands on his thighs, observing Astrid's convulsions with interest but no concern.

"*We need a doctor!*" Jenny cried. "*I can't hold her!*"

"Bosh," Jacobs said. There was a half-smile—the only kind he could manage—on his face. "Did you expect it to be easy? It's *cancer*, for God's sake. Give her a minute and she'll be—"

"There's a door in the wall," Astrid said.

The hoarseness had left her voice. Her eyes rolled back down in their sockets . . . but not together; they came one at a time. When they were back in place, it was Jacobs they were looking at.

"You can't see it. It's small and covered with ivy. The ivy is dead. She waits on the other side, above the broken city. Above the paper sky."

Blood can't turn cold, not really, but mine seemed to. *Something happened*, I thought. *Something happened, and Mother will be here soon.*

"Who?" Jacobs asked. He took one of her hands. The half-smile was gone. "Who waits?"

"Yes." Her eyes stared into his. "*She*."

"Who? Astrid, *who*?"

She said nothing at first. Then her lips stretched in a terrible grin that showed every tooth in her head. "Not the one *you* want."

He slapped her. Astrid's head jerked to the side. Spittle flew. I shouted in surprise and grabbed his wrist when he raised his hand to do it again. I stopped him, but only with an effort. He was stronger than he had any right to be. It was the kind of strength that comes from hysteria. Or pent-up fury.

"*You can't hit her!*" Jenny shouted, letting go of Astrid's shoulders and coming around the wheelchair to confront him. "*You lunatic, you can't hit h—*"

"Stop," Astrid said. Her voice was weak but lucid. "Stop it, Jenny."

Jenny looked around. Her eyes widened at what she saw: a delicate pink wash of color beginning to rise in Astrid's pale cheeks.

"Why are you yelling at him? Did something happen?"

Yes, I thought. *Something happened. Something most surely did.*

Astrid turned to Jacobs. "When are you going to do it? You better hurry, because the pain is very . . . very . . ."

The three of us stared at her. No, it was the five of us. Rudy and Norma had crept back into the East Room doorway, and they were staring, too.

"Wait," Astrid said. "Wait just a darn minute."

She touched her chest. She cupped the wasted remains of her breasts. She pressed her stomach.

"You did it already, didn't you? I know you did, because there *is* no pain!" She pulled in a breath and let it out in an incredulous laugh. "And I can breathe! *Jenny, I can breathe again!*"

Jenny Knowlton went to her knees, raised her hands to the sides of her head, and began to recite the Lord's Prayer so fast she sounded like a 45 rpm record on 78. Another voice joined her: Norma's. She was also on her knees.

Jacobs gave me a bemused look that was easy to read: *You see, Jamie? I do all the work and the Big G gets all the credit.*

Astrid tried to get out of the wheelchair, but her wasted legs wouldn't hold her. I got her before she could do a face-plant, and put my arms around her.

"Not yet, honey," I said. "You're too weak."

She goggled at me as I eased her back onto the seat. The oxygen mask had gotten twisted around and now hung on the left side of her neck, forgotten.

"Jamie? Is that you? What are you doing here?"

I looked at Jacobs.

"Short-term memory loss after treatment is common," he said. "Astrid, can you tell me who the president is?"

She looked bewildered at the question but answered with no hesitation. "Obama. And Biden's the vice president. Am I really better? Will it last?"

"You are and it will, but never mind that now. Tell me—"

"Jamie? Is it really you? Your hair is so white!"

"Yes," I said, "it's certainly getting there. Listen to Charlie."

"I was crazy about you," she said, "but even though you could play, you could never dance very well unless you were high. We had dinner at Starland after the prom and you ordered . . ." She stopped and licked her lips. "Jamie?"

"Right here."

"I can breathe. I can actually *breathe* again." She was crying.

Jacobs snapped his fingers in front of her eyes like a stage hypnotist. "Focus, Astrid. Who brought you here?"

"J-Jenny."

"What did you have for supper last night?"

"Sloop. Sloop and salad."

He snapped his fingers in front of her swimming eyes again. It made her blink and recoil. The muscles beneath her skin seemed to be tightening and firming even as I watched. It was wonderful and awful.

"*Soup*. Soup and salad."

"Very good. What is the door in the wall?"

"Door? I don't—"

"You said it was covered with ivy. You said there was a broken city on the other side."

"I . . . don't remember that."

"You said she waits. You said . . ." He peered into her uncomprehending face and sighed. "Never mind. You need to rest, my dear."

"I suppose so," Astrid said, "but what I'd really like to do is dance. Dance for joy."

"In time you will." He patted her hand. He was smiling as he did it, but I had an idea he was deeply disappointed at her failure to remember the door and the city. I was not. I didn't want to know what she had seen when Charlie's secret electricity stormed through the deepest recesses of her brain. I didn't want to know what was waiting behind the hidden door she had spoken of, yet I was afraid I did.

Mother.

Above the paper sky.

Astrid slept all morning and well into the afternoon. When she woke, she declared herself ravenous. This pleased Jacobs, who told Norma Goldstone to bring "our patient" a toasted cheese sandwich and a small piece of cake with the frosting scraped off. Frosting, he felt, might be too rich for her wasted stomach. Jacobs, Jenny, and I watched her put away the entire sandwich and half the cake before setting her fork down.

"I want the rest," she said, "but I'm full."

"Give yourself time," Jenny said. She'd spread a napkin in her lap and kept plucking at it. She wouldn't look at Astrid for long, and at Jacobs not at all. Coming to him had been her idea, and I have no doubt she was happy about the sudden change for the better in her friend, but it was clear that what she'd seen in the East Room had shaken her deeply.

"I want to go home," Astrid said.

"Oh, honey, I don't know . . ."

"I feel well enough. I really do." Astrid cast an apologetic look at Jacobs. "It's not that I'm not grateful—I'll bless you in my prayers for the rest of my life—but I want to be in my own place. Unless you feel . . . ?"

"No, no," Jacobs said. I suspected that, with the job done, he was anxious to be rid of her. "I can't think of better medicine than sleeping in your own bed, and if you leave soon, you can be back not long after dark."

Jenny made no further objection, just went back to plucking at her napkin. But before she bent her head, I saw a look of relief on her face. She wanted out as much as Astrid, although perhaps not for quite the same reasons.

Astrid's returning color was only part of the remarkable change in her. She was sitting upright in her wheelchair; her eyes were clear and engaged. "I don't know how I can ever thank you, Mr. Jacobs, and I certainly can't repay you, but if there's ever anything you need from me that's mine to give, you only have to ask."

"Actually, there are several things." He ticked them off on the gnarled fingers of his right hand. "Eat. Sleep. Work hard to regain your strength. Can you do those things?"

"Yes. I will. And I'm never going to touch another cigarette."

He waved this away. "You won't want to. Will she, Jamie?"

"Probably not," I said.

"Miss Knowlton?"

She jerked as if he'd pinched her bottom.

"Astrid must engage a physical therapist, or you must engage one on her behalf. The sooner she gets out of that damn wheelchair, the better. Am I right? Am I cooking with gas, as we used to say?"

"Yes, Pastor Danny."

He frowned, but didn't correct her. "There's something else you fine ladies can do for me, and it's extremely important: *leave my name out of this*. I have a great deal of work to do in the coming months, and the last thing I need is to have hordes of sick people coming up here in hopes of being cured. Do you understand?"

"Yes," Astrid said.

Jenny nodded without looking up.

"Astrid, when you see your doctor and he expresses amazement, as he certainly will, all you'll tell him is that you prayed for a remission and your prayers were answered. His own belief—or lack of it—in the efficacy of prayer won't matter; either way, he'll be forced to accept the evidence of his MRI pictures. Not to mention your happy smiling face. Your happy and *healthy* smiling face."

"Yes, that's fine. Whatever you want."

"Let me roll you back to the suite," Jenny said. "If we're going to leave, I better pack." Subtext: *Get me out of here*. On that, she and Charlie Jacobs were thinking alike; they were cooking with gas.

"All right." Astrid looked at me shyly. "Jamie, would you bring me a Coke? I'd like to speak to you."

"Sure."

Jacobs watched Jenny trundle Astrid across the empty restaurant and toward the far door. When they were gone, he turned to me. "So. We have a bargain?"

"Yes."

"And you won't DS on me?"

DS. Carny-speak for *down south*, meaning to pull stakes and disappear.

"No, Charlie. I won't DS on you."

"That's fine, then." He was looking at the doorway through which the women had gone. "Miss Knowlton doesn't like me much now that I've left Team Jesus, does she?"

"Scared of you is what she is."

He shrugged it off. Like his smile, the shrug was mostly one-sided. "Ten years ago, I couldn't have cured our Miss Soderberg. Perhaps not even five. But things are moving fast, now. By this summer . . ."

"By this summer, what?"

"Who knows?" he said. "Who knows?"

You do, I thought. *You do, Charlie.*

"Watch this, Jamie," Astrid said when I arrived with her soft drink.

She got out of the wheelchair and tottered three steps to the chair by her bedroom window. She held on to it for balance while she turned herself around, and collapsed into it with a sigh of relief and pleasure.

"Not much, I know—"

"Are you kidding? It's amazing." I handed her an ice-choked glass of Coca-Cola. I had even stuck a piece of lime on the rim for good luck. "And you'll be able to do more each day."

We had the room to ourselves. Jenny had excused herself to finish packing, although it looked to me as if the job was already done. Astrid's coat was laid out on the bed.

"I think I owe you as much as I owe Mr. Jacobs."

"That's not true."

"Don't lie, Jamie, your nose will grow and the bees will sting your knees. He must get thousands of letters begging for cures, even now. I don't think he picked mine out of the pile by accident. Were you the one in charge of reading them?"

"Nope, that was Al Stamper, your friend Jenny's old fave. Charlie got in touch with me later."

"And you came," she said. "After all these years, you came. Why?"

"Because I had to. I can't explain any better than that, except there was a time when you meant the world to me."

"You didn't promise him anything? There was no . . . what do they call it . . . quid pro quo?"

"Not a single one." I said it without missing a beat. During my years as an addict, I'd become an accomplished liar, and the sad truth is that sort of skill sticks with you.

"Walk over here. Stand close to me."

I did. With no hesitation or embarrassment, she put her hand on the front of my jeans. "You were gentle with this," she said. "Many boys wouldn't have been. You had no experience, but you knew how to be kind. You meant the world to me, too." She dropped her hand and looked at me out of eyes no longer dull and preoccupied with her own pain. Now they were full of vitality. Also worry. "You *did* promise. I know you did. I won't ask what, but if you ever loved me, be careful of him. I owe him my life, and I feel awful saying this, but I believe he's dangerous. And I think you believe that, too."

Not as accomplished at lying as I'd thought, then. Or perhaps it was just that she saw more now that she was *cured*.

"Astrid, you have nothing to worry about."

"I wonder . . . could I have a kiss, Jamie? While we're alone? I know I'm not much to look at, but . . ."

I dropped to one knee—again feeling like a swain in a romance—and kissed her. No, she wasn't much to look at, but compared to how she'd looked that morning, she was a knockout. Still—it was only skin against skin, that kiss. There were no embers in the ashes. For me, at least. But we were tied together, just the same. Jacobs was the knot.

She stroked the back of my head. "Still such wonderful hair, going white or not. Life leaves us so little, but it's left you that. Goodbye, Jamie. And thank you."

On my way out, I stopped to talk briefly to Jenny. Mostly I wanted to know if she lived close enough to Astrid to monitor her progress.

She smiled. "Astrid and I are divorce buddies. Have been since I moved to Rockland and started working at the hospital there. Ten years ago, that was. When she got sick, I moved in with her."

I gave her my cell number, and the number at Wolfjaw. "There may be aftereffects."

She nodded. "Pastor Danny filled me in. Mr. Jacobs, I mean. It's hard for me to get used to calling him that. He said she might be prone to sleepwalking until her brainwaves re-regulate themselves. Four to six months, he said. I've seen that behavior in people who overdo stuff like Ambien and Lunesta."

"Yes, that's the most likely." Although there was also dirt-eating, compulsive walking, Tourette's syndrome, kleptomania, and Hugh Yates's prismatics. So far as I knew, Ambien didn't cause any of those things. "But if there's anything else . . . *call.*"

"How worried are you?" she asked. "Tell me what to expect."

"I don't really know, and she'll probably be fine." Most of them were, after all, at least according to Jacobs. And as little as I trusted him, I had to count on that, because it was too late to do anything else. The thing was done.

Jenny stood on tiptoe and kissed my cheek. "She's *better*. That's God's grace, Jamie, no matter what Mr. Jacobs may think now that he's fallen away. Without it—without *him*—she would have been dead in six weeks."

Astrid rode down the handicapped ramp in her wheelchair, but got into Jenny's Subaru on her own. Jacobs closed her door. She reached through the open window, grasped one of his hands in both of her own, and thanked him again.

"It was my pleasure," he said. "Just remember your promise." He pulled his hand free so he could put a finger to her lips. "Mum's the word."

I bent down and kissed her forehead. "Eat," I said. "Rest. Do therapy. And enjoy your life."

"Roger, Captain," she said. She looked past me, saw Jacobs slowly climbing the steps to the porch, then met my eyes and repeated what she'd said earlier. "*Be careful.*"

"Don't worry."

"But I will." Her eyes on mine, full of grave concern. She was getting old now, as I was, but with the disease banished from her body, I could see the girl who had stood in front of the stage with Hattie, Carol, and Suzanne, the four of them shaking their moneymakers while Chrome Roses played "Knock on Wood" or "Nutbush City Limits." The girl I had kissed under the fire escape. "I *will* worry."

I rejoined Charlie Jacobs on the porch, and we watched Jenny Knowlton's trim little Outback roll down the road that led to the gate. It had been a fine melt-day, and the snow had pulled back, revealing grass that was already turning green. *Poor man's fertilizer*, I thought. *That's what we used to call it.*

"Will those women keep their mouths shut?" Jacobs asked.

"Yes." Maybe not forever, but until his work was done, if he was as close to finished as he claimed. "They promised."

"And you, Jamie? Will you keep your promise?"

"Yes."

That seemed to satisfy him. "Stay the night, why don't you?"

I shook my head. "I booked a room at Embassy Suites. I've got an early flight."

And I can't wait to get away from this place, just as I couldn't wait to get away from The Latches.

I didn't say this, but I'm sure he knew it.

"Fine. Just be ready when I call."

"What do you need, Charlie? A written statement? I said I'll come, and I will."

"Good. We've been bouncing off each other like a couple of billiard balls for most of our lives, but that's almost over. By the end of July—mid-August at the latest—we'll be finished with each other."

He was right about that. God help him, he was.

Always assuming He's there, of course.

Even with a change of planes in Cincinnati, I was back in Denver the next day before 1 PM—when it comes to time travel, nothing beats flying west in a jet plane. I woke up my phone and saw I had two messages. The first was from Jenny. She said that she had locked the door of Astrid's bedroom last night before turning in herself, but there hadn't been a peep from the baby monitor, and when she got up at six-thirty, Astrid was still conked out.

"When she got up, she ate a soft-boiled egg and two pieces of toast. And the way she looks . . . I have to keep telling myself it's not some kind of illusion."

That was the good message. The bad one was from Brianna Donlin—now Brianna Donlin-Hughes. She'd left it only minutes before my United flight touched down. "Robert Rivard is dead, Jamie. I don't know the details." But by that evening, she'd gotten them.

A nurse had told Bree that most people who went into Gad's Ridge never came out, and that was certainly true of the boy Pastor Danny had healed of his muscular dystrophy. They found him in his room, dangling from a noose he'd made from a pair of bluejeans. He left a note that said, *I can't stop seeing the damned. The line stretches forever.*

XII

Forbidden Books. My Maine Vacation. The Sad Story of Mary Fay. The Coming of the Storm.

About six weeks later I got an email from my old research partner.

To: Jamie
From: Bree
Subject: FYI

After you were at Jacobs's place in upstate New York, you said in an email that he mentioned a book called *De Vermis Mysteriis*. The name stuck in my head, probably because I took just enough Latin in high school to know that's *The Mysteries of the Worm* in plain English. I guess research into All Things Jacobs is a hard habit to break, because I looked into it. Without telling my husband, I should add, as he believes I have put All Things Jacobs behind me.

Anyway, this is pretty heavy stuff. According to the Catholic Church, *De Vermis Mysteriis* is one of half a dozen so-called Forbidden Books. Taken as a group, they are known as "grimoires." The other five are *The Book of Appollonius* (he was a doctor at the time of Christ), *The Book of Albertus Magnus* (spells, talismans, speaking to the dead), *Lemegeton* and *Clavicula Salomonis* (supposedly written by King Solomon), and *The Grimoire of Picatrix*. That last one, along with *De Vermis Mysteriis*, was supposedly the basis of H. P. Lovecraft's fictional grimoire, called *The Necronomicon*.

Editions are available of all the Forbidden Books EXCEPT FOR *De Vermis Mysteriis*. According to Wikipedia, secret emissaries of the Catholic Church (paging Dan Brown) had burned all but six or seven copies of *De Vermis* by the turn of the 20th century. (BTW, the Pope's army now refuses to acknowledge such a book ever existed.) The others have dropped out of sight, and are presumed to be destroyed or held by private collectors.

Jamie, all the Forbidden Books deal with POWER, and how to obtain it by means that combine alchemy (which we now call "science"), mathematics, and certain nasty occult rituals. All of it is probably bullshit, but it makes me uneasy—you told me Jacobs has spent his life studying electrical phenomena, and based on his healing successes, I have to think he may have gotten hold of a power that's pretty awesome. Which makes me think of the old proverb: "He who takes a tiger by the tail dare not let go."

A couple of other things for you to think about.

One: Up until the mid-seventeenth century, Catholics known to be studying *potestas magnum universum* (the force that powers the universe) were liable to excommunication.

Two: Wikipedia claims—although without verifying references, I must add—that the couplet most people remember from Lovecraft's fictional *Necronomicon* was stolen from a copy of *De Vermis* which Lovecraft had access to (he certainly never owned one, he was too poor to purchase such a rarity). This is the couplet: "That is not dead which can eternal lie, And with strange aeons, even death may die." That gave me nightmares. I'm not kidding.

Sometimes you called Charles Daniel Jacobs "my old fifth business." I hope you are done with him at last, Jamie. Once upon a time I would have laughed at all this, but once upon a time I thought miracle cures at revival meetings were bullshit.

Give me a call someday, would you? Let me know All Things Jacobs are behind you.

Affectionately, as always,

Bree

I printed this out and read it over twice. Then I googled *De Vermis Mysteriis* and found everything Bree had told me in her email, along with one thing she hadn't. In an antiquarian book-blog called *Dark Tomes of Magick & Spells*, someone called Ludvig Prinn's suppressed grimoire "the most dangerous book ever written."

I left my apartment, walked down the block, and bought a pack of cigarettes for the first time since a brief flirtation with tobacco in college. There was no smoking in my building, so I sat on my steps to light up. I coughed out the first drag, my head swimming, and I thought, *These things would have killed Astrid, if not for Charlie's intervention.*

Yes. Charlie and his miracle cures. Charlie who had a tiger by the tail and didn't *want* to let go.

Something happened, Astrid had said in my dream, speaking through a grin from which all her former sweetness had departed. *Something happened, and Mother will be here soon.*

Then, later, after Jacobs had shot his secret electricity into her head: *There's a door in the wall. The door is covered with ivy. The ivy is dead. She waits*. And when Jacobs asked who Astrid was talking about: *Not the one* you *want.*

I can break my promise, I thought, casting the cigarette away. *It wouldn't be the first one.*

True, but not this one. Not this promise.

I went back inside, crushing the pack of cigarettes and tossing it into the trash can beside the mailboxes. Upstairs, I called Bree's cell, prepared to leave a message, but she answered. I thanked her for her email and told her I had no intention of ever seeing Charles Jacobs again. I told this lie without guilt or hesitation. Bree's husband was right; she needed to be finished with All Things Jacobs. And when the time came to go back to Maine and fulfill my promise, I would lie to Hugh Yates for the same reason.

Once upon a time, two teenagers had fallen for each other, and hard, as only teenagers can. A few years later they made love in a ruined cabin while the thunder rolled and the lightning flashed—all very Victoria Holt. In the course of time, Charles Jacobs had saved them both from paying the ultimate price for their addictions. I owed him double. I'm sure you see that, and I could leave it there, but to do so would be to omit a much larger truth: *I was also curious.* God help me, I wanted to watch him lift the lid on Pandora's box and peer inside.

• • •

REVIVAL

"This isn't your lame-ass way of telling me you want to retire, is it?" Hugh tried to sound as if he was joking, but there was real apprehension in his eyes.

"Not at all. I just want a couple of months off. Maybe only six weeks, if I get bored. I need to reconnect with my family in Maine while I still can. I'm not getting any younger."

I had no intention of going near my family in Maine. They were too close to Goat Mountain as it was.

"You're a kid," he said moodily. "Come this fall, I'm going to have a year for every trombone that led the big parade. Mookie pulling the pin this spring was bad enough. If you went for good, I'd probably have to close this place down."

He heaved a sigh.

"I should have had kids, someone to take over when I'm gone, but does that sort of thing happen? Rarely. When you say you hope they'll pick up the reins of the family business, they say 'Sorry, Dad, me and that dope-smoking kid you hated me hanging out with in high school are going to California to make surfboards equipped with WiFi.'"

"Now that you've got that out of your system . . ."

"Yeah, yeah, go back to your roots, by all means. Play pat-a-cake with your little niece and help your brother rebuild his latest classic car. You know how summers are here."

I certainly did: slower than dirt. Summer means full employment even for the shittiest bands, and when bands are playing live music in bars and at four dozen summerfests in Colorado and Utah, they don't buy much recording time.

"George Damon will be in," I said. "He's come out of retirement in a big way."

"Yeah," Hugh said. "The only guy in Colorado who can make 'I'll Be Seeing You' sound like 'God Bless America.'"

"Perhaps in the world. Hugh, you haven't had any more of those prismatics, have you?"

He gave me a curious look. "No. What brought *that* on?"

I shrugged.

"I'm fine. Up a couple of times every night to squirt half a teacup of pee, but I guess that's par for the course at my age. Although . . . you want to hear a funny thing? Only to me it's more of a spooky thing."

I wasn't sure I did, but thought I ought to. It was early June. Jacobs hadn't called yet, but he would. I knew he would.

"I've been having this recurring dream. In it I'm not here at Wolfjaw, I'm in Arvada, in the house where I grew up. Someone starts knocking on the door. Except it's not just knocking, it's *pounding*. I don't want to answer it, because I know it's my mother, and she's dead. Pretty stupid, because she was alive and healthy as a horse back in the Arvada days, but I know it, just the same. I go down the hall, not wanting to, but my feet just keep moving—you know how dreams are. By then she's really whamming on the door, beating on it with both fists, it sounds like, and I'm thinking of this horror story we had to read in English when I was in high school. I think it was called 'August Heat.'"

Not "August Heat," I thought. "The Monkey's Paw." That's the one with the door-pounding in it.

"I reach for the knob, and then I wake up, all in a sweat. What do you make of that? My subconscious, trying to get me ready for the big exit scene?"

"Maybe," I agreed, but my head had left the conversation. I was thinking about another door. A small one covered with dead ivy.

Jacobs called on July first. I was in one of the studios, updating the Apple Pro software. When I heard his voice, I sat down in front of the control board and looked through the window into a soundproof rehearsal room that was empty except for a disassembled drumkit.

"The time has almost come for you to keep your promise," he said. His voice was mushy, as if he'd been drinking, although I'd never seen him take anything stronger than black coffee.

"All right." My voice was calm enough. Why not? It was the call I had been expecting. "When do you want me to come?"

"Tomorrow. The day after at the latest. I suspect you won't want to stay with me at the resort, at least to start with—"

"You suspect right."

"—but I'll need you no more than an hour away. When I call, you come."

That made me think of another spooky story, one titled "Oh, Whistle, and I'll Come to You, My Lad."

"All right," I said. "But Charlie?"

"Yes?"

"You get two months of my time, and that's it. When Labor Day rolls around, we're quits no matter what happens."

Another pause, but I could hear his breathing. It sounded labored, making me think of how Astrid had sounded in her wheelchair. "That's . . . acceptable." *Acsheptable.*

"Are you okay?"

"Another stroke, I'm afraid." *Shtroke.* "My speech isn't as clear as it once was, but I assure you my *mind* is as clear as ever."

Pastor Danny, heal thyself, I thought, and not for the first time.

"Bit of news for you, Charlie. Robert Rivard is dead. The boy from Missouri? He hung himself."

"I'm shorry to hear that." He didn't sound sorry, and didn't waste time asking for details. "When you arrive, call me and tell me where you are. And remember, no more than an hour away."

"Okay," I said, and broke the connection.

I sat there in the unnaturally quiet studio for several minutes, looking at the framed album covers on the walls, then dialed Jenny Knowlton, in Rockland. She answered on the first ring.

"How's our girl doing?" I asked.

"Fine. Putting on weight and walking a mile a day. She looks twenty years younger."

"No aftereffects?"

"Nothing. No seizures, no sleepwalking, no amnesia. She doesn't remember much about the time we spent at Goat Mountain, but I think that's sort of a blessing, don't you?"

"What about you, Jenny? Are you okay?"

"Fine, but I ought to go. We're awfully busy at the hospital today. Thank God I've got vacation coming up."

"You won't go off somewhere and leave Astrid alone, will you? Because I don't think that would be a good id—"

"No, no, certainly not!" There was something in her voice. Something nervous. "Jamie, I've got a page. I have to go."

I sat in front of the darkened control panel. I looked at the album covers—actually CD covers these days, little things the size of postcards. I thought about a time not too long after I'd gotten my first car as a birthday present, that '66 Ford Galaxie. Riding with Norm Irving. Him pestering me to put the pedal to the metal on the two-mile stretch of Route 27 we called the Harlow Straight. So we could see what she'd do, he said. At eighty, the front end began to shimmy, but I didn't want to look like a wuss—at seventeen, not looking like a wuss is very important—so I kept my foot down. At eighty-five the shimmy smoothed out. At ninety, the Galaxie took on a dreamy, dangerous lightness as its contact with the road lessened, and I realized I'd reached the edge of control. Careful not to

touch the brake—I knew from my father that could mean disaster at high speed—I let off the gas and the Galaxie began to slow.

I wished I could do that now.

The Embassy Suites near the Jetport had seemed all right when I'd been there the night after Astrid's miracle recovery, so I checked in again. It had crossed my mind to do my waiting at the Castle Rock Inn, but the chances of running into an old acquaintance—Norm Irving, for instance—were too great. If that happened, it would almost certainly get back to my brother Terry. He'd want to know why I was in Maine, and why I wasn't staying with him. Those were questions I didn't want to answer.

The time passed. On July Fourth, I watched the fireworks from Portland Promenade with several thousand other people, all of us *ooh*-ing and *ahh*-ing as the peonies and chrysanthemums and diadems exploded overhead and were doubled in Casco Bay, where they swayed on the waves. In the days that followed, I went to the zoo in York, the Seashore Trolley Museum in Kennebunkport, and the lighthouse at Pemaquid Point. I toured the Portland Museum of Art, where three generations of Wyeths were on view, and took in a matinee performance of *The Buddy Holly Story* at Ogunquit Playhouse—the lead singer/actor was good, but no Gary Busey. I ate "lobstah" until I never wanted to see another one. I took long walks along the rocky shore. Twice a week I visited Books-A-Million in the Maine Mall and bought paperbacks which I read in my room until I was sleepy. I took my cell with me everywhere, waiting for Jacobs to call, and the call didn't come. On a couple of occasions I thought of calling *him*, and told myself I was out of my mind to even consider it. Why kick a sleeping dog?

The weather was picture-perfect, with low humidity, innocent skies, and temperatures in the low seventies, day after day. There were showers, usually at night. One evening I heard TV weatherman Joe Cupo call it "considerate rain." He added that it was the most beautiful summer he'd seen in his thirty-five years of broadcasting.

The All-Star game was played in Minneapolis, the regular baseball season resumed, and as August approached, I began to hope that I might make it back to Colorado without ever seeing Charlie. It crossed my mind that he might have had a fourth stroke, this time a cataclysmic one, and I kept an eye on the obituary page in the *Portland Press Herald*. Not exactly hoping, but . . .

Fuck that, I was. I *was* hoping.

During the local news on July 25th, Joe Cupo regretfully informed me and the rest of his southern Maine viewing audience that all good things must end, and the heatwave currently baking the Midwest would be moving into New England over the weekend. Temperatures would be in the mid-nineties during the entire last week of July, and August didn't look much better, at least to start with. "Check those air-conditioning units, folks," Cupo advised. "They don't call em the dog days for nothing."

Jacobs called that evening. "Sunday," he said. "I'll expect you no later than nine in the morning."

I told him I'd be there.

Joe Cupo was right about the heat. It moved in Saturday afternoon, and when I got into my rental car at seven thirty on Sunday morning, the air was already thick. The roads were empty, and I made good time to Goat Mountain. On my way up to the main

gate, I noticed that the spur leading to Skytop was open again, the stout wooden gate pulled back.

Sam the security guard was waiting for me, but no longer in uniform. He was sitting on the dropped tailgate of a Tacoma pickup, dressed in jeans and eating a bagel. He put it carefully on a napkin when I pulled up, and strolled over to my car.

"Hello there, Mr. Morton. You're early."

"No traffic," I said.

"Yeah, in summer this is the best time of day to travel. The Massholes'll be out in force later, headed for the beaches." He looked at the sky, where blue was already fading to hazy white. "Let em bake and work on their skin cancer. I plan to be home, watching the Sox and soaking up the AC."

"Shift over soon?"

"No more shifts here for any of us," he said. "Once I call Mr. Jacobs and tell him you're on your way, that's it. Job over."

"Well, enjoy the rest of the summer." I stuck out my hand.

He shook it. "Any idea what he's up to? I can keep a secret; I'm bonded, you know."

"Your guess is as good as mine."

He gave me a wink as if to say we both knew better, then waved me on. Before I went around the first curve, I watched in the rear-view mirror as he grabbed his bagel, slammed the Tacoma's tailgate shut, and got in behind the wheel.

That's it. Job over.

I wished I could say the same.

Jacobs came slowly and carefully down the porch steps to meet me. In his left hand was a cane. The twist of his mouth was more severe than ever. I saw a single car in the parking lot, and it was one I recognized: a trim little Subaru Outback. On the back deck was a sticker reading SAVE ONE LIFE, YOU'RE A HERO. SAVE A THOUSAND AND YOU'RE A NURSE. My heart sank.

"Jamie! Wonderful to see you!" *See* came out *she*. He offered the hand not holding the cane. It was obviously an effort, but I ignored it.

"If Astrid is here, she leaves, and leaves this minute," I said. "If you think I'm bluffing, just try me."

"Calm yourself, Jamie. Astrid is a hundred and thirty miles from here, continuing her recovery in her cozy little nest just north of Rockland. Her friend Jenny has kindly agreed to aid me while I complete my work."

"I somehow doubt that kindness had much to do with it. Correct me if I'm wrong."

"Come inside. It's hot out here already. You can move your car to the parking lot later."

He was slow going up the steps even with the cane, and I had to steady him when he tottered. The arm I grasped was hardly more than a bone. By the time we got to the top, he was gasping.

"I need to rest a minute," he said, and sank into one of the Shaker-style rockers that lined the porch.

I sat on the rail and regarded him.

"Where's Rudy? I thought *he* was your nurse."

Jacobs favored me with his peculiar smile, now more one-sided than ever. "Shortly after my session with Miss Soderberg in the East Room, both Rudy and Norma tendered their resignations. You just can't get good help these days, Jamie. Present company excepted, of course."

"So you hired Knowlton."

"I did, and believe me, I traded up. She's forgotten more about nursing than Rudy Kelly ever knew. Give me a hand, would you?"

I helped him to his feet, and we went inside to where it was cool.

"There's juice and breakfast pastries in the kitchen. Help yourself to whatever you want, and join me in the main parlor."

I skipped the pastries but poured myself a small glass of OJ from a carafe in the huge refrigerator. When I put it back, I inventoried the supplies and saw enough for ten days or so. Two weeks if they were stretched. Was that how long we were going to be here, or would either Jenny Knowlton or myself be making a grocery run to Yarmouth, which was probably the closest town with a supermarket?

The guard service was finished. Jacobs had replaced the nurse—which didn't completely surprise me, given Jacobs's own increasingly iffy condition—but not the housekeeper, which meant (among other things) that Jenny must also have been cooking his meals and, perhaps, changing his bed. It was just the three of us, or so I thought then.

We turned out to be a quartet.

The main parlor was all glass on the north side, giving a view of Longmeadow and Skytop. I couldn't see the cabin, but I could glimpse that iron pole jutting up toward the hazy sky. Looking at it, things finally began to come together in my mind . . . but slowly, even then, and Jacobs held back the one vital piece that would have made the picture crystal clear. You might say I should have seen it anyway, all the pieces were there, but I was a guitar player, not a detective, and when it came to deductive reasoning, I was never the fastest greyhound on the track.

"Where is Jenny?" I asked. Jacobs had taken the sofa; I sat down opposite him in a wingback chair that tried to swallow me whole.

"Occupied."

"With what?"

"None of your beeswax now, although it will be shortly." He leaned forward with his hands clasped on the head of the cane, looking like a predatory bird. One that would soon be too old to fly. "You have questions. I understand that better than you think, Jamie—I know that inquisitiveness is a large part of what brought you here. You will have answers in time, but probably not today."

"When?"

"Hard to tell, but soon. In the meantime, you will cook our meals and come if I ring."

He showed me a white box—not so different in appearance from the one I'd used that day in the East Room, except this one had a button instead of a slide switch, and an embossed trade name: Notiflex. He pushed the button and chimes went off, echoing from all the large downstairs rooms.

"I won't need you to help me go to the toilet—that I can still do myself—but I'll need you standing by when I'm in the shower, I'm afraid. In case I slip. There's a prescription gel you'll rub into my back, hips, and thighs twice a day. Oh, and you'll have to bring many of my meals to my suite of rooms. Not because I'm lazy, or because I want to turn you into my personal butler, but because I tire easily and need to conserve my strength. I have one more thing to do. It's a large thing, a vitally important thing, and when the time comes, I must be strong enough to do it."

"Happy to make and serve the meals, Charlie, but as far as the nursing part goes, I assumed Jenny Knowlton would be the one to—"

"She's occupied, as I told you, so you must take over her . . . why are you looking at me like that?"

"I was remembering the day I met you. I was only six, but it's a clear memory. I made a mountain in the dirt—"

"So you did. It's a clear memory for me, too."

"—and I was playing with my soldiers. A shadow fell over me. I looked up and it was you. What I was thinking is that your shadow has been over me for my whole life. What I ought to do is drive away from here right now and get out from under it."

"But you won't."

"No. I won't. But I'll tell you something. I also remember the man you were—how you got right down on your knees with me and joined in the game. I remember your smile. When you smile now, all I see is a sneer. When you talk now, all I hear is orders: do this, do that, and I'll tell you why later. What became of you, Charlie?"

He struggled up from the sofa, and when I moved to help, he waved me away. "If you have to ask that, a smart boy grew up to be a stupid man. At least when I lost my wife and son, I didn't turn to drugs."

"You had your secret electricity. That was *your* drug."

"Thank you for that valuable insight, but since this discussion has no point, let's end it, shall we? Several of the rooms on the second floor are made up. I'm sure you'll find one to your taste. I'd like an egg salad sandwich for lunch, a glass of skim milk, and an oatmeal-raisin cookie. The roughage is good for my bowels, I'm told."

"Charlie—"

"No more," he said, hobbling toward the elevator. "Soon you'll know everything. In the meantime, keep your bourgeois judgments to yourself. Lunch at noon. Bring it to the Cooper Suite."

He left me there, for the time being too stunned to say a word.

Three days went by.

They were broiling hot outside, the horizon blurred by a constant haze of humidity. Inside, the resort was cool and comfortable. I made our meals, and although he joined me downstairs for dinner on the second night, he took all the rest in his suite. I heard the TV blaring loudly when I brought them, suggesting that his hearing had also gone downhill. He seemed especially fond of the Weather Channel. When I knocked, he always turned it off before telling me to come in.

Those days were my introduction to practical nursing. He was still able to undress and start the water for his morning shower himself—he had an invalid's shower-chair to sit on while he soaped and rinsed. I sat on his bed, waiting for him to call. When he did, I turned off the water, helped him out, and dried him off. His body was a wasted remnant of what it had been in his days as a Methodist minister, and his later ones as a carny agent. His hips stuck out like the bones of a plucked Thanksgiving turkey; every rib cast a shadow; his buttocks were little more than biscuits. Thanks to the stroke, everything slumped to the right when I helped him back to his bed.

I rubbed him down with Voltaren Gel for his aches and pains, then fetched his pills, which were in a plastic case with almost as many compartments as there are keys on a piano. By the time he'd gotten them all down, the Voltaren had had a chance to work, and he could dress himself—except for the sock on his right foot. That I had to put on myself, but I always waited until he'd hauled on his boxers. I had no interest in being eye-to-eye with his elderly schlong.

"All right," he'd say when the sock was pulled up to his scrawny shin. "I'll do the rest myself. Thank you, Jamie."

He always said thank you, and the TV always went on as soon as the door was closed.

Those were long, long days. The resort's pool had been drained, and it was far too hot to walk the grounds. There was a health club, though, and when I wasn't reading (there was a shitpoke excuse for a library, mostly stocked with Erle Stanley Gardner, Louis L'Amour, and old Reader's Digest Condensed Books), I exercised in solitary, air-conditioned splendor. I jogged miles on the treadmill, pedaled miles on the stationary bicycle, stepped on the StairMaster, curled hand weights.

The only station the TV in my quarters got was Channel 8 out of Poland Spring, and the reception was lousy, producing a picture too fuzzy to watch. The same was true of the wall-size job in the Sunset Lounge. I guessed there was a satellite dish somewhere, but only Charlie Jacobs was hooked up to it. I thought of asking if he would share, then didn't. He might have said yes, and I'd taken everything from him that I intended to. Charlie's gifts came with a pricetag.

All that exercise, and still I slept like shit. My old nightmare, gone for years, returned: dead family members sitting around the dining room table in the home place, and a moldy birthday cake that gave birth to huge insects.

I woke shortly after 5 AM on the morning of July 30th, thinking I'd heard something downstairs. I decided it was the remnant of my dream, lay back down, and closed my eyes. I was just drifting off when it came again: a subdued clatter that sounded like kitchen pots.

I got up, stepped into a pair of jeans, and hurried downstairs. The kitchen was empty, but I glimpsed someone through the window, descending the back steps on the side of the loading dock. When I got out there, Jenny Knowlton was slipping behind the wheel of a golf cart with GOAT MOUNTAIN RESORT decaled on the side. On the seat beside her was a bowl with four eggs in it.

"Jenny! Wait!"

She started, then saw it was me and smiled. I was willing to give her an A for effort, but that smile really wasn't up to much. She looked ten years older than when I'd last seen her, and the dark circles under her eyes suggested I wasn't the only one having sleep problems. She'd stopped dyeing her hair, and there were at least two inches of gray below the glossy black.

"I woke you, didn't I? Sorry, but it's your own fault. The dish drainer's full of pots and pans, and I hit it with my elbow. Didn't your mother ever teach you to use the dishwasher?"

The answer to that was no, because we never had one. What my mother taught me was that it's easier to let stuff air-dry, as long as there's not too much. But kitchen cleanup wasn't what I wanted to talk about.

"What are you doing here?"

"I came for eggs."

"You know that's not what I mean."

She looked away. "I can't tell you. I made a promise. In fact, I signed a contract." She laughed without humor. "I doubt if it would stand up in court, but I intend to honor it, just the same. I owe a debt, the same as you. Besides, you'll know soon enough."

"I want to know now."

"I have to go, Jamie. He doesn't want us talking. If he found out, he'd be mad. I just wanted a few eggs. If I ever have to look at another bowl of Cheerios or Frosted Flakes, I'll scream."

"Unless your car's got a dead battery, you could have gone to Food City in Yarmouth and picked up all the eggs you wanted."

"I'm not to leave until it's over. You, either. Don't ask me anything else. I have to keep my promise."

"For Astrid."

"Well . . . he's paying me a great deal of money for a little bit of nursing, enough to retire on, but mostly for Astrid, yes."

"Who's watching out for her while you're here? *Somebody* better be. I don't know what Charlie's told you, but there really are aftereffects from some of his treatments, and they can be—"

"She's well cared for, you don't need to worry about that. We have . . . good friends in the community."

This time her smile was stronger, more natural, and at least one thing came clear to me.

"You're lovers, aren't you? You and Astrid?"

"*Partners*. Not long after Maine legalized gay marriage, we set a date to make it official. Then she got sick. That's all I can tell you. I'm going now. I can't be away for long. I left you plenty of eggs, don't worry."

"Why can't you be away for long?"

She shook her head, not meeting my eyes. "I have to go."

"Were you already here when we talked on the phone?"

"No . . . but I knew I *would* be."

I watched her trundle back down the hill, the golf cart's wheels making tracks in the diamond dew. Those gems wouldn't last long; the day had barely begun, and it was already hot enough to pop sweat on my arms and forehead. She disappeared into the trees. I knew that if I walked down there, I'd find a path. And if I followed the path, I'd come to a cabin. The one where I'd lain breast to breast and hip to hip with Astrid Soderberg in another life.

Shortly after ten that morning, while I was reading *The Mysterious Affair at Styles* (one of my late sister's favorites), the first floor was filled with the chiming of Jacobs's call-button. I went up to the Cooper Suite, hoping not to find him lying on the floor with a broken hip. I needn't have worried. He was dressed, leaning on his cane, and looking out the window. When he turned to me, his eyes were bright.

"I think today might be our day," he said. "Be prepared."

But it wasn't. When I brought him his supper—barley soup and a cheese sandwich—the television was silent and he wouldn't open the door. He shouted through it for me to go away, sounding like a petulant child.

"You need to eat, Charlie."

"What I need is peace and quiet! Leave me alone!"

I went back up around ten o'clock, meaning only to listen at the door long enough to hear the cackle of his TV. If I did, I'd ask if he didn't at least want some toast before he turned in. The TV was off but Jacobs was awake and talking in the too-loud voice people who are going deaf always seem to use on the phone.

"She won't go until I'm ready! You'll make sure of it! That's what I'm paying you for, so *see to it!*"

Problems—and with Jenny, it seemed at first. She was close to deciding she'd had enough, and wanted to go somewhere. Back to the Downeast home she shared with Astrid seemed most likely, at least until it occurred to me that it might actually have been Jenny he was talking to. Which would mean what? The only thing that came to mind was what the verb *to go* often meant to people of Charlie Jacobs's age.

I left his suite without knocking.

What he'd been waiting for—what we'd all been waiting for—came the next day.

His call-chime went off at one o'clock, not long after I'd taken him his lunch. The door to the suite was open, and as I approached, I heard the current weather boffin talking about how warm the Gulf of Mexico was, and what that augured for the coming hurricane season. Then the guy's voice was cut off by a series of harsh buzzing sounds. When I walked in, I saw a red band running along the bottom of the screen. It was gone before I could read it, but I know a weather warning when I see one.

Severe weather during a long hot spell meant thunderstorms, thunderstorms meant lightning, and to me, lightning meant Skytop. To Jacobs, too, I was betting.

He was once more fully dressed. "No false alarms today, Jamie. The storm cells are in upstate New York now, but they're moving east and still intensifying."

The buzzing started again and this time I could read the crawl: WEATHER ALERT FOR YORK, CUMBERLAND, ANDROSCOGGIN, OXFORD, AND CASTLE COUNTIES UNTIL 2 AM AUGUST 1. POSSIBILITY OF SEVERE THUNDERSTORMS 90%. SUCH STORMS MAY PRODUCE HEAVY RAIN, HIGH WINDS, GOLF BALL–SIZED HAIL. OUTDOOR ACTIVITIES NOT RECOMMENDED.

No shit, Sherlock, I thought.

"These cells can't dissipate or change course," Charlie said. He spoke with the calmness of either madness or absolute certainty. "They *can't*. She won't last much longer, and I'm too old and sick to start over with someone else. I want you to bring a golf cart around to the kitchen loading dock, and be ready to go at a moment's notice."

"To Skytop," I said.

He smiled his lopsided smile. "Go now. I need to keep an eye on these storms. They're producing over a hundred lightning-strikes an hour in the Albany area, isn't that wonderful?"

Not the word I would have chosen. I couldn't remember how many volts he'd said a single lightning-strike produced, but I knew it was a lot.

In the millions.

• • •

Charlie's call-bell went off again a little after 5 PM. I went upstairs, part of me hoping to see him downhearted and angry, another part as damnably curious as ever. I thought that was the part that would be satisfied, because the day was darkening rapidly in the west, and I could already hear mumbles of thunder, distant but approaching. An army in the sky.

Jacobs was still listing to starboard, but excitement—he was fairly bursting with it—made him look years younger. His mahogany box was on the end table. He had shut off the TV in favor of his laptop. "Look at this, Jamie! It's beautiful!"

The screen displayed NOAA's projection of the evening's weather. It showed a tightening cone of orange and red that went directly over Castle County. The timeline projected the highest probability of heavy weather arriving between seven and eight. I glanced at my watch and saw it was five fifteen.

"Isn't it? Isn't it beautiful?"

"If you say so, Charlie."

"Sit down, but get me a glass of water first, if you will. I have some explaining to do, and I think there's just time. Although we'll want to go soon, yes we will. In carny terminology, we'll want to DS." He cackled.

I got a bottle of water from the bar refrigerator and poured it into a Waterford glass—nothing but the best for guests of the Cooper Suite. He sipped and popped his lips in appreciation, a leathery smack I could have done without. Thunder rumbled. He looked toward the sound, his smile that of a man anticipating the arrival of an old friend. Then he turned his attention back to me.

"I made a great deal of money playing Pastor Danny, as you know. But instead of spending it on private jets, heated doghouses, and gold-plated bathroom fixtures, I spent mine on two things. One was privacy—I've had enough of Jesus-shouting pagans to last me a lifetime. The other was private investigation firms, a dozen in all, the best of the best, located in a dozen major American cities. I tasked them with finding and tracking certain people suffering from certain diseases. Comparative rarities. Eight such illnesses in all."

"*Sick* people? Not your cures? Because that's what you told me."

"Oh, they tracked a representative number of cures, too—you weren't the only one interested in aftereffects, Jamie—but that wasn't their main job. Starting ten years ago, they found several hundred of these unfortunate sufferers, and sent me regular updates. Al Stamper minded the dossiers until he left my employ; since then, I've done it myself. Many of those unlucky people have since died; others replaced them. Man is born to illness and sorrow, as you know."

I didn't answer, but the thunder did. The sky in the west was now dark with bad intentions.

"As my studies progressed—"

"Was a book called *De Vermis Mysteriis* part of your studies, Charlie?"

He looked startled, then relaxed. "Good for you. *De Vermis* wasn't just a part of my studies, it was the basis of them. Prinn went mad, you know. He ended his days in a German castle, studying abstruse mathematics and eating bugs. Grew his fingernails long, tore out his throat with them one night, and died at the age of thirty-seven, painting equations on the floor of his room in blood."

"Really?"

He gave the one-sided shrug, accompanied by the one-sided grin. "Who knows for sure? A cautionary tale if true, but the histories of such visionaries were written by people interested in making sure no one else followed their paths. Religious types, for the most part, overseers of the Heavenly Insurance Company. But never mind that now; we'll speak of Prinn another day."

I doubt it, I thought.

"As my studies progressed, my investigators began a winnowing process. Hundreds became dozens. Early this year, dozens became ten. In June, the ten became three." He leaned forward. "I was looking for the one I've always thought of as Patient Omega."

"Your last cure."

This seemed to amuse him. "You could say so. Yes, why not? Which brings us to the sad story of Mary Fay, which I just have time to tell before we remove to my workshop." He gave a hoarse laugh that reminded me of Astrid's voice before he'd cured her. "Workshop Omega, I suppose. Only this one is also a well-equipped hospital suite."

"Run by Nurse Jenny."

"What a find she was, Jamie! Rudy Kelly would have been at a loss . . . or have gone yipping down the road like a puppy with a wasp in his ear."

"Tell me the story," I said. "Let me know what I'm getting into."

He settled back. "Once upon a time, in the seventies, a man named Franklin Fay married a woman named Janice Shelley. They were graduate students in the English Department at Columbia University, and went on to teach together. Franklin was a published poet—I've read his work and it's quite good. Given more time, he might have been one of the great ones. His wife wrote her dissertation on James Joyce and taught English and Irish literature. In 1980, they had a daughter."

"Mary."

"Yes. In 1983 they were offered teaching positions at American College in Dublin, as part of a two-year exchange program. With me so far?"

"Yes."

"In the summer of 1985, while you were playing music and I was working the carny circuit with my Portraits in Lightning gaff, the Fays decided to tour Ireland before returning to the States. They rented a camper—what our British and Irish cousins call a caravan—and set out. They stopped one day for a pub lunch in County Offaly. Shortly after they left, they collided head-on with a produce truck. Mr. and Mrs. Fay were killed. The child, riding behind them and strapped in, was badly injured but survived."

It was an almost exact replay of the accident that had killed his wife and son. I thought then that he must have known it, but now I'm not so sure. Sometimes we're just too close.

"They were driving on the wrong side of the road, you see. My theory is that Franklin had a beer or glass of wine too many, forgot he was in Ireland, and reverted to his old habit of driving on the right. The same thing may have happened to an American actor, I think, although I don't recall the name."

I did, but didn't bother to tell him.

"In the hospital, young Mary Fay was given a number of blood transfusions. Do you see where this is going?" And when I shook my head: "The blood was tainted, Jamie. By the infectious prion that causes Creutzfeldt-Jakob, commonly called mad cow disease."

More thunder. Now a boom instead of a mumble.

"Mary was raised by an aunt and uncle. She did well in school, became a legal secretary, went back to college to get a law degree, quit the program after two semesters, and eventually resumed her former secretarial duties. This was in 2007. The disease she was carrying was dormant, and remained so until last summer. Then she began suffering symptoms that are normally associated with drug use, a mental breakdown, or both. She quit her job. Money was in short supply, and by October of 2013, she was also suffering physical symptoms: myoclonus, ataxia, seizures. The prion was fully awake and hard at work, eating holes in her brain. A spinal tap and MRI finally revealed the culprit."

"Jesus," I said. Old news footage, probably watched in some motel room or other while I was on the road, began playing behind my eyes: a cow in a muddy stall, legs splayed, head cocked, eyes rolling, mooing mindlessly as it tried to find its feet.

"Jesus can't help Mary Fay," he said.

"But you can."

His answer was a look I couldn't read. Then he turned his head and studied the darkening sky.

"Help me up. I don't intend to miss my appointment with the lightning. I've been waiting for it my whole life." He pointed to the mahogany box on the end table. "And bring that. I'll need what's inside."

"Magic rods instead of magic rings."

But he shook his head. "Not for this."

We took the elevator. He made it into the lobby under his own power, then dropped into one of the chairs near the dead fireplace. "Go to the supply room at the end of the East Wing corridor. In it you'll find a piece of equipment I've been avoiding."

That turned out to be an old-fashioned wheelchair with a wicker seat and iron wheels that screeched like devils. I rolled it down to the lobby and helped him into it. He held out his hands for the mahogany box, and I handed it over—not without misgivings. He held it curled to his chest like a baby, and as I rolled him through the restaurant and into the deserted kitchen, he resumed his story with a question.

"Can you guess why Miss Fay quit law school?"

"Because she got sick."

He shook his head disapprovingly. "Don't you listen? The prion was still dormant at that time."

"She decided she didn't like it? Her grades weren't good enough?"

"Neither." He turned to me and gave his eyebrows an old roué's waggle. "Mary Fay is that heroine of the modern age, a single mother. The child, a boy named Victor, is now seven years old. I've never met him—Mary didn't want that—but she showed me many pictures of him while we were discussing his future. He reminded me of my own little boy."

We had reached the door to the loading dock, but I didn't push it open. "Does the kid have what she has?"

"No. Not now, at least."

"Will he?"

"Impossible to be entirely sure, but he's tested negative for the C-J prion. So far, at least." More thunder boomed. The wind had begun to pick up, rattling the door and making a momentary low howling beneath the eaves. "Come on, Jamie. We really must go."

The loading dock stairs were too steep for him to negotiate with his cane, so I carried him. He was shockingly light. I deposited him in the passenger seat of the golf cart and got behind the wheel. As we drove across the gravel and onto the downward-sloping expanse of lawn behind the resort, there was another clap of thunder. The clouds to the west of us were purple-black stacks. As I looked, lightning forked down from their distended bellies in three different places. Any possibility of the storm missing us was gone, and when it hit, it was going to rock our world.

Charlie said, "Many years ago I told you about how the iron rod on Skytop attracts the lightning. Much more than an ordinary lightning rod would. Do you remember?"

"Yes."

"Did you ever come here and see for yourself?"

"No." I told this lie without hesitation. What had happened at Skytop in the summer of 1974 was between me and Astrid. I suppose I might have told Bree, if she'd ever asked about my first time, but not Charlie Jacobs. Never him.

"In *De Vermis Mysteriis*, Prinn speaks of 'the vast machinery that runs the mill of the universe,' and the river of power that machinery draws on. He calls that river—"

"*Potestas magnum universum*," I said.

He stared at me, bushy eyebrows hiked to what had once been his hairline. "I was wrong about you. You're not stupid at all."

The wind gusted. Ripples raced across grass that hadn't been cut in weeks. The speeding air was still warm against my cheek. When it turned cold, the rain would come.

"It's lightning, isn't it?" I said. "That's the *potestas magnum universum*."

"No, Jamie." He spoke almost gently. "For all its voltage, lightning is a mere *trickle* of power, one of many such that feed what I call the secret electricity. But that secret electricity, awesome though it may be, is itself only a tributary. It feeds something much greater, a power beyond the ability of human beings to comprehend. *That* is the *potestas magnum universum* of which Prinn wrote, and it's what I expect to tap today. The lightning . . . and this"—he raised the box in his bony hands—"are only means to an end."

We passed into the trees, following the path Jenny had taken after she'd gotten her eggs. Branches swayed above us; leaves that might soon be ripped away by wind and hail were in agitated conversation. I abruptly took my foot off the cart's accelerator button, and it stopped at once, as electrically powered vehicles are wont to do.

"If you're planning to tap into the secrets of the universe, Charlie, maybe you should count me out. The cures are scary enough. You're talking about . . . I don't know . . . a kind of *doorway*."

A small one, I thought. *Covered with dead ivy*.

"Calm yourself," he said. "Yes, there's a doorway—Prinn speaks of it, and I believe Astrid did, as well—but I don't want to open it. I only want to peek through the keyhole."

"In God's name, *why*?"

He looked at me then with a species of wild contempt. "Are you a fool, after all? What would you call a door that's closed against all of humankind?"

"Why don't you just tell me?"

He sighed as if I were hopeless. "Drive on, Jamie."

"And if I won't?"

"Then I'll walk, and when my legs won't carry me any further, I'll crawl."

He was bluffing, of course. He *couldn't* have gone on without me. But I didn't know that then, and so I drove on.

The cabin where I'd made love to Astrid was gone. Where it had stood—swaybacked, slumping in on itself, tagged with graffiti—was a nifty little cottage, white with green trim. There was a square plot of lawn, and showy summer flowers that would be gone by day's end, stripped clean by the storm. East of the cottage, the paved road gave way to the gravel I remembered from my trips to Skytop with Astrid. It ended at that bulging dome of granite, where the iron pole jutted toward the black sky.

Jenny, dressed in a flower-print blouse and white nylon Nancy Nurse pants, was standing on the stoop, arms crossed below her breasts and hands cupping her elbows, as if she were cold. There was a stethoscope looped around her neck. I pulled up at the steps and walked around the golf cart's snout to where Jacobs was struggling to get out. Jenny came down the steps and helped me get him on his feet.

"Thank God you're here!" She had to shout to be heard over the rising wind. The pines and spruces were bending and bowing before it. "I thought you weren't coming, after all!" Thunder rolled, and when a flash of lightning followed it, she cringed.

"Inside!" I yelled at her. "Right now!" The wind had turned chill, and my sweaty skin was as good as a thermometer, registering the change in the air. The storm was only minutes away.

We got Jacobs up the steps, one on each side. The wind spun the thin remnants of his hair around his skull in whirlpools. He still had his cane, and hugged the mahogany box protectively against his chest. I heard a rattling sound, looked toward Skytop, and saw bits of scree, smashed out of the granite by the lightning strikes of previous storms, being tumbled down the slope by the wind and off the edge of the drop.

Once we were inside, Jenny couldn't get the door shut. I managed, but had to put some real muscle into it. When it was closed, the howl of the wind dropped a little. I could hear the cottage's wooden bones creaking, but it seemed sturdy enough. I didn't think we'd blow away, and the iron rod would catch any close strokes of lightning. At least I hoped so.

"There's half a bottle of whiskey in the kitchen." Jacobs sounded out of breath but otherwise calm. "Unless you've polished it off, Miss Knowlton?"

She shook her head. Her face was pale, her eyes large and shining—not with tears, but with terror. She jumped at every clap of thunder.

"Bring me a small taste," Jacobs told me. "One finger will be plenty. And pour one for yourself and Miss Knowlton. We'll toast to the success of our endeavor."

"I don't want a drink, and I don't want to toast anything," Jenny said. "I just want this to be over. I was crazy to get involved."

"Go on, Jamie," Jacobs said. "Bring three. And speedily. Tempus fugit."

The bottle was on the counter next to the sink. I set out three juice glasses and poured a splash into each. I very rarely drank, fearing booze might lead me back to dope, but I needed this one.

When I returned to the living room, Jenny was gone. Lightning flashed blue in the windows; the lamps and the overhead flickered, then came back bright.

"She needed to see to our patient," Jacobs said. "I'll drink hers. Unless you want it, that is."

"Did you send me to the kitchen so you could talk to her, Charlie?"

"Nonsense." Smiling on the good half of his face; the other half remaining grave and watchful. *You know I'm lying*, that half seemed to say, *but it's too late now. Isn't it?*

I gave him one of the juice glasses and set the one meant for Jenny on a table at the end of the couch, where magazines had been arranged in a tasteful fan. It occurred to me that I might have entered Astrid's body for the first time on the very spot where that table stood. *Hold still, honey*, she'd said, and then, *It's wonderful.*

Jacobs raised his drink. "Here's to—"

I tossed mine off before he could finish.

He looked at me reproachfully, then swallowed his—except for one drop that dribbled down the frozen side of his mouth. "You find me odious, don't you? I'm sorry you feel that way. More than you'll ever know."

"Not odious, scary. I'd find anyone scary who's monkeying around with forces beyond their comprehension."

He picked up the drink that had been meant for Jenny. Through the glass, the frozen side of his face was magnified. "I could argue, but why bother? The storm is almost upon us, and when the skies clear again, we'll be done with each other. But at least be man enough to admit you're curious. That's a large part of what brought you here—you want to *know*. Just as I do. As Prinn did. The only one here against her will is poor Jenny. She came to pay a debt of love. Which gives her a nobility we cannot share."

The door behind him opened. I caught a whiff of sickroom odors—pee, body lotion, disinfectant. Jenny closed it behind her, saw the glass in Jacobs's hand, and plucked it away. She swallowed with a grimace that made the tendons in her neck stand out.

Jacobs bent over his cane, studying her closely. "May I assume . . . ?"

"Yes." Thunder boomed. She gave a little scream and let go of the empty juice glass. It hit the carpet and rolled away.

"Go back in to her," Jacobs said. "Jamie and I will join you very shortly."

Jenny re-entered the sickroom without a word. Jacobs faced me.

"Listen very closely. When we go in, you'll see a bureau on your left. There's a revolver in the top drawer. Sam the security guard procured it for me. I don't expect you'll need to use it, but if you do, Jamie . . . don't hesitate."

"Why in God's name would I—"

"We spoke of a certain door. It's the door into death, and sooner or later each one of us grows small, reduced to nothing but mind and spirit, and in that reduced state we pass through, leaving our bodies behind like empty gloves. Sometimes death is natural, a mercy that puts an end to suffering. But all too often it comes as an assassin, full of senseless cruelty and lacking any vestige of compassion. My wife and son, taken in a stupid and pointless accident, are perfect examples. Your sister is another. They are three of millions.

For most of my life I've railed against those who try to explain that stupidity and pointlessness with prattlings about faith and children's stories about heaven. Such nonsense never comforted me, and I'm sure it never comforted you. And yet . . . there is *something.*"

Yes, I thought as thunder cracked hard enough and close enough to shake panes of window glass in their frames. *Something is there, beyond the door, and something will happen. Something very terrible. Unless I put a stop to it.*

"In my experiments I've glimpsed intimations of that something. I've seen its shape in every cure the secret electricity has effected. I even know it from the aftereffects, some of which you have noted. Those are trailing fragments of some unknown existence beyond our lives. Everyone wonders at one time or other what lies beyond the wall of death. Today, Jamie, we'll see for ourselves. I want to know what happened to my wife and son. I want to know what the universe has in store for all of us once this life is over, and I intend to find out."

"We're not meant to see." Shock had stolen most of my voice, and I wasn't sure he'd hear me over the rising wind, but he did.

"Can you tell me you don't think about your sister Claire every day? That you don't wonder if she still exists *somewhere*?"

I said nothing, but he nodded as if I had.

"Of course you do, and we'll have answers shortly. Mary Fay will give them to us."

"How can she?" My lips felt numb, and not from the alcohol. "How can she, if you cure her?"

He gave me a look that asked if I were really that clueless. "I *can't* cure her. Those eight diseases I mentioned were picked because *none* are amenable to cure by the secret electricity."

The wind rose to a shout, and the first erratic bursts of rain struck the west side of the house, hitting so hard they sounded like thrown pebbles.

"Miss Knowlton turned off Mary Fay's ventilator as we were coming here from the resort. She's been dead for almost fifteen minutes. Her blood is cooling. The computer inside her skull, wounded by the disease she carried from childhood but still marvelous, has gone dark."

"You think . . . you actually *think* . . ." I couldn't finish. I was flabbergasted.

"Yes. It's taken years of study and experiment to reach this point, but yes. Using lightning as a road to the secret electricity, and the secret electricity as a thoroughfare to *potestas magnum universum*, I intend to bring Mary Fay back to some form of life. I intend to learn the truth of what's on the other side of the door that leads into the Kingdom of Death. I'll learn it from the lips of someone who's been there."

"You're insane." I turned toward the door. "I won't play any part in this."

"I can't stop you if you really mean to leave," he said, "although to go out in a storm like this would be the height of recklessness. Would it help if I told you that I'll proceed without you, and that would put Miss Knowlton's life at risk, as well as my own? How ironic it would be if she were to die so soon after Astrid was saved."

I turned back. My hand was on the knob; rain was pounding against the door on the other side. Lightning printed a brief blue rectangle on the carpet.

"You *can* find out what happened to Claire." His voice was low now, soft and silky, the voice of Pastor Danny at his most persuasive.

The voice of a coaxing devil.

"You might even be able to speak with her . . . hear her tell you that she loves you. Wouldn't that be wonderful? Always assuming she's still there as a conscious entity, of course . . . *and don't you want to know?*"

There was another flash of lightning, and from the mahogany box, a poisonous greenish-purple wink of light shot through a gap in the latch, there at one second, gone the next.

"If it's any comfort to you, Miss Fay agreed to this experiment. The paperwork is in apple-pie order, including a signed affidavit giving me power to cease so-called heroic measures at my own discretion. In return for my brief and entirely respectful use of her remains, Mary's son will be taken care of with a generous trust fund that will see him well into adulthood. There are no victims here, Jamie."

So you say, I thought. *So you say*.

Thunder roared. This time, just before the stroke of lightning, I heard a faint clicking sound. Jacobs did, too.

"The time has arrived. Come into the room with me or go away."

"I'll come," I said. "And I'll be praying nothing happens. Because this isn't an experiment, Charlie. This is hell's work."

"Think what you want and pray all you like. Maybe you'll have better luck than I ever did . . . although I really doubt it."

He opened the door, and I followed him into the room where Mary Fay had died.

XIII

The Revival of Mary Fay.

There was a large east-facing window in Mary Fay's death chamber, but the storm was almost fully upon us now, and all I saw through it was a tarnished silver curtain of rain. The room was a nest of shadows in spite of the table lamp. My left shoulder brushed the bureau Jacobs had mentioned, but I never thought of the revolver in the top drawer. All my attention was taken up by the still figure lying in the hospital bed. I had a clear view, because the various monitors had been turned off and the IV pole had been pushed into the corner.

She was beautiful. Death had erased any marks incised by the disease that had infested her brain, and her upturned face—alabaster skin set off by luxuriant masses of dark chestnut hair—was as perfect as any cameo. Her eyes were shut. Thick lashes lay against her cheeks. Her lips were slightly parted. A sheet was pulled up to her shoulders. Her clasped hands lay on it, above the swell of her bosom. A snatch of poetry, something from twelfth-grade English, came to mind and chimed there: *Thy hyacinth hair, thy classic face . . . How statue-like I see thee . . .*

Jenny Knowlton stood beside the now useless ventilator, wringing her hands.

Lightning flashed. In its momentary glare I saw the iron pole on Skytop, standing as it had for God knew how many years, challenging each storm to do its worst.

Jacobs was holding out the box. "Help me, Jamie. We must be swift. Take it and open it. I'll do the rest."

"Don't," Jenny said from her corner. "For the love of God, let her rest in peace."

Jacobs might not have heard her over the drumming rain and screaming wind. I did, but chose to ignore her. This is how we bring about our own damnation, you know—by ignoring the voice that begs us to stop. To stop while there's still time.

I opened the box. There were no rods inside, and no control box. What had taken their place was a metallic headband, as thin as the strap on a young girl's dress shoe. Jacobs took it out carefully—reverently—and gently pulled it. I saw it stretch. And when the next stroke of lightning came, once more preceded by that faint clicking sound, I saw green radiance dance across it, making it look like something other than dead metal. A snake, maybe.

Jacobs said, "Miss Knowlton, lift her head for me."

She shook her head so hard her hair flew.

He sighed. "Jamie. You do it."

I moved to the bed like a man in a dream. I thought of Patricia Farmingdale pouring salt in her eyes. Of Emil Klein eating dirt. Of Hugh Yates watching as the faithful in Pastor Danny's revival tent were replaced by huge ants. I thought, *Every cure has its price.*

There was another *click*, followed by another flash of lightning. Thunder roared, shaking the house. The bedside lamp went out. For a moment the room was plunged into shadows, and then a generator clattered to life.

"Quickly!" Jacobs's voice was pained. I saw burns across both of his palms. But he hadn't dropped the headband. It was his last conductor, his conduit to *potestas magnum universum*, and I believed then (and now) that not even death by electrocution would have made him drop it. "Quickly, before lightning strikes the pole!"

I lifted Mary Fay's head. Her chestnut hair fell away from that perfect (and perfectly still) face in a dark flood that pooled on the pillow. Charlie was beside me, bending down and breathing in harsh, excited gasps. His exhalations stank of age and infirmity. It occurred to me that he could have waited a few months and investigated what lay on the other side of the door personally. But that, of course, wasn't what he wanted. At the heart of every established religion is one sacred mystery that supports belief and induces fidelity, even to the point of martyrdom. Did he want to know what lay beyond death's door? Yes. But what he wanted more—I believe this with all my heart—was to violate that mystery. To drag it into the light and hold it up, screaming *Here it is! What all your crusades and murder in the name of God were for! Here it is, and how do you like it?*

"Her hair . . . lift her hair." He turned accusingly to the woman cowering in the corner. "Damn you, I said to cut it!"

Jenny made no reply.

I lifted Mary Fay's hair. It was as soft and heavy as a bolt of silk, and I knew why Jenny hadn't cut it. She couldn't bear to.

Jacobs slipped the thin band of metal over her forehead, so it lay tight against the hollows of her temples.

"All right," he said, straightening up.

I laid the dead woman's head gently back on the pillow, and as I looked at those dark lashes brushing against her cheeks, a comforting thought came to me: It wouldn't work. Cures were one thing; reviving a woman who had been dead for fifteen minutes—no, closer to half an hour now—was another. It simply wasn't possible. And if a stroke of lightning packing millions of volts *did* do something—if it caused her to twitch her fingers or turn her head—it would be no more meaningful than the jerk of a dead frog's leg when electricity from a dry cell is applied. What could he hope to accomplish? Even if her brain had been perfectly healthy, it would now be decaying in her skull. Brain death is irrevocable; even I knew that.

I stepped back. "Now what, Charlie?"

"We wait," he said. "It won't be long."

When the bedside lamp went out a second time, thirty seconds or so later, it didn't come back on, and I could no longer hear the roar of the gennie below the roar of the wind. Now that he had slipped the metal band around Mary Fay's head, Jacobs seemed to have lost interest in her. He was staring out the window, hands clasped behind his back like a ship's captain on the bridge. The iron pole wasn't visible through the teeming rain—not even as a shadow—but we'd see it when the lightning struck it. *If* the lightning struck it. So far, it hadn't. Perhaps there *was* a God, I thought, and He'd taken sides against Charles Jacobs.

"Where's the control box?" I asked him. "Where's the connection to that pole out there?"

He looked at me as if I were an imbecile. "There's no way to control the power that lies beyond the lightning. It would fry even a titanium box to a cinder. As for the connection . . . it's *you*, Jamie. Haven't you guessed even yet why you're here? Did you think I brought you to cook my *meals*?"

Once he'd said it, I couldn't understand why I hadn't seen it before. Why it had taken me so long. The secret electricity had never really left me, or any of the people Pastor Danny had cured. Sometimes it slept, like the disease that had hidden so long in Mary Fay's brain. Sometimes it awoke and made you eat dirt, or pour salt in your eyes, or hang yourself with your pants. That small doorway needed two keys to unlock it. Mary Fay was one.

I was the other.

"Charlie, you have to stop this."

"*Stop?* Are you insane?"

No, I thought, *that would be you. I've come to my senses.*

I just hoped it wasn't too late.

"There's something waiting on the other side. Astrid called it Mother. I don't think you want to see her, and I know I don't."

I bent to strip off the metal circlet that lay across Mary Fay's brow. He grabbed me in a bearhug and pulled me away. His arms were scrawny, and I should have been able to break his grip, but I couldn't, at least not at first. He held me with all the strength of his obsession.

As we struggled in that gloomy, shadow-haunted room, the wind suddenly dropped. The rain slackened. Through the window I could see the pole again, and small rivers of water running down the wrinkles in the bulging forehead of granite that was Skytop.

Thank God, I thought. *The storm is passing by.*

I stopped fighting him just as I was on the verge of breaking free, and so lost my chance to end that day's abomination before it could begin. The storm wasn't over; it had only been drawing in a breath before commencing its main assault. The wind rushed back, this time at hurricane velocity, and in the split-second interval before the lightning came, I felt what I had on the day I'd come here with Astrid: the stiffening of all the hair on my body, and the sense that the air in the room had turned to oil. Not a *click* this time but a *SNAP*, as loud as a small-caliber gunshot. Jenny screamed in terror.

A jagged branch of fire shot from the clouds and struck the iron pole on Skytop, turning it blue. My head was filled with a vast choir of shrieking voices and I understood it was everyone Charles Jacobs had ever cured, plus everyone he'd ever snapped with his Portraits in Lightning camera. Not just the ones who'd suffered aftereffects; all of them, in their thousands. If that shrieking had gone on for even ten seconds, it would have driven me insane. But as the electric fire coating the pole faded, leaving it to glow a dull cherry-red like a branding iron fresh from the fire, those agonized voices also faded away.

Thunder rolled and rain swooshed down in a rush, accompanied by a rattle of hail.

"Oh my God!" Jenny screamed. *"Oh my God, look at it!"*

The circlet around Mary Fay's head was glowing a brilliant, pulsing green. I saw it with more than my eyes; it was deep in my brain, as well, because I was the connection. I was the conduit. The glow began to fade, and then a fresh bolt of lightning struck the pole. The choir shrieked again. This time the band passed from green into a coruscating white, too dazzling to look at. I closed my eyes and put my hands over my ears. In the darkness the afterimage of the circlet remained, now an ethereal blue.

The interior screams faded. I opened my eyes and saw the glow embedded in the circlet was fading, as well. Jacobs was staring at the corpse of Mary Fay with wide, fascinated eyes. Drool dripped from the frozen side of his mouth.

The hail gave a final furious rattle, then quit. The rain began to slacken. I saw lightning fork into the trees beyond Skytop, but the storm was already moving east.

Jenny abruptly bolted from the room, leaving the door open. I heard her crash into something as she crossed the living room, and the bang when the door to the outside—the one I'd had to struggle to close—flew open and hit the wall. She was gone.

Jacobs took no notice. He bent over the dead woman, who lay with her eyes shut and her sooty lashes brushing her cheeks. The circlet was only dead metal now. In the shadowy room, it didn't even gleam. If it had burned her forehead, the mark was beneath the band. I didn't think it had; I would have smelled charred flesh.

"Wake up," Jacobs said. When there was no response, he shouted it. "Wake up!" He shook her arm—gently at first, then harder. "Wake up! Wake up, damn you, *wake up*!"

Her head wagged from side to side as he shook her, as if in negation.

"WAKE UP, YOU BITCH, WAKE UP!"

He was going to pull her out of bed and onto the floor if he didn't stop, and I couldn't have borne that further desecration. I grabbed his right shoulder and hauled him away. We staggered backward in an awkward dance and crashed into the bureau.

He turned on me, his face wild with fury and frustration. "*Let me go! Let me go! I saved your miserable useless life and I demand you—*"

Then something happened.

From the bed came a low humming sound. I relaxed my grip on Jacobs. The corpse lay as it had lain, only now with its hands splayed out at its sides, thanks to Charlie's shaking.

It was just the wind, I thought. I'm sure I could have convinced myself of it, given time, but before I could even get started, it came again: a faint humming from the woman on the bed.

"She's returning," Charlie said. His eyes were huge, bulging from their sockets like the eyes of a toad squeezed by a cruel child. "She's reviving. She's *alive*."

"No," I said.

If he heard, he paid no mind. All of his attention was fixed on the woman in the bed, the pale oval of her face deep in the swimming shadows that infested the room. He lurched toward her like

Ahab on the deck of the *Pequod*, dragging his bad leg. His tongue lapped at his mouth on the side that wasn't frozen. He was gasping for breath.

"Mary," he said. "Mary Fay."

The humming sound came again, low and tuneless. Her eyes remained shut, but I realized with a cold chill of horror that I could see them moving beneath the lids, as if in death, she dreamed.

"Do you hear me?" His voice, dry with an almost prurient eagerness. "If you hear me, give me a sign."

The humming continued. Jacobs put the palm of his hand on her left breast, then turned to me. Incredibly, he was grinning. In the gloom he looked like a death's head.

"No heartbeat," he said. "Yet she lives. *She lives!*"

No, I thought. *She waits. But the wait is almost over*.

Jacobs turned back to her and lowered his half-frozen face until it was only inches from her dead one—a Romeo with his Juliet. "*Mary!* Mary Fay! Come back to us! Come back and tell us where you've been!"

It's hard for me to think of what happened next, let alone write it down, but I must, if only as a warning for anyone else who contemplates some similar experiment in damnation, and may read these words, and turn back because of them.

She opened her eyes.

Mary Fay opened her eyes, but they were no longer *human* eyes. Lightning had smashed the lock on a door that was never supposed to be opened, and Mother came through.

They were blue eyes at first. Bright blue. There was nothing in them. They were utterly blank. They stared at the ceiling through Jacobs's avid face, and through the ceiling, and through the cloudy sky beyond. Then they came back. They registered him, and some understanding—some comprehension—came into them. She made that humming sound again, but I hadn't seen her draw a single breath. What need? She was a dead thing . . . except for those inhuman staring eyes.

"Where have you been, Mary Fay?" His voice trembled. Saliva continued to drip from the bad side of his mouth, leaving damp spots on the sheet. "Where have you been, what did you see there? What waits beyond death? *What's on the other side?* Tell me!"

Her head began to pulse, as if the dead brain within had grown too big for its casing. Her eyes began to darken, first to lavender, then to purple, then to indigo. Her lips drew back in a smile that widened and became a grin. It grew until I could see all of her teeth. One of her hands trundled across the counterpane, spider-like, and seized Jacobs's wrist. He gasped at her cold grip and flailed for balance with his free hand. I took it, and thus the three of us—two living, one dead—were joined. Her head pulsed on the pillow. Growing. *Bloating.* She was no longer beautiful; she was no longer even human.

The room didn't fade; it was still there, but I saw it was an illusion. The cottage was an illusion, and Skytop, and the resort. The whole living world was an illusion. What I'd thought of as reality was nothing but a scrim, as flimsy as an old nylon stocking.

The *true* world was behind it.

Basalt blocks rose to a black sky punched with howling stars. I think those blocks were all that remained of a vast ruined city. It stood in a barren landscape. Barren, yes, but not empty. A wide and seemingly endless column of naked human beings trudged through it, heads down, feet stumbling. This nightmare parade stretched all the way to the distant horizon. Driving the humans were antlike creatures, most black, some the dark red of venous blood. When humans fell, the ant-things would lunge at them, biting and butting, until they gained their feet again. I saw young men and old women. I saw teenagers with babies in their arms. I saw children trying to help each other along. And on every face was the same expression of blank horror.

They marched beneath the howling stars, they fell, they were punished and chivvied to their feet with gaping but bloodless bite wounds on their arms and legs and abdomens. Bloodless because these were the dead. The foolish mirage of earthly life had been torn away and instead of the heaven preachers of all persuasions promised, what awaited them was a dead city of cyclopean stone blocks below a sky that was itself a scrim. The howling stars weren't stars at all. They were *holes*, and the howls emerging from them came from the true *potestas magnum universum*. Beyond the sky were *entities*. They were alive, and all-powerful, and totally insane.

The aftereffects are trailing fragments of an unknown existence beyond our lives, Charlie had said, and that existence lay close in this sterile place, a prismatic world of insane truth that would drive a man or woman mad if it were so much as glimpsed. The ant-things served those great entities, just as the marching, naked dead served the ant-things.

Perhaps the city wasn't a city at all but a kind of anthill where all the dead of earth were first enslaved and then eaten. And once that happened, did they finally die for good? Perhaps not. I didn't want to remember the couplet Bree had quoted in her email, but was helpless not to: *That is not dead which can eternal lie, And with strange aeons, even death may die.*

Somewhere in that marching horde were Patsy Jacobs and Tag-Along-Morrie. Somewhere in it was Claire—who deserved heaven and had gotten this instead: a sterile world below hollow stars, a charnel kingdom where guardian ant-things sometimes crawled and sometimes stood upright, their faces hideously suggestive of the human. *This horror was the afterlife, and it was waiting not just for the evil ones among us but for us all.*

My mind began to totter. It was a relief, and I almost let go. One idea saved my sanity, and I still cling to it: the possibility that this nightmare landscape was itself a mirage.

"*No!*" I shouted.

The marching dead turned toward my voice. The ant-things did likewise, their mandibles gnashing, their loathsome eyes (loathsome but *intelligent*) glaring. Overhead, the sky began to tear open with a titanic ripping sound. An enormous black leg covered with tufts of spiny fur pushed through it. The leg ended in a vast claw made of human faces. Its owner wanted one thing and one thing only: to silence the voice of negation.

It was Mother.

"*No!*" I shouted again. "*No, no, no, no!*"

It was our connection to the revived dead woman that was causing this vision; even in the extremity of my horror, I knew it. Jacobs's hand clutched mine like a manacle. If it had been the right hand—the *good* hand—I could never have freed myself in time. But it was the weakened left. I pulled with all my might as that obscene leg stretched toward me and that claw of screaming faces groped, meaning to yank me upward into the unknowable universe of horror that awaited beyond that black paper sky. Now, through the rip in the firmament, I could see insane light and colors never meant to be looked upon by mortal creatures. The colors were alive. I could feel them crawling over me.

I gave one final yank, freeing myself from Charlie's grip, and went tumbling backward. The empty plain, the vast broken city, the groping claw—they all disappeared. I was in the bedroom of the cottage again, sprawled on the floor. My old fifth business stood beside the bed. Mary Fay—or whatever dark creature Jacobs's secret electricity had summoned into her corpse and dead brain—gripped his hand. Her head had become a pulsing jellyfish with a human face crudely scrawled upon it. Her eyes were a lusterless black. Her grin . . . you would say no one can *actually* grin ear to ear, it's just a saying, but the dead woman who was no longer dead was doing exactly that. The lower half of her face had become a black pit that trembled and throbbed.

Jacobs stared at her with bulging eyes. His face had gone a cheesy yellow-white. "Patricia? Patsy? Where are you? Where's Morrie?"

The thing spoke for the first and last time.

"*Gone to serve the Great Ones, in the Null. No death, no light, no rest.*"

"No." His chest hitched and he screamed it. "*No!*"

He tried to pull back. She—*it*—held him fast.

Now from the dead woman's gaping mouth came a black leg with a flexing claw at the end of it. The claw was alive; it was a face. One I recognized. It was Tag-Along-Morrie, and he was screaming. I heard a tenebrous rustling sound as the leg passed between her lips; in my nightmares I still hear it. It reached, it stretched, it touched the sheet and scrabbled there like skinless fingers, leaving scorch-marks that gave off thin tendrils of smoke. The black eyes of the thing that had been Mary Fay were bulging and spreading. They merged over the bridge of the nose and became a single enormous orb that stared with blank avidity.

Charlie's head snapped back and he began to make a gargling sound. He stood on his toes, seeming to make one final, galvanic effort to free himself from the grasping hand of the thing that was trying to come through from that insane netherworld I now know is so close to our own. Then he collapsed to his knees and fell forward with his forehead against the bed. He looked like he was praying.

The thing let go of him and turned its unspeakable attention to me. It threw back the sheet and struggled to rise, that black insect's leg still extruding from its gaping maw of a mouth. Now Patsy's face had joined Morrie's. They were melted together, writhing.

I got up by pressing my back against the wall and pushing with my legs. Mary Fay's bloated, pulsing face was darkening, as if she were strangling on the thing inside her. That one smooth black eye stared, and reflected in it I fancied I could see the cyclopean city, and the endless column of the marching dead.

I don't remember yanking open the top drawer of the bureau; I only know that all at once the gun was in my hand. I believe if it had been an automatic with the safety on, I would have just stood there, pulling at the frozen trigger, until the thing arose, shambled across the room, and seized me. That claw would have pulled me into its gaping mouth and into that other world, where I would face some unspeakable punishment for daring to say one word: *No.*

But it wasn't an automatic. It was a revolver. I fired five times, and four of the bullets went into the thing trying to rise from Mary Fay's deathbed. I have reason to know exactly how many shots I fired. I heard the roar of the gun, saw repeated muzzle-flashes in the gloom, felt it jump in my hand, but all of that seemed to be happening to someone else. The thing flailed and fell back. The melted faces screamed with mouths that had merged. I remember thinking, *You can't kill Mother with bullets, Jamie. No, not her.*

But it was no longer moving. The obscenity that had come out of its mouth lay limp, trailing on the pillow. The faces of Jacobs's wife and son were fading. I covered my eyes and screamed, over and over again. I screamed until I was hoarse. When I lowered my hands, the claw was gone. Mother was gone, too.

If she was ever there in the first place, I hear you say, and I don't blame you; I wouldn't have believed it myself, if I hadn't been there. But I was. *They* were—the dead ones. And *she* was.

Now, however, it was only Mary Fay, a woman whose serenity in death had been destroyed by four bullets fired into her corpse. She lay askew with her hair fanned out around her head and her mouth hanging open. I could see two bullet holes in her nightgown and two more below them, in the sheet that was now puddled around her hips. I could also see the scorch-marks left by that terrible claw, although there was no other sign of it now.

Jacobs began very slowly to slide to his left. I reached out, but the movement felt slow and dreamy. I didn't even come close to grabbing him. He thumped to the floor on his side, knees still bent. His eyes were wide open but already glazing. An unutterable expression of horror was stamped on his features.

Charlie, you look like a man who just got a bad electrical shock, I thought, and began to laugh. Oh, how I did laugh. I bent over, grasping my knees to keep from falling. It was almost noiseless, that laughter—the screaming had blown my voice out—but it was genuine. Because it *was* funny; you see that, don't you? Bad electrical shock! A shocking development! Hilarious!

But all the time I was laughing—convulsed with it, sick with it—I kept my eyes on Mary Fay, waiting for the hair-tufted black leg to slither out of her mouth again, giving birth to those screaming faces.

At last I staggered out of the death chamber, and through the living room. A few broken branches lay on the carpet, blown through the door Jenny Knowlton had left open. They crunched like bones under my feet and I wanted to scream again, but I was too tired. Oh, I was so tired.

The stacked stormclouds were moving away to the east, throwing down random forks of lightning as they went; soon the streets of Brunswick and Freeport would be flooded, the storm drains temporarily clogged with chips of hail, but between those dark clouds and the place where I stood, a rainbow bent its many-colored arc over the entire breadth of Androscoggin County. Hadn't there been rainbows on the day Astrid and I had come here?

God gave Noah the rainbow sign, we used to sing during our Thursday-night MYF meetings, while Patsy Jacobs swayed on the piano bench and her ponytail swung from side to side. A rainbow was supposed to be a *good* sign, it meant the storm was over, but looking at this one filled me with fresh horror and revulsion, because it reminded me of Hugh Yates. Hugh and his prismatics. Hugh who had also seen the ant-things.

The world began to darken. I realized I was on the verge of fainting, and that was good. Perhaps when I woke up, my mind would have blotted all this out. That would be even better. Even madness would be better . . . as long as there was no Mother in it.

Death would be best of all. Robert Rivard had known it; Cathy Morse had, too. I remembered the revolver then. Surely there was a bullet left in it for me, but it seemed like no solution. Perhaps it would have, if I hadn't heard what Mother said to Jacobs: *No death, no light, no rest.*

Only the Great Ones, she had said.

In the Null.

My knees unhinged and I went down, leaning against the side of the doorway, and that was where I blacked out.

XIV

Aftereffects.

Those things happened three years ago. Now I live in Kailua, not far from my brother Conrad. It's a pretty coastal town on the Big Island. My place is on Oneawa Street, a neighborhood quite distant from the beach and an even longer stretch from fashionable, but the apartment is spacious and—for Hawaii, at least—cheap. Also, it's close to Kuulei Road, and that's an important consideration. The Brandon L. Martin Psychiatric Center is on Kuulei Road, and that's where my psychiatrist hangs out his shingle.

Edward Braithwaite says he's forty-one, but to me he looks like he's thirty. I've found that when you're sixty-one—an age I will reach this August—every man and woman between the ages of twenty-five and forty-five appears to be thirty. It's hard to take people seriously when they look as if they're barely past their Terrible Twenties (it is for me, anyway), but I try hard with Braithwaite, because he's done me quite a lot of good . . . although I'd have to say that the antidepressants have done more. I know that some people don't like them. They claim the pills muffle both their thinking and their emotions, and I can testify that they do.

Thank God they do.

I connected with Ed thanks to Con, who gave up the guitar for athletics and gave up athletics for astronomy . . . although he's still a volleyball monster, and not bad on the tennis court, either.

I've told Dr. Braithwaite everything you've read in these pages. I held back nothing. He doesn't believe much of it, of course—who in his right mind would?—but what a relief in the telling! And certain elements of the story have given him pause, because they are verifiable. Pastor Danny, for instance. Even now, a Google search for that name will yield almost a million results; check it yourself if you don't believe me. Whether or not any of his cures were genuine remains a matter of debate, but that is true even of Pope John Paul, who supposedly cured a French nun of Parkinson's while alive, and a Costa Rican woman of an aneurysm six years after he died. (A good trick!) What happened to many of Charlie's cures—what they did to themselves and what they did to others—is also a matter of fact rather than of conjecture. Ed Braithwaite believes I wove those facts into my narrative to give them verisimilitude. He almost said as much one day late last year, when he quoted Jung to me: "The world's most brilliant confabulators are in asylums."

I am not in an asylum; when I finish my sessions at Martin Psychiatric, I'm free to leave and go back to my silent, sunny apartment. For this I am grateful. I'm also grateful to still be alive, because many of Pastor Danny's cures are not. Between the summer of 2014 and the fall of 2015, they committed suicide by the dozens. Perhaps by the hundreds—it's hard to be sure. I'm helpless not to imagine them reawakening in that other world, marching naked beneath the howling stars, harried along by terrible ant-soldiers, and I am very glad I am not among them. I think that gratitude for life, whatever the cause, indicates that one has managed to hold on to the core of one's sanity. That some of my sanity is gone forever—amputated, like an arm or a leg, by what I saw in Mary Fay's deathroom—is a fact I have learned to live with.

And for fifty minutes every Tuesday and Thursday, between two o'clock and two fifty, I talk.

How I do talk.

On the morning after the storm, I woke up on one of the couches in the lobby of the Goat Mountain Resort. My face hurt and my bladder was bursting, but I had no desire to relieve myself in the men's room across from the restaurant. There were mirrors in there, and I didn't want to glimpse my reflection even by accident.

I went outside to piss and saw one of the resort's golf carts crashed into the porch steps. There was blood on the seat and the rudimentary dashboard. I looked down at my shirt and saw more blood. When I wiped my swollen nose, a maroon crust flaked off on my finger. So I had driven the golf cart, and crashed it, and bumped my face, although I could remember doing none of that.

To say I didn't want to go back to the cottage near Skytop would be the understatement of the century, but I had to. Getting into the golf cart was the easy part. Driving it back down the path through the woods was more difficult, and every time I had to stop and move fallen branches, it was harder to get going again. My nose was throbbing and my head was thumping with a tension headache.

The door was still standing open. I parked, got out of the cart, and at first could only stand there, rubbing at my poor swollen nose until it began to ooze blood again. The day was sunny and beautiful—the storm had washed away all the heat and humidity—but the room beyond that open door was a cave of shadows.

There's nothing to worry about, I told myself. *Nothing will happen. It's over.*

Only what if it wasn't? What if the *something* was still happening?

What if *she* was waiting for me, and ready to reach with that claw made of faces?

I forced myself up the steps, one at a time, and when a crow cawed harshly from the woods behind me, I cringed and screamed and covered my head. The only thing that kept me from bolting was the knowledge that if I didn't see what was in there, Mary Fay's deathroom would haunt me for the rest of my life.

There was no pulsing abomination with a single black eye. Charlie's Patient Omega lay as she had when I last saw her, with two bullet holes in her nightgown and two more in the sheet around her hips. Her mouth was open, and although there was no sign of that horrible black extrusion, I didn't even try to tell myself I had imagined it all. I knew better.

The metal band, now dull and dark, still circled her forehead.

Jacobs's position had changed. Instead of lying on his side next to the bed with his knees drawn up, he was propped in a sitting position on the other side of the room, against the bureau. My first thought was that he hadn't been dead after all. The terror of what had happened in here had brought on another stroke, but not an immediately fatal one. He had come to, crawled as far as the bureau, and died there.

It could have been, except for the revolver in his hand.

I stared at it for a long time, frowning, trying to recall. I couldn't then, and I have refused Ed Braithwaite's offer to hypnotize me in an effort to recover my blocked memories. Partly this is because I'm afraid of what hypnosis might release from the darker regions of my mind. Mostly it's because I know what must have happened.

I turned from Charlie's body (that expression of horror was still stamped on his face) to look at Mary Fay. I had fired the revolver five times, I was sure of that, but only four bullets had gone into her. One had gone wild, not surprising when you consider my state of mind. But when I lifted my eyes to the wall, I saw *two* bullet holes there.

Had I gone back to the resort, then returned the previous evening? I supposed it was possible, but I didn't think I could have brought myself to do that, even in a blackout. No, I had fixed this scene before I left. *Then* I went back, crashed the golf cart, staggered up the steps, and fell asleep in the lobby.

Charlie hadn't dragged himself across the room; I was the one who did the dragging. I propped him against the bureau, put the gun in his right hand, and fired it into the wall. The cops who would eventually discover this bizarre scene might not test Charlie's hand for gunshot residue, but if they did, they would find it.

I wanted to cover Mary Fay's face, but everything had to be left exactly as it was, and what I wanted most of all was to escape that room of shadows. I took a moment longer, though. I knelt beside my old fifth business and touched one of his thin wrists.

"You should have stopped, Charlie," I said. "You should have stopped a long time ago."

But could he have done that? It would be easy to say yes, because that would allow me to lay blame. Only I'd have to blame myself as well, because I hadn't stopped, either. Curiosity is a terrible thing, but it's human.

So human.

"I hadn't been there at all," I told Dr. Braithwaite. "That's what I decided, and there was only one person who could testify that I had been."

"The nurse," Ed said. "Jenny Knowlton."

"I thought she'd have no choice but to help me. We had to help each other, and the way to do it would be to say we'd left Goat

Mountain together, when Jacobs started raving about turning off Mary Fay's life support. I was sure Jenny would go along with that, if only to make certain I kept quiet about her part in it. I didn't have her cell number, but I knew Jacobs would. His address book was in the Cooper Suite, and sure enough, her number was in it. I called and got voicemail. I told her to call me back. Astrid's number was also in his book, so I tried her next."

"And also got voicemail."

"Yes." I put my hands over my face. Astrid's days of answering her phone had been all over by then. "Yes, that's right."

Here's what happened. Jenny drove her golf cart back to the resort; Jenny got into her Subaru; Jenny drove to Mount Desert Island without stopping. All she wanted was the comfort of home. That meant Astrid, and sure enough, Astrid was waiting for her. Their bodies were found just inside the front door. Astrid must have plunged the butcher knife into her partner's throat as soon as Jenny walked in. Then she used it to cut her wrists. She did it crosswise, not the recommended technique . . . but she cut all the way to the bone. I imagine them lying there in pools of drying blood while first Jenny's phone rang in her purse, then Astrid's on the kitchen counter below the knife rack. I don't *want* to imagine that, but I am helpless to stop it.

Not all of Jacobs's cures killed themselves, but over the next two years, a great many did. Not all of them took loved ones with them, but over fifty did; this I know from my research, which I shared with Ed Braithwaite. He would like to write it off as coincidence. He can't quite do it, although he is happy to dispute my own conclusion from this parade of madness, suicide, and murder: Mother demands sacrifices.

Patricia Farmingdale, the lady who poured salt in her eyes, recovered enough of her vision to smother her elderly father in his bed before blowing her brains out with her husband's Ruger. Emil Klein, the dirt-eater, shot his wife and son, then went out to his garage, poured lawnmower gas over himself, and struck a match. Alice Adams—cured of cancer at a Cleveland revival—went into a convenience store with her boyfriend's AR-15 and unloaded, killing three random people. When the clip was empty, she pulled a snub-nose .38 from her pocket and fired it into the roof of her mouth. Margaret Tremayne, one of Pastor Danny's San Diego cures (Crohn's disease), threw her infant son from the balcony of her ninth-story apartment, then followed him down. Witnesses said she uttered not a sound as she fell.

Then there was Al Stamper. You probably know about him; how could you have missed the screaming headlines on the supermarket tabloids? He invited both of his ex-wives to dinner, but one of them—the second, I believe—got caught in traffic and showed up late, which was lucky for her. When she walked in the open door of Stamper's Westchester home, she discovered Wife Number One roped to a chair at the dining room table with the top of her head caved in. The ex–lead singer of the Vo-Lites emerged from the kitchen, brandishing a baseball bat slimed with blood and hair. Wife Number Two fled the house, screaming, with Stamper chasing after her. Halfway down the residential street, he fell to the pavement, dead of a heart attack. No surprise there; he was a heavyweight.

I'm sure I didn't find all the cases, scattered across the country as they were, and buried in the outbreaks of senseless violence that seem more and more to be a part of daily life in America. Bree could have found others, but she wouldn't have helped me even if she had still been single and living in Colorado. Bree Donlin-Hughes wants nothing to do with me these days, and I totally get that.

Shortly before Christmas last year, Hugh phoned Bree's mother and asked her to come up to his office at the big house. He said he had a surprise for her, and he certainly did. He strangled his old lover with a lamp cord, carried her body into the garage, and slipped her into the passenger seat of his vintage Lincoln Continental. Then he got behind the wheel, started the engine, got some rock on the radio, and sucked exhaust.

Bree knows I promised to steer clear of Jacobs . . . and Bree knows I lied.

"Let us suppose it's all true," Ed Braithwaite said during one of our recent sessions.

"How daring of you," I said.

He smiled, but stayed on point. "It still wouldn't follow that the vision you saw of that hellish afterlife was a *true* vision. I know it still haunts you, Jamie, but consider all the people—not excluding John of Patmos, author of the Book of Revelation—who've had visions of heaven and hell. Old men . . . old women . . . even children claim to have peeked beyond the veil. *Heaven Is for Real* is basically the afterlife vision of a kid who almost died when he was four—"

"Colton Burpo," I said. "I read it. He talks about a horsie only Jesus can ride."

"Make fun all you want," Braithwaite said, shrugging. "Lord knows it's an easy account to make fun of . . . but Burpo also met a miscarried sister whom he knew nothing about. That's verifiable information. Like all those murder-suicides."

"Many murder-suicides, but Colton only met one sister," I said. "The difference is one of quantity. I never took a course in statistics, but I know that."

"I'm happy to assume the kid's vision of the afterlife was false, because it supports my thesis that your vision of it—the sterile city, the ant-things, the black-paper sky—was equally false. You see what I'm driving at, don't you?"

"Yes. And I'd love to buy into it."

Of course I would. Anyone would. Because every man and woman owes a death, and the thought of going to the place I saw has done more than cast a shadow over my life; it has made that life seem thin and unimportant. No—not just my life, *every* life. So I hang on to one thought. It's my mantra, the first thing I tell myself in the morning and the last thing I tell myself at night.

Mother lied.

Mother lied.

Mother lied.

Sometimes I almost believe it . . . but there are reasons I can't quite manage to do so.

There are *signs*.

Before going back to Nederland—where I would discover that Hugh had killed himself after murdering Bree's mother—I drove to the home place in Harlow. There were two reasons for this. After Jacobs's body was discovered, the police might get in touch with me and ask for an accounting of my time in Maine. That seemed important (although in the end, they never did), but something else was more important: I needed the comfort of a familiar place, and people who loved me.

I didn't get it.

You remember Cara Lynne, don't you? My great-niece? The one I carried around at the Labor Day party in 2013 until she fell asleep on my shoulder? The one who held out her arms to me every time I came near? When I walked into the house where I'd grown up, Cara Lynne was between her mother and dad, sitting in an old-fashioned high chair that I might have sat in once myself. When the little girl saw me, she began to scream and throw herself from side to side so violently that she would have tumbled to the floor if her dad hadn't caught her. She buried her face against his chest, still screeching at the top of her lungs. She only stopped when her grandfather Terry led me out onto the porch.

"What the hell's *that* about?" he asked, half-humorously. "Last time you were here, she couldn't get enough of you."

"Don't know," I said, but of course I did. I had hoped to stay a night, perhaps two, sucking up normality the way a vampire sucks blood, but that wasn't going to work. I didn't know exactly what Cara Lynne sensed in me, but I never wanted to see her small, terrified face again.

I told Terry I'd just stopped by to say hello, couldn't even stay for supper, had a plane to catch in Portland. I'd been in Lewiston, I said, slop-recording a band Norm Irving had told me about. He said he thought they had national potential.

"And do they?" he asked.

"Nah. Strictly lo-fi." I made a business of looking at my watch.

"Never mind the plane," Terry said. "You can catch another one. Come on in and have dinner with the family, little brother. Cara will settle down."

I didn't think so.

I told Terry I had recording gigs at Wolfjaw that I absolutely could not miss. I told him another time. And when he held out his arms to me, I hugged him hard, knowing chances were good I'd never see him again. I didn't know about the murders and suicides then, but I knew I was carrying something poisonous, and would probably carry it for the rest of my life. The last thing I wanted was to infect the people I loved.

On the way back to my rental car, I stopped and looked at the dirt strip between the lawn and Methodist Road. The road had been paved for years, but the strip of dirt looked just as it had when I used to play there with the toy soldiers my sister gave me for my sixth birthday. I had been kneeling there and playing with them one day in the fall of 1962, when a shadow fell over me.

That shadow is still there.

"Have *you* murdered anyone?"

Ed Braithwaite has asked me this question on several occasions. It is, I believe, what's called *incremental repetition*. I always smile and tell him no. It's true that I put four bullets into poor Mary Fay, but the woman was already dead at the time, and Charles Jacobs died of a final cataclysmic stroke. If it hadn't happened that day, it would have happened on another, and probably before the year was out.

"And you obviously haven't committed suicide," Ed continues, smiling himself. "Unless I'm hallucinating you, that is."

"You're not."

"The impulse isn't there?"

"No."

"Not even as a theoretical possibility? One that comes to you in the dead of night, perhaps, when you can't sleep?"

"No."

My life these days is far from happy, but the antidepressants have put a floor under me. Suicide isn't on my radar. And given what may come after death, I want to live as long as possible. There's something else, too. I feel—rightly or wrongly—that I have a lot to atone for. Because of that, I'm still trying to be a do-right daddy. I cook at the Harbor House soup kitchen on Aupupu Street. I volunteer two days a week at the Goodwill on Keolu Drive, next to the Nene Goose Bakery. If you're dead, you can't atone for anything.

"Tell me, Jamie—why are you the special lemming who feels no urge to jump off the cliff? Why are you immune?"

I just smile and shrug. I could tell him, but he wouldn't believe me. Mary Fay was Mother's door into our world, but I was the key. Shooting a corpse kills nothing—not that an immortal being such as Mother *can* be killed—but when I fired that pistol, I locked the door. I said *no* with more than my mouth. If I told my shrink that some otherworldly being, one of the Great Ones, was saving me for some final and apocalyptic act of revenge because of that *no*, said shrink might begin thinking about involuntary committal. I don't want that, because I have another duty, one I consider far more important than helping out at Harbor House or sorting clothes at the Goodwill.

At the end of each session with Ed, I pay his receptionist by check. I can afford to do this because the itinerant rock guitarist turned recording engineer is now a wealthy man. Ironic, isn't it? Hugh Yates died without issue, and left a substantial fortune (handed down from his father, grandfather, and great-grandfather) behind. There were many small bequests, including gifts of cash to Malcolm "Mookie" McDonald and Hillary Katz (aka Pagan Starshine), but a large part of the estate was to be divided between me and Georgia Donlin.

Given Georgia's death at Hugh's hands, that particular bequest could have provided probate attorneys with twenty years' worth of legal munching and tasty fees, but since there was no one to kick up dickens (I certainly wasn't going to), there was no wrangle. Hugh's lawyers got in touch with Bree and told her that, as the deceased was her mother, she arguably had a valid claim on the loot.

Only Bree wouldn't argue. The lawyer who handled my end of the business told me Bree claimed Hugh's money was "tainted." Perhaps so, but I had no compunctions about taking my share of it. Partly because I played no part in Hugh's cure, mostly because I consider myself tainted already, and feel it's better to be tainted in comfort than in poverty. I have no idea what happened to the several million that would have gone to Georgia, and have no desire to find out. Too much knowledge isn't good for a person. I know that now.

When my twice-weekly session is finished and my bill is paid, I leave Ed Braithwaite's outer office. Beyond is a wide carpeted hall lined with other offices. A right turn would take me back to the lobby, and from the lobby to Kuulei Road. But I don't turn right. I turn left. Finding Ed was just happenstance, you see; I originally came to the Brandon L. Martin Psychiatric Center on other business.

I walk down the hallway, then cross the fragrant, beautifully maintained garden that is the green heart of this large facility. Here patients sit taking the reliable Hawaiian sun. Many are fully dressed, some are in pajamas or nightgowns, a few (recent arrivals, I believe) wear hospital johnnies. Some engage in conversations, either with fellow patients or with unseen companions. Others merely sit, looking at the trees and flowers with vacant, drugged-to-the-gills stares. Two or three are accompanied by attendants, lest they hurt themselves or others. The attendants usually greet me by name as I pass. They know me well by now.

On the other side of this open-air atrium is Cosgrove Hall, one of three Martin Center in-patient residences. The other two are for short-termers, mainly people with substance-abuse problems. The usual stay in those is twenty-eight days. Cosgrove is for people with issues that take longer to resolve. If they ever do.

Like the corridor in the main building, the one in Cosgrove is wide and carpeted. Like the corridor in the main building, the air is chilled to perfection. But there are no pictures on the walls, and no Muzak, either, because in it some of the patients hear voices murmuring obscenities or issuing sinister directives. In the main building's corridor, some of the doors are open. Here, all are shut. My brother Conrad has been residing in Cosgrove Hall for almost two years now. The Martin Center administrators and the psychiatrist in charge of his case want to move him to a more permanent facility—Aloha Village on Maui has been mentioned—but so far I have resisted. Here in Kailua I can visit him after my appointments with Ed, and thanks to Hugh's generosity, I can afford his upkeep.

Although I must admit my walks down the Cosgrove hallway are a trial.

I try to make them with my eyes fixed on my feet. I can do that, because I know it's exactly one hundred and forty-two steps from the atrium doorway to Con's small suite. I don't always succeed—sometimes I hear a voice whispering my name—but mostly I do.

You remember Con's partner, don't you? The hunk from the University of Hawaii Botany Department? I didn't name him then and don't intend to now, although I might have done if he ever visited Connie. He doesn't, though. If you asked him, I'm sure he'd say *Why in God's name would I want to visit the man who tried to kill me?*

I can think of two reasons.

One, Con wasn't in his right mind . . . or in any mind at all, for that matter. After hitting the hunk over the head with a lamp, my brother ran into the bathroom, locked the door, and swallowed a handful of Valium tablets—a *small* handful. When Botany Boy came around (with a bloody scalp that needed stitches, but otherwise not much the worse for wear), he called 911. The police came and broke down the bathroom door. Con was passed out and snoring in the tub. The EMTs examined him and didn't even bother to pump his stomach.

Con didn't try very hard to kill either Botany Boy or himself—that's the other reason. But of course, he was one of Jacobs's first cures. Probably *the* first. On the day he left Harlow, Charlie told me that Con had almost certainly cured himself; the rest had been a trick, pure huggermugger. *It's a skill they try to teach in divinity school*, he'd said. *I was always good at it.*

Only he lied. The cure was as real as Con's current state of semi-catatonia. I know that now. *I* was the one Charlie conned, not just once but again and again and again. Still—count your blessings, right? Conrad Morton had a lot of good stargazing years before I woke Mother. And there's hope for him. He plays tennis, after all (although he never speaks), and as I said, he's a volleyball monster. His doctor says he's begun to show increased outward response (whatever that is when it's at home), and the nurses and orderlies are less likely to come in and see him standing in the corner and striking his head lightly against the wall. Ed Braithwaite says that in time Conrad may come all the way back; that he may *revive*. I choose to believe he will. People say that where there's life, there's hope, and I have no quarrel with that, but I also believe the reverse.

There is hope, therefore I live.

Twice a week, after my talks with Ed, I sit in the living room of my brother's suite and talk some more. Some of what I tell him is real—a kerfuffle at Harbor House that brought the police, a particularly large haul of almost-new clothes at the Goodwill, how I've finally gotten around to watching all five seasons of *The Wire*—and some of it is made up, like the woman I'm supposedly seeing who works as a waitress at the Nene Goose Bakery, and the long Skype conversations I have with Terry. Our visits are monologues rather than conversations, and that makes fiction necessary. My real life just won't do, because these days it's as sparsely furnished as a cheap hotel room.

I always finish by telling him he's too thin, he has to eat more, and by telling him that I love him.

"Do you love me, Con?" I ask.

So far he hasn't answered, but sometimes he smiles a little. That's an answer of a kind, wouldn't you agree?

When four o'clock comes and our visit is over, I reverse course and walk back down to the atrium, where the shadows—of the palms, the avocados, and the big, twisted banyan at the center of it all—have begun to grow long.

I count my steps, and I take little glances at the door ahead of me, but otherwise keep my gaze firmly fixed on the carpet. Unless I hear that voice whispering my name.

Sometimes when that happens, I'm able to ignore it.

Sometimes I cannot.

Sometimes I look up in spite of myself and see that the hospital wall, painted soothing pastel yellow, has been replaced with gray stones held together by ancient mortar and covered with ivy. The ivy is dead, and the branches look like grasping skeletal hands. The small door in the wall is hidden, Astrid was right about that, but it's there. The voice comes from behind it, drifting through an ancient rusty keyhole.

I walk on resolutely. Of course I do. Horrors beyond comprehension wait on the other side of that door. Not just the land of death, but the land *beyond* death, a place full of insane colors, mad geometry, and bottomless chasms where the Great Ones live their endless, alien lives and think their endless, malevolent thoughts.

It's the Null beyond that door.

I walk on, and think of the couplet in Bree's last email: *That is not dead which can eternal lie, And with strange aeons, even death may die.*

Jamie, an old woman's voice whispers from the keyhole of a door only I can see. *Come. Come to me and live forever.*

No, I tell her, just as I told her in my vision. *No.*

And . . . so far, so good. But eventually something will happen. Something always does. And *when* it does . . .

I will come to Mother.

April 6, 2013–December 27, 2013

Author's Note

CHUCK VERRILL is my agent. He sold the book, and provided aid and comfort along the way.

NAN GRAHAM edited the book with a sharp eye and an even sharper blue pencil.

RUSS DORR, my tireless researcher, provided information when information was needed. If I screwed something up, it was because I failed to understand. In such cases blame me, not him.

SUSAN MOLDOW took all my calls, even when I was being a pain in the ass, and urged me ever onward.

MARSHA DeFILIPPO and JULIE EUGLEY mind my real-world affairs so I can live in my imagination.

TABITHA KING, my wife and best critic, pointed out the soft places and urged me to fix them. Which I did, to the best of my ability. I love her a bunch.

Thanks to all of you, and special thanks to THE ROCK BOTTOM REMAINDERS, who taught me you're never too old to rock and roll and have kept me high-stepping to "In the Midnight Hour" since 1992. Key of E. *All* that shit starts in E.

—Bangor, Maine